WRECKED
Cast Away

USA TODAY BESTSELLING AUTHOR
EMMANUELLE SNOW

Smart Lily
Publishing

SURFER BOY

SUMMER LOVE!!!

T THE AUTHOR

MEDORA BEACH
SUMMER FEVER
SURFING DAY

Cast Away
Emmanuelle Snow

Copyright © 2023 by Emmanuelle SNOW

First edition - January 2024 (V_1) (2025 update)

ISBN eBook: 978-1-998077-00-7

ISBN paperback: 978-1-998077-01-4

Editors: Shalini G. and SLE

Cover: SMART Lily publishing inc.

Published by SMART Lily Publishing inc.

———

Emmanuelle Snow
emmanuellesnow.com

MEDORA BEACH UNIVERSE

Wrecked series
Cast Away
Ride For a Fall

Touchdown series
(coming soon)

All titles available at
emmanuellesnow.com

OTHER BOOKS BY THE AUTHOR

ALL TITLES AVAILABLE AT EMMANUELLESNOWSHOP.COM

CARTER HILLS BAND UNIVERSE

Carter Hills Band series

False Promises

Blindsided

Forevermore

Whiskey Melody series

Sweet Agony

Cruel Destiny

Beautiful Salvation

Wild Encounter

Brittle Scars

Upon A Star series

Last Hope

Midnight Sparks

Love Song For Two series

Fallen Legend

Rising Star
Snowbound

———

MEDORA BEACH UNIVERSE

Wrecked series
Cast Away
Ride for a Fall

Touchdown series
Kickoff

———

All titles available at
emmanuellesnow.com

TRIGGER WARNINGS

Disclaimer

My books are realistic and emotional love stories.

I'm an advocate for mental health, and some topics could be sensitive for certain readers since they are portrayed as close to real life as possible.

I've listed the potential trigger warnings for each title on my website.

Be advised that those trigger warnings could potentially be spoiler alerts for the storylines.

Those sensitive topics have been written with the utmost care and respect. Please reach out if you have questions or comments.

The Medora Beach universe contains sexuality, mature

content, and language not intended for people under 16 years of age.
For other readers' sake, please avoid spoilers in your reviews.

Thank you and have a wonderful day!

Emmanuelle

emmanuellesnow.com

*To you, who dances in the light
and plays in the dark,
remember there is no day
without the night.*

BECOME A VIP

TO NEVER MISS A THING

Snow's VIP

Join **Emmanuelle Snow's VIP newsletter**

Be the first to know about new releases, giveaways, sales, and special events. And step into a space where big emotions are celebrated, love is messy and beautiful, and stories linger long after the last page.

emmanuellesnow.com

Snow's Soulmates

Join Emmanuelle Snow's Facebook VIP group, **Snow's Soulmates**, to chat with her and other readers, get updates, and more bonus content.

facebook.com/groups/snowvip

WRECKED SERIES

He set himself out to ruin me.
But I'm not going down without a fight.

When my parents sent me away, little did I know it would turn out to be the best and most heartbreaking summer of my life.

My complicated existence began once I moved to Feather Lake, North Carolina. A job offer and a bus ticket and I was gone for the entire summer. My parents just forgot to mention my "vacation" would last for more than a week. A little detail that didn't sit well with me.

My nightmare started that day. When I got hauled away from the perfect summer with my friends and had to leave with only two pieces of luggage and an angry heart.

From there, everything went down the rabbit hole.

It took two days. Two days once I arrived there for me to notice him the first time. And to never forget him afterward. Two days for him to infiltrate my heart, dig his claws into its beating parts, and bleed it to death.

I've decided not to let him spoil my summer vacation. And my new friendships. Because there's a boy who lights up my days and makes me smile, and with him, I'm feeling things I never did before. And right now, I'm addicted.

Chapter 1

Thirteen year old

January 19

Dear Ava,
I can't believe I've missed your birthday again this
year. I'm so sorry about the change of plan. I was
looking forward to spending the entire weekend with
you. I swear, since we moved down south, we barely
ever make it to Michigan anymore. There's always
something coming up. Not that I miss the chilly

winters, though. I prefer the warmth of the weather here.

Before winter break, I went to school wearing only a hoodie and sneakers. I could've never done that in Elk River in December. Can you imagine it? I'm sure you're covered in ten layers right now because you're always cold.

How was your winter break? Did you like spending your vacation in Aspen? I wish we could have come with you guys, but Dad's business has just started picking up, and I understand it was better and more logical for my parents to stay here. Not for me, though. I really wanted a white Christmas. Hopefully, next year we'll be able to go together.

My friend Riri and I decorated a palm tree with blue lights because I thought it would look good. I'm sure you would have approved.

You probably have received your gift by now. Well, I'm sure Mom sent you something pretty to wear, but I wanted you to have something I made. I used purple, white, and navy-blue threads because I know they're your favorite colors. I made a matching one for myself too, so it means we're connected even though we live far apart.

Riri helped me with the wrapping. We talk about you all the time. Sometimes it feels like you're here with us. I can't wait for you to visit and you two to meet. I'm sure you will get along just fine.

Mom and I recently redecorated my room, and now I have a bigger bed. Do you remember the old one in the cottage our parents rented that summer? So cramped it was when both of us tried to fit in it. I just had a flashback of the time you fell off the bed in the middle of the night, and we decided to lie in our sleeping bags on the floor instead. No, I still say I didn't push you. And no matter what you believe, I don't kick in my sleep. But now when you come over, there is enough space, and we can share my bed.

Do you have plans for next summer? Maybe I could come visit you for a week or two. It would be fun to spend some time together like we used to. I'll talk to my parents. See if they agree. I'll be fifteen so it makes more sense if I'm the one who makes the bus ride on my own. I wouldn't want you to travel alone.

I miss you.
Happy thirteenth birthday, Ava!
I wish you all the best.

Love,
Cici xxx

P.S. Call me after you read this letter.

P.P.S. Riri says hello.

P.P.P.S. Don't forget to write back.

March 6

Ava!!!!

You won't believe it. I auditioned for the cheer-leading squad for next year, and I got in. Riri helped me practice until I knew the choreography by heart. This was so stressful. I thought my heart would jump out of my chest. But I did it. I made the team.

How are you doing? Did your parents agree to let you spend your spring break with Iris at her cottage? I heard Mom talking to your mama about it the other day.

Last Friday, during lunch break, I was reading your letter, and some friends at school were asking why we write letters to each other instead of emails. And when I said it was more exciting to receive a real envelope through the mail than a chime on a computer, they looked at me like I was crazy. I wish you had been here that day because you would have thought it was funny. Their faces... OMG. I almost told them we use pigeons to deliver the mail (you know, like in that movie), and I'm pretty sure they would have believed me. Anyway, thanks for the pumpkin cookie recipe you sent in your last letter. I can't wait to try it with Mom.

Dad promised we'd talk about my coming to visit you

next summer. He's not really enthusiastic about this cross-country journey at my age. But he's being a good sport and said we'd discuss it. Cross your fingers. Hope he says yes. Cross your toes too, Ava. Just in case.

Or maybe...just maybe...the three of us will come to Michigan, and it will all be like it used to be. Sleepovers and camping nights in your backyard. And painting our nails and doing our faces. Dressing up. Having scary movie marathons.

Oops. Look at the time. I gotta go. I'm not done with my math homework. And I really need to finish that novel for my English lit class tomorrow. I hate tests.

See you soon (hopefully).
Fingers and toes crossed until then!

Love,
Cici xxx

P.S. There's a new boy in my English class, and his name is Camden. He has blue eyes, and he invited me to the movies on Friday night. I said yes. I'll keep you updated.

P.P.S. Oh, I forgot. My friend Riri and I finished in second place at the school science fair last week. Life is awesome these days.

———

April 3

Dear Ava

Okay, there's so much I need to tell you. Remember when I told you Camden, the new boy in class, invited me to the movies? Well, the following week, we played mini golf together, and he kissed me. And now I have a boyfriend. I'm sure you would approve. He's nice and sweet and always wants to hold my hand and carry my backpack. I'm super happy, and I wish you were here to hang out with us. And meet him.

Well, I want you to meet all my friends. You should move down here. You would like it since it's summer almost all year-round.

I received the silly pictures you sent me and the one of us when we were little kids. I can't believe we were that small.

I was thinking that when we're both in college, or some time after, we should be roommates. Imagine how much fun it would be to spend all this time together and have our own place... I know it's a few years from now, but it's never too early to start planning. And maybe we can also go to see the Eiffel Tower together after graduation. Have a girls' trip. Let's talk about it when I visit you this summer and we make a list of all our dreams.

I miss you.

Can you believe I have a boyfriend? I don't. LOL.
Mom is here and says hi. She's making your favorite
dish for dinner.
Tell Iris I said Happy Birthday.

Love,
Cici

P.S. I wish you were here.

P.P.S. Dad said he'd call your father next weekend
to figure something out for our summer vacation.
Fingers and toes crossed. For real this time!

Sixteen years old

The blade fell from my grip, landing next to the discarded letters on the floor as I watched the line of blood dotting my fair skin and trickling across the surface of my forearm. I held my breath, waiting for the sting of pain. The one I couldn't seem to run away from. Something that would remind me I was alive. In the last three years, I had become an addict. To physical pain.

Every time the memory of who I'd lost took over my thoughts, it twisted my insides. Made me vulnerable. I couldn't think straight, disconnected from my emotions, but dying to feel something. Anything.

Blood dripped onto the floor, and I followed the path, hypnotized by the pattern.

Still, I felt nothing. Blank.

My head spun, and I blinked.

My gaze drifted to my arm, mentally begging for the aftershock to kick in. For the physical pain to erase the mental one.

After what seemed like forever, the twinge on my forearm, just below the crease of my elbow, finally hit me. Oxygen returned to my lungs as I took a deep inhale, escaping the prison of numbness that had suffocated me seconds ago.

My eyes flitted to the mirror above my dresser. I looked haunted. Shadows undermined my eyes. And a sadness—though I wished it would vanish—lingered in my irises.

The first time I used a blade was the summer after my thirteenth birthday. At the time, I had no idea how to cope with my grief. Until a girl from my gym class shared how she relieved the paralyzing emotions that sometimes crippled her after her mother's death.

She put into words the feelings that were drowning me inside. The ones I refused to talk about because they hurt too much. Her words resonated with me. For once, they made sense to the confused and heartbroken girl I was back then.

In a way, grief broke me. It made me weak. And ashamed of myself when I let my emotions rule me. The ones I tried to conceal deep inside for as long as I could remember. Until I couldn't bury them anymore. That was the moment I started cutting myself. Because in a twisted manner, it helped relieve the suffering from the crater lodged deep inside me. And to soothe my troubled mind.

That spring, my favorite person in the world had been taken from me.

In the most hurtful way.

She didn't get a chance to fight back. That chance was stolen from her.

She didn't have the opportunity to say her goodbyes. No one had heard her last words.

She had been forced to put all those dreams of hers to rest. Forever. We would never visit Paris together. Nor would we ever be roommates once in college. She never came to visit me that summer, and I never met all her friends.

Three years later, all those memories still haunted my nightmares. Sometimes. Most times.

I lost not only her that day, but also a part of myself. And the people I considered to be second parents. They all disappeared from my life. And I had no idea if I'd see them again someday. I knew it was for my own good that they stayed away. I was suffering. So lost in my own pain that just the idea of seeing them was enough to send me back spiraling. But the realization didn't hurt any less.

Eyes brimming with tears, my heart fractured in my chest. I hated everything about being me right now. I was failing myself. Again. In so many ways. My teeth dug into my lower lip as I swallowed the sobs about to wreck me.

Harming myself wasn't a habit of mine. I had only done it seven times in the past. When the pain became unbearable and too hard to hide, when I felt like I was falling down the rabbit hole, it helped me remember I was still here. Alive. And that all those chances she would never have were still waiting for me.

"I miss you," I said to a picture of us that we'd taken on my eleventh birthday. Wearing matching blue polka-dot dresses, both of us grinning at the camera. The last one we celebrated together.

Dizziness filled me, and for an instant, I thought I would faint.

The cut should have already started clotting by now. Instead, a thick film of blood covered my skin, oozing down my forearm.

My hand clamped onto my desk, my body growing weaker by the second.

Ohmygod, what have I done?

How deep did I cut this time?

It was usually only a surface scratch, but right now it felt to be much deeper than that. My fingers shook as I wiped the mess off my skin, trying to stop the bleeding.

My bedroom whirled around me.

Trying to stay calm, I fixed my gaze on the photo. Could she see me hurting from wherever she was? If she were here, she would be so disappointed in me. She loved life. Always cheerful and dancing around for the smallest of things. Everything gave her joy. Thinking happy thoughts. And befriending everyone.

My eyes darted to the injury I'd inflicted upon my body. Chills worked through me. I didn't wanna die. Just the thought scared the shit out of me. I wanted to live.

I watched my forearm. "Please, blood, stop. I'm sorry." Tears burned the back of my eyes. My heart did some awkward jump inside my chest. Tremors shook me.

How did I end up here? Again?

The cut stung, and pain radiated from the wound.

Sadness wrapped around me, suffocating every piece of my being.

I needed to do better. Be better.

I hated feeling like I had no grip on my own life.

I was done being sad. And miserable. I was done wreaking pain upon myself, thinking it would help. I had to take back control of my life. For me. For her. She wouldn't want to see me like this. Broken and suspended in time. Everything hurt so bad. Inside and out. Blood trickled down my arm. I was getting light-headed. Grief seemed like a weight, crushing me. I needed to fight. For both of us. She wasn't given the chance to reach for her dreams. Why was I forfeiting mine? It sounded selfish to waste a life when hers had been stolen. She would tell me to fight back. Yeah, she certainly wouldn't want me to drown and give up.

Using the heel of my hand to put pressure on the wound, I let my sobs out. I squeezed my arm in a vice. The bleeding wouldn't stop.

Shame filled me. I had let the letters get to me. I hated the idea I hadn't been strong enough to deal with the emotions today with a clear mind.

Tears drenched my face, and I used my shoulders to clear my foggy vision.

I needed my mom.

With slow and unsteady steps, I staggered toward the kitchen where my parents were making breakfast. I had draped a black T-shirt over my arm to conceal the result of my actions. A chill crawled up my back. Cold sweat pearled on my forehead. Suddenly, I felt so tired.

The smell of bacon hit my nose first. Followed by the crisp aroma of freshly brewed coffee.

Dad stood with the frying pan in his hand, listening to my little brother Collin's retelling of his last soccer game, while Mom was busy pouring caffeine into mugs. I could hear them, but it was hard to understand what they were saying. Like I was standing in some sort of bubble, far away from them. The numbness I felt inside was now spreading to my physical body.

I tried to move forward but was paralyzed, my feet heavy.

My body overheated. As if lava was traveling in my bloodstream. Seconds later, my teeth chattered when the heat was replaced by cold shivers.

Bracing myself and doing my best not to collapse, I neared them. Black dots danced in my vision. Breathing became harder. My pulse pounded in my head.

"Morning, Miss Sunshine," Dad called out when his eyes landed on me, the carefree grin drawn on his lips slowly dissolving. Worry swam in his eyes.

I stood there with drenched cheeks, holding my arm tight and wishing for the bleeding to stop. The pain to leave. And the fog filling me to recede.

I wished the wound would heal.

The pan dropped from his hand. Mom seemed to be alerted by the ruckus because she turned around at once. A gasp passed her lips, and her eyes rounded when she looked at me. In seconds, they were both standing by my side.

"What happened?" my father asked, his strong arms enveloping me and helping me stay upright as a new surge of dizziness made my head spin. "Are you hurt?"

Time slowed down.

Once again, I heard their voices, but they sounded distant.

I saw their faces, mere inches from mine, but they looked to be miles away from here.

Dad lifted me in his arms. I buried my face in his chest, my safe place, while he carried me to the living room and sat me on the sofa, my hand still clamped tight over the T-shirt covering the wound on my forearm.

"Ava, talk to us," my mother urged, kneeling before me. She combed my hair back with her fingers as her eyes roamed over my face. "What happened?" Her attention drifted to my T-shirt-covered arm, and she asked a silent question as she stared at me.

I shook my head, never releasing the pressure on the slit across my flesh. My gaze was stuck to the corner of the chevron-patterned rug underneath the coffee table. I refused to admit what I had done. But I also knew I had to tell her how bad it was. Another wave of exhaustion hit me. The stickiness of the blood made it through the cotton fabric.

Dad sat next to me, carefully removing the piece of clothing around my arm. His eyes widened, overflowing with worry as he took in the wound.

"I'm sorry," I whispered, unable to look at any of them.

"She needs stitches," I heard him tell my mother.

More shame grew roots inside me, and I mumbled, "For...for a moment...I...I missed her and wanted to be with her." I swallowed the constriction in my throat. "I found the last letters... And life seemed unfair. I don't want to hurt every time I think about what happened. I can't do this anymore."

He fastened his arms around me, holding me closer. His lips descended to rest on the top of my head. "It's okay. We'll get you more help, okay? We'll figure it out. I'm sorry, baby. We're here."

In a heartbeat, Dad was bandaging my forearm, Mom providing him with gauze and tapes from the first aid kit. The entire time, I rested my head on my father's chest, fighting the sleepiness invading me.

"Ava, put pressure on it," he said while he secured the bandage with the last piece of medical-grade tape.

With my eyes closed, I could hear my mother's whisper. "Okay, I'll drive Collin to the Jensens'. I'll meet you at the clinic." She kissed my forehead. "I love you, honey."

I was lifted from the couch, and seconds later, I felt myself lying on the backseat of the car.

My lids stayed close the entire ride. I refused to see the pain on my father's face as I felt the weight of his gaze through the rearview mirror. None of it was his fault. Or my mom's.

Growing up, I just happened to be an expert at masking my pain. And my feelings. Instead of talking about it, I would plug music into my ears and escape to another world where I was safe. And nothing could hurt me.

My parents were my anchors, and I knew if I opened up to them, they would help me through this ripping pain affecting me. This void I sometimes felt inside. They did save me once. Could they save me a second time?

Soon, exhaustion won the battle, and my mind took me far away from here. The last thing I heard was my father's panicked voice saying, "Ava, wake up. Stay with me. Come on, Miss Sunshine, open your eyes," while he lifted me from the backseat, and everything went black.

Chapter 3

Seventeen years old

S played over my pink suitcase, I pressed with all my weight, praying it wouldn't rip as I zipped it up, the fabric strained to its maximum capacity. With a sigh, I surveyed my bedroom, sadness hitting me. The steel-blue walls framed with white trims and matching faux wood furniture looked foreign now. As if I was noticing them for the first time. The lime-green, bright-pink, and sunshine-yellow pillows sprinkled on the navy-blue comforter brought a touch of joy to the room. A far cry from the old décor consisting of charcoal walls and a black bedspread. Last year, when I decided it was time I took back control of my life, Mom offered to redecorate my bedroom with more colorful accents. To bring some happiness into my life, she had said.

"A, I don't understand why you gotta move," my best friend Iris said, perched on my bed, her arms around her folded legs, and her chin propped up on her knees. "Who the hell do your parents think they are? Robbing us of our last real summer together. We've talked about this since freshman year. I even indulged in that tiny piece of purple bikini because we were supposed to be wild and say yes to every opportunity." Her bottom lip swelled in a pout, and she pushed her dark hair over her shoulder. She blinked, her honey-colored eyes filling with questions. "Maybe I should talk to Mr. and Mrs. P. Do a presentation, show them our vision board. Or ask my mom if you could come to stay with us for the summer."

I sighed and sat on my *about to burst open any minute* luggage. "I told you. My therapist agreed too. I need the closure. Also, Uncle Mason offered me a job. I just had no idea my visit with my aunt and uncle would last three months when I suggested it. My parents say they need to figure out some things on their end, so I guess the timing is right. Dad keeps repeating the work experience will be good for my college application next year." I emphasized the word *good* with air quotes. Because, how could working thirty hours a week for the next few weeks be better than a summer of endless fun with my friends? I still had no clue. Following my stint in therapy, after I relapsed and harmed myself for the last time a year ago, I'd decided I would get stronger. Both physically and mentally. I wanted to do better.

I was desperate to recover.

Through my mental health journey, I realized that even though I believed I had fully healed, grief still had its claws deeply embedded into my heart. Despite myself, I kept being its prisoner, as darkness had an invisible pull on me. Over the years, pain had just become less obvious than it used to be. It wasn't until I stood two feet in that the truth hit me. I needed more help. Alone, I wouldn't succeed in chasing the demons of my life away.

Once a week, for a little less than a year, I met with Dr. Koffman, the therapist who treated me from the age of thirteen to fifteen. Until the terror of my nightmares left. For good this time.

Five weeks ago, I concluded that the closure I so desperately needed should happen this summer. I shared the idea with my parents at dinner one night, and the next thing I knew, I had a bus ticket and a job waiting for me in North Carolina mere days after the school year ended.

Talk about kicking your daughter out. It wasn't the plan I had in mind when I voiced it.

If I'd been a rebel-on-a-mission teen giving them anxiety attacks, I might have understood their wanting me to spend some time away. But nope. Not me.

Straight A student. Barely complaining about curfews on the weekends. Never arrested for public indecency or driving under the influence.

They had no valid reason to kick me out. To cast me away for the summer.

The sunshine that was now back in my life disappeared six days ago. When my parents sat me down and announced I would be going away for the entire summer.

"Ava, listen. We know you might not agree with this, but we've decided, as your parents, it would be best for you to go to Feather Lake for more than a week."

I parted my lips to argue, but my mother raised a hand to shut me up before I could express my disagreement. "We're happy you're thriving again. But there are things we need to tackle. Adult stuff. Uncle Mason and Aunt Melinda are ecstatic at the idea of having you over for a little while. Don't get mad. We checked with your thera-pist and she agreed it could do you good too."

Even though their words made sense, it didn't mean I had to approve of their decision. For me. I had plans of my own. Go there for a week. Come back here and enjoy my vacation with Iris. Now, all of that had all gone up in smoke.

"Good?" Iris whined. "Your uncle owns a garage, for God's sake, not a prestigious law firm or a research facility where you could help find a cure for Alzheimer's."

I buried my face in my hands, forcing shut my lids to keep the burning tears at bay. Soon my stupid emotions would ruin the last day with my best friend. I could express my feelings nowadays. It wasn't always an easy feat, but I was getting better at it. Even though I still disliked when people witnessed my being vulnerable, I could let go when things overwhelmed me.

My dad…well, stepdad…but nah…in my heart, Craig had always been my father in every way that counted, said my emotions were wired differently, and I had to learn how to deal with mine in my own way. At my own pace.

I inhaled, chasing away my sour mood. The lump in my throat dissolved a little, and I brought my focus back to my friend.

Since my parents would drop me at the bus station first thing in the morning, Iris and I had less than twenty-four hours with each other, and I intended to make the most of it.

"Bonfire tonight?" I asked, forcing some pep into my words.

Iris jumped to her feet and circled me with her arms, peppering kisses all over my head.

"Stop, dummy. Yuck. Stop," I begged, my sadness forgotten for now and replaced by a train of chuckles. "I'm not your chihuahua. Don't kiss me like that. It's troubling. And disgusting."

She stepped back and picked up the phone she'd discarded earlier on the bed. "Yay, your smile has returned. Let's not spoil these fourteen hours and thirty-seven minutes we have left."

I raised an eyebrow. "Did you set a timer?"

She shrugged. "What? Didn't want to lose a second of the shortest summer we had together."

I pulled her into my arms.

"Anyway, you're not going away without a proper goodbye."

"Geez, you are speaking like I'm about to die. Can you just not make me feel like I'm leaving forever, please?"

She dropped her shoulders in defeat. "You're right. But adding a little drama makes things more exciting." She flicked her wrist, going back to the device in her hand. "I made plans. Bonfire. Midnight swim. Late pizza delivery. Night in the cargo bed of Lucas's truck, because you guys will be apart for three months. Imagine all the times he'll have to fuck his own fist thinking about you."

I threw a pillow at her. "Shut up. Don't scream that for the entire town to hear. My parents would freak out if they knew we talked about having sex."

Iris gasped. "Do you think if they knew, they'd still send you away?"

"Yep. They'd send me further away." I poked my tongue out. "An all-girls boarding school on a remote island." I paused and inhaled. "About Lucas…we're not together anymore. We decided to no longer date."

Iris's inquisitive gaze darted to me. "A, are you okay? What does it mean, *no longer date*?"

"Two weeks ago, we realized we were better off as friends. Even though we talked about sex, neither of us was ready for the next step. He's just not the guy for me. We're not going to force things. He wants me to enjoy my summer without having to miss him all the time. Anyway, it's not like we'll be together in college either. He's moving to England to stay with his dad next year." I shrugged. "Maybe it's a good thing. It's no big deal."

She held my hands in hers and blinked. "Whoa, you guys are on a break. You would tell me if it was more than that, right? I know your penchant for romance, A. Your heart must be in pieces right now. Two weeks? Why didn't you say anything?"

"I'll be fine. Lucas and I, we're still friends. We'll always be friends. No matter what happens. So, I'm not losing him. We chose to wait until the end of the school year. To avoid the rumor mill and make things awkward amongst our friends."

"It sounds like an excuse for him to bang other chicks while you're away."

"The truth is that I don't love him as much as I thought I did. I'm telling you. No one is getting heart-broken over this. It stung at first, and I shed a few tears, but it didn't last. Deep down, I'm sure it was the right call. We'll see how it goes once school resumes in the fall. If he were my true love, wouldn't I be shattered right now?"

Iris offered me a concerned expression. She knew about my episodes.

I smiled at her to prove I was okay. "And I'm not. I'm rather kinda relieved. Don't worry, okay?"

She tugged at my hand, and we both lay on my bed, staring at the ceiling for a long beat.

Iris was the only person who knew about my history and why I acted the way I did. She was my confidante and a sister to me.

"Is your breakup with Lucas part of the reason your parents are sending you away for that long?"

I shrugged. "I guess it's one of the contributive factors. If I were to relapse, going to Feather Lake would be the main trigger. Or it'll be the closure I need. We'll see how it goes, but I'm confident I can do this. I feel stronger and better about myself. There's no darkness looming around anymore, and the nightmares are gone too. I'm excited to see my aunt and uncle again. I've missed them a lot in the last few years."

"A, this summer won't be the same without you. Who's gonna listen to me speak for hours about art exhibitions on my wish list or how my little sister is getting on my last nerves when she practices her violin? I better get a girlfriend now, or you know me. I'll spend my free time at the library or hide in my room working on my jewelry line and miss all the fun."

We both flipped to our sides, facing each other, and entangled our fingers. "I'll miss you too." A new mass, growing bigger and sturdier, took root in my throat. My stomach clenched as a fresh surge of emotions swirled inside me. A fat tear escaped from Iris's eye, and the dam I'd been working hard to contain broke. Soon, a heartfelt sob escaped my lips.

We hugged for what seemed like hours. Until my best friend pulled back and wiped her eyes with her fingers. "Girl, we gotta go. No way are we missing tonight. We said this summer would be all about getting outside our comfort zone. *A Summer to Remember*. Better start now."

I nodded, my throat still too raw to speak a word.

Iris and I had been best friends since fifth grade. One September, she moved six houses down mine, and over the years, we'd been inseparable. We'd never been apart for long. Each summer, when we were younger, we attended day camp together. When we went on vacation, she would often tag along. If her family did, I would get an invite too.

So, this…this summer away from each other, when we knew we'd be in colleges on different coasts of the country in a little over a year, was a hard pill to swallow.

And for the first time in all my seventeen years of existence, I kinda resented my parents. They'd organized my vacation without my consent. While Collin, my thirteen-year-old brother, was spending the next two months in soccer camp, a few hours' drive from here, I was being shipped to the other end of the country for twelve weeks.

I changed into a pair of coral shorts and an off-white T-shirt with pink and orange palm trees stamped on the front. While I braided my hair over my shoulder, I looked at my reflection in the mirror and made sure no traces of the tears I'd cried minutes ago were left on my face.

"Ready?" my friend asked once we both regained our composure and fixed ourselves.

I surveyed my room as waves of nostalgia hit me. "All packed. Sure, let's go." I breathed out and followed her downstairs.

"Where are you girls going?" Dad asked as we crossed paths in the kitchen.

"Out," I said, my tone missing the usual cheerfulness. Right now, I was upset and couldn't fake being happy. For the longest time in my life, I pretended I was fine when I wasn't. Part of learning how to express my emotions better was to stop faking them when I didn't mean them. It was still a work in progress, but I was getting there.

My dad's face fell. "But dinner is almost ready. I made your favorite meal. Iris can stay too. We wanted to spend the evening together with you. Since it's your last night in town. Celebrate the beginning of the summer vacation and your trip."

I shrugged, fetched two apples from the wooden basket on the kitchen island, and tossed one to Iris. "Sorry. Usually, I would. But tonight, I can't. We have plans. Don't wait for me."

Craig ate the distance between us and held my upper arms. "Ava…it doesn't have to be this way. We know you're upset to be sent away for longer than expected. But Uncle Mason is happy to have you over. He's been looking forward to showing you the basics of running a business. For years, you've said you'd like to be an entrepreneur. Here's your chance. You'll get to see how much you like it before you apply to college next year. Decide if you still wanna pursue business management as your major. Think about it. It will be a wonderful experience and will look great on your application too."

I turned my head, avoiding his eyes, aware my heart wouldn't be able to ignore the pain I suspected was filling his eyes, but decided not to back down for once and hold my own. I was angry. My parents had to deal with it. They created the situation. My heart rattled in my chest. I hated confrontations. But by messing with my life, they should have expected my retaliation.

"And you'll get paid. You'll be able to buy that car you've been talking about. Or save it for some other grand project in the future. Trust me, I wouldn't have agreed to this if I didn't think it was a wonderful idea."

Pinching my lips together, I sucked in a long breath through my nose, doing my best to avoid showing my dad how much his words affected me.

His shoulders dropped when our gazes connected.

I glared at him, or at least, I tried to. Why wasn't I able to tell him how mad I really was? Instead, I averted my eyes, hoping my silence was enough to project my thoughts. See? Work in progress.

"Fine. Go out." He sighed. Knots tied around my stomach. I hated seeing him defeated. "We're leaving at seven tomorrow. Just make sure you're back here on time. Curfew is canceled tonight. You girls be safe. Call me if you need a ride later."

Every cell in me strained, my body about to rip at the seams and expose my leaking heart.

I fought with everything I possessed to keep my poker face on and the glower in my eyes.

Keeping my back straight, I said, "I'm sorry. Gotta go." The only words I could muster right now without revealing the conflicted emotions surging inside me. Anger, sadness, confusion, pain. Emotions I needed to sort out before they consumed me.

In one swift movement, I jerked away from my dad's grip.

His arms went slack at his sides, and I saw the subtle shake of his head as I put more space between us.

Just as Iris and I were about to exit the house through the kitchen door, we bumped into my mother.

"Hey Mrs. P," my friend said in her usual cheerful voice.

"Girls. Where are you going? We were about to eat. Craig cooked all aftern—"

I strode out the door, avoiding a glance in her direction, knowing I was breaking their hearts, but unable to stop my escape. There was just too much going on at once, and it screwed with my composure. I had to walk away and breathe on my own. I was sure my parents would understand when I explained. Later. Much later. Once the anger was expended.

I was well-aware my fleeing could paint me as a coward, but my parents hurt me too. Right now, I couldn't deal with everyone else's desires.

I exhaled the air in my lungs.

They chose to send me away, and I needed time to accept the idea. Yep, they should've told me weeks ago, not six days before the departure date. We should have talked about it. I should have been allowed to have a say. It was my life. My summer. They meddled with all of it. A new wave of hurt rose in the depths of me.

"I'll be back in time to board that bus," I barked, slamming the door and bruising my own heart in the process.

Chapter 4

Mom hugged me for what felt like hours while I stood still in her arms. She cried against my shoulder, and tears pooled in my eyes, no matter how hard I tried to keep them locked in. "You'll arrive in Feather Lake tomorrow afternoon. Uncle Mason will be there to welcome you. You have cash and your credit card in case of emergency. Do you need anything else?"

I shook my head.

"I'll miss you, baby. Please enjoy your summer, okay? Be safe, and we'll see you soon. Don't give a hard time to Uncle Mason and Aunt Melinda. I love you."

I nodded, refusing to speak. Hot tears flowed down my

cheeks, and I fidgeted with the thread bracelet around my wrist, desperate to ground myself and not break down.

Dad pulled me in next, fastening his arms around me. "Ava, I'm sorry you feel like we're doing this to get rid of you. One day, you'll realize it was an opportunity that many don't get in a lifetime, and you'll be happy you did it. In the meantime, just don't be harsh with your mother. She has a lot on her shoulders right now. She needs some time to figure things out. It's for the best. For all of us. We would never do anything to hurt you or your feelings on purpose, Miss Sunshine."

"Dad," I said, unable to hide my exasperation at the pet name he'd been using since the day he held me for the first time, minutes after I was born, considering me his, as he often repeated over the years.

He leaned back. "Finally. A reaction." His large fingers dried the tears rolling down my cheeks. "I love you, kiddo. We all do. Please be safe and tell my brother I said hi."

I nodded and brought my focus to my black Chucks. The ones on which I had written inspiring quotes with a gold permanent marker last summer. Today, I had opted for a bland outfit. One that fitted my mood. Washed-out denim cut-offs and a white T-shirt underneath a large black hoodie, so big on me that it covered my hands.

After I hugged Collin, I turned up the volume of my phone, stuck my earbuds in, and boarded the bus that would drive me from Michigan to North Carolina.

Sitting by the window, I dropped my backpack on the seat next to mine, hoping people would get a hint and sit anywhere but next to me. I needed my space. And room to breathe. I had almost a thirty-hour journey in front of me, and I refused to share it with anyone.

With the sleeve of my hoodie, I wiped the last traces of moisture from my eyes and shut my eyelids, rested my head against the window, and got lost in my mind. Due to the fact that I barely slept an hour last night, I fell asleep before the bus even took off.

The smooth vibration of the tires on the pavement turned gravelly before the bus came to a stop, jerking me out of my slumber. *What the—*

How long had I been out?

I wiped the drool that had dried at the corner of my mouth and rubbed my fists over my heavy eyelids. When I opened them, the sun shone brighter and directly on my face through the glass, blinding me. From its high position, I'd guess it was close to noon. Why did we stop?

Rotating my neck, I stretched and got rid of the tension that had accumulated in my shoulders in the last few hours. I cocked my head to the side when people moved to their feet to exit the vehicle, only to be captured by two sky-blue irises fixated on me.

It took me a fraction of a second to realize I hadn't been alone all this time.

I removed my earbuds while my gaze swooped over him from head to waist.

"Nice to see you alive," the curly-haired surfer-looking blond guy said with a smirk. "You snored so bad I was tempted to put one of my socks into your mouth to silence that muffler."

He winked, and I glared at him, not sure whether he was teasing me or not.

"You coming?" he asked.

I blinked. "Where?"

"Pit stop. The driver announced a fifteen-minute break. Guess that music was too loud, or that muffler of yours needs some tuning." His lips stretched wider as he pointed to my earbuds.

"Reel in your grin. I wasn't snoring." I crossed my arms over my chest and upped my chin in defiance.

"Says who?"

Right now, I wished I could scratch that smile off his full lips. "I wasn't. You're hearing things. You should see an ear doctor. Just to make sure."

The upturn of his mouth never faltered as amusement danced in his eyes.

"Wanna bet?" he asked in a breezy tone that sounded like nails on a chalkboard to me.

I glared at him, his over-cheerfulness annoying me after a sleepless night.

"Stop."

The hot-looking stranger arched a brow. "Stop what?"

"You know what. Don't pretend you don't."

He mimicked my stance, his arms now folded over his broad chest the same way I did. "No idea what you're talking about. Care to speak in English."

I frowned, never breaking eye contact. "How can you be so infuriating?" I groaned. "Stop looking at me like that. Like you're some big shot and I'm an angry person or something."

"Angry person or something…" He scratched his temple. "Not sure what you mean."

I harrumphed. "Whatever. Move." I scanned the area around me as I motioned to stand. This break would help stretch my legs. "Wait? Where's my bag? What did you do with my stuff?"

He extended his arm. "First, let's be civil. I'm Joseph. My friends call me Joe. Sometimes Joey. Or Curry, like the spice."

I stared at his hand, not sure if I was ready to make a new friend just about now. Too soon.

"Come on, it's just a handshake. I won't bite you.

Unless you're scared my happiness will rub off on you. If that's the case, I get why you're afraid. Being happy is a shame."

I huffed. "Don't try to psychoanalyze me. I'm not in the mood for your cheerfulness, hot stuff. Doesn't mean I'm unhappy."

"Oh, you're a germophobe then. Afraid my hand will infect yours." He seemed to think for a long second. "Would sanitizer help? I have some in my bag."

I huffed. "I'm not scared of germs. Stop fabricating explanations about who I am that you can't back up. You know nothing about me."

"Still waiting," he said, waving his proffered hand.

"Fine." I slid my palm into his. The warmth of his hand transferred to me, sending goose bumps up my forearm. "Happy now?"

"Almost. What should I call you? Grump? Sulk-Master?"

I rolled my eyes and blew out a long breath. "Ava."

"Ava. I love your name." Sparks flashed in his blue eyes. They were the same color as the sky on a summer day. "Where are you going, Ava?" He pronounced each syllable slowly.

"None of your business." I peeled my hand back, wiping it over the back of my shorts, trying to rub off the remaining current from his touch.

Joseph shook his head, the grin still anchored to his handsome face. Sun-kissed skin, as if he spent all his time outside, square jaw, long neck, he looked like he had come straight from the California shores.

"Ava, come on. I'm not a psycho. I'm just trying to make conversation here. We'll be bus neighbors for God knows how long, better find some company to make it less boring. Everybody needs a sidekick. Let me start over. I'm

Joseph. From Traverse City, Michigan. Moving to North Carolina to live with my dad and his new wife. They just had a baby. I guess it makes me a new big brother. Your turn?"

Okay, Joseph didn't have a murderer vibe—the one Dad always warned me about—emanating from him. What did murderers look like anyway? Creepy and sketchy, I guessed. No, Joseph didn't fit the profile.

"I'm from Elk River and going to North Carolina too. For the summer. Happy now?"

Joseph bobbed his head, his lips tilted up. For the first time, I noticed the single dimple marking his chin. "We're best friends now," he added in a teasing tone. "Told ya, it's better to be friendly since we're going to be stuck together for a long while. See? It wasn't that hard."

My earlier question rushed back to my mind, which had been too busy being charmed by the stranger sitting next to me. "My stuff? Where is it?"

Joseph moved to his feet and offered me a hand. "Up there," he said pointing to the compartment above our heads. "Now let's go, bestie. We just have time to pick up food and exercise our legs before we hit the road again."

That's when I realized we had stopped in front of a gas station and people were climbing back into the bus with pizza slices in cardboard trays, cans of soda, and snacks.

My stomach grumbled at the smell of greasy junk food. My breakfast this morning had consisted of a banana and a cup of coffee, so anything edible sounded like heaven right now.

Joseph pulled at my hand and led me outside. "My treat. Pick whatever you want."

I halted and waited until he spun to face me.

"What?"

"Why are you being nice to me? You don't even know me."

His amusement dropped a notch. "You look like you might need a friend. I'm just applying for the job."

I forced a hint of a smile to my lips. "Thanks." And against all odds, he might just be right.

———

"If you could live anywhere in the world, where would it be?" Joseph asked as we shared a bag of gummy bears.

I reflected on it for a minute, the gears in my brain working hard to think about every country I had ever heard of. "Australia. No. Africa. I don't know the exact place, but someplace where I can help endangered animals."

"Thanks for asking." He poked his tongue out playfully.

I scowled. All this small talk was exhausting, but Joseph was determined to keep going.

"Mine is Thailand," he added before I could say anything. "Those beaches. Life seems so chill there. Favorite movie?"

"*It Happened to Us.*" I exhaled and forced the question out. "Yours?" I asked with an exaggerated curl of my lips.

"Oh, so you're a drama and tearjerker masochist? Interesting." Joseph pushed a handful of jellies into his mouth. "Why doesn't it surprise me?" he asked with a mouthful. "Mine is *Wavelength*. The surfing biopic."

I poked his shoulder. "Geez, swallow before speaking. It's disgusting. I can see all those murdered bears in there."

He opened his mouth wider. "Like that?"

I closed my eyes and shook my head.

"Any siblings?" he asked next.

"Yes. You?"

He swallowed the remaining of his gummies before speaking again. "See, you can master the art of conversation. You're a natural."

I frowned.

His grin grew wider.

Whatever.

"A half brother and twin half sisters on my mom's side. A ten-year-old stepsister named Kelly and a three-month-old baby sister on my dad's side. Her name is Scarlett. I can't wait to meet her. Brothers or sisters?"

"A younger brother. Collin. And Iris, my best friend. We're more like sisters. She's my favorite person."

Joseph's fist hit his chest. "I thought *I* was your favorite person. I'm wounded, Ava."

I sighed at his theatrical display. "On this bus, on this journey, you are my only friend. You can steal the best friend spot if you wish."

"Taken. It's mine. For as long as we both shall live."

"And now you're turning into Shakespeare. Entertaining being your friend."

"I'm full of surprises. Wanna watch something? I have a couple of movies downloaded on my laptop. I'll let you choose. I don't have *It Happened to Us*, but I bet you can find something else that you can bawl your eyes to."

"Oh, and now you're a gentleman. I'll never be bored with you in my life."

"Told ya. I'm the *best* best friend you'll ever get. Better call Iris and tell her she's now second best. Think she'll ever forgive you?"

"Cockiness suits you. Can you give this friendship a couple more hours so we know for sure it's the real deal before claiming your new title out loud?" I asked, giving him a pointed stare. "Stop rushing it."

Joseph slid his laptop out of his backpack and positioned it over his thighs. "Fine, I'll give you till tomorrow to get used to this new reality, bestie."

Turning it on, he grinned.

Why was he so gleeful?

I grabbed the rest of the gummy bears from the bag and stuffed them into my mouth with a shrug, never returning his smile. "Works for me."

———

The bus stopped at around six in the evening in the parking lot of different food chains so we could grab dinner. Joseph and I had gotten to know each other a little over the last few hours. I found out he really loved talking about everything and anything. He showed me pictures of his family. Of his friends back in Michigan. Talked me through the art of throwing the perfect football and about his favorite music bands. Every time I thought he was done and put music back into my ears, he would pull at my earbuds, asking a new question. Or sharing a new piece of information I never asked for. I had to admit he was entertaining, all his stories full of colorful details.

How could he not get I was desperate for silence? And time to sulk on my own—without interruption. The fake smiles and yawns didn't deter him. No, it seemed to encourage him to fill the periods of silence even more.

A part of me wished I could tell him to gimme a break. To let me be. While the other half loved the distraction and the comfort that had settled between us.

With my eyes trained outside, I surveyed my food options, an old country song playing in my ears, when my seat neighbor removed my left earbud.

"What?"

He grabbed my hand. "Come on, let's go and eat."

"Since dinner is my treat, according to your rule, how about sushi?" I asked once we exited the vehicle.

He winced. "Nah. Too fancy. What about cheeseburgers, fries, and milkshakes? Typical American teenager's food choice."

Already, the whiff coming from the burger place permeated my nose.

"I was about to suggest a salad." A pout formed on my lips.

"Where's the fun in that? We're on our own, no parental figure to supervise what we eat, and you pick a salad? Are you sure you're not sick? Where's your sense of adventure and risk? Please tell me you're joking. That it was a test. To see if I would fall for it."

I rolled my eyes. "Are you majoring in theatre?"

"Maybe."

"Okay. Fine, you win. I was just testing you. A burger sounds good."

"Ha, ha. I knew it." Joseph watched me. "Avalon is a prankster. Noted. Follow me."

We ate on a tiny patch of grass next to where the bus was parked. The sun, giant and orange, glowed on the horizon, painting the sky in pinkish brush strokes.

"Beautiful, isn't it?" my new friend said.

I nodded, unable to avert my eyes. I grabbed my phone to immortalize this moment when he stole the device from my hand.

"Let me. Turn around, and I'll snap a picture of you."

I shook my head, feeling warmth creeping up my cheeks. "You don't have to."

"Ava, I want to. Now smile."

For a moment, we remained silent. Was Joseph Curry a genuinely nice person, or was it all an act? How could he still wanna be friends with me after I'd been keeping him mostly at arm's length all day, never striking up a conversation of my own and only answering his questions when I had to?

"Beautiful." Joseph handed me back my phone.

"Thanks," I said, fidgeting with my fingers and avoiding his eyes as I sensed his piercing gaze on me. "We should get back on the bus."

After we gathered our stuff and threw away our empty food packaging, we returned to our seats.

We stayed silent for a long while, and I plugged my buds into my ears, my head pressed against the window, watching the scenery and the night falling upon us.

"No. Not good enough. This stops now," Joseph said after a long while, tugging my earbuds out of my ears. Again.

Slowly, I tilted my head to look at him, not sure what he meant.

"This," he said, motioning to the space between the two of us. "No more ignoring each other. We're besties, remember? We're traveling buddies. And we're already spending the night together. Not that I usually put out on the first date, but hey, in this case, I might make an exception. Because of you."

At his wit, I relaxed my shoulders and grimaced. "Sorry. Sometimes I need some space. To zone out."

"Ava, you look sad. As your new best friend, I gotta know if I should worry."

"I'm fine." I wasn't, but I wouldn't tell him. It was none of his business. The fight with my parents, it ate me up from the inside. I was still angry about being shipped away without my consent. Not sure when I'd get over this one. If I thought too much about it, no doubt a new wave of sadness would invade me. Changing the subject sounded like my best option. "And for what it's worth," I said, curling my lips with a hint of a smile and trying to diffuse his worries, "and since you are my *best friend*—according to your definition of seat neighbors—for another twelve hours or so, I'll say this. I don't put out on the first night either."

Joseph laughed out loud, and the sound erased some of the uneasiness overwhelming me.

"Mind if you share your music?" he asked after an instant. "I'll share my shoulder for the night. Seems like a fair deal, don't you think?"

I blew out a long breath. "Sure." A version of me loved the idea I wasn't alone on this trip. Joseph was kind of nice, and if I was being honest with myself, he made this unwanted road trip a lot less boring than it could have been. It gave me no time to mope over my situation.

Yeah, Joseph, by pushing himself into my bubble and with his over-the-top cheerfulness, made me forget about my anger for the time being.

"Thanks. For your shoulder pillow."

He plugged the earbud I handed him into his ear. His fingers reached for mine, and I didn't jerk them away. His presence soothed the wound in my heart. Even though it made no sense. Not breaking apart, with my head pressed against his shoulder and our hands linked, we fell asleep listening to the music, the inky night outside now plunging the bus into a comforting cover of darkness.

For the first time since I had learned I'd be going away this summer, I didn't feel alone on the journey.

Chapter 5

"**G**ood morning, sleepyhead" were the first words I heard the moment I pried my lids open. It took me a long minute to get my bearings and recall where I was.

"Sleep well? I bet. My shirt is drenched in drool."

My eyes sprang open.

Joseph.

I pushed away from his shoulder, rolling my jaw back and forth to remove the strain that had settled there while I slept.

Cranking my neck to the side, I looked outside. "What time is it? Is it even legal to wake up at this hour?" I asked through a yawn as I firmed my back and angled myself to watch him.

"Six." His voice dropped to a whisper "Don't scream, please. Most people are still out of it. Or a bit groggy without their daily caffeine shot."

I blinked at his early morning joy. Could this guy ever be moody? Since we met, his smile hadn't left his lips.

Another yawn escaped me, and I stretched my arms over my head to get rid of the lingering effect of sleep from my body.

"Did you sleep at all?" I asked as Joseph offered me a muffin from the pack he had bought the previous day.

"Yep. I'm an early riser. Love to hit the waves at sunrise in the summer. Or the gym in the winter."

"Ah, I knew it," I exclaimed too loud, cupping my mouth with a hand. My gaze traveled all around us. "Sorry," I whispered. "I should have bet you were a surfer. You have the look."

Joseph fanned the air in front of him. "Oh Avalon, you're smart, sweet, and beautiful, but that morning breath is a deal breaker."

My face flushed. I felt scorching heat taking over my cheeks. Gosh, now was the moment I should dig a hole in the ground and bury myself in it.

I placed a hand before my mouth and blew into it, trying to gauge how deep this grave of mine should be.

Joseph's laughter added another layer to my let-me-die vow.

"Avalon, you should see your face. I'm just messing with you."

I pinched my lips together and killed him with my eyes only. In the last week—since I had learned I'd be gone for almost three months—I had mastered this new skill. "You jerk. What's with the Avalon?"

He shrugged. "Don't know. Sounds ethereal. Like you. Dark blonde hair. Soft aqua eyes. Sinful lips." His focus descended to my mouth for a flash-second before resuming their ascension to my eyes. Electricity traveled through me. For a reason that escaped me, I loved the way he looked at me. I averted my eyes, the intensity of his gaze burning my skin. "Anyway, for me, you're Avalon. Believe me, Ava is a beautiful name, but Avalon suits you better."

"Huh, thanks. That was nice. Everything you said."

"I'm *that* person. Selfless, compliment-giving, good-looking Joseph Curry."

The bus stopped, and the driver's announcement cut our discussion short. "Breakfast break. Fifteen minutes, folks. Be back in time."

Joseph caught my hand in his. "Come on, bestie. Let's get some food."

Inside, I bought two toothbrushes and a travel-size toothpaste tube because my toiletry kit was in my bag. "Here," I said, slapping one on my new travel companion's chest. "Better be clean than sorry." I put on my fakest smile.

Joseph replied with a disapproving stare.

"Avalon," he tsk-tsked at me. For a moment, I held my breath, thinking I might have offended him, but in the next second, his intoxicating grin—the one displaying that chin dimple—came back in full force. "Just kiddin'. Thank you. I'm touched to know my hygiene is a concern for you."

"What are best friends for?" I remarked, sarcasm bleeding from my words.

His palm hit his chest. "Love it when you recognize our bond."

"Ohmygod, you never stop."

He emptied the shelves into my arms, and I followed him around as we argued about what we should get. "Are you having a growth spurt?" I asked when he added a box of cereals to the pile.

He winked and led me toward the cashier, carrying two to-go coffee cups. "Like you said, better be fed than sorry."

Side by side, we boarded the bus.

"What are your plans for the summer?" Joseph asked once we were back on the road. A bag full of snacks, drinks, and gas station knickknacks, which was supposed to keep us busy for the last few hours of this trip, rested at our feet. "You never told me why you are spending time far away from home."

I sighed, the residual anger of last week resurrecting at the thought of wasting my summer away. Pushing it down, I gave him a simpler explanation. "Long story short. I decided to visit my aunt and uncle for a week. My parents changed my stay to a three-month-long one instead. They thought I should work for my uncle and gain experience. The girl working the front desk left two weeks ago, and they all agreed I should be her replacement this summer. Without consulting me first."

"I see. Are your parents going through a divorce?"

I popped a piece of croissant into my mouth. "Nah, why?"

"One day, when I was around ten, my parents sent me away to spend a month at my grandparents'. They were divorcing and wanted to deal with it without my witnessing the messiness of the situation. Just sayin'."

I shook my head. "No. No way. Craig and my mom love each other. They were high school sweethearts. You're wrong."

"If you say so." Joseph tossed a handful of dry cereals into his mouth and chewed before speaking again. "You said Craig and your mom. Why not Mom and Dad?"

I sighed. "My biological dad died. Just after my mom learned she was pregnant with me."

"Oh fuck. Sorry, Avalon."

I half-smiled at the term of endearment. "Don't be. Craig is my father. I usually call him Dad. It's just—I'm upset at them. When I am, I tend to call him Craig instead. Don't read too much into it. It's childish."

"Where are you staying? I'll be in Medora Beach. That's where the waves are the best. It's a small town along the coast. Dad manages a surf school on the beach, and he and his wife own a restaurant by the pier. If you're staying close, maybe we could see each other again. I know a few people in town, but it could be fun to have my best friend around." Joseph tilted his lips, expectation filling his eyes.

"Maybe," I said, my gaze turning somber, not wanting to commit.

He shook his head in dramatic fashion. "Avalon, girl. You're hurting me. I thought we were already best friends forever, you and I. After all, we agreed. We even shared music and a shoulder last night. How much closer than that can it get?"

"I'll be in Feather Lake. Seems like a boring, small town surrounded by thick forest and lakes."

"Therefore, you should visit the beach on your days off. Because you have a reason to come." He pointed to his chest with his thumb. "Wouldn't want you to miss me too much."

"Okay."

"Okay? Can you, for once, look happy?" he asked.

I fake-grinned, showing way too many teeth, and added an unconvincing "Yay."

Joseph shifted on his seat and closed his arms around me. "Friend, we have a deal." He pulled back and extended his hand. "To the start of a great summer and our new friendship"

I shook his palm and couldn't hold back my smile this time. "To being friends."

He took his phone out and draped an arm around my shoulders. "I'm making this relationship official." He snapped a picture of us. "Now gimme your number so I don't have to search the entire state for you once we both go our separate ways."

He winked, and I punched my number into his phone, feeling a bit better about the next three months of my summer vacation slash prison sentence, now that I had an ally.

———

A few hours later, we climbed out of the bus. The bright sun's rays burned my flesh. Joseph handed me my backpack and helped me grab my suitcase from the compartment underneath the vehicle.

Uncle Mason waited for me with my name written on a cardboard sign in black ink and a bag of pink cotton candy. My lips stretched of their own accord, and my heart did a happy dance in my chest because he remembered I would kill for the sugary treat.

"Hey kiddo," he greeted me with the biggest smile. Even though I was upset with my parents, none of this was his fault. We hadn't seen each other in four years, and right now, he looked so much like my dad, but with grayed temples.

Abandoning my baggage on the ground, I nestled against his chest, his loving arms enveloping me.

"Look at you. You've grown so tall." At five-foot-eight, I had reached a respectable height. He leaned back to study me, twirling a strand of my dark blonde hair around his finger. "I'm sure Craig must be chasing those boys away with a baseball bat. Because I know I would. You look so much like your mama. I'm so glad you're here, kiddo."

I nodded as we broke apart. "Thanks for having me. I hope it wasn't too much trouble for you."

"You're kidding, right? I'm so excited you're here. Melinda is ecstatic to have another woman in the house. C'mon, Ava, let's go home and get you settled. Are you hungry?"

"A little."

"We'll stop by The French Toast first to grab a bite." His arm circled my shoulders. "We've missed you. As long as you live here, our home is your home, okay?"

I nodded. Unlike my parents, at least Uncle Mason and Aunt Melinda really sounded like they cared to have me around this summer.

We reached his pickup truck, and Uncle Mason slid behind the wheel after placing my luggage in the backseat.

Joseph called my name before I could haul myself into the passenger seat.

"Hey Avalon, wait up." He jogged my way, the smile I now recognized as his personal trademark illuminating his face. "Let's meet up again. Dusty's." His hand rested on the frame of my open door. "One week from now. It's where all the locals go. Our favorite hangout spot. Drinks are cheap, and chicken wings are tasty. I'll text you the address. You better show up, or I'll come and find you."

"Okay."

"Love it when we have overenthusiastic conversations," he said with a wink. He hesitated for a short instant before leaning forward and kissing my cheek. "It's a date, best friend."

He closed the door after I climbed into the idling truck. Cold air hit me, and I relished how it cooled my sweaty self. Getting used to the warm and humid temperature of the South would take some time.

"Who was that?" Uncle Mason asked with one raised brow.

I offered him a non-committal shrug. "A friend."

He cleared his throat. "A friend? Mind being more specific?"

I felt my cheeks heating up. "Joseph. We traveled together. He's moving here. We agreed to meet again. Nothing super exciting."

"Let's talk about that later." He gave his head a tiny shake. "You've been in town for five minutes, and I'm already sensing boy troubles."

"Nothing like that. I promise."

"Yeah, we'll see."

———

Iris texted me just after I exited the shower and was about to empty my suitcase in the room Aunt Melinda decorated for me. Whitewashed walls—with touches of purple dotting the space, from pillows to picture frames—white comforter, a white chest of drawers with a rectangular mirror above. A seashell wind chime hung in the window that was framed by silk curtains. The room connected to a three-piece en-suite bathroom, which I really enjoyed. I never had a chance not to share a bathroom before. The room also included a private entrance, accessible from the front of the house. Somehow, it was like having my own apartment, and I loved that the room afforded privacy.

Mine was the only bedroom on the main level of the bungalow with a steel-blue exterior. Outside, white trims outlined the windows, and white columns over brick pillars supported the wrap-around porch. The lawn was green and freshly cut, its scent permeating the air. The kitchen was at the back of the house and had a door leading to the garden, a garage, and a backyard. Uncle Mason told me they usually used that entrance to come and go since they had more parking spaces at the back of the house.

Grayish-teal walls and maple wooden floors gave the entire house a peaceful ocean-vibe charm. Handcrafted wood furniture, black and soft pink accents made it look country-chic. The room adjacent to mine was an office with a Murphy bed to transform the space into a guest room when needed. Upstairs were two more bedrooms, the master and a smaller one, which had been converted into a little sanctuary with a variety of plants, a reading corner, and rows of family photos occupying the length of one wall.

The bungalow wasn't big, but I already felt at home the moment I stepped inside. After Uncle Mason gave me the grand tour earlier, it consolidated the feeling.

Even though Feather Lake wasn't a coastal town and was mostly set in acres of wood, my bedroom had a fresh and soothing atmosphere. I loved everything about it. It enveloped me with warmth—and calm.

IRIS

Hey A, are you there yet? You sent me a one-line message hours ago and then nothing. Are you okay?

ME

Yep. Just a sec.

I took a picture of my new bedroom and sent it to my friend.

IRIS

Wow, I love the decor. It's super you. Still upset?

ME

Yes. But met this guy on the bus. Joseph. Funny and sweet. For a moment, he made me forget about my parents casting me away. With a friend in town, maybe things won't suck too much.

IRIS

Joseph? You met someone? Already? You didn't lose any time. Perhaps you'll still be able to go wild this summer. Who knows. Is he cute?

I checked my other messages and realized Joseph hadn't sent the picture of us yet.

ME

I'll send you a pic. Once I get the one he took. He has a chin dimple and a surfer boy look. He's a bit too cheerful. But hey, it sort of balanced out with how I was feeling. All fine, I guess.

What about you? Anything new in the last thirty-something hours?

IRIS

I wish. I got the job at the gift shop. I'm starting on Monday.

Oh, gotta go. Mother is calling my name. She sounds mad. Text me tomorrow once you're settled. Love you x

ME

Love you too xx

A soft knock on my door snapped me out of my train of thought. The ones about my life, plans, and dreams I'd left behind. My anger had somehow evolved since I left my hometown. Here, I had no one to complain to. Even though I had family around, people who loved me and, from what it seemed, were glad to have me here, I had no idea how I'd survive this summer on my own. Without Iris.

"Come on in," I called out, hanging the last piece of clothing in the closet.

Aunt Melinda's head peeked through the door. "Hey honey. Dinner is ready." She padded into the room and sat on the edge of my bed. "Do you miss anything?"

I glanced around and shook my head. "I'm fine." I paused before joining her. My aunt had long brown hair and turquoise eyes, almost the same shade as mine on a sunny day. Except for the hair color, people who didn't know any better always thought we were related by blood since we looked very much alike. Growing up, she had always been my favorite relative. She had a calmness about her and an assurance nobody else I knew possessed, and I'd always loved how it rubbed off on me. "Thanks for the room. It's beautiful. You didn't have to do that."

She brushed my hair behind my ear with her fingers. "Honey, it's my pleasure. I consider you a daughter, and I couldn't wait to transform this room into something beautiful. Just like you."

"I-I love what you did in the bedroom upstairs," I said.

Our eyes locked. We both knew it must have been hard for her and Uncle Mason to erase all traces of the past from those walls. She squeezed my hand, and I bowed my head in understanding.

"Ava, you're gonna spend a lot of time here this summer. I know it isn't what you had planned and you're upset about it. Believe me, I would be too if my parents had uprooted me without a warning, but I hope you'll still enjoy your time with us. I also know I'm not your mama, but you and I have always been close in the past. Just keep in mind that I'm here. Whenever you need me. Friends, shopping, work, hair, boys. If you need someone to listen to you without judging, one who's the very best at keeping confidences, I'm your woman. I know things haven't always been easy for you in the last few years, and living with us can trigger memories, but just know we're here for you. I hope you'll make the most of your stay." She moved to stand. "Need a hand with anything before we go and eat that lasagna I made?"

"Nope, I'm done. Did you—"

"Yes, honey. I added bacon the way you like it. Uncle Mason says it's disgusting, but you and I, we are the only ones with real taste in this family. Come on, let's go. I'm starving, and I'm sure a full night's sleep will do you good. I bet sleeping on the bus wasn't comfortable."

After dinner, I went back to my room, exhausted. As long as adrenaline had coursed in my bloodstream, the fatigue had stayed at bay. But now that I was lying on my bed, listening to music, my eyelids grew heavy, and sleep claimed me before I could even comprehend what was happening.

My dreams were filled with an enthusiastic and handsome blond-haired guy, who a part of me couldn't wait to see again. Because with his light, he chased my dark clouds away.

And the memories about the girl who used to live here. In the bedroom upstairs.

Chapter 6

The smell of buttery pancakes and maple syrup drifted to my nose and woke me up from my sleep the next morning. Dressed in night shorts and a long-sleeved T-shirt, I met Uncle Mason and Aunt Melinda in the kitchen.

"Morning," I said, still groggy while running a forearm over my eyes. "Is that for me?" I asked through a yawn as Uncle Mason pushed a mug of coffee my way on the kitchen island.

"All yours. Did you have a restful sleep?"

I brought the hot liquid to my lips, blowing on the steam before running the risk of burning my tongue. "Yes."

"Honey, I'm glad," my aunt said. "Color has returned to your face since last night. Hungry?"

I nodded.

"Sit down." She placed a plate of pancakes topped with fresh blueberries in front of me.

"This smells divine," I said, leaning forward to take a big whiff. "But you guys didn't have to go into this much trouble for me."

Aunt Melinda tapped my shoulder from behind. "You kiddin', right? We're just super excited to have you around. Since you know—"

My back tensed, and I swallowed hard, waiting for her next words.

"Well, you know—" She seemed to think better and instead went with, "Let's just say we're ecstatic you are here with us this summer. Please let us spoil you a little, okay? We'll try not to go overboard."

I pinched my lips together and met her gaze. "Okay."

"Awesome." Tension left her shoulders, and I could see each one of her muscles relaxing.

The knots in my back dissolved too. For an instant, I wondered if she would bring up the topic we hadn't addressed yet. Sure, I was ready to deal with the past, but maybe not on my first day in town.

"What do you wanna do today?" Aunt Melinda asked. "I have the entire morning free for you."

"You'll come to the garage with me on Monday morning," Uncle Mason chimed in, "so I can show you around and explain everything to you in detail. How does it sound?"

I felt bad for my lack of enthusiasm for the job he offered me. With a deep inhale, I plastered what I hoped looked like a genuine grin to my lips. "Perfect. Thank you for doing this."

"Anytime, kiddo."

Aunt Melinda took the seat on my left. "Honey, you and I can drive around town, and we can get our hair done or our nails. Hang out and gossip. Your call. Unless you wanna be left alone to do whatever pleases you. Think about it."

Uncle Mason sat down and fished something out of the pocket of his jeans. "Before I forget. Here," he said.

"What is it?" I asked once he dropped a set of keys into my palm, frowning.

"House key. Garage key. And the third one is a surprise. As long as you're staying here, it will be yours to use."

I blinked, taking in the logo. "For real?"

"It's not new. It had a whole life before you, but we restored it at the garage, and it's working like a charm. I thought you might like to have some independence."

I blinked again. "For me?"

He nodded.

"Ohmygod. Ohmygod." I sprang to my feet and wrapped my uncle in a hug. "Thank you, thank you, thank you."

"It was Melinda's idea actually."

"Thought it could help make the move less bitter," she said. "There's no bus service around here, and you'll need to be able to drive yourself."

I pulled them into my arms, and they enveloped me in their embrace. For a whole minute, I was back to being Ava, the happy teen, instead of the gloomy version of myself I had become in the last week as my heart danced with warmth at the contact.

"And it might be useful to go see that boyfriend of yours," Uncle Mason said in a teasing tone.

"He's not my—"

"Boyfriend? Already? What did I miss?" my aunt asked.

I returned to my seat. "Nothing," Uncle Mason and I said at the same time with a chuckle.

"I can already predict this summer will be memorable," my aunt said, unable to hide her smile. She stood up and draped her arms around my shoulders from behind. "I've missed you, Ava. A lot. I'm glad we're doing this."

I nodded, my short-lasting cheerfulness now evaporating at the thought I had been sent away. "Me too."

We finished eating and decided we'd just drive around this morning so I could figure out how to orient myself until I became familiar with the town. I showered and dressed in a pair of denim cut-offs and a cream tank top with lacy straps, braided my damp hair over my shoulder, and added a coat of mascara and some lip gloss.

"You look beautiful, honey," Aunt Melinda complimented when I joined her. "Ready?"

"Have fun, you two." Uncle Mason kissed his wife and opened the door for us.

The kitchen door led to a large driveway and a detached double-door garage. The property was a flat land, delimitated by rows of thick and high trees. Colorful flower beds and wooden planters, filled with what I assumed to be vegetables and spices, were on the opposite side of the driveway. Behind the garage was a path leading to the pond Uncle Mason told me about when I first arrived here that was invisible from where we stood. The vast piece of land was covered by manicured green grass. A large oak stood in the middle of the backyard, a swing hanging from one of its branches. In my mind, I could picture a little girl perched on it, her daddy pushing her as she begged him to push higher.

I halted when my eyes landed on an old, restored teal pickup truck in the middle of the driveway. "Is this…?" I asked, with my hand over my heart.

"Yes. You like it?" my aunt asked.

"I love it." I spun to face her. "How did you know?"

"Remember that summer we went camping by the ocean? The manager had one just like it, and you'd said when you grow up, you'd like to have one of your own. I hoped you hadn't changed your mind."

"Can I take her for a ride later?"

"Her? So, it's a girl? And yes, you can. As Mason said, it's yours to use."

"She has too much personality to be a guy. Now I gotta figure out a name. I'll let you know later what we agreed on, she and I."

Aunt Melinda unlocked her car with the key fob, and we both slid in. She backed from the driveway and looked at me before pulling into the street. "As I said, I have plans this afternoon, so you can drive around and get acquainted with whatever-her-name is during that time. Sounds good?"

"Yep." Perhaps, just perhaps, being here for three months wouldn't be so bad after all.

Aunt Melinda and I chatted about anything and everything as we drove around town together. Friends. School. My life. Her life. Things to do around here. It was like we'd never been apart. I had decided to let go of my anger for a few hours and roll with it. She didn't ask any questions about my mental health, but once we stopped in a parking lot, I chose to open up a little so she wouldn't worry about me. There was something about the cozy confines of a car that made it easier to confide about my past struggles.

"It broke my heart, honey. To know you were suffering so much and that there was nothing I could do to make it go away." She dabbed under her eyes with a tissue. "Many times, I wished I could have gotten on the next plane and hugged you, but your mom explained what your therapist said, and I understood. Didn't mean it wasn't hard feeling helpless." She paused for a long moment, closing her eyes and inhaling through her mouth before bringing her attention back to me. "And in all honesty, we were so devastated. I'm not sure I would've been a great help to you. My heart…it was in pieces. It still is. But every day, I'm a little better at dealing with the pain. And the loss." Her throat worked as she swallowed. "I'm glad you're doing better too. Right now, that's what matters the most to me. Still…I'm sorry I let you down for so long."

I pinched my lips together to contain my emotions and reached for her trembling hand. We remained silent as the weight of the words—and the event that changed our lives forever—passed between us.

"You didn't need to worry about me on top of everything else. I'm sorry I scared you."

She squeezed my hand back. "Never say you're sorry, Ava. It wasn't your fault. I'm just glad you're healing and offered to come here. Just promise me you'll tell me if you ever feel overwhelmed, okay? Don't keep it all inside. Please."

I nodded. "I promise. I'm a work in progress, but I'm getting there. I haven't felt like…you know…for quite some time. My heart is happier nowadays. I found other ways to cope when I'm in pain. Or when life becomes too much."

After going to the nail salon for some French mani-pedis, we bought new shades and had lunch at The French Toast on Main Street. On our ride home, we picked up donuts at the bakery downtown and slushies at the gas station. When Aunt Melinda and I parted ways, I climbed into Destiny…no, Felicity…yes, better…and went for a drive on my own. My aunt had programmed a few places I might like into my phone, including the lake shore where there was a sandy beach and a park.

"There are quiet spots along the shore. Can come in handy when you need time away from the world," she told me earlier. "During the weekends and at night, people your age hang out there. Parties, barbecues, boat rides, bonfires, name it. It's always busy."

I wasn't the most extrovert person, so meeting new people gave me a bit of anxiety, but I also was aware that spending all my free time by myself would turn out to be boring as hell. I had Joseph, but unless he sent me that picture of us, I had no way of contacting him because, like a fool, I hadn't added his contact to my phone, assuming he would message me sooner.

Aunt Melinda dropped me home and left for her appointment. Armed with a towel, sunblock, and a book, and wearing a bikini underneath my clothes, I decided to spend my afternoon at the lake to see what the buzz was all about.

Being Saturday, the makeshift parking lot—just a patch of ground covered in pine straw—was already pretty full, so I drove a bit further and found an empty spot away from the crowd.

I killed the engine and climbed out. Adjusting my sunglasses, I shouldered my bag and neared the shore following a narrow path through the trees toward the glimmering water that I could now see from a distance. My breath caught in my lungs at the beauty of it. The lake looked majestic, like a precious diamond hidden from any curious eyes who drove by. Blue sky, dark trees, sandy shore. I heard faint voices and music on my right. The smell of barbecue hit my nostrils, no doubt coming from the other side of the thick woodsy area where all the cars were parked.

The spot I found was deserted—like the ones my aunt described. A small wooden dock was set above the water. An old hammock was hung in the shadow between two mature trees, in front of a fire pit made of rocks and full of ashes and half-burned logs.

The sweet scent of blooming flowers and tree moss tickled my nose in the most delicious way.

The sun shone high and bright, and after removing my top and applying sunscreen, I spread my towel on the dock and lay on my back, my book in hand, and music in my ears.

Through the years, music had become one of my coping mechanisms. It helped me evade my mind when things overwhelmed me.

I swiped my phone and clicked a picture and sent it to my best friend back home.

ME

[picture]

IRIS

OMG I'm so jealous right now. I changed my mind, can I come to NC too? Looks amazing. And that bikini, girl, you look phe-no-me-nal. I hope you'll be able to flaunt it on the beach.

I snorted and decided not to engage in this line of conversation when another text message came in.

IRIS

Any news from your new friend? Still waiting for that picture?

ME

Yep. He hasn't sent it yet. I'll forward it to you as soon as I receive it.

We have a date next week.

IRIS

Date? Like date, date? You didn't waste any time. Tell me everything.

ME

Not what you think. Just as friends date. I'll call you later, okay?

IRIS

Sure. Have fun.

Adjusting my ear buds, I closed my eyes, basking in sun's heat when a cracking sound from the edge of the woods, about ten feet from where I lay, startled me. Could it be an animal? Fear slithered down my back. Aunt Melinda had said nothing about having to carry pepper spray around. She also said alligators didn't usually live in the area—none had been spotted here in the last decade— and it was safe to go swimming at the lake.

Springing to a sitting position, I held my breath, my gaze zooming in on the moving tree branches. I jumped to my feet and hurried off the dock where I had discarded my stuff earlier. Two figures walked out, a guy and a girl, and stopped in front of me. The girl fixed her skirt, giving her companion a doe-eyed look and a sultry curve of her lips.

But it was the guy who caught my eye and made me his prisoner.

Tousled light brown hair, tanned skin, dressed in all black except for the brown leather cuff around his left wrist. Aquamarine eyes under a pierced brow found mine and stole every particle of air from my lungs. I gasped as he and I stared at each other for endless seconds, flames licking the space between us. His lips, the color of ripe strawberries, stole my attention.

His eyes widened…in recognition? But how could that be? We'd never met before, so it was impossible he knew who I was. Still, the look on his face resembled shock. And something else.

"Who the fuck are ya?" The girl barked the question. Her glance, filled with judgment, glided over the length of me. "Never saw you before around here. This isn't a hangout spot for losers. Forgotten your way?" She flicked her wrist. "Wherever you came from, leave. Now. It's a private beach. Our private spot. And you aren't invited."

Private beach, my ass. From the mocking tone in her voice, I could tell she was just screwing with me. On purpose.

The stranger grabbed a joint from his pocket and lit it up. Amusement danced across his features, his attention flicking between the two of us.

The girl's eyes threw daggers at me, and her disdain rippled from every inch of her bare skin. I swallowed my hesitation and firmed my back, remembering I wore nothing else other than a tiny bikini top and a pair of shorts.

In a forest-green bikini, even tinier than mine, leaving nothing to the imagination, she was beautiful. In an edgy way. With jet-black hair, smudged red lipstick, and black kohl around her eyes. Her surly attitude didn't impress me. I knew people like her. She was just another bully. I would ignore her and not give her the time of the day. It usually did the trick.

The guy stood motionless next to her, a protective grip around her waist. His throat bobbed once. Twice. His lips pursed, and I became transfixed by the angles of his face.

As if someone had sculpted his features. His heated attention covered my skin in goose bumps. The silent exchange spread shivers of excitement through me, and I hated myself for relishing their intensity.

Unable to escape the hold he had on me, I stayed rigid, my eyes lost in the green abysses of his. As if only the two of us existed on this earth. Sparkled with gold, their aquamarine hue was alluring, changing colors ever so often. Now devoid of any warmth, they were laser-focused on me. Deadly. Cleaving my body yet leaving me gasping for more. My senses felt alien to me, with the sudden rush of heat pooling in my core. The swirl of feelings was new and scary. Yet I craved more of it. I couldn't break this hold he had on me. And I didn't want to.

Until the girl strode forward, causing his eyes to drift to her, and I was no longer his prisoner. I was left shaken and had to take a step back. What was happening to me? I sucked in a deep breath as I looked at the girl, waiting for her next move. That was sure to come. I hated confrontations and had no intention of making enemies on my first day in town.

Whatever this girl had against me, it had no weight. Still, my stomach churned at the idea she was looking for a fight. The little voices in my head told me to step back and add more space between us. Not wanting to show any fear and give her power over me, I shut them down and forced myself to stay still, right where I was.

Returning his attention to me, the mysterious stranger tightened the arm around her and held her back. She bounced back to his side with a "What the fuck" mumble and a scowl, and stole the blunt from his grip, taking a long drag. I watched their interaction, my eyes going back and forth between them and wondering what their deal was.

Once again, I got lost in the depths of green irises that

swallowed me whole and froze me, unable to do anything but study each detail of his profile.

I moved forward and stopped. He did the same.

"Hey," I said, my voice shaky and low.

He blinked, his lips parting to say something when the girl cut him off. "Are you like dumb? Or do you speak English? What are you still doing here?" She sighed, rolling her eyes, her facial expressions hard and her annoyance unconcealed.

She looked at him, probably expecting him to back her up, but he remained stoic next to her.

She cursed under her breath, but her boyfriend didn't seem affected by her antics, ignoring her, his eyes appraising me as if searching for clues. About what? I had no idea.

She stomped her foot, exasperation pouring out from her.

My jaw dropped, and no matter how bad I told myself to clamp my mouth shut, the muscles refused to listen to anything my brain ordered.

It was like this boy had taken over the control center of my body without my permission.

Beside him, the girl grew impatient and tugged at his sleeve.

As if someone had stung him, the guy's eyes moved away from mine and broke the last thread of connection we shared. I blinked. *What just happened?* Everything inside me tightened, compensating for the high only his attention provided me. My pulse went ballistic, and I struggled to take a full breath in.

My heart raced in my chest. All my senses were attuned to him.

The fascination on his face dissolved, and an angry frown took over.

"Grab your things and get the fuck away from here," he threatened, his tone vicious, not open for argument. The low baritone of his voice vibrated through me and sent a rush of heat to my belly. It quickly melted away as his words registered, and the cruel tilt of his lips sent chills down my back. Whoever he was, he had *Don't mess with me* written all over his face. His sudden change of attitude confused me. A lot. His earlier surprise had morphed into aversion, matching his girlfriend's expression.

Who was he, and what did I do to end up on his bad side? Seconds ago, we were locked in a staring contest. Was he upset, annoyed, or just being a dick? Because I had no clue how to interpret any of his moods.

"Now." A single word. But one that acted like a punch to the stomach. Bands of steel wrenched my heart at the viciousness of his tone—and his words—when he spoke again. "This is a private beach. There is a kids' park a quarter of a mile from here with a swing set. That seems more like your scene."

I gasped but stayed put, refusing to move or listen to him.

My heartbeats got wilder behind my ribs. I wasn't one to engage with someone—even less a stranger—for the sake of it, but right now, I didn't care.

Surprise flashed in his irises, now a darker shade of green, and a shadow passed across them, warming them up. Once again, I wondered why it felt like we already knew each other. Was he not used to people standing their ground when he bossed them around?

A split second later, the glow vanished, and I blinked again, not sure if I'd imagined it.

Making no attempts to move, I studied him as if I could solve the mystery he was.

Lost in my contemplation of him, he said something

else I didn't catch and pointed to my bag at his feet. I followed his movements, focusing on his lips.

His eyes recaptured mine, still mesmerizing. "Don't forget your diaper bag on your way out." This time, I heard what he said. His lips twisted, and he looked pained. His words lacked their angry sneer. Like he had no choice but to get rid of me, and fast.

Shivers clambered up my spine. Not from fear, but fascination. One I couldn't explain. *Hot and cold.* The only way to describe him.

The girl burst into a devilish laugh, a smug expression shaping her lips, breaking the face-off. Until now, I had forgotten about her presence. "I think she's a slow learner. Do you think she's mentally unstable?"

The guy said nothing and swooped down to pick up my shirt at the same time I squatted. Our fingers brushed, and heat spread through me, as if I was on fire.

He didn't move his hand from mine. He was ensnared too. A low growl formed in his throat, snd a whimper parted my lips. I had no idea what was happening. It freaked me out as much as it got me curious. Never before did a stranger have this much effect on me.

For a fleeting second, his annoyance dissolved as we stilled, eyeing each other. His attention went back and forth from my eyes to my mouth. Feeling self-conscious under his gaze, I chewed my lower lip.

His breathing hastened.

I couldn't shake away the tension that was rising between us. Was this how attraction felt? No. It couldn't be. The rapid beating of my heart and sudden awareness were just my body's instinctive reactions to a stranger. It had to be smart enough to ever feel the pull toward such a boy. An angry, good-looking one with a passive-aggressive problem.

Get away from him, Ava. He's dangerous.

His hand pressed harder on mine, and my fingers twitched under his touch.

We were connecting in the most awkward manner, and yet, it sent mixed signals to every part of my body. A lure, bordering on obsession—obsession to know how it would evolve—developed deep inside me.

His nonverbal cues made me believe he felt it too. The lust. The tremors of my digits. My sharp intakes of air.

His tongue swept over his lower lip, and I followed the motion. Glints shone in his irises. Air barely made it to my brain. A jumbled chaos awoke in my chest. His mouth opened, and I got transfixed by the sight, but no sound came out. My body temperature skyrocketed, and I couldn't feel the breeze on my skin anymore.

As if he couldn't resist the pull, the guy leaned toward me, his proximity overwhelming my senses. I moved forward, my need to be closer to him pushing me in his direction. His body grew closer, and closer, when the girl behind him cleared her throat, and we both jostled back.

My attention reverted to his face in time to witness the glower steeling his features. Upright and emotionless, he stepped back and returned to her side.

"Are you deaf?" His strained voice rendered me speechless. I tried to speak up, but all my words died on the tip of my tongue before I could express them. My mouth went dry.

"Seriously, just get lost. Go annoy someone else. Move." He averted his eyes for a quick second, all the while tapping his foot on the dusty ground.

Gone was his nonchalant slash angry vibe. Now he looked agitated, desperate for me to be gone. Even his words sounded clipped. "Are you dumb, or is a simple request too hard for your brain to process?"

He picked the joint back from the girl's grip, sucking on the tip.

He glared at me as if daring me to reply. To fight him. But I refused to engage in whatever this bully-off was. His eyes darkened with every passing second, as if they could see inside me. Read my secrets. And my fears. I blinked, in a weak attempt to refuse him access.

Everything around me seemed to turn silent. The water licking the shore and the birds chirping in the trees. The scent of sunscreen and flowers didn't reach my nose anymore, buried by a faint scent of leather.

How could I be super aware of him?

My body temperature soared another degree. I was about to ask him who he was when he beat me to it, irritation heavy in his tone. "You should go back to where you came from. This isn't your town, and you're not welcome." He exhaled the smoke in my face.

What a jerk.

Looking away to hide my hurt and annoyance, I groaned and shoved everything into my bag. "Asshole," I grumbled while I hurried down the path leading to my truck, my pulse thrumming from the encounter.

"Oh, so you *aren't* mute." His voice resonated behind me.

I clenched my fists, refusing to give him the satisfaction of seeing any reaction from me.

With long strides and a firmed back, I walked away, pretending I wasn't affected.

Even if the rude jerk annoyed the shit out of me, a tiny part of me, the masochistic one, wished we could meet again. Because no matter how crazy it sounded, the look he gave me sent a rush through my being like nothing else had before. A thrill I couldn't define with words. Never before had I ever felt a pull so strong toward something clearly toxic. As I risked a last glance over my shoulder, I caught him giving me a slow once-over, his gaze following my exit, trained on my butt, his face still a mask of stone.

For a fraction of a second, our gazes collided, and I felt more alive than I ever did in my life.

I turned around, scurrying away.

———

After dinner, I relaxed in my room, listening to music while replaying the earlier scene from the lake as I wrote in my journal. I hadn't done it in almost a week, and it was long overdue. My therapist came up with this idea last year. At first, I was reluctant, thinking it was childish to write to a stack of lifeless paper, but then she compared it to the pen pal letters I used to send when I was younger, and I agreed to give it a shot. She was right. It helped when I put my feelings and thoughts on the pages. To let it out instead of keeping it all inside. Today's entry was inspired by the lake encounter.

Dear Diary

I'm sorry I haven't written to you in days. My life has been hectic in the last week, and I'm just getting used to my new reality.

Today has been a very weird day, and I have no idea where to begin... I'm in Feather Lake, NC, for the summer. I made the journey on my own. Not that it was my choice, but now that I'm here, I feel a little bit better about the whole thing. Whatever. I'm still upset with Mom and Dad about how they shipped me here without a warning, and I'm trying hard to forgive them. Work in progress. It should be my personal mantra, I guess.

On my trip here, I met Joseph. At first, he annoyed the shit out of me because—let's be honest—he was too damn happy. Yeah, I know, I didn't think being too cheerful was a thing either. Until I met him. He wouldn't let me sulk on my own and did his best to entertain me the entire ride. In the end, it worked. Now, he's my only ally around here.

He invited me to hang out with him and his friends next Friday. Some place called Dusty's. Is it weird we clicked so fast? I'm telling you, the light pouring out from him is contagious, and I love how he makes me feel. Calm. Even though I didn't tell him that. Perhaps he figured it out by himself. Why else would he invite me to spend time with him?

And then there is this other guy. A stranger I met earlier today. He was dark, mysterious, and mean. Cruel, even. But if I'm being truthful, he fascinated me. More than he should have. Why? I have no clue. Every word he spoke was meant to hurt me and my feelings. He treated me like I was an inconvenience in his life. His girlfriend too. But his eyes told me another story. They were hypnotizing. A shade of green that reminded me of the deep end of the ocean. Dangerous and lethal. When he looked at me, it was like he knew what was inside my head. I never experienced something like that before. A part of me was scared, and the other half was mesmerized. Hard to explain...

And that's not all, but you'll think it's silly. It was like we already knew each other. I know it makes no sense. Not at all. I'm sure I'm mistaken. Not mistaken, but wrong because it's impossible.

When our fingers brushed, the weirdest sensation crept through me. It was so powerful. I didn't remove my hand because I loved how it made me feel. Excited. Alive.

I don't know his name, and I have no idea if I'll ever meet him again. Even though he intrigues me, his attitude problem is enough to keep me away. The last thing I need, while I'm here, is to make enemies. I'll lie low and do my own thing. Hopefully, I'll meet people my age who don't have a chip on their shoulders and are friendlier.

I'll let you know how the next few days go. Gimme some time to get used to my new life, and I'm sure I'll have plenty to say. The last few days have been exhausting. I think I need the rest.

Going to bed.
Night
Ava (who can't wait to see how her summer in Feather Lake will unfold) xx

Lying on my back under the covers, I replayed my day.

My heart went wild every time I closed my eyes and relived the unspoken connection the handsome and not-so-friendly stranger and I shared. For a short moment, I pretended he was nice—and the girl didn't exist. That it was just the two of us on the lakeshore. I wondered how different our meeting would have been. But then my sanity kicked back in, and I hated myself for being captivated by him. For still thinking about him hours later.

Despite myself, my mind kept wandering back there. Curiosity got the better of me. I grabbed the journal I'd discarded on the bedside table and wrote at the bottom of today's entry—in big, bold, underlined letters.

Who is he? And what's his deal?

I closed my journal when I felt I was being ridiculous and should forget all about him before he consumed my thoughts even more than he already had.

After fighting the pillows and covers for what appeared to be hours, my eyelids weighed heavy, and my brain lost the fight as sleep claimed me.

Chapter 7

On Monday morning, I woke up early, rested, and ready to start my day. Jitters filled my stomach at the thought of beginning my new job in less than three hours. Yesterday, I'd been conditioning myself to show a little excitement at the idea in between my talking with Iris over video chat and driving around town. When I passed the lake, I was tempted to make a detour to see if the stranger was there, but then my conscience made a comeback, and I abandoned the idea before making a fool of myself. Or risking another unwanted confrontation.

In front of the full-length standing mirror in the corner of my room, I examined my outfit. After I changed twice, I decided on a yellow empire summer dress with a jeans jacket in case the office was too cold. I tied my hair into a high sleek ponytail and added a coat of mascara and my favorite cherry-flavored pink lip gloss.

There. I looked professional enough.

Aunt Melinda made a sound of approval when I walked into the kitchen. "Up early, you. Sleep well?"

I grabbed the mug of coffee waiting for me on the island, fidgeting with the handle. "I think so."

"Anxious about today?" she asked.

Uncle Mason walked in at the same time, pressing his hands on her shoulders from behind and kissing her cheek. "Ava, don't be nervous," he said, picking a raspberry scone from the basket. "You'll see, it will go on smoothly. I promise. The last thing I want is for you to stress over this job."

I appreciated his making an effort not to rush me into this. He turned to face his wife. "Big day at the office?" he asked.

She sighed. My aunt worked as a PR for the Red Wolves, the professional hockey team. "I fear it will be. With the stunt Saxon pulled last week, I'm sure the press will still be all over it. Gosh, I hate it when grown-up men turn into idiots. He shouldn't have presented Eddie McGillis, football superstar, to the world as his partner only to cheat on him the next day with some basketball college recruit. Now the quarterback is on a self-sabotaging mission, thanks to Sax. His coach and the organization are getting involved after the contract he just signed. It's a clusterfuck with a capital *C*."

"I'm sorry you have to deal with all this. At least they make your job interesting." He planted a kiss on her nose, and her arms wrapped around his neck.

Like my own parents, my aunt and uncle were disgustingly in love. I blamed the Pierce genes for the lovesickness. After all, Uncle Mason and Dad were brothers.

I sat on a stool, and Aunt Melinda pushed the basket full of scones in front of me. "Take one, Ava. You can't go to work on an empty stomach."

I breathed out and indulged, my insides so tight that I wondered how I'd even get a bite in.

Uncle Mason neared the kitchen door. "Ava, meet me when you're ready. You don't have to come to work until nine. Take the time to relax. This summer internship should be fun, not something to develop a rash over."

I nodded, taking small bites to avoid my stomach churning.

"Love your dress, by the way," Aunt Melinda said as she sat next to me. "I have a benefit later this summer. If you're interested, we could go shopping together. I need a new gown. If you'd like to come, you're more than welcome. You'll need a gown too, and I'm the one inviting, so it will be my treat."

"You don't have to."

She shook her head with vigor. "I insist. I wanna do this. It makes me happy. If Celeste… Anyway, if you're free and would love a five-course dinner prepared by some of the most distinguished chefs in the country, live music, and getting pampered, let me know. The invite isn't going anywhere. The Red Wolves organization never do anything half-ass."

I cupped my heart with one hand. "Wow. That's very generous of you. I'd like that. I've always wondered how it must feel to transform into a princess for a night."

"Deal. We'll talk about it later. I gotta run." She put her empty dish in the sink and pivoted to look at me. "And Ava? Just breathe. Have fun today."

I nodded. She left, and my appetite returned. Aunt Melinda always had a way to make me feel comfortable. We used to see each other often. She and my parents and

Uncle Mason all grew up together. In the small town of Elk River, Michigan. Mom and Craig were supposed to attend college together and live happily ever after, but he broke her heart by keeping information from her. They ended their relationship, and she left alone for college. For years, they avoided each other. During her junior year, she met my biological dad—or bio-dad as I often called him. They fell in love, and Mom got pregnant with me five years later. Bio-dad was diagnosed with a very aggressive form of colon cancer, and he died two months later. Heartbroken, Mom returned to her hometown to pick up the pieces of her life. She and Aunt MelindaShe and Aunt Melinda— who used to be best friends—rekindled their friendship, and since Craig and Uncle Mason were brothers and my aunt was dating him by then, they all saw each other almost every day. Craig helped Mom out when she moved into her own apartment. He gave her a hand when she was confined to bed rest at thirty weeks and couldn't run errands or set up the nursery. He slept on the sofa in case she had a craving or needed something in the middle of the night. Slowly, they learned to be in each other's lives all over again and realized there was still love between them. Craig proposed one night, so they got married in the hospital's little chapel mere hours before I was born. I took on his last name, and he's been my father ever since.

When I was younger and Collin was still little, I used to spend a lot of my free time with Uncle Mason and Aunt Melinda until they had to move when she received a job offer she couldn't turn down. Then tragedy hit their lives, and for quite some time, they didn't visit anymore. I was aware a lot had to do with me and my health. For almost four years, we only talked over the phone on rare occasions. Now that things were running smoother for all of us, I was thankful we finally reconnected.

Taking my time on my way to work, I grabbed a box of pastries from the bakery on Main Street. The parting words from my aunt and the small detour helped settle my nerves.

Uncle Mason welcomed me the moment I parked my truck.

"How is she doing?" he asked. "Giving you any trouble?"

"Nah. She's perfect. I love her."

"Glad to hear it." He took the box from my hands. "You shouldn't have, but I'm sure the guys will appreciate the gesture. Ready?"

I firmed my back and lifted my chin. "As ready as I'll ever be."

"Let's go then."

I spent the morning familiarizing myself with the garage, meeting some of the mechanics on duty today and one of the salespersons, and getting accustomed to the basics of the accounting system.

Uncle Mason took his time to explain everything in detail and answer all my questions. He gave me a minute to take notes so I wouldn't forget all the steps as quickly as I learned them.

At lunch, we walked to a small Mexican eatery two blocks from the garage. As we sauntered back, a man stopped us and asked my uncle something about a carburetor he'd ordered. "Go ahead, Ava. I'll meet you in a bit. Will you be all right to manage on your own for now?"

I nodded. "Sure."

"If you have questions, ask for Ride. He should be there by now."

"Ride. Oh, okay."

I walked the last block, the sun's rays grazing my skin. Two girls about my age walked past me and waved. I returned the gesture. My earlier jitters had receded, and working at the garage and living in Feather Lake all summer didn't sound so bad anymore.

When the printer announced it was short of paper, I headed toward the supply room at the back where I knew all the extra office materials were stacked.

When I turned the corner, I bumped into a wall. One made of muscles and bones. Towering over me by a few inches. Hooded aquamarine-green eyes locked on mine and stole my ability to talk.

I blinked, and all the air left my lungs as if someone had punched me in the stomach. I blinked again, now quite sure it was a mistake. Some hallucination.

My blood iced in my veins, and I swallowed my uneasiness.

No, it wasn't a dream. He stood there, pressed against me, the heat from him radiating down my body.

Straightening my back, I braced myself for the words that would leave his mouth.

Chapter 8

Say something, I told myself, but all the words were stuck inside. I parted my lips, then closed them, unable to come up with a coherent thought. Even though I wanted to deny the truth, I couldn't. This guy was one of the most beautiful specimens I had ever seen. Even more so from this close, where our breaths mingled, no matter if he wore his frown like a fashion accessory. A curl of his hair fell over his forehead, hiding half of his left eye. My fingers itched to push it away so I could admire each of his features without distraction.

I pursed my lips, and once again, I found myself at a loss for words. His gaze traced the length of me, and I noticed the pulse leaping at the base of his throat.

He jerked his hand away, the one gripping my hip and

keeping me upright and anchored to the floor. When did it even get there, and how long had it been there? At the lost connection, I stumbled forward, one hand flying to his heart to keep my balance. My chest brushed against his hard one as I took a deep breath in. In other circumstances, I would have called touching him a bold move and would have never attempted it, but right now, my body had a mind of its own.

His heart raced under my fingertips. Jitters woke up in my core. For the first time, I understood the words raw magnetism.

Because even though he wore his stupid frown like his armor, it wasn't annoyance I saw in his stormy eyes, but heat. Fiery. So hot that it could burn me alive. And I would be glad for it.

And possessiveness. Dark and potent.

But then, with the little life experience I had, maybe I was wrong, and this was hate.

If it was, then how could someone dislike a person they never met before so much that it bled from them?

My feet felt heavy like they were made of concrete.

My arm dropped to my side.

I had no idea where we were or what I'd been doing minutes ago.

The air surrounding us got charged with thick particles of heat.

Even the room seemed to spin around us at a dizzying speed.

Until he spoke and killed the spell we were under.

"You?" Disgust dripped from his tongue, erasing every trace of the moment that had taken us hostages. "Thought I told you to scram. Can't you sense when you're not welcome somewhere, or are you just too much of a baby to understand commands?"

"I…it's not—"

I shut my eyes, loathing myself for not being able to put this guy in his place and tell him to go fuck himself.

"What's wrong, baby girl, you haven't learned to talk yet? I thought I heard you curse me the other day. My bad."

How could each word exiting his mouth be a mockery?

He quirked a thick brow, and my focus moved to his piercing, before lowering to his mouth, watching him run his tongue over his upper teeth. His shoulders slumped for a short instant, and his features relaxed. He glanced down and shook his head as if this confrontation wasn't a will but a necessity.

When his focus returned to me, he leaned in, his lips nearly touching mine, yet not. I sucked in a shaky breath of air, all my senses awakening at his dangerous proximity.

His fingertips grazed mine, and a low grunt escaped his mouth. Like the last time, electricity zinged where our hands connected. I took a deep inhale, stunned by the confirmation I hadn't dreamed of the sparks between us at the lake. Once again, I had no clue how to explain it because my body relished every second. My heart thudded in my chest. While my brain told me to run away, I stayed put, addicted to the sparks shooting through me. I lifted my eyes to his in recognition. No matter the mockery shining in them or the rigidity of his posture, this stranger didn't scare me. I felt oddly comfortable next to him. Something brewed between us that I couldn't figure out.

"Baby girl, if I were you, I'd—"

A strong hand clapped my shoulder from beside me, and I jumped back. "Oh hey, I see you two have met," Uncle Mason said with a blazing smile directed at both of us.

He moved behind me, pressing my shoulders with both

hands now. "Ride, this is my niece, Ava." *He* was Ride? And *he* worked here? "The one I told you all about, and who's staying with us for the summer and working here at the garage."

The tension in Ride's back mirrored mine as we both stood still, speechless, the air between us thick enough to be cut with a knife.

Uncle Mason, oblivious to Ride's full-of-venom words, continued, "I am counting on you to make her feel welcome here. Whatever Ava needs, you provide, okay? She's part of the team now, and she's family."

No. *No, no, no.* This was a bad idea.

Ride's eyes flitted to mine and stayed there. Contempt shone in them. I knew he was going to be contrary, but I would let nothing, and nobody, stand in my way this summer. Or treat me like a doormat.

Maybe I could take advantage of this opportunity.

I took a deep breath in, needing some courage to speak up and not miss my chance to put him in his place.

"Uncle Mason, Ride was showing me the ropes. In fact, he just invited me to grab ice cream with him later so he could show me around town. Be my personal guide. Aren't you sweet, *Riiidde*?" I couldn't help taunting him, stretching the syllables of his name. Who the hell named their child Ride anyway?

Fire burned in the depths of his irises. Victory coursed through my veins, a delicious rush. Getting a rise out of him felt amazing.

"It's Ryder." Fury underlined his words. "Only friends call me Ride, and you are not one. Are you, baby girl?"

Uncle Mason, who now stood next to me, observed our exchange, his head ping-ponging between us in amusement. "Guess this summer just became a lot more interesting," he said with a chuckle. "Kids, keep it civilized. Banter all you want. Even fight. But be respectful." Something sparked in his gaze. "I truly hope you two get along. Anyway, you will be able to continue this conversation later because Ride is having dinner at our place tonight. Like every Monday and Thursday night."

I gasped and choked on my own breath.

Ryder flashed me a smug smirk. That devilish look told me he would set himself up for ruining me. I'd have to grow a tougher skin—and quick.

"Nice. We can grab that ice cream afterward." My body tensed, while my face displayed the biggest fake smile I could muster. I nodded to my uncle, then marched toward the front desk, my head held high.

Behind my back, I heard Uncle Mason's whispered warning. "Ride, I won't tell you twice. We talked about it. You're not messing with Ava. She's a good girl. Don't play mind games with her, and treat her like a little sister. Show her around, and have her back. If she needs help, you volunteer. Every time. We're all family, and she's my guest and my niece, so give her the respect she deserves. Don't be a prick. Have I made myself clear enough?"

"Yes, sir," Ryder said. His tone had lost all traces of defiance. It conveyed respect—and admiration.

His change of attitude surprised me. That and the fact Uncle Mason acted like a paternal figure around him.

Once I reached the safety of the front of the garage, I facepalmed. Why did I trick myself into spending some alone time with him?

Day four of my stay here and already I'd made a fool of myself and been insulted. I also gained an enemy. Or two. Amazingly great.

"Everything okay?" Uncle Mason asked once he joined me.

I avoided glancing at him, busying myself with filling the business card holders.

"Yep. All good."

"Ava, listen… Don't worry about Ride. He looks intimidating and dangerous, and he can be a pain in the ass, but I swear he's not. He's harmless. He's had a hard life and sometimes forgets to be cordial."

I nodded.

And that's when what my uncle had said earlier finally reached my conscious mind.

Ride is having dinner at our place tonight. Like every Monday and Thursday night.

I shivered at the reminder. I disliked the idea of spending any more time around the insensitive jerk, but my curiosity got the better of me, and I couldn't wait to be around him again. If only to see what Uncle Mason liked about the guy. Or because his closeness did things to my body that nobody else ever did before.

———

After we closed the garage, I drove myself back home, while Uncle Mason went to run some errands. It was the first time I thought of Feather Lake, North Carolina, as home. Somehow. I'd been in town for seventy-two hours, but it felt longer. My anger toward my parents had faded a little since I landed here. But whenever I thought about all the plans I had with Iris, things that would never happen now, it came back in full force. Dad had texted me twice, but I still hadn't written back anything more than "I'm okay" or "Good" or "I love you too." Short answers. No details about my stay. A girl needed time. And maybe I hoped they would understand I should be part of the decision process when it concerned me and my life.

I refused to be anyone's puppet, and so far, the silent treatment had worked better with my parents than any tantrums or heated discussions. A small win. For me.

Living at Aunt Melinda and Uncle Mason's had its perks, though. My little brother wasn't around to annoy the shit out of me and go through my stuff without my permission. Also, Mom couldn't nag me about doing my chores or driving Collin to soccer practice. Here, I had my own space, and I was treated like a grown-up.

I missed Iris the most. I wasn't used to her not climbing through my bedroom window around nine, just so we could share the tub of ice cream she brought over or get our gossip in check before the next day. Share dreams and fears. First times and secrets.

"Honey, you're home," Aunt Melinda greeted me when I entered the house through the kitchen door. "How was your first day? Did Mason give you time to adjust, or did he bury you in work?"

She kissed my cheek before handing me a glass of lemonade. "Freshly made. Hope it's still your favorite."

"Yes. Thanks." I downed half of it. "I missed this," I said, pointing to my almost-empty drink. "First day was good. I learned how to create invoices and send quotes, and where everything was located. I should get the gist of it quickly."

She pulled my hand and led me to sit with her at the kitchen island. "I know it's a lot of work, but you'll learn so much. Owning a business is more than just what the eye sees. A huge part of the work is done backstage, and it's not always the most fun part. It requires sacrifice, time, and energy, but that's where the magic happens. At the end of the day, it's rewarding to know you made it through another day, another week, another year and to see all the progress you've accomplished. Dedication is the keyword. And passion. If you have both, you're halfway there."

I perused the room and glanced at the four places set at the table.

Aunt Melinda followed my line of vision because she offered an explanation. "We're having company tonight. In fact, every Monday and Thursday and other days in between. Have you met Ryder yet? He works with Mason. Sweet kid."

A mass lodged at the back of my throat, and a zing traveled across my back at the mention of the enemy. The memories of our bitter encounters crept along my vertebras.

Sweet would be the last adjective I'd use to describe him. Arrogant. Despicable. Passive-aggressive. But no, sweet didn't even cross my mind.

"We have. Met, I mean."

"Well, he's part of this family. A son to us. I hope you two get along."

Not a chance. He clearly hates my guts. I kept this part to myself.

A son? Would I have to deal with him the whole summer? Perhaps Ryder and I just started on the wrong foot, and we'd be able to keep things friendly. Sooner than later.

"Can I help you with dinner?" I proposed, trying to lock away the images of Ryder and his mesmerizing eyes, permanent frown, and full lips by changing the subject.

"Sure. Can you make the salad? I'll start the grill outside. Mason should be here any second to put his special touch to the steaks."

I gathered all I needed, humming the song I played on my phone, the tension of the day's work finally dissipating. I swayed my hips while chopping tomatoes, unable to erase the new Jessa Hart song out of my head. Carrying the bowl, I turned to the table when, for a second time in mere hours, I bumped into a human wall. The one made of poisonous barbs.

I froze, my eyes widening at his sight.

"Don't stop on my account, baby girl. Keep the show going. I kinda enjoyed the view," he said with a twist of his lips, bringing a bottle of beer to his mouth after licking the drops that had splashed on his hand.

Looking away, I cursed under my breath. "Dick—"

"What did you say?" Ryder asked with the closest thing to a smile his lips could draw.

"You heard me just fine." I placed the salad bowl on the table, crossed my arms, and huffed a breath.

"Someone's panties are knotted. You should go commando. It would remove your pissy attitude."

"Pissy attitude? Me?" My thumb pointed at my chest. "For all I know, it only comes out when you're involved. Could be a good idea to grab a mirror to help you remove your head from your ass if you don't know where to start."

I cupped my mouth. Where did those words come from? I blinked. And blinked again.

"Sorry," I mumbled, shaking my head and avoiding his stare.

"Don't be sorry, baby girl. I'm glad I could help you flush that out of your system. It's unhealthy to keep so much spite inside." He searched my eyes. "What? Baby girl isn't used to being defiant?" He spoke in a childish voice, ridiculing me.

Ire fired my bloodstream. My tongue was tied, and not a single word came out.

"You should stay away. I could pervert your mind." His eyebrow twitched. "What? Did you lose the use of your voice? Or are you not able to follow a conversation?

Go ahead, insult me. I love it when you're angry with me."

He winked, and my jaw hung open at this boldness.

"You should close your mouth. Unless you want me to stuff it shut."

"I—" Did he just say what I thought he said? "You—"

"Me what?"

I charged at him, pushing his chest with both hands. Ryder was solid as an oak and didn't even budge. "You disgust me. Keep your dirty words for someone else. Not interested in anything related to you. God, I wouldn't touch you even with a pole."

A loud chuckle left his mouth. "Your hands don't seem so repelled right now."

Both our eyes drifted to my palms still splayed over his hard chest, and I yanked them away and stepped back, putting as much distance between us as possible.

An aggravated noise passed my lips. I inhaled to keep my boiling fury from pouring out. "What do you want with me? You've been an ass since the day we met. Haven't you learned the basic rules of civility? What? Dear Mommy and Daddy forgot that part of your education?"

His jaw flexed, and a gloomy look passed through his eyes. His hands balled at his sides. *Did I hit a nerve?* I had the upper hand right now, and I wasn't about to stop.

"Need a class? I'm sure you can enroll in one at School for Dummy Bullies."

"Care to join me? I heard they have 'buy-one get-one' deals."

I blew a long breath. "Nice try. Perhaps they'll agree to your taking it twice. In case you flunk the first time. Want me to call and check with them?"

Amusement played on his face.

It sent a new wave of irritation through me.

"What's wrong with you?" I was about to lose my temper. "Tell me. Are you so bored with your own existence that meddling in other people's lives is your hobby?"

His perfect lips—I hated the fact the guy had amazing features—stretched into a conceited tilt. One I couldn't detach my eyes from. One I wanted to rip from his face. With my nails. "You."

My brows furrowed in confusion. "Me what?"

He sighed. "My problem is *you*. Want me to spell it out?"

"You're lying. You don't even know me. Stop projecting your insecurities on me." Since when was I able to tell someone else, a stranger nonetheless, the thoughts I usually kept to myself? "Perhaps it's not a class you require but a whole degree." I tapped my chin with my finger, pretending to think. "Yep, sounds about right."

"Who would have thought you could spit venom?" he asked, the edge in his voice cutting through me. "Baby girl can be bad. How surprising."

"You know nothing about my character."

He scoffed, igniting a fresh surge of fury inside me. "Oh, you wish."

"What does that even mean? Keep talking in clues that lead nowhere. Really mature. Glad you're having your own fun. Now beat it. I've seen your mug enough for one day." I snapped my fingers in his face. "Shoo. Out of my way. Bye and don't hesitate to never come back while I'm here."

He snorted. "Tsk-tsk. Sheathe those claws, tiger. I wouldn't want you to hurt yourself."

I skewered him with my eyes. "God, you're infuriating."

Only when I heard the back door open and Aunt Melinda and Uncle Mason's voices come closer did I realize Ryder and I had gravitated toward each other.

Our chests rose and fell, brushing with each intake of air.

Ryder leaned in and whispered in my ear, "And yet, here you are, unable to stay away."

I blinked and inhaled through my mouth to kill the balls of anger swimming in my stomach and stepped back. My skin tingled. Everywhere. His eyes never left mine. Not even for a second.

"I hate you," I whispered back.

He winked. "You wish."

I jabbed my fingertip into his hard chest. "Stay the fuck away from me."

"Or?"

"Or… You'll see."

"This is so scary."

"You dick."

"Wanna take a peek?"

"*Arghhhh*… Stop talking already."

"Stop being so fun to mess with." That smirk again brightened his face.

"Why are you still here?"

"Baby girl, you'd miss me if I left. Tonight will be amazing, I can feel it. Don't you?"

"I feel nothing other than the urge to punch your smug face right now."

"So romantic."

"I'm done with you. Once and for all."

Spinning around, I returned to the kitchen. I could feel Ryder's stare burning holes in my back. With my hand over my head, I flipped him the bird. *Take that, jerk.*

Right now, I had no idea who the girl giving this arrogant boy what he deserved was. A wide smile spread on my face. Parts of me kinda liked the badass version I projected when I was around him. It felt empowering. And liberating.

I grabbed a pile of plates from a cupboard, and when I pivoted, Ryder stood behind me. Again.

"Can't you take a cue?" I sighed and once again, his eyes captured mine.

He opened his mouth, and I grimaced, not sure if I was ready for the verbal diarrhea that would come out.

Instead, he smirked and took the plates from my hands. "Here, let me give you a hand."

I froze, my jaw hanging open, blinking as he grabbed the dishes from my grip and turned around.

"I think the word you're looking for is *Thank you*," he said over his shoulder, followed by a wink.

I didn't move, too floored by his change of attitude.

"You're welcome, baby girl. See? We're making progress."

Chapter 9

Ryder's lips parted slightly, and for a brief instant, I wished I could feel them on mine. The tension between us was affecting my common sense.

His smoldering gaze pierced the walls I tried to build around me.

My breathing hitched. My heart flipped in my chest, its beat irregular.

I wiped my moist hands on my black shorts and adjusted my pink top I had changed into, praying for the supercharged air surrounding us to ebb.

My body was betraying me.

When Ryder watched me with that much intensity, my brain turned into jelly.

With a shake of my head, I escaped the pull he had on me, reeling in my stupid thoughts.

I stumbled back, using the countertop to keep my balance, putting much-required distance between us, and groaned in annoyance.

"Oh, you're both here. Glad you two are getting acquainted," Uncle Mason said, a plate of juicy steaks in one hand and a bottle of beer in the other.

"Let's eat," my aunt said, her lips stretched wide.

We followed them to the dining room, and she took a seat next to her husband, leaving me to sit beside the person who had quickly become the pollution in my universe.

As if he hadn't tortured me with his words for the last ten minutes, Ryder chatted with my family like he belonged here. Like he'd been sitting at this table for a long time. He cracked jokes, exchanged stories, and even smiled.

None of this persona was anything like the guy I'd met before. The one thrusting poisonous barbs.

Keeping my focus on my food, I pictured his face every time my fork stabbed a piece of meat or a carrot. It calmed some of my murderous thoughts.

"Ava, are you all right?" Aunt Melinda asked. "You're awfully silent tonight."

I plastered an upward curl to my lips and nodded. "All good. Just a bit tired," I lied.

"You had more fight in you earlier, baby girl. What happened? Did the big bad wolf scare you?" Ryder asked.

If looks could burn, I'd turn him into ashes right about now.

"All fine," I said, my tone harsher than normal. "Let it go."

He raised his hands in surrender. "Just sayin'. Loved that feisty personality you got going on today."

My devotion returned to the food on my plate, not before noticing the frown marring my aunt's forehead.

"Did you hear from that boy of yours?" Uncle Mason asked.

A warm flush spread over my face. No doubt my cheeks were crimson now.

Ryder's head snapped in my direction, and Aunt Melinda watched me with interest.

"You still haven't told me anything about him," she said.

"Nothing to say. We're friends, and I don't have his number. He was supposed to text me. Guess he forgot…or he's busy."

With three pairs of eyes fixated on me, I tried to melt into my seat, without success.

"Well, when you talk to him, if you wanna invite him over, just know it's fine with us," Uncle Mason continued. "He looked like a charming boy."

"He is," I agreed through clenched teeth.

Ryder's stare drilled holes into my skull. An annoyed mask covered his face now. I bet it could break into pieces if I poked it.

I washed the last bite of food down with a sip of water, the iciness of the liquid easing the burn lining my throat.

And breathed easier.

I took another sip when fingers rubbed the side of my thigh, and I dropped the glass. After splashing water all over my clothes, it fell on the table before rolling down to the floor, shattering into pieces.

I yelped and jerked up from my seat. Aunt Melinda gasped. Uncle Mason leaped to his feet, ready to help. Ryder too stood up and leaned forward until his face rested an inch from mine when I bent over to pick up the broken pieces.

"Well played, baby girl. If you wanted to catch my attention, no need to make a show of it. You could have just asked. Or shaken that ass like you did earlier."

His closeness stole all the air from the room. It spun around me, its walls closing in on me. I gripped the table to avoid either kissing that stupid, smug expression off his face or slapping him.

Twinkles danced in his eyes before they released me. "I'll do it," Ryder proposed. "Let me clean up the mess."

I exited whatever state I was in and spoke with my most sweet-as-honey tone. "I'm sorry. Don't be silly, Ryder. I'll do it." I reached for the shards of glass when he pushed me back. "What's that for?"

An expression I never saw before painted his face. He looked pained. "Don't touch it."

"Why? I'm old enough to clean up a mess."

"You could cut yourself. Leave it to me."

"Why do you care?"

"Never mind." His voice hardened. "I don't." I straightened up, and he followed suit, his attention not faltering away from me. "Move, I'll do it."

Uncle Mason shook his head as he neared us with a broom. "You kids have fun. I heard earlier you had an ice cream date. Go crazy. We'll deal with this."

Oh yeah, the ice cream idea I'd thrust on Ryder this afternoon. Did I really have to roll with it now, or could I pretend I was too exhausted to go out?

"I think I'll call it a night," I said, faking a yawn. "Raincheck?" I looked at him, my eyes pleading with him to play along. After all, he owed me that. And so much more.

"Don't be silly. We won't be out too late. Come on, I don't offer pretty girls to eat treats with me every day."

Jerk.

And I'm the one who came up with the fake scheme, I told him with a glare.

He returned my challenge with another one of his it-could-pass-for-a-smile smirks.

"Ava, I think you should go," my aunt said, putting to rest the war we had been fighting in silence. "Tasha works at the ice cream parlor. I'm sure you two will get along. It's never too early to make friends, honey. I already told her you were coming to town when I saw her and her mama the other day. She's a social butterfly, and she'll introduce you to everyone."

"Huh, I'll ask for her," I said, fidgeting with my fingers.

Ryder's hand pressed against the small of my back, and heat shot through me in powerful jolts as he led me toward the door. "Let's go."

What was that?

I held my breath as the imprint of his palm left a lingering burn.

"Have fun," Uncle Mason said.

I sidestepped, putting much-required room between Ryder and me until I could breathe some air not tainted by his scent. Arrogance and fury. Why was he acting all sweet in front of my family but treating me like hell every other time?

He moved toward the passenger side of his car and opened the door for me to get in. I glowered at him when he said, "Jump in, baby girl."

"Don't break a sweat, Romeo. I'm fully capable of opening my own door. No need to pretend you actually tolerate me."

"Oh, but I tolerate you just fine." He winked, and the

blazing fury I felt each time he stood in my vicinity returned. "After all, this little idea was all yours. I wouldn't want to deceive you and derail your super mischievous plan to spend some time alone with me."

"I wasn't—it's not what you—stop talking already." With a sigh, I hauled myself in and thanked the music he blasted through his speakers that averted the need for all conversation.

Ryder drove fast, with a stiff back and laser focus. The muscular cords of his forearms strained when he changed gears, and I found it almost impossible to look away. His jaw was set in stone, accentuating the square line. With each mile he covered, his body became terse, precision defining every one of his actions. A faint whiff of leather and spice drifted to my nose. Masculine and dangerous. A scent that fit him perfectly. One I would forever link to him. That I knew.

The hint of recklessness in his driving spread shivers along my back. It sent my heart into overdrive, and I loved every second of it. Adrenaline shot through me. For a short moment, I shut my eyes and reveled in his careless yet full-in-control driving. Each time he pressed the gas pedal harder, a zing only danger could bring traveled through my being. An intoxicating feeling few things or situations in my life provided.

I admired his profile. His tousled dark hair looked as if he'd just gotten out of bed or run his fingers through it too many times. His jaw ticked and set into a firm line. The faint shadow of stubble grazed his skin. The sleeves of his T-shirt did nothing to hide his bulging biceps when his grip around the steering wheel tightened.

A million sensations I wished I could quash swam inside me. Lust. Curiosity. Admiration. Nothing I should have felt where Ryder was involved. The guy had been a dickhead since the minute we met, yet here I was, impressed by his driving skills.

A gasp passed my lips when he rotated the car in a one-eighty tire-screeching maneuver. The centripetal force glued my back to the seat and planted goose bumps over my arms. Holding on to the center console and door handle, I let out a trembling breath once we stopped in a parking spot and Ryder killed the engine. My heart kicked in my chest, and I had no idea when or if I'd ever felt a thrill like this before.

"Kid not used to getting a little fun?" He shook his head and stepped out after replying to an incoming text message, not even waiting for me to join him.

After I regained some control over my deafening heart, I ran after him.

"Two waffled vanilla-chocolate swirls. One with a cherry on top. The other without," Ryder ordered before I could even read the menu.

He paid and grabbed the two cones, ignoring me as he skipped the picnic tables outside and sat on the curb ten feet further away. I joined him, keeping a distance of two feet between our bodies.

"You know I can order for myself," I said, partly annoyed at how he'd dismissed me so easily even though I was standing next to him. So much for introducing myself to the girl working behind the counter like my aunt had suggested.

Ryder handed me the cone with the cherry on top, and I offered him a quizzical stare. "Kids love this shit."

I pinched my lips into a thin line, but soon a traitorous curve broke free. Okay, said like that, it actually sounded kinda nice.

I swallowed the fact I didn't get to order what I usually

would have and accepted the treat as a peace offering. "Thanks."

Dressed in dark jeans and a black T-shirt, Ryder looked so out of place amongst the colorful picnic tables, yellow exterior, and royal-blue awnings of the ice cream shop.

His eyes glistened with mischief as he watched me—like, really watched me—licking the ice cream now melting over my fingers. My entire body was aware of every flicker of the gaze aimed at me.

My stomach vibrated with flutters.

The sick part of me enjoyed being the object of his devoted attention.

"Why are you looking at me like that?" I asked after a long stretch of silence.

"Like what?"

"Huh… I don't know. Like you know something about me or… Never mind it's ridiculous." *Shut up, girl. Say nothing else. Why are you trying to solve the mystery of him? Get over with this not-date, and go back home where you're safe.*

"Say it." Ryder watched me, waiting for an explanation.

"It's hard to explain," I finally said.

"Try me."

"Like… huh…I'm a game to you. Or a…" I scratched my forehead, not sure where I was going with this. "Or you're aware of something I'm not."

"Whoa, it's a lot of—"

My phone chimed from where it was placed beside me on the grass, and I thanked this universe for the distraction. I hesitated to check it, sure it was another attempt from my parents to get me to talk to them, but it went off again, and Ryder made the decision for me.

"Hey, gimme that," I said, trying to grab the device from his grip.

His face turned to stone as he studied something on the screen. The muscle of his jaw twitched.

"Who's that?" he asked, flipping the screen in my direction so I could take in the picture.

I chastised myself mentally. Why hadn't I reinstated the auto-lock function earlier when I listened to music while prepping dinner? I needed a diversion. Anything to convince Ryder to give back my phone.

The biggest grin I could manage—and I was certain it would piss him off—curved my lips. "A friend," I answered.

"A friend?"

I couldn't fail to notice the expression of doubt taking over his face.

"Yeah, right."

"Gimme that," I said, succeeding this time at retrieving my device.

The picture of us Joseph took on the bus stared back at me.

Finally. Now I'd have a way to communicate with the only ally my age around here.

JOSEPH

Avalon *smiley face emoji* So sorry it took me forever to get back to you. Long story. All set now.

The reminder of the term of endearment he used sent warmth through me.

JOSEPH

How's the new living situation?

I started typing when Ryder chose to stick his nose where it didn't belong and snatched my phone. His fingers tapped the screen violently.

I leaned over him, using my other arm to deter his newfound mission. In vain.

"Stop. What do you think you're doing? Give it back. You can't do this. Stop."

The chime announcing the message had been sent froze my blood, and I turned livid at the sight of what he wrote.

ME

Your Avalon is busy. Doesn't have time to waste on a loser like you. Leave her the fuck alone. I won't tell you twice. She has better things to do. Goodbye.

P.S. And her name isn't Avalon, you idiot.

Wrath coiled around my stomach. "Are you for real?" I whisper-screamed. "What's that? Joseph is my friend. My only friend around here. You have no right to interfere in my personal life. You cannot do this."

Ryder took my phone away from me. Once more. "I'm doing you a favor."

It felt like my brain would explode, my blood pounding into my skull at his nonsense. "A favor? How? Why are you being mean? Can you not meddle in my life?"

"One day, you'll see. And you'll thank me. If your head isn't too far gone into your ass by then. Anyway, if we're together, you're not flirting or chatting or indulging in anyone else, much less another guy. Understood?"

I shook my head violently. Ohmygod, his ego. I dragged a hand over my face and inhaled through my mouth, trying to find my composure that slipped away every time Ryder was in the picture. "Together? How are we even together? What are you talking about? We're here because I tricked you into this when I thought it would never happen or that you would agree to the scheme, and then you bought me this"—my chin pointed to the half-eaten cone—"without asking what I'd like first and assumed I'd want a cherry on top. For you, I'm just a kid with no backbone, and you've decided controlling my life could be a nice hobby." I inhaled after unloading my annoyance on him all at once. "And we're not even *talking* talking."

"I'm here, aren't I?"

"Yeah, sure. Physically. Otherwise, it's like I'm on my own. All you do is invade my privacy and text *my* friend on *my* phone. Unless you bring some substance into the conversation, keep your mouth shut. Silence is much more enjoyable when you're involved." I took another bite of my ice cream. "Oh, and no bossing me around. News flash. I'm not your pet project. Stop interfering in my life. Got it?"

He shrugged, his heavy gaze nailing me to the spot.

"*Arghhhh*, you're so infuriating. Did you even understand a word I said?" No response, no acknowledgment. Nothing. I could feel my blood turning into lava with each ticking second. Why was he ignoring me? He angered me so much that all I wanted was to scream at him. I swallowed my wrath. "Say. Something."

"No."

"No? Why not? You usually don't shy away from your opinion."

Cool as a cat, Ryder said nothing, engulfing his ice cream cone in one giant bite.

Pig. Even though I hated him at this instant, the movements of his tongue mesmerized me, and I forgot for a split second why we were fighting, and what we were fighting about.

After a minute, he leaned into my space, his thumb grazing the corner of my lips. Shivers followed the curve of my spine. His face neared mine. I held my breath. What was he doing? My heart rate accelerated, and I couldn't tell if I was excited or scared. A million butterflies awoke in my chest. The faint scent of leather emanating from him was all I could smell. *Do something, Ava.* I had no idea what I should do. Lean in or lean back? Our eyes met, and I thought I'd dissolve right there under the intensity emanating from him. I couldn't breathe on my own anymore.

As if Ryder was a magnet and I was a weak piece of steel, I met him half-way. Just a couple of inches separated our faces.

My hands trembled, and my grip around the cone tightened.

His breath fanned my nose. We were sitting close. Too close.

His digit, still resting at the corner of my mouth, felt like a hot iron branding my skin. He caressed the length of my jaw with his fingertips. I leaned into the touch, loving how it felt, and unable to resist.

What was going on with me? Why did he always find a way to affect me? Ryder was the enemy, not a boy I had an interest in.

One moment, I wanted to rip his head off, and now I wasn't sure I could look away, even if the building behind us caught fire or the entire town burned to ashes.

Time idled.

I tried to move but couldn't find in me the strength to pull away. I refused to be a pawn in whatever sick game Ryder was playing, but I also wanted to know what he'd do next.

His lips parted, and he moistened the lower one with his tongue.

That was it. The moment he would do something out

of character and surprise me or confirm my suspicion he was not to be trusted at any point.

His teeth bit into the full flesh, and his pupils dilated.

Was he about to kiss me? But mostly, did I want him to?

My thoughts swirled in my head, and I couldn't think clearly anymore, adrenaline pumping into my bloodstream.

If Ryder kissed me, would I slap him or indulge in it? Would he kiss me like he meant it, with the same passion he showed while fighting me, or would it be another one of his twisted actions to torture me?

Kiss. Ryder. Passion. Those words didn't belong together.

And yet, if I tilted my head just a little, our mouths would connect.

Ohmygod, I had no clue what to do, how to act, what to say. Why was I analyzing everything?

A car honked, breaking the moment. Ryder brought his thumb to his lips. "You had ice cream there." He licked his digit clean. Liquid heat filled my belly. Oh geez, I would die. I missed the burn of his touch when he pulled back.

What was wrong with me? How did I forget we weren't friends?

The vehicle stopped beside us, the engine idling, stealing our attention. The driver saluted Ryder, and a girl exited from the passenger side. A cold chill lined my spine when I noticed who it was.

"You," she said with disgust pouring out from her. Guess the feeling was mutual. "That's who you're spending your free time with, Ride? Seriously, you ditched me for this skank?"

The tires screeched as the car pulled away.

Ryder discarded my phone on the grass strip next to

me and moved to his feet. He wiped his hands over his jean-clad legs before draping an arm around the girl's shoulders. She batted her lashes and rose to her tiptoes to smack her lips on his, the imprint of her scarlet lipstick marking him.

Together, they sauntered away, not a care in the world about my existence.

"Where are you going?" I screamed after them. They both kept ignoring me. I walked past them, and throwing the last bite of my cone away, I rested my fists on my hips. "Ryder? Talk to me. Are you leaving?"

"Yes, we are, kid," the girl answered in his place while his gaze raked over me in a painful sweep. One that left a burn in its trail.

"What am I supposed to do now? Walk home?"

The girl snickered. "It's actually a decent idea. Get lost while you're at it." She threw a five-dollar bill at me. "Or buy yourself a bus ticket out of here."

"Ride—"

"Yeah. I don't care. The exercise will do you good. And don't call me Ride. We're not friends. Already warned you." The cruelty of his words revealed his real face, hardening my heart. Not that I would consider us friends, but I thought maybe we could be civil to each other.

I blinked too many times. "Are you being serious right now?"

He shrugged. "Sorry, baby girl. My car has only two seats. Next time, think about it before tricking me into taking you out."

Tears burned the sensitive flesh around my eyes, but I refused to let him see how much his actions affected me. For infinite seconds, I stood there, speechless as they climbed into the car, not sparing me a glance.

Fighting the wave of nausea hitting me and the humiliation of having been played, I rushed out of the parking lot, ready for the three- or four-mile walk home, and prayed I wouldn't get lost as violet streaks tinted the sky. Soon, darkness would settle in, and I hoped I could make it back in time.

The distinctive sound of the horsepower and the heat of Ryder's smoldering stare passed by me, but I refused to acknowledge him. Plugging music into my ears, I texted Joseph, hoping he wouldn't hold Ryder's rudeness against me.

I wasn't a freaking doormat, so I had to find a way to put him in his place—and fast—or Ryder would make this summer a living hell. I wouldn't let him.

"Screw you, jackass," I screamed at his retreating car and stormed away.

Chapter 10

My phone rang, and I killed the music to take the call, not recognizing the number. Darkness blanketed me now, and thanks to the flashlight on my phone, the occasional passing cars, and my not-too-shabby sense of direction, I estimated I had about one mile left to reach home.

"Hey you," Joseph's voice greeted me. It warmed my insides and erased the specks of anger still swirling inside me. How could his voice act like a soothing balm and be powerful enough to ease me every time? "I thought it would be better to talk rather than your typing in the dark."

He had offered to pick me up many times in the last

hour, but I didn't want to be a bother—and I needed time to get my anger under control. The walk would do that.

"Are you almost there? I'm not liking the idea of your walking in the dark all by yourself."

I sighed. "I'm fine. Just not the night I pictured. Anyway, almost home. I think. The signal isn't that good around here, so the GPS on my phone keeps reloading, never giving me a real-time location."

"I can't believe the guy just upped and left. What a jerk."

"Yep. My mistake. I thought I was playing him by making him take me out. Now I know better." I pushed away the images of Ryder and his girlfriend flying through the parking lot earlier, leaving clouds of dust behind. "How's surfing school? Are you already the coolest guy in your beach town by now?"

His easy laughter warmed me inside. "Nah, not even close. Sorry to disappoint you. Between the surf lessons and helping at the restaurant, when my head hits the pillow at night, I'm already asleep. And it's only day two. I'll get used to it, just gimme a week or two." He paused. "Still coming on Friday night?"

More of my annoyance dissolved at the idea of spending time together. "Sure. And you know what? Uncle Mason fixed a truck for me. For the duration of my stay, it's mine to use."

"Nice. I'm kinda sad I don't have to come to pick you up, though," Joseph teased.

"One day, I'll let you do the honors. In the meantime, I sh—" A car honked, and the sound startled me. When my gaze locked on the driver, my improving mood died. "Fuck."

"Hey, what's wrong? Are you okay?" Joseph asked on the other end of the line, worry in his voice.

"Yeah. Whatever."

"Avalon, what is it?"

Ryder slowed down beside me and asked, "Wanna go for a ride, baby girl?"

With his window all down, his bent arm resting on the frame, and the wind sweeping his dark hair, he resembled a movie star. My heart went crazy in my chest. With a shake of my head, I chased the picture away and reminded myself I was mad at him, and that he was enemy number one. And that he acted like a dickhead most of the time. No. Scratch that. Who was I trying to convince? Ryder *was* a jerk.

"Who's there?" Joseph asked.

"No one."

"Stop being a brat and get in," Ryder continued.

"Avalon, don't climb into someone's car. Please," Joseph pleaded.

"It's fine. Just the a-hole who abandoned me earlier," I said, running a hand over my face and closing my eyes, praying when I opened them up, Ryder would have disappeared. Not a chance.

"Who are you talking to?" Ryder asked, his car nearing me. "Just get in."

"Avalon—"

"I don't wanna see you," I told Ryder.

"What?" Joseph asked in my ear.

"Not you. Him."

Ryder sighed. "Stop acting out."

"Avalon, who's with you?" Joseph asked.

"Nobody I care about."

"Are you coming?" Ryder asked.

"Leave."

"Avalon. What's going on?"

"Joseph, I need to go. I'll text you later. I'll be all right.

Don't worry." I hung up before he could argue and folded my arms over my chest. "Ryder, I'm not going with you. Go back to your socially impaired girlfriend instead. I'm good on my own."

His gaze threw bullets my way. "Are you going to make things harder all summer than they already are? Stop being a snob, and get in the car."

"Harder? Harder than what?" I was screaming now. "You speak no sense. Take your own advice. Get lost. Forget about me, and I'll stay out of your way."

He hit the gas, and the car flew forward before stopping at a weird angle and blocking my route.

He stormed out toward me, fury wrapped tight around him, not even taking the time to close the door. "Get. In. the. Fucking. Car. It's dark. It's late. It's not so safe."

Digging my heels into the ground, I refused to move. "And now you care about my safety. How convenient."

Before I could realize what he was doing, he scooped me over his shoulder, my feet kicking the air behind me and my fists hitting the middle of his back.

"Let go of me," I hollered. "Kidnapping is a serious offense in the United States."

He snorted and only released me after he dropped me onto the passenger seat of his idling car.

I fought him with slaps and blocks. "Get your dirty paws off me."

He raised his hands in surrender, rounded his car, and drove it back on the road before I could comprehend what had just happened.

Minutes later, Ryder parked beside my truck in the driveway. "Let's do this some other time. I had a blast tonight," he said, his eyes turning to slits and his mouth crooking at one end.

I bet he was having the time of his life screwing with

my existence. "Let's not," I countered, hurrying out of the car, my shoes pounding against the cobblestones and my pulse deafening me.

A creepy laugh broke the silence of the night, making my hair stand on end all over my body.

Not in the mood to fake a happy demeanor, I entered the house through the outer door connected to my bedroom and locked myself in before shooting Joseph a text message.

ME

Home. Safe. Jerk gone. Friday can't come fast enough. I'll talk to you tomorrow. Glad to have a best friend in this town.

JOSEPH

Awesome. Can't wait to show you around. It's a date then, bestie.

Yeah, it's a date, I repeated, for my own sake, feeling the heat pooling in my cheeks as I popped the picture of us on my screen and studied it for a long beat.

———

The next morning, I was calling clients about their upcoming appointments when Ryder entered the garage, not even sparing me a glance. The entire time he crossed the reception area, I held my breath, unable to draw oxygen in. As he retreated, my gaze was trained on his jean-clad ass, the coil around my stomach loosening. The door clicked after him, and I caught a full intake of air.

He was the most confusing human being I had ever encountered. How could I be fascinated with someone I couldn't stand?

With a shake of my head, I banished the images of him from my mind and concentrated on my work.

"Everything all right?" Uncle Mason asked when he joined me at my desk and handed me a cup of freshly brewed caffeine. "Any client giving you trouble? You look preoccupied."

"Nah, everything's good."

"Have you called your father yet?" he asked, rolling a chair next to mine and taking a seat. I shook my head. "Wanna talk about it?"

"Not really."

"Ava, your parents love you. Never would they send you away to punish you. They're going through some things right now. Nothing you should worry about, okay? All I can tell you is that it breaks their hearts that you're avoiding them. I get why you're angry, but once that anger evaporates, can you just dial them? I think they would be really happy to hear your voice and not be updated by text messages exclusively."

I swallowed hard, all his words making sense. I wasn't a girl who held grudges against other people. I had no clue why this time around it felt important to show my parents I didn't agree with their decision. Once I called them, I wouldn't be able to hold on to my anger for much longer. They would get through me and shatter it to bits. They always did.

"I'm still mad. I have no idea how to forgive them this time. Usually, I do. But this summer, they pushed their luck. I met Joseph on the bus. You and Aunt Melinda have been welcoming, and I feel at home with you guys. None of my wrath is aimed at any of you. I don't appreciate their sending me away without consulting me. It was a low blow. Iris and I have been talking about our summer plans all year. They knew, and they still made the decision behind my back, keeping me in the dark. When I'm ready, I'll call them. For now, they have to accept being updated by text messages is my meeting them halfway."

"For the record, I understand your frustration." Uncle Mason clapped my shoulder. "Call them, text them. Whatever feels right with you, kiddo. Do you think you can lock this place up tonight? I have an appointment and gotta leave early. Ryder should be here, but sometimes he leaves early on Tuesdays. Just in case, let me show you how to proceed."

I followed him to the back of the garage and took notes on my phone about how to set the alarm and which doors to lock and lights to turn off.

The rest of the day went by quickly. I spent almost an hour on the phone with the technician to resolve a printer issue and waved goodbye at Uncle Mason when he left around three thirty. The two remaining mechanics went home at five, and then it was just me. Alone. The garage was divided into two separate departments. Car fixing and used vehicles resale. The reception desk was set between the two, opening onto a small administrative office, where I completed and filed paperwork in between answering phone calls and greeting customers.

After locking the front door as Uncle Mason had instructed, I made my way to the back door to make sure Chuck and Sean, the mechanics, had locked it at the end of their shift.

When I passed Uncle Mason's office, I heard noises from behind a door on my right. My hands clenched at my sides, and taking a ratchet from the toolbox next to the car lift, I padded toward the source of the faint music I could hear now. Nobody should be here besides me. I debated calling my uncle but decided fear wasn't an option. Perhaps someone forgot to turn off the radio.

With my hand around the doorknob, I turned it in slow motion, my heart thundering in my chest. I licked my lips, trying to bring moisture back to my mouth.

Holding the tool in the air above my head, I yanked the door open, thinking if a thief stood on the other side, the surprise would be enough to scare them away.

I exhaled when no one appeared before me. Instead, I was met with a staircase, the flickering light bulb attached to the ceiling infusing me with a new wave of fear.

With careful steps and a white-knuckled grip on the banister, I climbed the stairs one by one, praying none would creak and betray my presence.

The faint scent of car oil and dust permeated my nostrils. The old staircase would make a perfect prop in a horror movie. It had just that uninviting, sketchy vibe about it. A chill traversed me, and I firmed my back, projecting the confidence I lacked.

Once I reached the top, I repositioned the ratchet over my head, ready to knock out any intruder in my path. If one existed.

On the landing was a doorway on my left, and when I turned the corner, I came across a small kitchen. Outdated but looking well-kept. Dark-wood cupboards, a set of black appliances, a circular wooden table surrounded by three mismatched chairs.

Not the place where thieves would hang out without anyone at the garage noticing them.

The whiff of tomato sauce in a pan on the stove filled my nose. Nearing it, I realized, with a touch of my hand, it was still warm.

The sink was filled with a few items.

I swiveled to scan the place. It was modestly furnished, but everything appeared to be in decent shape. A navy-blue couch, a coffee table, and a wall-mounted TV. The hardwood floor was worn in places, and the drapes framing the window were faded from the sunlight.

In the living room, I spotted the source of the punk rock music I could hear from downstairs.

I was about to turn it off when a deep growl scared me from behind.

I spun around with a start and lost my footing. Instead of scaring the intruder with the tool in my hand, it fell to the floor at my feet with a loud thud.

I jumped at the sound. Being a cop was clearly not a career path I should pursue.

Staring at my weapon on the floor, it took me a few seconds before I brought my eyes up to look at the person standing in front of me. My heart rate decreased at the sight of him.

"You?" I asked, blinking. "You gotta be kidding me."

His tone, unwelcoming and rough, worked through me. "Babies shouldn't visit bad guys' apartments without being invited. I thought Mason said you were a smart one."

"You?" I repeated as his scent, leather and spice, tickled my nose. "What are you doing here?"

Ryder glared at me while using the towel in his hand to remove the excess moisture from his damp hair. That's when I realized he stood before me in nothing but dark jeans, the elastic of his boxer briefs peeking at the waistband. Rivulets of water licked his bare chest and caught my gaze as I followed their slow descent.

He sported a set of sculpted abs enveloped in bronze skin, with a tattoo on his ribcage and a scar along his left collarbone.

Warm flutters invaded my belly.

"You should get dressed," I said. "Walking around half-naked is inappropriate."

Kill me now. For all I knew, I had stepped inside *his*

apartment. I straightened my posture. No, I wouldn't back down. Ryder was distracting. And he really should put a shirt on.

"Care to repeat that?"

"No. You heard me right the first time."

Geez, how could my tongue loosen every time he was involved? Why couldn't I keep my mouth shut? Since when did I pick fights with people on purpose? Around him, I often barely recognized myself.

With any other half-naked guy standing a yard before me, I'd be tongue-tied right now. And blushing tomato-red. Then I would scurry away without a second thought. Not with him, though. I just could not.

"Something wrong with your hearing?" I asked. "Put. A. Shirt. On."

"No. And I'll ask the questions now. What are *you* doing here? You haven't learned to knock? Unless you wanted to ogle me. Or join me in the shower."

Warmth crept up my cheeks, and I used my hands to ease the burn.

"Don't be a douchebag. I was tasked to lock the garage before leaving."

"And my apartment is your responsibility? How? Please enlighten me," Ryder said, his sarcastic tone raking on my last nerve.

I groaned and pivoted on the balls of my feet, ready to bolt out of the enemy's territory.

A strong hand gripped my elbow and shook me around before I could make my escape. I lost my footing, but he prevented me from crashing onto the floor, his grip on me tightening. Tingles arose from his touch. I refused to let my body enjoy the reaction he provoked within me.

"Don't ever fucking come back here without an invite, baby girl." His cruel words were a contradiction to the expression shadowing his face. Dilated pupils took over the entire green—almost blue—hue of his irises and teeth digging into his bottom lip. Even his voice sounded deeper than usual. More masculine. More gravely. "You've been warned." A simple command that sounded more like a dark promise than a threat.

He growled, his attention not faltering.

I jerked my elbow away from his fingers and turned to look at him, feeling defiant. "Or else?"

His smirk sent shivers through me. He rolled his shoulders back, towering over me, his stance rigid and menacing. Yeah, Ryder could scare the shit out of me. So why did I still feel a pull toward him when he tried to intimidate me?

I suffered from some kind of sickness because I relished the standoff.

Air crackled around us. It thickened with unsaid words that neither of us dared to acknowledge.

With a step forward, Ryder closed in on me. Our chests almost touched with each intake of air. His tongue peeked out, and I held my breath, waiting for his next move. Would he get closer? Would he scoop me over his shoulder like a caveman and carry me outside like he did before? Or would he simply stare at me, tongue-tied, not used to being challenged?

For the tiniest sliver of time, the zing between us overshadowed our disagreement. Until he spoke and killed the moment.

"Don't make me show you."

"You don't impress me."

His finger traced a line from my chin to my collarbones, and I swallowed the gasp about to exit my mouth before he let go of me.

"Don't forget to lock up after yourself. I'm not in the

mood to be woken up in the middle of the night if the alarm goes off because you forgot to lock the garage door." Without another word, he disappeared down the hall, leaving me there in the middle of his kitchen, speechless and confused.

The spot where his skin had touched mine buzzed, and I used my other hand to erase the memory of the imprints of his fingers on my bare skin.

The thump of my heart quickened. Unable to avert my eyes, I glared at his back for a long beat.

A part of me wanted to run after him. To have the last word.

Another part of me couldn't wait to get the hell out of there fast enough.

Self-preservation won, and minutes later, after I engaged the alarm, I sat in my truck, cursing the one person I could easily kill with my bare hands if given a choice. The one who had the ability to make my summer hell if I gave him the chance.

Time to grow a spine and show Ryder he had no power over me. N.O.N.E. None.

I had summer plans back in Michigan. Right now, as I drove home, I decided to stick with it. One way or another, I would make the best out of these twelve weeks. "Just stay out of my way, Ryder Whatever-Your-Name."

After dinner, I retreated to my room to call my best friend.

"Please pick up." Voicemail. I sighed. "Guess I'll vent some other time."

In the next hour, I tried Iris twice and even sent her three text messages, but she never picked up or replied. I had to tell her all about my hatred for the guy living above the garage. The one poisoning my existence.

Next, I texted Joseph.

ME

Hey, how was your day? Surfing any good?

JOSEPH

Bestie, I was thinking about you.

How about a private surf lesson?

ME

Me? I'm not a sports person.

My earlier resolution made an appearance just in time. *A Summer to Remember.* That was supposed to be Iris's and my tagline for the next three months.

I inhaled a long gulp of air and typed fast before I changed my mind.

ME

You know what? I'd love to.

Surfing was not something I'd ever thought I would try one day. Here was my chance, and I wouldn't miss it. Yeah, I could do this. Or try to.

JOSEPH

Perfect. Friday night at Dusty's. And if you're free this weekend, I could give you your first lesson. I usually work the lunch shift at my parents' restaurant on Saturdays. We could go surfing early in the morning, and you could spend the day with me if you like. I'm usually off by two. What do you think?

Spending my day with Joseph would prevent me from bumping heads with Ryder every chance I got. And I'd love to spend time in Joseph's company. Somehow, I felt like we'd known each other for longer than a bus ride across the country. So far, he had proven he preferred to make me smile instead of awakening a thirst for murder inside me, which I liked a lot.

ME

Awesome. AI can give you a hand during lunchtime.

JOSEPH

You don't have to.

ME

I insist. After all, you're my best friend, remember? And friends help each other out. Any distraction to avoid Ryder this summer is welcome.

JOSEPH

Arguing with you doesn't seem like a smart idea. Why is that?

ME

Because I'll have the last word. Don't even try. It's a waste of your time.

Take that, Ryder Whatever-Your-Name. I think you could use a hint.

JOSEPH

Can I text you later? I'm on babysitting duty tonight. Scarlett is having colic, and it's hard to type with just one hand.

ME

Sure. No problem. How's the bonding with your sisters going?

JOSEPH

Great. So far. Ask me tomorrow. I need to put a ten-year-old chatterbox to bed and feed a baby.

ME

Next time, let me know. I can help out. I've babysat lots of kids. Lay Scarlett over your forearm, like a football, and swing her slowly back and forth. It should help. Mom used to do that with Collin when he was a baby.

JOSEPH

I'm trying that as soon as we end this conversation. Let's hope you're a baby whisperer.

By the way, I'll pick you up. Don't refuse. I insist. Good night.

ME

Good night. Call me if Scarlett doesn't feel better.

I discarded my phone, but an incoming message pinged, and I picked it back up.

On the screen was a picture of Joseph with both his sisters. Scarlett had teary blue eyes, a painful expression shadowing her face. Kelly was blonde with big curious eyes and sported a genuine smile.

ME

This is adorable.

On my back, spread on my comforter, I stared at the ceiling. Thinking about Collin made me miss my family. A lot. I had never been away from them for more than a week, and usually, my absences meant staying at Iris's, not being on my own in another state.

Scrolling through my phone, I looked at the pictures of everyone I missed back home. After I took a big gulp of air, I dialed my parents.

Chapter 11

"Miss Sunshine," Dad greeted me when he answered after the third ring. Strings of knots tightening my stomach loosened. Just the sound of his voice sent moisture to my eyes. I sealed my lids, breathing through my mouth to calm my jittery heart. "Are you okay?" I could hear the concern in my father's voice.

I cleared my throat, trying hard to keep my composure and not give in to my overwhelming emotions. My bottom lip trembled, and I bit it as I regained some control over myself. "Yeah." My voice sounded weaker than intended. I blew out a long breath. I reminded myself I was mad at them, and they shouldn't get away with sending me here against my will so fast. "I am. I'm sorry for leaving like I did. For skipping our last dinner together." More tears pooled in my eyes. My voice cracked as I added, "I hate being upset with you, but you left me no choice. You had no right to uproot me without my consent. I'm not five anymore. I have a voice, and I should be able to use it."

Was all the bantering with Ryder giving me some spikes?

I usually wasn't the teen arguing with my parents and holding her own.

This time I wanted to be heard.

Guess Ryder was useful at something after all.

"Your mother and I never meant to send you away against your will. The last thing we wished for was to hurt you. We have a matter to deal with, and the opportunity presented itself. We also thought it'd be a great experience for you. It's just for three months, not a lifetime."

"Iris and I had plans. There are no excuses. It wasn't fair you didn't tell me sooner."

My father sighed. "Think you'll forgive us by the end of summer?"

I shrugged even though he couldn't see me. "Maybe." I breathed in some air filled with a hefty dose of courage. "If you want updates, just text me. For now."

"Huh, okay. Wanna talk to your mother? I'm sure she'd be delighted to hear your voice."

I shut my lids, firmed my back, and exhaled. "No. Not tonight. Some other time. I just called to let you know I'm fine, so you don't have to worry."

Wow, I was holding my position. My heart hit the wall of my ribcage. It hurt like hell to upset my parents, though, but they had to hear me loud and clear. I was not kidding when I argued that their decision sucked and should have been discussed beforehand with the one person it concerned, aka me.

"Night," I said when my dad turned silent.

"Take care, Ava. We love you. Never doubt it."

"Yeah. Love you too."

I hung up and blew out a long breath, twisting my bracelet around my wrist to soothe the discomfort swirling in me.

After I showered to flush away the last traces of my uneasiness, I slipped my tired self under the covers and grabbed my phone to set the alarm. The low battery notification flashed on the screen. Before I plugged it by the side of the bed, I shot Joseph a text.

ME

Hope Scarlett is doing better. Night, bestie.

I hit *send* and shook my head at the screen. A side of me loved the idea that Joseph and I could become friends this summer. He had a way of bringing sunshine into my cloudy days with his bottomless happiness.

He answered seconds later.

JOSEPH

Ah, I knew I was irresistible. Bestie, huh?
See, not hard being honest with yourself.
Glad you can admit I am your best friend.

This guy. Could he ever have bad days? Everything he said always sounded cheerful. Even his text messages displayed his happy demeanor.

ME

It was a test. To see if you were already deep asleep or buried under a mountain of dirty diapers.

JOSEPH

Nice try, Avalon. Lie to yourself all you want, but I know the truth.

I gotta wake up early. Need my beauty
sleep. Can we talk tomorrow?

ME

Sure. I'll be free after work. Night.

Holding on to the hope I wasn't alone on my summer journey, I fell into a deep slumber.

———

The next morning, I was busy classifying invoices when Ryder walked by the reception desk and dropped a to-go coffee cup on the desk. I turned to look at him with a raised brow, not sure why he would address me after the disastrous encounter of the previous night.

"I heard you like caffeine. Peace offering. Yesterday, I went to visit my mom. It always puts me in a sour mood. It had nothing to do with you. Poor timing on your part when you walked in without being invited."

He stuffed his hands in his pockets, looking uncomfortable.

"Thanks, but you didn't have to. Not sure we'll ever become friends anyway. You made it pretty clear."

"Don't get used to it. It's a one-time thing. And perhaps Mason said I wasn't making an effort to welcome you."

Not touching the cup, I swiveled my chair, returning to my task and ignoring him.

He didn't budge and gave me a look hard to interpret when I watched him over my shoulder because I could still feel his stare on me. I huffed my annoyance.

Ryder said nothing, his face expressionless and his eyes boring into mine with a heaviness that propelled shivers down my back, swallowing me whole.

Uncle Mason walked by before Ryder could leave, our staring contest still fully on.

"Hey guys. How is it going this morning? Do I sense a truce between you two?"

I snorted and rolled my eyes.

Ryder's jaw clenched. His gaze stayed locked on mine.

Heat enveloped me, and I felt like I'd melt in my seat.

Using his most syrupy voice, he said, "I was bringing your niece her morning coffee. Thought she'd appreciate the gesture. Turns out she's giving me attitude instead of a thank you."

He shrugged and hung his head as if I'd hurt his feelings, then brought his eyes back to mine with a challenge glinting in them, all traces of friendliness gone.

Wrath boiled in my veins.

Such a hypocrite. The audacity of Ryder. Portraying me as the bad guy. I wouldn't let him walk all over me without a fight. Two could play this game.

Faking a smile, I returned his poised attitude and rolled my shoulders back, playing unaffected. "I'm just waiting for it to cool down a bit. Wouldn't want to burn my tongue. Don't be so quick to judge my actions, *Riiidde*."

Uncle Mason lifted both hands before him. "Fine. No truce. Keep up the good work, though. Ava, this afternoon, we'll go through more complicated functions in the accounting software. I have a meeting at lunchtime, but we'll get to it once I'm back. How does it sound? Ready for the next step?"

I nodded. "Sure."

"Awesome. Okay, you two, just remember if you keep fighting, be civilized about it." He let out a chuckle and left us.

Before I could add anything else, both Ryder and Uncle Mason had retreated to the back of the garage, leaving me alone with my murderous thoughts about the guy who reveled in screwing with my existence daily.

Unable to resist the aroma of caffeine infiltrating my nostrils, I grabbed the to-go cup and relished the scorching liquid as it went down my throat.

How could Ryder know things about me that I hadn't spoken out loud, including my weakness for caffeine?

I feared the idea he could read me and that he could find out what made me tick.

Earlier, Aunt Melinda had asked me to invite Joseph for dinner the next day. She said she'd like to meet him before agreeing to let me spend my Friday night and Saturday in his company.

"Well, Mason and I talked. We'd like to officially meet him before letting you hang out with a stranger. Your safety is important to us," she had said.

I should be thankful she cared. Even though it felt awkward to have them approve of my friendship with a boy.

I saved my work and gathered my phone and purse. It was a beautiful sunny day, and on my first drive to work, I had spotted a small Thai eatery I was dying to try. The garage was mostly empty at lunchtime, except for a few mechanics finishing their work orders due in the afternoon.

As I walked away from the building, with music in my ears, an odd sensation prickled at me, and my stomach knotted. Like I was being observed. A quick perusal around the parking lot confirmed I was being paranoid. No none was there.

Until I did a one-eighty with my head and caught the dark eyes on me belonging to a broody silhouette. My heart thundered in its cage as we both engaged in one of our staring duels.

My breaths quickened. Why did we always end up in

the same dance? It was getting old. Despite it all, neither of us seemed to be able to stop.

From the short distance, I took in the scowl and hard set of his jaw and tried to come up with a decent explanation as to why Ryder would be mad at me today.

What appeared like disappointment flashed on his face, but he reeled it in as fast.

Except for the coffee encounter this morning, nothing exceptional happened between us. We didn't even cross paths all morning.

I scanned the length of him. Even with a scowl and dressed down in a navy coveralls tied at the waist over a white T-shirt molding the planes and ridges of his chest, he looked hot. More than he was allowed to. If I wasn't careful, my clothes would burn under his heated stare. Feeling self-conscious and not wanting him to imagine things that didn't exist between us, I stopped ogling him and noticed he held two wrapped sandwiches and bottles of soda. Too engrossed in the puzzling sight of him, I had missed it at first.

Did he bring me food? Did Ryder really think we were cordial enough that I would agree to spend my lunch break with him?

I was reading the situation wrong. I had to be. Ryder told me many times to stay away from him. Why would he want us to share lunch and spend time together? With a shake of my head, I erased the images of him and walked away, each foot I put between us releasing the uneasiness swirling in my abdomen.

That night, I stayed back at work to finish the day's paperwork after I promised my uncle I'd lock the place up.

Too focused on my task, I hadn't even noticed the blue sky and warm sun had been taken over by angry gray clouds and hail pellets. With my purse, I covered my head as I rushed to my truck, my only goal being to escape the attack from the gods above.

I slammed the door shut and settled in my seat, hypnotized by the *thud, thud, thud* of the bouncing pearls of ice hitting my windshield.

I turned the key in the ignition. Nothing. I tried again. Still nothing.

"No. No. Not tonight. Please, Felicity. I'm not in the mood. I am tired and hungry. Just start. I'll get you checked tomorrow." I turned the key and pressed the gas pedal. "Please, please, please." Nothing. I hit the steering wheel in frustration. I was desperate to get home. I looked around, trying to find an explanation as to why my battery could be dead when I noticed the position of my headlight switch. It was ON. *Ohmygod. Did I really forget to turn it off earlier?* Damn it. These old trucks were tricky since the lights had to be turned on and off manually, and I wasn't used to doing so in Dad's car.

I'd seen my father boosting his car battery with cables before, and I was sure I could manage it with a little help before having to call Uncle Mason to my rescue. After all, I was still in the garage's parking lot, so I had every tool I might need right under my nose.

On my phone, I searched *How to jump a car battery* on the internet. Plenty of step-by-step tutorials and videos appeared on the screen. I checked a few before concluding that, I was a resourceful woman and I could indeed do it myself. I recalled seeing those portable battery packs on a shelf at the back of the garage.

The hail outside had decreased, but the dark clouds were still lingering above, more threatening than before. A clap of thunder startled me just as I neared the building, and the first droplets of rain hit my face.

Within a few minutes, I had gathered the cables and

battery pack and was making my way back to my truck. The downpour had increased, soaking me in seconds. Under the lifted hood of my pickup truck, I found partial shelter from Mother Nature's onslaught.

Once again, I studied the photos on the tutorial carefully before positioning the clamps on each pole of the battery as instructed. A tiny flutter of pride ran through me. The version of me I'd been in Michigan would have never attempted to fix a car herself. I usually relied on my parents when I faced challenges.

Present-Ava was trying very hard to be more assertive, thanks to Ryder always getting a rise out of me, and to own her independence. Right now, I concluded I had the situation under control. That I could deal with the battery by myself.

My finger hovered over the on/off switch of the battery pack once I finished setting up the cables as instructed. I took a deep breath in, ready to test if the lesson from the internet was any good when a rough voice spoke up from behind me. One that sent a flock of butterflies swirling in my chest, and goose bumps to blossom all over my body.

"What do you think you're doing? Do you have a death wish?"

I jumped back in surprise.

In the slowest motion possible, I turned around and folded my arms, ready for the face-off with Ryder that I had no way of running away from.

He stood there, drenched in the rain, his usual frown bunching his dark brows together. His hair was plastered to his skull, giving the devil his due. His eyes were ready to singe me—in anger or something else, I couldn't tell.

My hormones woke up. How could he look hot even wet? Ryder was the biggest contradiction in this world.

A pulse started in my body, a rhythm that responded to his. I was helpless to do anything but hide it. Nonchalance painted my face as I strove to keep it as blank as possible, not wanting him to read me. It was raining. I should have been shivering, but the trembles that started in my core were anything but that. I refused to answer him, lest my voice reveal its secrets.

"I asked you a question, baby girl." His usual disdain flooded me like thick poison every time he turned his attention to me.

I scrunched up my face as I tried to make sense of his sudden appearance. My hand moved to my forehead, shielding my eyes from the rain assault.

"Not your problem," I snarled. In the few days I'd been in Feather Lake, I had turned into a version of myself I barely recognized when Ryder lurked in my peripheral vision, and getting worse as soon as our eyes connected. Never before had I relished a verbal fight like I did with him.

He shook his head, and I used the interlude to memorize every detail of his, from his angular jaw to the stiff position of his shoulders, his now-transparent white T-shirt molded to each ridge of his abdomen, and down to the jeans now glued to his thighs that displayed the lean muscles of his long legs.

"Having your death on my conscience isn't something I'm excited about." His words snapped me out of my careful perusal of his toned body.

"Unlike the preconceived notions you made about me —which are false, by the way—I can do this." I waved my phone in front of his face. "Thank you, but I should be able to jump a dead car battery on my own. I'm following the steps. Thank you for worrying, but you can leave now."

He folded his arms over his chest, not budging.

I mimicked his stance. "Told you to go. I'm not some circus monkey, and entertaining you isn't on my to-do list."

He made no move to leave, standing there with his gaze fixed on me—no visible trace of threat in his expression.

I groaned. "Get the fuck away. Are you deaf? Let me do my own thing."

"Keep going, baby girl. I love it when you spit your venom at me. It's kinda hot when you get mad. You're all flustered and bothered, and it suits you. Who knew you could bite?"

My gaze should have skewered him on the spot. God, how much more infuriating could he possibly be?

His voice sounded like nails on a chalkboard when he said, "You sure you know what you're doing?" He lifted one of his eyebrows.

I rested my fists on my hips and nodded. "Yep. Leave."

He raised his hands in surrender. "Don't mind me then. And don't electrocute yourself."

My eyes sprang wider. "Electro-what? This is you messing with me, right? Please tell me it's not an issue, that it's safe to boost a battery."

Turning on his heels, he sauntered away without another look at me.

"Ryder?" I hollered, running after him. "What did you mean by that?"

Chapter 12

The idea I could harm myself while using the battery pack was enough to kill the excitement I experienced minutes ago. I hurried after Ryder, needing to convince him to help me out. When he slowed his retreat and turned around, his presence was powerful enough to steal all the viable oxygen around us. His irises shone darker than usual. Even without uttering a word, his intoxicating energy wrapped itself around me. He glared at me, waiting for me to say something, and I could barely recall what I was about to ask him.

"I-huh…" I closed my eyes and sucked in a breath before I decided to abandon my pride. For now. "Help me. Please. I've never done this before. I could use your advice. Only this time, though." Great. Now I had resorted to begging him. Funny how things turned around quickly whenever he was involved.

Rain poured over our heads, but neither of us made a move to find shelter as we faced each other. Droplets of water clung to his thick eyelashes. My fingertips tingled to comb the damp strands of his hair adhering to his forehead to the side. He took a step forward, killing the remaining space separating our bodies. I swallowed. He did too.

Time slowed.

His lips parted, and his gaze glided all over my face, freezing on my mouth before snapping back to my eyes. He did that down-and-up sweep two more times. His throat bobbed, and he tilted his head to the side. For a fraction of a second, I wondered why he was watching me like that. The air around us became supercharged with a thrill I could feel deep in my bones. If my pounding heart could slow down its beating, I was sure we could hear the crackles under our rushed breaths.

His lips appeared fuller, and no doubt they would devour me alive if they claimed mine. What would they taste like? Why was I even thinking about kissing Ryder? It wasn't just my truck that was having a breakdown right now, but my sanity too.

Gone was the arrogant jerk I had gotten used to. The guy standing in front of me appeared younger. And timid. Though it did nothing to tame the lethal attitude he projected.

The masochistic side of me ached to discover how bad Ryder would burn me if I got too close. The idea of danger I associated with him was an unknown rush that intrigued me as much as it scared me.

My lips ached to feel the softness of his.

I balled my hands at my sides, not knowing what do to with them as they itched to touch him.

"Baby girl, you shouldn't—"

"Shut up."

His eyes grew bigger. His stupidly gorgeous face tensed, and I lost every bit of self-control I had left.

The magnetism between us reached a new level, and after losing the tug of war in my head, I leaned in.

A raindrop hit my eye, and my senses kicked back just in time. With a shake of my head, I broke the spell, and we both took a step back.

Ryder's voice, when he finally spoke, sounded colder than the hail that fell earlier. "And now, after brushing me off, you're asking for my help?" No mention of the… *What was it anyway? A pull…an almost-kiss…? No, it couldn't be.* No mention of whatever we experienced seconds ago. Did I dream the moment? Nah. Why did he choose to act as if it never happened? The lure on his face had vanished, replaced by a stare that could slay me if aimed at me for too long.

I cleared my throat, trying to escape the last vestiges of the hold he still had on me. "It's not like I have other choices." My voice sounded deeper than usual, almost aroused. The last thing I needed was for Ryder to notice how hot and bothered our interaction had made me. I cleared my throat again for good measure. "Dying is not on my wish list either."

"You always have choices. In life, there are always other options."

By the intensity of his glower, I wondered if we were still talking about my truck's dead battery or not.

"Right now, I don't. Will you help me or not?"

"God, you're the most maddening person I've ever met. You fucking drive me nuts."

"Whatever."

Not ready to show any more weaknesses around him or make him aware how his words stung, I straightened my back and pushed my hair away from my face.

"What's your game plan?"

"Plan? All I'm asking for is your help to boost my truck battery."

"You're infuriating."

I snorted. "And you think you aren't?"

The air surrounding us thickened, suffocating me. My body temperature shot up, and I relished the feel of the rain on my skin. We were both soaked, neither of us backing down from the imminent verbal fight I could feel coming because that was what Ryder and I did best: argue and banter. And drive each other crazy.

How could my temper only wake up when he was involved? I cursed under my breath at the realization. "And yet, you're the one always choosing to insult me," I added, my words wrapped in multi-layered bitterness.

He sighed and relaxed his stance. "You know what, baby girl? Just deal with it on your own. If I'm so toxic to you, I should stay away. Good luck. Time to shine. Show me what you're made of." He leaned against a tow truck parked a few feet away from where I stood, the nonchalance he wore so well pouring out from him.

"You're joking. You gotta be."

"Nope. Sorry to disappoint you." He raked his fingers through his wet locks, breaking eye contact.

"How am I supposed not to electrocute myself? I thought I had done it right. I followed the steps…"

He snorted. "You'll figure it out. Start over. Or don't. Are you willing to take the risk?" The smirk I grew to hate made an appearance, eliciting a surge of annoyance inside me.

I remained silent, considering my options, not sure what to do.

His voice cut through me. "Find that confidence back, baby girl. I have faith in you."

With one long stride, I stepped into his space. Take that for confidence. I pressed my fingertip between his pectoral muscles. "You work at a garage, and you won't even give me a hand. It's lame. Even coming from you."

His hand enveloped my finger, keeping it against his torso. "For all I know, you work at a garage too, no?" He cocked his pierced brow, and at that moment, I wished I could rip it off his skin.

His lips twisted, and I was about to blow a gasket due to the rage he provoked in me. "Geez, stop smirking. It's annoying. And you…you are…whatever, just stop."

"A subject. A verb. A complement. How can you not form complete sentences at your age?" He gave his head a shake. "Deceiving."

"Ohmygod, I hate you. I hate you so much right now. There's no word to express how bad I wanna strangle you."

One of his fingers tucked a wet strand of my hair behind my ear, his hand almost cupping my jaw as it lingered against the side of my face for way too long to be accidental.

I fought the urge to press my cheek into his palm, all my attention focused on keeping my breathing slow and even.

Another clap of thunder broke the silence—a confirmation of the hatred we shared—and we jumped apart.

Shutting my lids, I pivoted so he couldn't see my face. I clenched my hands into fists at my sides and forced some oxygen into my lungs, praying it would ease the time-ticking bomb about to rip me to pieces. When my eyes opened again, I studied the battery pack and cables I'd set up. And looked at the picture on my phone screen. It looked similar. What was Ryder seeing that I couldn't? Where was I going wrong?

Deciding that dying wasn't in my plans tonight, I pushed the remaining bits of my pride aside and spun around, praying Ryder would still be behind me, waiting. Who was I kidding? I didn't have to look to be certain he was there. I could feel the prickles of his presence all over my back. The thought I was always so aware of him all the time sent goose bumps over my arms, and I pushed the realization away. Whatever.

With one stride forward, Ryder's body caged me against the hood of my truck, his proximity stealing my breath away, and confusion infiltrating my thoughts.

He ran a finger along my eyebrows, wiping the raindrops away. I shivered underneath his touch. He dropped his hand, but it traced the length of my ribcage instead of releasing me. I arched my back, unable to stay indifferent to the turmoil rising in my core. I hated how my body responded to his. Always. Ryder possessed some power over me, a force I had no clue how to escape from.

"See, you don't hate me."

My voice was a shaky whisper. "Yes, I do. I truly hate you."

"Nah. You think you do, but you don't." He paused. "Ask me again."

His words vibrated through me, and I loathed how his voice alone could ignite something deep within me. A burn so addictive I could feel the flames licking my insides. "W-why?"

Something pulsed between us. Right now, I couldn't explain it. It just turned bursts of wrath into the bedlam of a wildfire. A blaze hard to contain. And it confused me because I couldn't tell whether it was attraction or hate. Lust or disdain.

Everything about him made me jittery—and uncertain.

"Because." He shrugged. "I like it when you beg me."

"I was right. I hate you. Oh God, you're a jerk. The worst."

"Fully aware."

"I can't stand you."

"You already made it pretty clear, and still, you need me."

"No." I huffed. Damn, I really needed him this time.

He wiggled his eyebrows, waiting for me to acknowledge I did.

I groaned and wished I could kick myself. I couldn't believe I was about to indulge in his stupid power game. "Want me to beg on my knees?"

He glanced at his crotch and then at me and smirked. "Not this time, baby girl. Wouldn't want you to get your knees wet the first time."

I would murder him. Now I was certain.

"You are a disgusting pig."

"Well, this pig is tired of wasting his time." He pointed to his chest with a finger. One I'd break if I were a violent person. Soon I would become one if he kept riling me up.

That inflated ego. How he could pass through the doorway every morning baffled me.

His lips lifted into a sneer. Yeah, he had to know how angry he made me.

"Don't refer to yourself as a pig. It dilutes the effect."

"Deep down, you wish I was a horn dog, don't you?"

"Stop. With. The. Sexual. Innuendos. It doesn't affect me."

"You sure?" That cocky smile of his returned.

How could he infuriate me so much all the time?

I folded my arms over my chest, pretending I was building a wall between us.

"Stop."

He lifted his hands in surrender. "Okay."

"Okay? That's all you gotta say?"

"Yep." He popped the *P,* and I wanted to claw his eyes out.

Closing my eyelids for a quick second, I took a cleansing breath in. When my attention drifted back to the most annoying human to have ever walked the surface of this planet, I fixed the fakest smile on my lips. "Help me. Please. Happy now?" I was disgusted with myself for partaking in that silly game of his.

His smirk turned into a full-blown grin. "When asked so nicely, how can I refuse?" We fixated on each other for endless seconds, neither of us averting our eyes first. "Wasn't so difficult after all." His tone had lost the playfulness. Something was happening, and once again, I couldn't get a grip of it.

Heat swirled through me. Ryder stood so close that the warmth of his exhale tickled my skin. All my anger left me as we breathed the same air.

"Thanks," I murmured in a weak voice that didn't sound like mine.

Ryder nodded, and with both hands around my upper arms, he swept me to the side as if I weighed next to nothing. When he let go of me, shivers started where his hands had grabbed me seconds ago.

He spoke, and it stole my attention. "See, the handles must be positioned vertically. Not horizontally. You don't want them touching each other or any piece of steel."

Beside him, I stood still, studying the steady movements of his hands, impressed by the confidence he showed.

"That's all?"

"Yeah."

"Other than that, I did okay?"

Ryder stepped back with a nod. "Yep. Ready to push that button?"

"You sure it's safe now?"

He stuffed his hands into his pockets and bobbed his head twice. "Affirmative. Jump in and start the engine when I tell you. Let's see if you were right and the battery was dead."

I did as instructed, and a few seconds later, my truck roared to life.

Ryder removed the clamps and shut the hood with a loud thud and watched me with a grave expression. Turning the wipers on, I brushed the rain away, and unable to tame my proud smile, I gave him a thumbs-up through the windshield before exiting my vehicle to meet him. "Thanks. For helping me out. That-that was nice of you."

He rubbed the skin of his nape. "Yeah, well…Go home, baby girl. It's almost dinner time, and you're soaked." He avoided my eyes, looking everywhere but me.

I studied him with a puzzled look. Why did he seem conflicted? Ryder was such a complicated mystery to uncover.

"Well, you're right. I should get going," I said, pointing behind me with my thumb before rubbing the bracelet around my left wrist. "Again, thank you for saving me from getting…huh…electrocuted."

"Anytime."

I almost hugged him in that instant, but before I could do something so out of character and complicate our already explosive dynamic, I hauled myself behind the wheel and used my hand to dry my face as much as possible. When I pulled away from my parking spot, the rain stopped, and rays of sunshine pierced through the heavy clouds. With my foot on the brake pedal, still in the garage's parking lot, I admired the rainbow forming on my left, a contrast to the earlier darkness. With a tilt of my head, I searched for Ryder, wishing he was witnessing the hopeful display chasing the gloominess of the day away. But he was long gone, as if he were never here. Feather Lake weather and he were very similar. Moody. Sometimes dark and menacing. And sometimes, colors shone through, pushing the heaviness aside and reminding me life was a happy and beautiful contradiction. The last thought brought images of Joseph to my mind, and I breathed easier.

Ryder personified the stillness in the air before a storm, the darkness after the moon, while Joseph was the calming sun breaking the night.

Right now, after the storm that just hit me, I craved sunshine in my life.

Once home, the hot jets of the shower relieved the residual tension from my upper back. I dressed in a pair of pink shorts and a simple V-neck tee. Feeling calmer, I lay on my bed and called Joseph.

"Miss me already?" he asked as a greeting. Just the sound of his voice added a sparkle to my day.

"Always," I replied, sarcasm coating my words. "Life would be so boring without my bestie in it."

He burst into a fit of giggles, and unable to resist, I joined in.

"I have something to ask you," I said, once our laughter died down.

"Ask me anything, Avalon."

"My aunt and uncle wanna meet you before they agree to my hanging out with you on Friday night. How do you feel about having dinner with us tomorrow? I know it's short notice, but Friday is in two days, so—"

"White or pink?"

I blinked and frowned. "What?"

"The flowers for your aunt. Which color?"

"Oh, that. Forget it, you don't need to."

"I insist. If they're nice enough to have me over, it's the least I can do. So, what will it be?"

"If you insist. Pink. Can you be here around six? I'll text you the address."

"I'll be there. And Avalon? I'm excited to spend time with you again."

Before I could reply, I heard faint voices in the background.

"I gotta go," he said. "Dinner's ready. Can I call you later? I'm not on babysitting duty tonight, so I should be free from any distractions."

"Sure. I need to help with dinner anyway. Bye."

I met Aunt Melinda in the kitchen. "I can cook tonight," I proposed. "How about a pasta salad?"

"Oh, I'd like that. You sure, honey?"

"I want to. Grab yourself a drink and just relax. I'll come to get you when it's ready."

"Thank you."

"Huh," I said before she exited the kitchen. "Before I forget, Joseph agreed to come tomorrow night."

A large smile stretched her lips. "Chicken Marsala or orange beef?"

"Chicken."

"Great. I'll be outside if you need me."

———

The next day went by quickly. Excitement filled me—the good kind—at the idea of Joseph coming over and meeting my family. I was hoping they'd get along great because I could see myself spending a lot of time with him during my stay in Feather Lake.

I drove back home early that afternoon, Uncle Mason offering to take over for the last hour of my shift so I could make sure everything was ready for tonight. Back home, Mom and Dad knew most of my friends since we'd been hanging out together forever. I didn't recall the last time I had to introduce them to someone new, much less a boy who was a friend.

In a hurry to start dinner and be ready when Joseph arrived, I showered quickly and was wrapped in a towel when I heard the notification chime of my phone that I'd forgotten in the kitchen.

Thinking it could be Joseph, I almost tripped over my own feet as I hurried, the floor slippery under my wet feet. I turned the corner and bumped into a wall. Again. Ryder stood there, a crooked smile grazing his lips, his hands locked around my waist. I scanned the length of him. Dark jeans and a fitted navy-blue T-shirt. A simple outfit that on anyone else would be dull. On him, it only increased his charm and mystery. Go figure. I snapped out of my admiration of his appearance and barked a "You?" I couldn't refrain from emphasizing the annoyance in my tone. "What are you doing here?"

I noticed the pulse throbbing in his neck, hypnotizing me for an instant. I swallowed when the heat from his palms shot through me. Jerking away from his grip, I stepped back.

"Don't look so happy to see me, baby girl."

I roasted him with my stare.

"Oh, come on. We were good yesterday. I helped you

out. Saved you from a painful fate. Have you forgotten already?" he asked, his cocky assurance wrapped around each word passing the rims of his full lips.

His eyes traveled the length of me. Dilated pupils. Slack jaw. *Kill. Me. Now.* I was wearing nothing else other than a way-too-short towel. A stifled growl passed his lips, and I was suddenly aware of our closeness. Were my cheeks crimson? Trying to put some distance between us and to make sure I wouldn't flash him, I crossed my arms over my chest and sighed, doing my best to appear unaffected.

"Looking for this?" he asked, waving my phone above his head.

"How? Gimme that." I jumped to catch my device, the towel around me dipping low.

His eyes widened.

Ryder was taller than me, and no way could I reach for his hand. Refusing to expose another inch of me to his eyes, I fixed the hem of the towel and returned to my previous pose, hip tipped forward, arms folded, and my face fixed in a scowl. "Stop taking my phone and reading my messages. Why are you being such a pain in the ass?" *And why did I always turn off the auto-lock function? Didn't I learn my lesson the last time?*

He brought down his arm and started reading the message using a high-pitched voice. "*Avalon.* What's with that name again? It sounds stupid. *On my way. Let me know if you need anything, I can make a pit stop and get it.* Oh, sweet. You landed a very well-mannered boyfriend, baby girl. Congrats."

"Joseph isn't my boyfriend, but it's none of your business anyway. Now leave before he arrives."

Ryder waggled his finger inches from my face. "Tsk-tsk. Not happening. I'll wait for him right here."

With both hands, I pushed him toward the kitchen door. "No. Leave. I'm serious. For once, do what is asked of you. Get lost. Far from here."

His laughter traveled through me. Baritone. Spreading shivers all over my arms.

"Not a chance. Why would I miss spending a night with you?"

"Spend the night? Are you drunk or something? Anyway, go and find someone to harass elsewhere. I'm busy tonight. Without you."

"Like I said, I'll be right by your side the entire time."

"No." I closed in on him and with a palm flat on his chest, pushed him to the side. "This was fun, but I have plans, and they don't include you. I'm sure you don't have friends, but if you do, find them. Or pay a visit to mommy dearest and forget I exist. I'm sure she's the only one missing you right now."

He balled his hands at his sides, his eyes ready to pulverize me to pieces. "Don't talk about my mother. Ever," he said, his words clipped.

"Geez, chill out already."

He ground his jaw back and forth. His attention drifted to my hand still resting over his heart, and after a beat, he relaxed. He didn't move to leave, though. Instead, his trademark smirk traced his lips, and he propped himself against the counter. "What day is today?"

I blew out a long and annoyed breath. "I'm not up for games, *Riiidde.*" I could muster a class A, full-of-sass, syrupy tone when he riled me up.

"Ryder." His eyes turned to slits, the air around us thickening with explosive tension. He quirked one brow. "Not Ride, baby girl. You haven't earned it. We're not friends, remember?"

"Yeah, that's what I said. *Riiidde.* So, Thursday. That's

today. Happy? Now scram. Go and play bully somewhere else. Or better yet. Get lucky with your lady friend."

He snickered, the sound devoid of humor. "You wish. But no. Did you forget what happens on Thursdays?"

I groaned. "What does that mean?"

"And for the record, I'm citing Mason: *Ride is having dinner at our place. Like every Monday and Thursday night.*"

"Oh, you gotta be kidding me."

His smirk stretched. "Nope. I'm having dinner with you and your little friend. No way would I miss it."

The gears of my brain accelerated. *Think, Ava.*

"What do you want? Anything. Name it and I'll do it. In exchange, you skip dinner tonight."

"Date. You and me."

"Wait. No. Not happening. Last time, you ditched me and left with someone else. Not that it was a date, but still, I was left to walk home on my own."

"False. I came back to pick you up."

My eyes narrowed. "Sure. After you got your dick sucked." The words tumbled out before I could stop them, and I silenced myself with a hand over my mouth.

An amused expression painted Ryder's face. "Who would have thought you had it in you? Dirty talk. And a naughty mind. Maybe baby girl isn't so innocent after all." A glint shone in his eyes. "Are you offering? I could really use the release."

My arms shot over my head. "No. Gross. You are gross. And rude. And vulgar. Where did you get your manners from? A dumpster?"

"Keep going. You're flushed. Red is a good color on you. And, for your information, I got my manners from a box of cereals. You know, those trivia questions on the backside of the boxes? Great source of information. Less filthy."

I groaned, unable not to react to his comment.

Ryder's humor died down. "About that date, when should I pick you up?"

After I blinked a thousand times, I crossed my arms over my chest, standing my ground. I wouldn't let his earlier words rattle me. "Not going on a date with you. Find something else."

"Kiss me."

"Ugh. Why would I do that?" I shook my head with too much velocity. "No. Never. Forget I offered you a way out."

"You said anything." He shrugged.

I grumbled under my breath. "Well, I lied. There are things I'll never do for or with you. I can clean your living room. Cook food and stack your refrigerator for a week. Wash your car. Run your errands. But I'm never kissing your stupid mouth. Forget it. Not interested in spending time with you either."

"Isn't that what you're doing just now? Don't you think our banter sounds like foreplay?"

I groaned, dropping my arms in defeat. Exasperation bubbled inside me. "Too late. The offer doesn't stand anymore. Go away. And you get nothing in exchange." I turned to leave but remembered my phone, so I pivoted to steal it from his grip. In a hurry to put much-required space between us, I stomped away but lost my balance, the floor still wet.

A strong arm caught me from behind, winding around my waist. With my back pressing into his front, I could feel Ryder's strong heartbeat against my shoulder blade. We both stood there, frozen. The warmth of his breath caressed my nape. Despite myself, I relished the sensation. And the safety his embrace provided.

His lips grazed the skin of my bare shoulder.

A million tingles rose inside me.

Tracing the length of my bare arm, his hand electrified my skin.

Heat swirled inside my core, and I thought I would combust, his touch a trail of fire.

Unable to break the spell, we stood there, immobile.

My hand enveloped his, still holding me against him.

Our breaths quickened.

I felt dizzy.

"What's happening?" I asked once I found my voice. "What are you doing?"

As if prodded by a hot poker, Ryder jumped back, cold air replacing the warmth of his body. "Nothing. Don't get ideas in your head. I just prevented you from falling face-first on the floor. Now get dressed, and stop hitting on me."

I blinked, hurt piercing my heart. "You're the one who asked me on a date. And to kiss you. Need me to refresh your memory?" I asked, my words tinged with spite.

"It was just a test. As if I'd go out with a kid. Or want your mouth on mine. Anyway, I already warned you I'm the big bad wolf from the children's storybooks. Stay the fuck away."

Without another word or look in his direction, I ran back to my room, slamming the door behind me. Throwing myself on the bed, I punched the mattress and screamed my hatred for Ryder into a pillow. I yelled until the lining of my throat became raw with the exertion, and then I screamed again, just for good measure.

There. Better.

Once my irritation decreased to a manageable level, I dressed in a white cotton summer dress with spaghetti straps and wooden buttons at the front that landed mid-thigh. I added a little makeup and returned to the kitchen, with my chin high, doing my best to ignore my nemesis. He wouldn't enjoy getting a rise out of me again tonight.

Ryder's gaze swept over me, taking in every inch of my body, the slow perusal feeling like a burning caress.

"What?" I asked, trying to sound irritated. Deep down, I enjoyed how he undressed me with his eyes.

"What are you wearing?"

My brows furrowed at his stupid question. "Huh, an astronaut suit, isn't it evident?"

"You should go and change."

My eyeballs almost popped out of their sockets. The boldness of this boy. "Why? Gimme one good reason."

"Because… I don't…"

I pinched my lips together to avoid smiling. Did I render Ryder speechless? In my head, I high-fived myself. For once, I'd have the last word. "Yeah, right. Keep your mouth shut. It's better for everyone."

Deciding to ignore him, I busied myself with prepping dinner. The entire time, he stood behind me, close enough I could feel his presence, but far enough our bodies wouldn't touch. Every time I spun around, I bumped into him, and he just shrugged. Gone was the aquamarine-green hue of his irises as they appeared almost black.

"Move." I'd been asking a dozen times, and he still refused to budge.

"No. I'm all good here. Admiring the view."

"Well, there's nothing to admire. Get lost."

I chose to pretend he wasn't here and continued to follow the recipe Aunt Melinda had left on the counter this morning.

Ryder's arm slid by the side of my face to grab a beer while I was fetching ingredients from the refrigerator. I twirled until our faces were aligned. "Enough. Stop trying to intimidate me or whatever game you're playing. It's not working. Find another victim for your bullying ways. Now since you're not living here, feel free to leave the premises of this house while I prep dinner."

We stood too close for comfort, and I saw dark glints shining in his eyes.

"One problem with your great plan, baby girl. Mason asked me to come home early to give you a hand because Melinda is stuck at work for another hour. Suit yourself, but I'm not going anywhere."

"You're lying."

"Sue me," he said in his trademark cocky manner with a smirk on his face.

Chapter 13

Ryder and I worked side by side without a word or a look in each other's direction. The room buzzed with hostility. I was sure if someone were to light a match, the house would explode. Neither of us said anything for at least twenty minutes, and I'd never enjoyed silence as much as I did right now.

I was chopping celery for the rice when I started chuckling despite myself.

"What the fuck are you laughing at?" Ryder's voice broke my train of thought. "What amuses you so much?"

With the knife, I diced a rib slowly.

"You hear that?" I chopped another one. "In slow motion, it sounds like tiny bones cracking. I'm just imagining they are yours, and it brings me great joy."

He froze, then relaxed his muscles. Questions swirled in his eyes. "Are you sick or something?"

I waved the knife in my hand. "Nah, I'm just enjoying your imaginary suffering. See? I don't need to insult you. All I gotta do is chop celery, and I get the same rush."

"You sound like a fucking psycho."

"Takes one to know one."

That did the trick because he shut up and focused on his task without arguing. After I ordered him to slice mushrooms and chop shallots and garlic, I busied myself with preparing the chicken breasts, keeping my back to him the entire time, pretending he didn't exist. At one point, the silence felt too heavy, so I scrolled through my phone, and music started playing on the wireless speaker mounted on the kitchen wall.

Better. I could now block Ryder's brain from communicating with mine without my consent in case he had some special power I'd ignored for so long. Deep down, I feared he could read my mind even if I stayed mute. That seemed to be the case the first time we met by the lake.

Letting my hips sway to the rhythm of the music, I forgot all about my unwelcome guest. Aunt Melinda arrived at five forty-five, followed by Uncle Mason minutes later.

"Smells divine in here," he said as he entered the kitchen and fished a beer out of the refrigerator after kissing his wife. "I can see you make a great team when you put your differences aside."

"What differences?" Aunt Melinda asked. "I thought you two got by just fine."

"Let's say I noticed some tension," he continued. "The four of us are family, so keep your disagreements for when you're out of here, okay?"

Ryder and I both nodded. "Fine," we said at the same time.

"See? Super easy. Problem solved. Our house is Switzerland. Wanna argue? Don't see eye to eye on something? I don't care. Go outside. Hatch it out."

The doorbell startled us all. "Go, Ava. I'll take over," Aunt Melinda said. She fixed my hair with her fingers before taking my place by the stove, removing the wooden spoon from my hand.

With each step toward the front door, my pulse spiked, and a thin layer of sweat lined my back. My throat felt parched, and I swept my tongue over my lips to remove the dryness, and breathed out. I could do this.

I just hadn't thought the next time Joseph and I met, we'd have an audience watching us. I ran a hand over my face, straightened my dress, and opened the door.

Joseph's familiar warm smile loosened the knots in my upper back. His presence comforted me. It chased the clouds Ryder's presence brought my way. We barely knew each other, but I felt at ease around him.

"Hey Avalon," he greeted me, pulling me into a one-arm hug and dropping a kiss on the side of my head, an arrangement of mixed pink flowers in his other hand. He looked really handsome wearing a pale-yellow T-shirt with a distressed surfboard on the front and gray cargo shorts. His curly blond hair was disheveled, and I was dying to run a hand through the messy strands. "I missed you. It's been too long."

My lips curled into a smile at his words. This boy. How could he miss someone he only had met once? But still, it was so typical of his personality and refreshing that it didn't surprise me.

We broke apart when someone cleared their throat behind me.

The sound dampened the excitement running through my bloodstream. Why did Ryder always have to ruin everything good whenever he was around? Like he couldn't wait to screw with me and my life.

"Hi, I'm Joseph," my friend said, extending his hand for a shake.

The latter stayed impassive for a beat, studying his profile before meeting his palm. "Ryder."

Joseph's eyebrows furrowed. "Oh, you're the charming ice cream date."

I cupped my mouth with a hand, muffling my giggles, the sarcasm in Joseph's tone impossible to miss.

"Love the text messages you sent me, by the way," Joseph continued. "Too bad I'm not into douchebags, or you and I would've been instant best friends."

"You two know each other?" Uncle Mason asked as he joined us in the entryway. He looked at all of us.

"Long story," I muttered.

He shook Joseph's hand next.

"Nice to meet you, sir."

"Nice to see you again, son. Please call me Mason. One fair warning and I'll say it before witnesses. Don't hurt Ava. Don't think about doing it. Don't try doing it. If you do, you deal with me. Understood?"

"Absolutely. Just so you know, it's not my intention and it never will be."

"Glad we're on the same page here. Come on in. I'll introduce you to my wife." My uncle's hand landed on Joseph's shoulder while he led him to the kitchen. "Want something to drink?"

As soon as they turned the corner, I faced Ryder, my fists going to my hips. "Don't be your usual despicable self."

He raised his hands. "Relax already. Don't get your panties in a twist. I'm no monster. I just don't like the guy."

My hands flew to my sides. "You don't even know him," I said through clenched teeth.

"No need. I can sense these things. Be careful, *Avalonnnn.*"

My eyes turned into weapons. How many times could I cut him to shreds in my mind in a day?

I shook my head, not in the mood to even reply to his mockery, and spun around to return to the kitchen, the sound of laughter reeling me in.

"These flowers are beautiful, Joseph," Aunt Melinda said, bringing the bouquet to her nose and taking a big whiff before arranging them in a vase. "You didn't have to but thank you."

Joseph winked at me and mouthed, *Told you so.*

I returned his grin.

"You guys take a walk or do something while I finish here," my aunt said. "Dinner will be ready in fifteen minutes. Just be back by then."

Outside, Joseph and I decided to tour the acre-sized property. There was a pond in the northwest corner I wanted to show him. It was peaceful there. And far enough from the one person I wanted to dismiss.

"I like your family," Joseph said after we walked in silence for a minute, his hands stuffed in his pockets. "They're welcoming and they care about you a lot. It shows. You're lucky to have them."

"Thanks. They're important to me," I replied, toying with the bracelet around my wrist.

When I was little, we used to see each other all the time. I was obsessed with Aunt Melinda. She and Uncle Mason would take me everywhere with them. When they moved, we only saw them once or twice a year. After things got difficult, we lost touch, and I was glad we reconnected now. I didn't feel like sharing snippets of my life even with Joseph. I had learned in the last few years that trust was something you cherished, not gave away easily. After everything that went down in my life, I had a tough time confiding in people outside my close circle.

Joseph didn't push me for more information. We remained silent until he asked, "Why is that jerk here again? Is he their son, or does he just enjoy messing with you on purpose?"

I exhaled. "Truth? I have no clue. They have some sort of long-lasting relationship I can't explain. My aunt and uncle consider Ryder a son, but I have no idea why, though. He's been nothing but a pain since I showed up here. He treats me like I'm a child and he's what...two years older than me at the most. I have no clue what his deal is, but I'm doing much better when we're not sharing the same air." Speaking about Ryder somehow had loosened my tongue. I had to vent to someone since Iris wasn't returning my calls these days.

"Well, I'm here now, so he better not monkey around you, or he'll get a piece of my mind."

"I can fend for myself. So far, he only barks but never bites. I think he's trying to look tough when he's not. Forget about him. He's not worth our time. Anyway, he comes to dinner here twice a week. I didn't remember about it when I invited you. I learned he'd be here about an hour ago myself."

"How do you like Feather Lake so far?" Joseph asked after a beat.

"It's growing on me." I hadn't been in Feather Lake long enough to make friends or go out and stuff, but I liked how folks were nice and chilled here. Especially the customers and the people I worked with.

"Think your aunt and uncle will let you come to Dusty's tomorrow night? It's a local hangout spot. Where we go to avoid tourists. When I was a kid, we vacationed in Medora Beach every summer. Two years ago, my dad traveled here. He met Amanda, they fell in love, and he moved here full-time. He bought a surfing school because he thought it was cool, and after Amanda and he married, they took over the beach restaurant that used to belong to her family. Surfing is something my father and I have always bonded over. Most of the friends I've made during my summer vacations still live here. Brody, Leslie, Carmen, Roni, Diego. They should be there tomorrow. Could be fun for you to have more than one friend in town. The girls are great. You'll love them."

"I'm sure they'll agree to it. After all, wasn't that why they invited you over tonight?"

Joseph shrugged. "I guess." He fished out his phone from the pocket of his shorts. "We should go. Your aunt said fifteen minutes." He looked around.

The pond was on our left, surrounded by thick woods, with a wooden bench on its bank with the word *Celeste* etched into the backrest. A clamp tightened around my heart at the sight of it.

"It's beautiful here. And peaceful." Joseph brought his attention back to me. "You okay, Avalon? You look pale."

I shook the wave of discomfort away. "All fine." Grabbing his hand, I motioned him forward. "Let's eat. I'm starving."

Chapter 14

Conversation flew easily around the dinner table that was big enough to seat six people. It was like Joseph had had dinner with us many times in the past. Like he belonged amongst us. Other than Ryder being his broody self, everyone else was in a cheerful mood.

Even I couldn't stop smiling.

"Ava told me you're a surfer," Uncle Mason said.

"I should've guessed," Ryder mumbled through clenched teeth.

"What?" my uncle asked.

"Nothing," Ryder continued. I could feel the annoyance pouring out from him.

"I used to hit the waves when I first moved here."

Sadness passed through Uncle Mason's eyes. He hung his head for a quick second, breathed in, and it was gone.

"My dad owns a surfing school. I'm in charge during the summer. He and his wife, my stepmom, just had a baby, so I'm giving them a hand."

"I'd like to look it up one day," Uncle Mason continued.

"Whenever you're free. I have some sick boards we ordered. They got delivered this morning. Can't wait to try them out."

"How will I resist?" Uncle Mason said with a chuckle. "I miss the waves."

"Just come by. I'll send you the contact details. On Saturday morning, I'm giving Ava her first lesson."

Ryder choked on his water, and my irritation toward him multiplied.

"Oh, that's wonderful. Your parents moved here?" Aunt Melinda asked.

Joseph started explaining his family situation, answering all their questions.

My stare drifted to Ryder sitting opposite me. Our eyes locked. I sucked in a big gulp of air, the wall I'd built between us dissolving under the strength of his attention.

His gaze darkened. His lips thinned.

His face was unreadable.

What's your problem? I mouthed.

He stayed impassive, his stare burning through me.

Goose bumps blossomed on my skin.

My throat felt dry, and clutching the glass in my hand, I took a hefty gulp.

Mind you own business, I added.

Why? I'm just expressing my thoughts.

No. False. You're judging him. Me. Everyone.

Ryder shook his head. *Nope. Don't get all dramatic. I just don't agree with your choice of friends.*

I turned my head, ignoring him and his attempts to keep the conversation going.

Joseph said something I didn't quite get and smiled at me. Under the table, a foot hit my shin as I returned the curl of his lips.

As if stung by a bee, my head jerked in Ryder's direction. A smug expression painted his features.

Stop interfering in my life, I added with a glare impossible to mistake. *You're ruining everything.*

You need no help in that department.

I rolled my eyes. *You're such a drama queen. Grow up.*

His face hardened, and somehow, lava pooled in my belly at the sight. Ryder's chair scraped the floor as he pushed it back and moved to his feet, his features strained. "Ready for dessert?" he asked. He cleared the table, the sound of plates banging together filling the otherwise silence.

With the towering pile of dishes, he disappeared into the kitchen and my eyes trailed his back.

I breathed easier once he wasn't too close to me anymore.

Through the wide windows framed by shimmery pink curtains, I watched the sunset casting a bright orange glow over the line of trees in the backyard, then turned my full attention to the people still seated around the table.

"Do I get the pleasure of picking up Ava tomorrow?" Joseph asked. "We'll go to Dusty's and meet some friends. I'll drive her back around midnight at the most and be here at six on Saturday to pick her up for her surf lesson."

My eyes rounded. "Six? Like in the morning?" I asked, alarm clear in my voice.

"The best waves are early," my uncle chimed in.

"Six?" I repeated.

"You'll do good," Joseph said in a reassuring tone. "You'll see. It's easier than it looks." His hand connected with mine over the table, giving it a reassuring squeeze.

"I hope so," I said, my lips stretching into a fake smile I hoped wouldn't betray the uneasiness brewing in my stomach.

"Don't stress over—" Joseph began, only to be interrupted by Ryder bringing a dish of hot chocolate pudding on the table with a "Careful, it's hot" warning. Stepping between us, we couldn't continue our conversation, and Joseph had to break our hand contact. Ryder didn't have to come between Joseph and me, as his side of the table was free, but deep down, I knew it was an intentional move. Part of his Annoy-Ava plan.

Not ditching his scowl, he made it his mission to serve us dessert from his spot next to me, forcing himself into my space. The entire time, the heat from his body scorched mine where our skin touched.

"I can't believe how much of a jerk he can be," I complained when I accompanied Joseph to his pickup truck after he said goodbye to everyone a bit later. "It's like he feels entitled to fuck with my days."

Joseph let out a loud chuckle. "He's something, I agree. Ignore him. He'll find someone else to bother if you don't give him the time of day. You'll see. Can you blame him? A hot girl moves in with his pseudo-family, and now he must share his favorite slash only child spot with her. He's reacting. And he's probably disarmed around you. Guys feel threatened all the time by pretty girls, and we're not always smart about it."

"You think he'll warm up to my presence? That it's just a phase? Because so far, he's done a pretty good job of making my stay hell."

He grabbed my upper arms. "I'm sure. Don't let him walk all over you, though."

I nodded.

He pulled me against him and kissed my forehead. From the moment we met, Joseph had always been super affectionate toward me, not something I was used to, and I hardly knew how to reciprocate his affection.

"I'll be here at six thirty tomorrow night. We could grab something to eat first—just the two of us—and then head to Dusty's. What do you think?"

"Sure. Sounds good."

"Fantastic. Thanks again for the invite."

He leaned forward and kissed my cheek.

My heart fluttered in my chest.

Joseph's breaths picked up.

I backed away, offering him a tight-lipped smile. "Thanks for coming tonight. I had a great time."

"Anytime, Avalon. See you tomorrow."

He climbed into his truck and waved at me as he pulled away.

Ryder neared me just as I was about to get inside the house. My body ignited the more he closed in on me, and I hated how it reacted to his presence without my permission. I stepped to the side, away from him, and schooled my features to give nothing away.

"This is a fucking joke." The anger coating his voice sliced through me.

I blinked, surprised at his sudden bout of aggravation. "What?"

"You know exactly what I'm talking about."

My pulse went crazy at his admission. Even without his confirming anything, I could tell what had riled him up. How could he have something against Joseph? All night, he never gave Joseph a chance to befriend him.

Whatever went down between us since I moved to town and how sour our *non*-relationship was, he had no right to make Joseph the scapegoat.

Without another word to me, he hauled himself into his car, started the engine, and drove away, leaving a cloud of dust—and a bewildered me—in his trail. My heart sunk in my chest, plummeting down at a vertiginous speed because none of his actions and interactions tonight made sense. One second, he couldn't stand me, and the next, he acted like a possessive jackass. How much more puzzling could Ryder be?

I sighed and pushed him out of my mind.

Spending time with Joseph was what I should focus on. Harmless fun. No drama. And a good time.

———

Dear Diary

I saw Joseph again tonight. Since arriving in Feather Lake, we hadn't spent any time together. He was still as cheerful as what I remembered from our bus trip across the country. And his smile was as blinding as the first time.

He came over to have dinner at my place, and it felt natural to have him there. Aunt Melinda and Uncle Mason seemed to like him a lot.

When he's by my side, I feel happier and calmer, and I end up smiling too.

And then Ryder happened. He was his usual broody self and made it his mission to try to sabotage our night. Seriously, something is wrong with him. I just can't figure out why he loves to mess with my life so much. The guy is such a mystery. I hate that my eyes are attracted to him, and that my heart beats fast when he's around.

We shared a moment earlier. I think we did. He asked me to kiss him, but I'm sure it was a test. Or not.

Something else also happened. His arm wound around me when I slipped and almost fell face first on the floor, and he breathed into my neck. I felt a connection for the first time. For just a minuscule, almost non-existent, instant. I am convinced I didn't dream it. Whatever it means to him, it means nothing to me. Ryder is a jerk, and I must remember that.

I must go to bed soon because I have a full day tomorrow. Joseph asked me out on a date. We'll dine together, and then we'll meet his friends. I'm a bit nervous about it, but Joseph is kind and protective—I witnessed it tonight with Ryder—so it's all good.

On Saturday morning, he's gonna teach me how to surf. This is exciting, even though it freaks me out a bit. I'm not a sports person, so I can't wait to see how it goes. That's not all. I'll have to wake up at like five. In the morning. Can you imagine? Yeah, I know, it's crazy. Spending time with Joseph hope-fully will make up for the early hour. I'll keep you *updated in a few days and tell you how it went. I'm calling Iris now because you don't talk back and sometimes, I need a friend who can help me out.*

Night,
Ava (who can't believe she's going on a date and will learn to surf) xx

———

"Okay, you gotta help me," I told Iris over video chat while I was getting ready to go to bed. "What should I wear? I have two dates with Joseph, and I wanna look cute, but not desperate. I have never dated anyone except Lucas. I've never even kissed anyone except Lucas. This is my having no clue whatsoever about what I'm doing."

"Do you like him?"

I shrugged. "Yes. Maybe. He's a bit too cheerful, but on him, it works. He makes me smile, something not many people can pull off."

She clasped her hands. "Good enough. Enjoy whatever you two are. Or will be. *A Summer to Remember*, A. Repeat after me."

"*A Summer to Remember*."

"See, super easy. Now show me what you brought on this trip, and we'll start from there." I turned the camera around. "And, A, breathe. It'll be fine. He sounds like a great guy."

"Going on a date with a guy I barely know, meeting a bunch of strangers, learning how to surf. How is any of this a good idea? Please tell me to cancel, and I will."

Iris's loud giggle resonated through the speaker. "Come on, A. You're doing what we said we would. Enjoying your summer. Just because we are apart, it doesn't mean you have to forget all about the plan. Kiss a hot guy. Learn how to ride a board. Meet new people. Get a job. Move away for three months. Those are all the experiences that create memories for your old days. Stop idling, and let's start with which bikini you should wear."

After we came up with different outfit options, I slouched on my bed, dressed in pink night shorts and an oversized T-shirt, and propped my phone on a pillow.

"That Joseph guy is definitely kissing material," Iris said, batting her eyelashes. "Don't miss your chance if he makes the first move. Carpe diem, they say. Or something like that. Seize the day. Take advantage of an opportunity. Live in the now. Anyway, you get the idea."

"How about you? Met anyone? You never answer my texts or my calls."

"The delivery girl at the gift shop…she's kinda cute. We've been hanging out. There's one tiny problem, though."

"What is it?"

"Don't tell anyone. My parents would have me locked up in my bedroom for the next fifteen years if they knew."

"What is it?" I repeated.

"She's twenty years old."

"Twenty?"

"Yep." She winced. "She's funny, charming, and she gets me. She's an introvert and loves to read. We fit. We kissed today. I swear all those butterflies swirled inside me when our lips touched." Iris rested her hand over her heart, a dreamy expression dancing in her eyes.

"Iris, you kissed someone. I'm so proud of you. I've been away for what? A week? And already you have that smitten look on your face. Who cares if she is seventeen or twenty? You did it. Took you long enough," I teased.

"How is it going with Mr. *Broody Should Be My Middle Name*? Found other ways to play with your patience lately?" she asked, changing the subject without an ounce of subtlety.

"He's been his usual self. I don't know what his deal is. He's friendly with everyone else, and then we cross paths, and he becomes a dickhead. We had a moment earlier. Something passed between us. I can't explain it. I was still wet, just out of the shower. I lost my footing, and he caught me around the waist before I fell on my face and humiliated myself. I swear I could feel his breaths on my neck."

Iris brought her phone closer to her face, entranced by my retelling of the events. "Then what? Don't leave me hanging."

"He accused me of hitting on him. Just after he asked me out on a date. And asked me to kiss him."

"A date? And a kiss? What am I missing? Since when did your life become a TV reality series? Explain yourself, A."

And I did. I told her everything about my heated encounter with Ryder earlier and the coffee and dead car battery episodes of the previous day.

"Okay, you won't like what I'm gonna tell you," she said after she reflected on it for a few minutes. "The guy is into you."

"No, he's not. I swear. He hates my guts."

"He brought you coffee as a peace offering. It was done clumsily, I agree, but he said he was sorry. Not sure guys like him say sorry often. He's intimidated by you."

"He's not. Why would he be? I'm this almost boring teenager. He has his own place. Works full-time. Probably receives head in the woods by the lake. I'm just plain me. And we fight all the time. Your theory makes no sense. Find a better one."

"A, listen to me. Are you blind? I don't think so. He was angry and felt threatened because you had another guy coming over."

"Joseph said something before he left. That Ryder is disarmed around me because I crash-landed in his life and took the place that was exclusively his."

"Maybe. But I still believe my version is more accurate. Think about it. It's logical. You can't deny it. He's testing your boundaries. See where the limit is. The more you engage in his behavior, the more he'll indulge. Perhaps fighting—getting a rise out of you—is what turns him on. Some people enjoy weirder fetishes."

"I do hope you're wrong. On all accounts. Because why would I go out with someone I'm barely able to tolerate? Or whose dick grows hard while insulting me?"

Her mouth popped open.

"Shush. Don't answer."

"A, I'm seeing a whole lot of trouble in your near future. Who could have guessed your *Summer to Remember* would turn out so interesting after all?"

Someone knocked on my bedroom door. "It's open," I said.

Aunt Melinda's head peeked inside. "Ava, when you're done with your call, can we have a chat, you and I?"

"Sure. Gimme a couple more minutes."

"Come and get me when you're ready. It's kinda important we talk about this."

I nodded, and she closed the door after her.

"What is this about?" Iris asked. "Did you kiss surfer boy in the middle of the kitchen? Or did I'm-a-jerk say something about your little encounter?"

"I have no idea. Guess I better find out. Geez, I hope it's not something bad." I pinched the fabric of my shirt to fan myself. "See, now I'm getting all sweaty. Wish me luck."

"Luck, girl. Keep me updated. I'm really wondering what you did. Your aunt sounded so serious."

"She's usually pretty chill." I fanned my body again. "Night, Iris."

"Text me once you're done, okay? Don't forget."

"I will."

We hung up, and I left my room to have the talk with Aunt Melinda. I felt I was about to enter the death row. I stopped mid-step when I heard her having an agitated conversation with her husband in the living room.

"…they're just kids," she said in a soft voice.

"Yeah, well, I've been that kid once. You witnessed my actions. Don't deny it," my uncle replied, his tone harsh.

"It was just a phase," she said, intertwining her fingers with his. "You grew out of it."

"For you." He shook his head. "Still, I'm not sure it's a good idea that—" He noticed me and didn't finish his sentence. "Hey kiddo. Everything all right?"

"Hmmm… You guys are busy." I brought my attention to my aunt. "Do you prefer we do this some other time?" I suggested, praying she would say yes.

"She's all yours," Uncle Mason said. He stood up and kissed his wife, and when he passed me, he tapped my shoulder before exiting the house. "I'll see you two later."

When Aunt Melinda looked at me, her smile reached both ears. "Honey, let me grab two mugs of tea and meet you in your bedroom."

"Oh…okay. Thanks."

With my pulse racing and air barely reaching my lungs, I made a dash for my room and took a seat on my bed, waiting for my aunt to join me.

A weird feeling weighed heavy in the pit of my stomach. Was I the reason they were arguing?

Chapter 15

Aunt Melinda sat beside me, offering me a mug of tea. "Ava, since you're staying here with us this summer, I feel like we must have a talk. There are things we can agree on. I'm not here to be a buzzkill, but to find an agreement that fits all of us, Mason included. This way, we can all respect one another's boundaries and know what is allowed and what's not."

I nodded and tried to swallow the lump forming in my throat. I hated these talks. So far, I'd never had those with anyone other than my parents. It felt weird to have my aunt playing parent. Even though I understood why she was doing it, and I respected her for it, it didn't mean I liked where I knew this was going.

"Let's start with curfew," she said. "How about eleven

on the weekdays and one o'clock on the weekends? School is off, but you have a job now, so you gotta be responsible. I trust you to be smart. If you're running late one night, let us know, and we'll deal with it. What do you think?"

"Sounds fair. I'm not a party person. In the past, curfew hasn't really been an issue."

"New town, new friends. You never know how your life can change once you find yourself in a brand-new environment. I'm happy we're on the same page here. What about boys?"

"What about boys?" I repeated.

"Ava, I saw the way Joseph looked at you. And how you looked at him. You guys have some intense chemistry going on for two people who've just met."

I said nothing, avoiding her gaze and tracing the stitches on the comforter with my fingertip.

"I'm sure you two will see each other a lot in the next three months, so we should come up with rules."

"Okay."

"First, no boy sleeping over without asking first. And not on weekdays."

"I'm not—I don't—"

She raised a hand. "Let me finish, then we'll discuss it. No parading without clothes in the house. If you have sex, because I know at some point it might happen, I prefer it takes place under our roof than in a shady and unsafe back alley somewhere. As long as it's respectful and you're not doing anything you're not comfortable with. If you have a sleepover elsewhere, you tell us first."

Heat rushed to my cheeks. I swallowed hard. Could my aunt sense the discomfort in me?

"Noted," I said, my voice so low I wondered if she could hear me.

"Also. Condoms, contraception, safety. Let me know if

you have questions," Aunt Melinda said. "I wouldn't be a great aunt if I didn't make sure you were informed about these things. You're seventeen."

"Mom had that talk with me when I turned fifteen. If it can reassure you, I've never been reckless, and I won't start now. I swear. And I promise not to jump into things I'm not ready for. I never did it, and I don't think I'm quite there right now. Even if I was, I don't have a boyfriend."

"Sometimes, when you like someone, one thing leads to another, and it happens before you know it. I just wanna make sure you know what to expect. An hour of fun comes with great responsibilities. If you can't accept these risks and be an adult about it, it means you're not ready."

"For your information, I'm already on the pill because I have bad cramps. One less thing to worry about," I said, trying to ease her worries.

"Ava, I trust you. Never doubt it. Neither the condom nor the pill is a foolproof method, but it helps decrease the chances of an unplanned pregnancy or diseases. When you combine both, that's when you're most protected."

"Got it."

"Do you have questions? Comments? Things you wanna discuss?"

I shook my head. "No. Not at the moment."

Aunt Melinda grabbed my hand between hers after she placed her mug on the floor. "I'm happy you're here with us, and I hope I didn't scare you with the birds and the bees talk. All Mason and I want is for you to be safe and feel free to be able to talk to us about anything bothering you."

"You're doing a great job so far."

She blinked the moisture in her eyes. "Thanks. It means a lot."

We hugged for the longest time.

"What did you think of Joseph?" I asked once we returned to our previous positions.

"What did I think? He's a nice young man. Polite, funny, kindhearted. We both liked him very much. I'm relieved you're making friends. I wouldn't want you to spend all summer on your own, only working and being home alone. Not that I don't enjoy your presence, but you're young. You should have fun with people your age."

I brought the mug to my lips and took a sip.

"Thank you. For everything. We should do this more often. Girl chat."

"I'd like that. Now go to bed. You have a full day tomorrow and a busy weekend ahead of you. Good night, Ava."

"Night."

She closed the door after her, and alone in the dark, I dreamed about my summer here in Feather Lake. Was Iris onto something when she said Ryder had a crush on me? No, she wasn't. It made no sense. My thoughts drifted to Joseph when images of Ryder polluted my dream feed. My subconscious and I needed to have a talk because this was not okay. With my eyes closed, I prayed for Joseph's face to make an appearance. Aquamarine-green eyes battled with sky-blue irises as I relived my night in my mind, and I chose to zoom in on the ones that were loaded with unabashed happiness.

Chapter 16

Creak. The sound of a door opening woke me up. My heart hammered in my chest as I pulled the covers to my chest and sprang into a sitting position. This was definitely the door leading to the outside. "Who's there?"

My hand patted the bedside table until I found my phone and turned on the flashlight, blinding the intruder standing on the threshold.

"Put that down, baby girl," Ryder's strained voice said.

"You? What are you doing here?"

"Shhh. Turn down your volume. Geez, no need to wake up everyone."

"You're in my room." I looked at the time on the screen. "At one sixteen in the morning. Care to explain?"

Leaning to the side, I turned on the bedside table lamp, casting the bedroom in a golden glow.

"I don't have my phone and my car, and walking here seemed like a good idea at the time."

"Why didn't you use the front door? This is *my* room."

"If I did, I would have woken up Melinda and Mason. My head is killing me, so drop the interrogation, will you?"

"How did you get in? I locked the door myself." I remembered double-checking it before going to bed.

He lifted a brow. "Really?"

"Never mind, I don't wanna know."

"Can I use your en-suite? I'll be quick."

"Huh…" Before I could answer, my brain still asleep and unable to think clearly, Ryder had removed his T-shirt. I watched him stumbling toward the bathroom, when the light beam from the night lamp revealed a dark bruise on his ribcage and a cut on his shoulder. "What's that?"

"Nothing."

"Stop." I sprang to my feet and neared him, inspecting the wounds after I flipped the light switch on. "It's not *nothing*." I sighed at his stubbornness. "Who did that to you?"

"Mind your business. I'll wash it and be out of your way if you stop interfering."

"Where did you go tonight? After you left?"

"Again, none of your business."

"You should get someone to look at it. Your ribs could be broken." I surveyed the bruise, taking in the purplish-red discoloration.

"Been taking care of myself for a fucking long time. I'll live." He shook his head. "Someone's debt had to be paid. And *I* paid the price. Debt is clear now. It was the last time."

I yelped. "You got beaten up? For someone else's actions?"

"Not all of us are born equal." He shrugged. "In my world, the lines can get blurry sometimes."

"I know… I don't understand why someone would do that to you."

"You mess with them; they mess with you. That's how it works."

"It shouldn't."

"Like I said, I can take care of myself."

"Doesn't mean you should, though. You should tell Uncle Mason. He could help you."

"Nah, he's done enough already. This is my fight. Leave him out of it. Don't get him involved. Not a word to him, you understand me? I'm not joking."

I nodded. "Okay." I entered the bathroom and beckoned him with a finger. "Come. I'll fix you up."

"Why?"

"You shouldn't have to do this by yourself. And let's say I have experience with wounds."

"How so?"

"You're not the only one with secrets."

Ryder and I remained silent while I cleaned his cut with a warm washcloth and soap. He hissed, and I blew on the gash to ease the sting.

After I bandaged the wound, I tiptoed to the laundry room to grab one of Uncle Mason's T-shirts and tossed it at him. "Wear this."

"Thanks."

"Can I ask you a question? Why come here and not go to your mom?"

"She—she's not here."

"Does she live in town?"

His tone hardened. "Stop with the twenty questions already."

"I'm just curious."

"Well, don't be. Stay out of my fucking business. Already warned you."

"Relax. I'm just trying to help."

"You did enough."

"Fuck you."

He hung his head. "Sorry. It was nice of you to help me. Not a lot of people care."

"It was nothing."

"For me, it was not nothing." He picked up his discarded shirt and motioned to leave.

"Where are you going?"

"Somewhere."

"Where's your car?"

"Not here."

I wouldn't get much more information from Ryder tonight. Gathering the second pillow from my bed and a pile of blankets from the closet, I handed them to him. "Sleep here. Tonight only." Surprise flashed on his face. "On the floor," I specified.

Ryder studied me for a minute. "You sure?"

"Yeah. I'll drive you home in the morning. It's a one-time offer. Don't get used to it."

"Why?"

"No clue. As you said, not everyone has the same opportunities in life. Take it or leave it. We can go before everyone wakes up."

"Thanks."

"Night."

———

The next morning, Ryder and I left early and stopped to grab take-out breakfast before driving to the garage together.

"How are you feeling?" I asked after we stopped to eat in an empty parking lot offering a perfect view of the lake. Shiny water and blue sky, the view was stunning at this hour. Perched on the hood of my truck, we sat side by side, last night's events bridging our differences. For now.

The morning air sent chills through me, and I was glad I wore an oversized hoodie over my work outfit consisting of a sleeveless mint-green dress and a jeans jacket. The sleeves covered my hands as I sipped on my to-go coffee, the heat emanating from the cup warming me up.

"Good as new."

Birds chirped in the trees, the echo of a lawn mower could be heard in the distance, and the sound of little kids laughing filled our silence. It wasn't awkward, but rather somehow comfortable. Lost in my thoughts and my contemplation of the view, I didn't feel like talking, and from his short answers, I was pretty sure Ryder didn't either.

Were Ryder and I only good at conversing if we argued?

His back was pressed against my windshield, and his long legs were stretched before him, crossed at the ankles. His eyes were closed, his face angled toward the sun. His dark hair was a tousled mass on the top of his head, begging to be tamed.

He didn't look pissed at the world right now, but calm. And serene. This was the version of Ryder I had never met before. One that intrigued me because it was so far from the boy I'd met until now.

My eyes traced his profile, and I wondered who had hurt him and if deep down, he was as broken as I was, and what the words of last night meant. *In my world, the lines can get blurry sometimes.*

The idea he had no family outside of mine pained me. Nobody should be fending for themselves with no one in their corner to cheer them up. At least I knew Uncle Mason and Aunt Melinda cared for him. That much had been evident since the first day I walked on him at the garage and later at dinner that night.

They really did love him like a son.

"Ready to go?" he asked, not opening his eyes. "Unless you're not done trying to figure me out."

"I am… I'm not… Yes, we can go."

He jumped from the hood and held out his hand. "Gimme the keys. I'm driving."

Not in the mood to spoil the morning, I did as he asked and sat in the passenger seat.

"Are we good?" I asked when we entered the garage from the side door and Ryder turned off the alarm.

"As long as you keep your mouth shut about last night, we are."

"I won't tell anyone. I swear."

Without another word, he turned the corner and climbed the stairs to his apartment. I watched him leave, not so sure if our friendship had evolved in the last seven hours or if this was just a glitch and everything would be back to normal in no time.

Chapter 17

"I could have driven there," I told Joseph when he picked me up later that night. Dressed in a powder-blue short-sleeved shirt that made his irises pop and black cargo shorts, he looked super cute. He steered me toward his pickup truck and opened the passenger door for me to climb in. "It's only a twenty-five-minute drive, I checked."

He circled the vehicle and hauled himself behind the wheel, pulling away. "What's the fun in asking you to hang out with me if we meet there? I wouldn't get the pleasure of spending these extra twenty-five minutes with you."

"Okay. Huh… Thanks." I could feel my cheeks turning a bright shade of red.

"And by the way, you look pretty tonight."

My face grew warmer at the compliment.

Iris and I had decided last night I'd wear a denim skirt with a black tank top and sneakers. I had braided my hair and applied a coat of glimmery gloss and mascara.

"You don't look so bad yourself."

Joseph bowed. A tiny smile broke free on my face, removing the tension in me and flushing the rocks piling in my stomach. Could I do that? Put my trust in a guy I only spent a few hours with? Could I let down my guard and just enjoy the night?

I fidgeted with the bracelet around my wrist, feeling a bit out of my element. Sure, Joseph and I had fun together in the past, but this felt different.

He kept stealing glances at me, and these wordless exchanges confirmed I could do this. With him. Trust and let go a little. Even though we agreed this was a night between friends, it felt awfully like a *date* date.

He spoke first, and I sighed in relief. "Avalon, I have one super important question for you before we get there."

"Go ahead. Ask me," I said.

"Pizza, burgers, or tacos?"

Oh, I hadn't seen that one coming. I tapped my finger against my chin. "Hmmm, let me see. Pizza."

He pumped his fist. "I was hoping you'd say that because I know the perfect place."

We drove for thirty minutes before Joseph parked his truck. From where we stood, I could admire the ocean and the rays of the low sun dancing across its surface. Exiting the vehicle, salty air clung to my skin and filled my nose. With a look around, I took in the cedar shakes building with cobalt-blue trims, doors, and banister. Surrounded by green foliage bushes and decorative palm trees, it was beautiful. Wooden swings tinted with the same natural color as the cedar walls were hung on the wrap-around porch. Ocean Mist was written in big cobalt-blue letters on a sign hanging from a three-foot tall pole next to the small cobblestone alley.

"Wow, I'm speechless. It's the most charming place I've ever been to."

"Come on. Let's sit."

Joseph grabbed my hand and pulled me forward.

Inside, the hostess led us to a small table on the covered back deck overlooking the ocean. From our spot, we saw seagulls fighting for clams under the pier on our right. A family, with two kids running around, trying to fly a kite on the mostly deserted beach. A young couple kissing, walking hand in hand, and an older man jogging shirtless, a black Labrador running at his side.

Pink brush strokes painted the sky. The view stole my breath away.

The tables were made of recycled wood, and the chairs were painted a mix of soft pastel shades. Whiskey-colored beams crossed the whitewashed plank ceiling.

Inside, a few booths lined one of the walls, the seats covered in a sand-colored, seashell-patterned fabric.

I relished the ocean breeze brushing my skin and the sound of the waves hitting the shore.

"How is it going tonight, Joseph?" the server asked as she brought us two glasses of water and a pitcher of lemonade.

"Great. Thank you, Glenda."

The lady winked at my friend. "I'll be back in a few minutes to take your order."

The man working behind the bar waved at us next, and Joseph returned the gesture.

"Wow, you're on a first-name basis here. Wait, is this your family's restaurant?" I asked. "Or do you befriend everybody wherever you go?"

"Yes, it's my—"

A woman in her thirties walked toward us. She was beautiful with shoulder-length brown hair and a contagious smile. "Joseph, you came. I was hoping to see you two tonight."

He moved to his feet to hug her.

"Amanda, this is my friend Ava, the one I was telling you all about. Ava, this is my stepmom, Amanda. She's Kelly and Scarlett's mom. And she owns the place."

"It's nice to meet you, Ava," Amanda said, leaning forward to pull me into a hug. Now I knew where Joseph inherited his hugging inclination. It was a family trait, no doubt. "You two let me know if you need anything. Order all you want. It's on the house. And once again, I'm glad to meet you, Ava."

"Thank you, Mrs. Curry."

"Call me Amanda, sweetheart. I'm too young to be called by my last name."

"Thank you, Amanda, it's generous of you to have us tonight."

"My pleasure," she said. "We're so happy Joseph decided to move here. We missed him a lot when he was up north." They exchanged a genuine smile. From the way they both interacted, I could tell how close they were. "I was lucky enough to replace a server who didn't show up tonight and meet you guys. I'll be inside. I hope to see you again soon."

"Me too," I said, more comfortable around Joseph's family members than I could ever have predicted. Hopefully, if I met his dad one day, he would be as easy-going and welcoming.

"Wow, I think I just had my first girl crush," I said, once Amanda disappeared inside.

"She's the best. Dad is about the same. I swear,

nothing seems to deter them. They're a great match. When my father moved in with Amanda and Kelly, they'd offered me the apartment above the garage when I visited. Now it's fully mine. I live with them, but I sorta have my own place at the same time. With the newborn and Kelly, who talks a mile a minute, I love having my own space."

"The best of both worlds."

When Glenda came back to take our order, we both asked for spinach and extra bacon on our pizza.

"How is it even possible?" Joseph asked after she left. "I've never met anyone ordering the same exact thing as me before."

I shrugged. "Guess we were destined to meet," I teased.

He clinked his glass of lemonade with mine. "Let's drink to that. I like the idea our meeting was all planned by the universe up above."

The rest of the dinner passed too quickly. The food was delicious and the company, charming.

"Dusty's?" Joseph asked as we made our way toward the exit.

"Yes."

Amanda joined us at the front door. "How was the food?"

"Excellent," I said.

"I like to hear that," she replied before pulling me into another hug before I could add anything else. "Joseph told me he's giving you a surf lesson tomorrow. Come over and order breakfast when you're done. I'll be here all morning."

"I'd like to give you a hand during lunchtime. If it's okay with you. Joseph will be working anyway, so better make the most of my time here."

"You sure? You could just relax on the beach, perfect your tan, or read a book."

"Nah, I'd much prefer helping out."

"Okay then. We're always short of staff. I'll see you tomorrow," Amanda said before wishing us a good night. "I gotta go back to my girls."

We parked at Dusty's. The lot was half-full. From outside, the shack almost seemed abandoned. The red paint was chipped in most places. The wooden trims around the windows were in dire need of sanding and a fresh coat of paint. The flower beds were filled with weeds. Even the whitewashed sign above the front door only hung on one side.

I grimaced and glanced at Joseph. "You sure we're at the right place?"

He snickered. "Don't let the exterior scare you away. I swear it's the best hangout spot in town. If it was too clean and didn't look like a shit hole, all the tourists would invade our special place. As long as they think it's unsafe, they'll stick to the overpriced tourist traps and let us be in peace."

"Well, in that case, show me the way."

Inside, the dive bar looked nothing like its exterior. Wooden plank walls and tables with red-leathered booths, black wrought iron chandeliers, and at the back, an antique jukebox was set in a corner, next to a small, empty space I believed to be a dance floor.

A group of people was busy throwing darts, next to the pool and foosball tables.

Country music played, and I recognized one of my favorite singers.

Joseph pointed to the two booths before us. "These are my friends. Most guys are lifeguards, so you might see them if you spend some time at the beach. Diego and Carmen are siblings, and all their friends hang out together. The girls have a wild side, but don't worry, they're great people. Come on, let's go and say hi. Then we can either sit with them or play a game of pool or chat by the bar."

His fingers intertwined with mine, and I enjoyed the assurance they provided me.

A Summer to Remember, I repeated in my head at the sight of all those people already familiar with one another, chatting and laughing.

My pulse pounded in my head at the realization I was the outsider. This was a big step for me, meeting a bunch of strangers all at once. Not that I was super shy, but I preferred small groups of people to big gatherings. With a breath I wished was deep enough to carry some courage along with it, I fixed a curl to my lips as Joseph introduced me to everybody, never letting go of my hand. As if he was aware I was slightly out of my element and required his comfort. Most of them rose to their feet and hugged me. What was with all the hugs tonight? I'd never been hugged by strangers before, but here, it felt normal.

We sat in a booth, and Leslie and Veronica were quick to include me in their conversation. After a moment, I eased into their presence and answered their questions. Joseph squeezed my hand under the table and whispered in my ear. "Told you, you'd fit right in."

I bowed my head, my wariness chipping away.

"Thanks for inviting me." I was thankful he brought me along to spend time with his friends tonight. He didn't have to, but I appreciated he did. It meant something to me. My other hand returned to the straw in my glass, and I punctured a cherry at the bottom and lifted it to my lips, listening to the stories the girls were cheerfully sharing.

Around ten, Joseph leaned closer and asked, "Wanna get out of here? It's almost time for me to drive you back home, and I want to spend a few moments alone with you before we have to leave. Walk on the beach?"

"Sure, I'd like that."

We hugged everyone goodbye, and after the girls made me promise to come back another time, Joseph and I followed a small path behind the bar leading to the sandy beach. A sliver of the moon shone high in the sky, basking us in a white glow.

The sound of the surf washing the shore was a relaxing melody.

As if we'd done it multiple times before, my fingers laced through his.

"This is beautiful," I said, my gaze roaming the expanse of white sand and water around us. "We should do this again," I said, feeling bold for once in my life. "Go out."

"Yeah." He caught me glancing at him sideways. "I bet you'd like it here."

"I do."

We halted and turned to face each other, cast under a spell only the moon witnessed. "Can I kiss you?" Joseph asked after what felt like a long time. "I've been dying to all night."

His hand rested on my cheek, his thumb grazing the skin there, his stare boring into mine. In the silver light, his blue irises appeared steel gray.

"You don't have to ask," I said, my voice barely above a whisper.

"Yes, I do."

I traced my bottom lip with my tongue. "Then the answer is yes."

In slow motion, Joseph's other hand molded to my waist, and he stepped forward, leaving no space between our bodies.

The thrumming of my heart vibrated through my entire self.

I sucked in a shallow breath when he tilted his head forward and skimmed his lips across mine. I fisted the front of his shirt, my head spinning, and held him to me as his mouth shaped to mine, more confident this time.

My other arm looped around his neck, deepening the connection we shared.

Shivers of pleasure ran through me.

I could barely breathe on my own anymore.

On my tiptoes, I pulled Joseph closer, our mouths never breaking apart as we tasted each other for the very first time.

Stars danced before my eyes.

One of Joseph's hands entangled in my hair, holding me in place as he savored my mouth. When his tongue teased my lips, I parted them to welcome him in.

I'd never felt so unsteady on my feet than in that instant. Even my heart turned giddy.

Time stopped existing as we lost ourselves in the feeling of us.

"God, it's even better than in my dreams," Joseph murmured against my mouth as we moved apart to catch some fresh air.

"You dream about me?" With a finger, I traced the length of my lips, now sore and swollen, trying to ease the sting.

"All the time."

My heart galloped wild in my chest at his confession. "I dream about you too," I admitted.

We exchanged a soft laugh.

"I should drive you back home."

"Can you kiss me one last time?" Who was this girl? I'd

never been that assertive before in my life. I kinda loved the self-assured version of myself I'd been turning into lately.

"You won't have to ask me twice."

Before I could drag a full breath in, Joseph's lips were back on mine, exploding my world into a splash of vibrant colors.

Both his hands were around my waist now, and my arms looped around his neck.

"You were right," I said when we broke apart. "I am going to enjoy my summer here." I looked away, and Joseph kissed my forehead.

"I was hoping you'd say that. It happened twice so far tonight. I think we'll get along just fine, you and I."

I knitted our fingers. "We already do."

Parked in front of my house a little before midnight, Joseph and I kissed some more.

My lips were numb, and my heart, about to explode.

"Night, Avalon. I'll pick you up at six. Bring warm clothes. We could light up a bonfire tomorrow night and grill some marshmallows or sausages."

"I'll be up and ready. Not sure I'll be able to sleep tonight, though. I think my head will replay our date for the next few hours."

"That will make two of us," he added with a wink. He walked me to the front door and claimed my lips one last time before driving away once I got inside the house.

I texted my best friend the moment I slid under the covers, fresh-faced and showered.

ME

I kissed him.

She replied within a minute.

IRIS

The surfer boy?

ME

Who else?

IRIS

Grumpy-Asshole. Whatever. How was it? I want details.

I related all the events of tonight.

IRIS

On the beach? Sooo romantic. My heart loves it. A LOT.

ME

I knew you'd approve. We're really doing it? Making this summer one to remember?

IRIS

Ab-so-lu-te-ly. Are you still surfing in the morning, or did you change your plans for an intensive make-out session instead?

ME

Plans haven't changed. Who knows, maybe we can do both? We're spending the entire day together.

How is it going with delivery girl? What's her name? You never told me.

IRIS

Tuscana.

ME

Oh, exotic. Love it.

IRIS

She's from Maryland. Nothing exotic about it. *winking emoji*

ME

laughing out loud emoji

Gotta go, I must be up and ready by six.

IRIS

Six? Like S-I-X, six?

Are you sure you're okay? Did you bump your head?

ME

Yep. And no. Waves are supposed to be better in the morning. It's a tide thing.

IRIS

Okay. You must really like him if you agreed to this.

ME

We said we'd do things out of our comfort zone this summer. Surfing at dawn is a combination of two things I've never done before.

IRIS

You go, girl. Keep me updated and send me a picture of that man of yours in nothing but swim trunks so I can attest to just how badly you're screwed.

ME

He's not my man.

Not yet at least.

IRIS

But he will be. I can feel it. Sleep tight. Or not. Your hormones must be having a blast right now. Enjoy the party. *winking emoji*

ME

Speak for yourself, Miss Dating-an-Older-Girl. Night xx

Shhh. I'm deleting this conversation in case
my parents decide to spy on my phone.
Good night x

Still surfing, no pun intended, the high of kissing
Joseph, I tossed and turned for the next hour. I saw the
minutes changing on the screen of my phone. No matter
what I did, I couldn't find a soothing position.

Desperate to catch some sleep, I closed my eyes and
relived the kiss on the beach over and over again. My body
warmed up. My hand slid between my thighs into my night
shorts. With hastened circular movements, I rubbed the
part of me that throbbed as the images invaded my brain
for the umpteenth time.

Broody green eyes replaced the sky-blue ones.

And dark hair pushed away blond locks.

With a shake of my head, I tried to scare away the new
images my brain was forming. In vain. Unlocking my
phone, I scrolled until my gaze landed on the picture of us
Joseph sent me. But as soon as my lids closed again, it was
Ryder's face that usurped my fantasies. A fresh wave of
pleasure invaded me at his sight.

A loud groan left my mouth. This was not happening.

I could have stopped the movement of my fingers, but
the more Ryder's face filled my mind, the hotter I got and
the more sensitive I became. Damn it. He was even
screwing up with my sexual scenarios.

Wet heat coated my fingers. My body was eager to
pretend they were his.

The deep baritone of his voice was all I could hear.

Oh God, this was bad. I was sick or something.
Because why would Ryder infiltrate my fantasies otherwise?

My breaths picked up, and I nipped my lower lip to
keep the moans in.

This wasn't right, yet it sent an addictive thrill through me. Each time Ryder's face took over my imagination, the more my body overheated, and the closer I got to a release. But touching myself with him in my mind felt like a betrayal. A subconscious one. On the other hand, no matter what I did, his face wouldn't fade away, and I really craved that climax.

I rubbed my clit faster, letting my head fall into the pillows as my back arched and ribbons of pleasure wrapped around me, taking me hostage.

I pushed my conscience aside and focused on the stormy eyes trained on me, those pouty lips that looked delicious, and the appealing chest muscles he paraded before me the other day when I entered his apartment.

The friction between my legs became too much. I increased the pace of my fingers until I exploded into a state of rapture. My heartbeat drummed faster. I couldn't suck a full breath in, exhausted by the orgasm that shot through me. Never before had I made myself come this hard. As if all my nerve endings were connected.

I prayed it was a glitch in my head—a one-time thing —and Ryder wouldn't become the source of my sex dreams. Damn, I refused to give him any more power over me. Joseph should be the only one allowed in my fantasies since he cared enough about me to treat me with decency and make me smile.

My conscious mind took over. I knew it was all a mistake when it switched the images in my mind. It had to be.

Within minutes, my body got heavier, my mind quieted, and I finally let myself drift into sleep.

Chapter 18

My eyes sprang open before my alarm went off. What time was it? No sign of daylight coming through the crack between the curtains. In the dark, I searched for my phone.

Five twenty-two.

Relishing the comfort and warmth of my bed, I flipped to my side, trying to make the most of the fifteen minutes of sleep I had left. In vain.

Excitement bubbled inside me.

I was not only going to learn how to surf today, but I would see Joseph again. Every minute before he arrived felt like a lifetime.

I jumped into the shower, wishing the hot water would

relax the knots in my shoulders. Even though I was longing for this day, some parts of me were still anxious about how it'd go.

Dressed in a pair of unbuttoned denim cut-off shorts and the powder-blue bikini Iris helped me choose the other night, I padded toward the kitchen, my shirt hanging from my fingers. Caffeine would help settle my nerves while I got ready.

I stopped in my tracks and gulped a big intake of air at the scene playing before my eyes.

What was going on?

Wearing jeans hanging low on his hips and a tight black T-shirt that left nothing to the imagination, Ryder stood there with his back resting against the kitchen counter. His eyes were trained on me, a mug in one hand and a smirk shaping his lips.

He nodded and hummed at something Uncle Mason, who was facing the sink, was telling him, my uncle oblivious to my sudden arrival.

Images of last night flashed before my eyes. That traitorous face. The one my brain conjured when I had my hand between my thighs.

Fury awoke in the depths of me.

The last thing I needed was to see his smug expression this early—and on my day off.

I clenched my hands so tight I feared I'd draw blood.

His eyes glinted, and his lips took on a devilish tilt. Could he tell? Could he guess I had pleasured myself with him in mind? I bet he had done this—invaded my thoughts and my privacy—with some voodoo shit only he could come up with.

I sealed my lids for a fraction of a second, hoping his presence in my kitchen was a mirage. With a grimace, I opened one eye and screamed internally. Ryder wasn't a product of my imagination or a remnant of last night's session. He stood there, watching me with an amused expression.

He pinched his lips together, and I could see the gears of his brain working and the challenge illuminating his eyes. It screamed bad news. For me.

"Going for a swim at five in the morning?" he asked, the tone mocking, a contrast to the heated gaze scanning me from head to toe.

My skin sizzled underneath his perusal, but I chose to ignore whatever feeling he provoked in me. More anger spread inside me at the thought he could make me feel things I never wanted to feel.

"No. What?" Uncle Mason asked, before turning on the balls of his feet and facing me. "Morning, Ava. Up early?" He scratched his forehead. "Oh, I forgot about the surf lessons. Sleep well?"

I felt heat creeping up my neck and cheeks. Seriously, could any of them guess what I'd been up to last night? No, how could they? Unless it was written all over my face.

I schooled my features as best as possible, aware I was a shitty liar. "Yeah."

"No, you didn't," Ryder chimed in. If I could teleport him anywhere else right now, I would. Okay, this time, I was sure he could read my mind and had psychic powers. *Shit.* I kept my cool even though inside, I was about to burst at the seams. I refused to let him know I had those kinds of thoughts about him. "You look like you've been up for days. Or all night. Anything on your mind?" A lift of the pierced brow and a crooked tilt of the lips accompanied his words. He took a sip of his coffee while keeping his gaze fixed on me. Waiting for my answer. As if. I would have loved to wipe that smirk off his face. Maybe scrape it with my nails or my teeth.

Was he trying to stir me up? To provoke a reaction out of me to confirm what he suspected?

Ohmygod, why was I so hot right now? As if my skin had caught fire.

Uncle Mason wasn't paying any attention to us, busy working the coffee maker, but I would never fight with Ryder in front of him. No matter what. It felt wrong, and I didn't wanna include my uncle in whatever was brewing between us.

My heart rate went wild behind my ribs.

Ryder waggled his eyebrows as if to encourage me to indulge him. It was bad enough I suspected he could perceive my inner thoughts. With a deep inhale, I plastered my most disinterested face on, wishing it would reveal nothing.

I needed to flee the scene—and fast—but my heels were glued to the floor. This had to be a nightmare. I had to wake up. As subtly as I could, I pinched the side of my thigh. *Ouch.* It. Was. Real.

No matter how much I told myself to run, I seemed to be frozen on the spot.

Casting a glance down to escape the powerful hold Ryder had on me, I noticed I still hadn't put my shirt on. I dressed in record time, not meeting his eyes this time when I accepted the shot of caffeine Uncle Mason handed me.

"Here, kiddo."

"What are you guys doing?" I asked, turning my back to the stranger in our house. Could I pretend he wasn't here? I risked nothing by trying.

"Remember I said we wanted to renovate the kitchen? Well, Ride offered to help me out and thought it would be a great idea to start today. So here we are. It will be a bit of a construction zone for the next two weeks, but we'll get through this."

"Oh. You should've told me. I could've given you a hand."

"It's a two-man job, baby girl," a low voice said from behind me. "We can't have you breaking a nail."

I jumped around, ready to strangle him. Ryder laughed at his own words. The sound vibrated through me. How could I despise someone that much?

I hate you, I mouthed, not shying away from the true feelings that concerned him.

Wanna bet? He mouthed back the question, his cockiness on full display.

I saw fire-engine red. That smirk.

Repeating in my head he wasn't worth my time or my energy—not today and certainly, not at this hour—I groaned and took a step back, escaping his gravitational field.

"When Joseph arrives, I'll be in my room," I said, spinning around and hurrying away before I could do or say something I'd regret later.

"Ride, don't be a jerk," I heard my uncle say. "I know you guys like to get a rise out of each other, but Ava is good people. Have her back. Please."

I closed the door before I could hear his answer. In my head, it sounded something like "She's not worth the trouble" or "She's just a kid, tantrums are expected." Or "She's making herself come thinking of me. Let me enjoy this moment."

I flipped the bird at the door, my breathing returning to normal. Almost.

Busying myself, I filled my backpack with a towel, underwear, a hoodie, and a pair of jeans.

A knock on my door put to rest the hatred I felt toward Ryder.

"Come on in," I said, thinking it to be my aunt.

I pivoted and came face to face with the boy I hated the most.

"No. No, no, no. Out. Now. This is *my* room, and you're not invited. Leave." I pushed his chest with both palms, but he didn't budge. I pushed harder.

He circled my wrists with his hands, and I lost the fight. We both breathed hard as we stood there, barely six inches apart.

"Get out. Go, annoy someone else." I held his piercing gaze. Unless he was an idiot, he couldn't miss the wrath radiating from every inch of me. "Are you deaf? I asked you to leave. Twice. Why won't you?" I cocked my head to the side, escaping the dark abysses of his eyes. The ones about to ruin me if I got lost in them.

"Well, aren't you an angry little kitten early in the morning?"

"I'm not."

"Yes, you are. Stop denying it. You're all feisty, and it's kinda cute."

"What do you want?" I asked, unable to hide my annoyance under pretty words.

"To talk to you."

"No, you don't." I eyed him with disdain.

He stepped forward, and I stepped back.

"Don't come any closer." I feared if he neared me, my night fantasies would be ruined forever. That the perfect angles of his face would haunt my thoughts for the rest of time. Hard pass.

Ryder took one more step forward, and I took one more step back. We did this dance three times until my back was pressed against the wall.

It took all I had not to bring my attention to him. He still held my wrists, preventing me from putting more distance between us. In another attempt, I tried to yank my arms away, but Ryder's grip on them tightened. My forearms were pressed on each side of my head.

Even if I tried, I had nowhere to escape, his intoxicating energy enveloping each of my cells.

Ryder's voice sounded rougher as he asked, "Who would have thought you'd be such a headache after only a week in town?"

His words hit me because even though I chose not to, my eyes snapped to his of their own volition. *Stop it, Ava,* I told myself. Over and over. No matter what, I couldn't ignore him when he stood so close and his body was pressed against mine.

Get away from him, Ava, I repeated to myself. The traitorous part of me relished this little act he was putting on.

Why was my body not agreeing to my commands? Couldn't it listen to me for once?

I pushed my shoulders back. Ryder wouldn't have the last word. Not if I could prevent it.

"Me? A headache? How about you being a walking nightmare? You *are* the one driving me insane. You *are* the one searching for a fight every time we cross paths. Not me. So, take a good look in the mirror."

He chuckled. My blood boiled in my veins at his audacity.

"You are impossible. It's all your doing. Angering me. Driving me nuts. You are the worst person I've ever met. You take pleasure in bullying people. No, scratch that. From what I've witnessed so far, you're only bullying me." I held my chin high when I said, "Tell me right now you don't take pleasure in it. Come on, say it."

He snorted. "See, you can be zesty when you put your mind to it. I knew you had it in you. It suits you."

He chose to ignore my dig at his character. Couldn't he own up for once? Admit he loved torturing me.

I glared at him, but the fire in his eyes melted my resistance.

With a sigh, I dropped my shoulders. "Let me go, or I'll be late."

"Not until you hear me out."

I shook my head. "Sorry, did you say something? I see your lips moving, but there's no sound coming out."

Surprise flashed on his face, but he replaced it with a scowl.

"What was I saying?" I asked. "Oh yes, that I can't stand you and you gotta let me go. I have plans that don't involve you, and right now, you're about to make me late. Leave me alone. Forget I exist."

"Impossible." Seriousness took over his face, and something resembling hurt flashed in his eyes. He blinked, and it was gone. Was that an emotion other than annoyance that I'd witnessed? "As long as you're here, I'm not going anywhere, baby girl. Get used to it."

"Why?" The doorbell rang, cutting short our confrontation. "See, my ride is here. Release me. Whatever point you're trying to prove, let's just pretend it worked, okay? I'm done playing your mind games."

I turned my head toward my bedroom door, hoping someone would knock and break the awkwardness of the moment when Ryder held my wrists with one hand and used the other to clamp my chin and force my head in his direction. My back was still pressed against the wall, so I had no choice but to comply.

"Look at me."

I closed my eyes.

"Come on, baby girl. Before you attacked me with your words, I came in here to tell you that I'm sorry."

This did the trick because my eyes popped open.

"I was out of line earlier with the breaking a nail comment. If you hadn't gone all aggressive on me, I would have told you sooner and been out of your room by now. Guess you like having me here after all." He winked before leaning even closer, his body flush with mine and his breath caressing the shell of my ear as he spoke. "Does the banter turn you on? Do you touch yourself thinking about me after we're done? Is that why you can't sleep at night? Because I invade all your dirty dreams?"

My wrath returned, and my eyes threw daggers at him. How could he? Was it written all over my face? My neck heated up. Ryder lifted one brow, waiting for my reply.

Now I was sure he had mind-reading psychic powers.

I swallowed and chose to change the topic. "Well, at least be honest. You can't help it. Aggravating me is your favorite hobby. Just say it."

"You wish."

"I wish not." I heard voices coming from the kitchen and knew Joseph had arrived. Trying to get away from the intruder in my bedroom, I switched to a warm-honey tone. "Can I go now? I have more important things to do than waste my time around you. Some of us actually have places to be."

"You sound like a brat."

We glowered at each other for another couple of seconds before Ryder finally released me. I rubbed my wrists to get rid of the stiffness there—and the memory of his touch.

Without a word or a look at him, I shouldered my bag, pushed past him, exited my bedroom, and kissed Uncle Mason's cheek, joining Joseph in the entryway.

My heart skipped a beat when his eyes landed on mine.

His lips tilted up, and I bet everybody in a ten-mile radius could sense the happiness ping-ponging between us in that instant.

He took my bag from me and opened the front door. "Ready?"

I bobbed my head, my excitement about the day returning, and my hatred for Ryder fading away. Joseph grabbed my hand, and flutters woke up in my core. I couldn't wait to be far away from here.

When I caught Ryder's eyes through the kitchen window while closing the door, he looked troubled as he watched me, his hands deep in his pockets, and his shoulders slumped forward.

Ryder never projected the same joyful energy that Joseph did. He wasn't caring or humorous, but there was a force emanating from him I couldn't deny. A dark side of him that a tiny part of me wished I could unwrap to see if his heart was really made of thorns or rather burnished gold treasured under layers of harsh life experiences.

I pushed the thought away. Ryder was a living contradiction. One I had no intention of resolving, and one I should avoid. At all costs.

Joseph and I stood side by side on the beach as the ocean displayed its majestic beauty with the slow cresting and rolling of its tides on the shore under the first rays of sunshine. A handful of surfers were already catching waves on our left.

"I'm not sure I'll be able to do that?" I said, pointing to a girl riding a pink board with ease.

"We might not even go into the water today. We'll

practice your pop-up technique. On the sand. It's easier to do it in water if you master it on land first."

In the early morning light, I enjoyed the sight of him. Longish golden hair swept by the ocean breeze, sky-blue irises, tanned skin, toned muscles, low board shorts. I could watch Joseph all day without blinking. Holding two surfboards under his arms, he could be the sport's perfect poster child.

My attention drifted to his mouth, hypnotized by the pink hue of his lips, as he explained the four steps to achieve the perfect surfer stance.

Things had been slightly awkward since he picked me up earlier. I could still feel the tension dancing between us, but neither of us had made any move to continue things from where we left them last night.

"Can you repeat the steps?" Joseph asked. "You seem a bit distracted this morning."

"You *are* distracting," I admitted, cupping my mouth with my hand, surprised by the bluntness with which I spoke the truth.

Dropping the boards on the beach, Joseph came closer. "Avalon, you want me to kiss you?"

I nodded, unable to get a word out.

"I was hoping you hadn't changed your mind since last night."

Heat swirled around us.

My heartbeat pounded in my head.

When his hands wrapped around my waist and his lips lowered to mine, I lost touch with reality.

Joseph stepped back before I could deepen our connection.

"Better?" he asked with a smile lifting the corners of his lips.

"You're still distracting," I said, breathless. "But I think I can pay attention now."

"Good. We'll work on the distraction part later." He winked.

Heat crawled up my cheeks. No doubt I was blushing bright red right now.

"Let me demonstrate what I mean. If you don't listen to my words, at least watch my body as I move."

That I could do. He lay down on one of the boards. Yes, I could watch him as his bronze skin and lean muscles captivated me. "This is the press-up position. See how I align my hands with my chest. It's a bit like a yoga pose." I followed the placement of his hands. "Next, you press up until your arms are straight. You want your eyes to look forward and your head tilted up. Just watch." He moved into position. "Now, you gotta pop up. That's the hardest step because it requires balance. In one swift movement, once your arms are extended, you bring your knees to your chest and pop up on your feet." He did it. "Let me start over from the beginning. The sequence is super quick. That's what we'll practice today. Once you're on your feet, all you gotta do is position yourself on the board a bit sideways. Always place your leading foot in front just like you would do on a snowboard or a skateboard."

"Leading foot? I've never been on any board before."

"Super easy. We'll find out in just a second. Watch one last time as I do the sequence, then we'll be ready to go."

I followed each movement as Joseph went from lying on his front to standing on the board.

He neared me and rubbed my upper arms in a comforting gesture. Could he read the alarm on my face?

"Avalon, you'll do great. I'll be by your side the whole time. Ready to find out which foot is your dominant one?"

I nodded.

"Good." He moved to stand behind me and held my waist. Goose bumps blossomed there. "I'll push you forward. Don't resist. Just a gentle push, I promise. You won't fall, but it'll give us the much-needed information about your stance. Ready?"

With both palms flat on my back, Joseph pushed me. I braced myself on my left foot.

"Good. You're a regular rider."

His hands locked back around my waist, and he pulled me to him. The beating of his heart reverberated through me.

"Wanna try?" he asked, his voice a murmur as he spoke next to my ear.

My own pulse grew crazy in my chest.

"Yes."

His lips skimmed my cheek. "Good. Let's get to it."

We broke apart, and I felt the withdrawal of his touch as soon as he let go of me.

Swallowing and wetting my lips with my tongue, I tried to restore my control.

After a few tries and Joseph's help to correct my posture and give me hints, I removed my hoodie, the rising sun and the exercise warming me up. Flat on my front on the board in only my denim shorts and a see-through white T-shirt over my bikini, I practiced my stand-up position again and again.

Even without glancing in his direction, I could sense Joseph's eyes sweeping over my silhouette in appreciation.

"Avalon, you're a natural. Let's take a break, and then we'll try it in water."

Knots tied my stomach. "Water? Like riding waves?"

He let out a heartfelt laugh. "No. No waves for a while. I'll stand beside you and hold the board while you move into the surfer stance. You'll see how different it feels while in the water."

"Oh, okay. For a moment, I got scared."

"I told you I'll be right there with you the entire time. If we catch a wave later, it'll be for fun, and I'll be on the board with you. Deal?"

I nodded. "Yep."

Sitting on the sand side by side, our legs folded and our arms locked around our knees, Joseph offered me a granola bar and a bottle of water as we admired the surfers at work.

"Can I ask you a question?" he asked after a minute, breaking the silence.

"Sure."

"Did you sleep at all last night? Because I'm not sure I did. I had a girl on my mind the entire time."

I returned his grin. "I don't think I did either. Not a lot, at least. I had a *boy* on my mind the entire time." I kept my eyes trained in front of me, refusing to risk a look in his direction and his being able to call bullshit on me. If I was being honest, I didn't lie to him. Not completely at least. He really occupied my thoughts. Until I chose to take advantage of the fantasies and my brain mixed things up. It was just a cognitive malfunction. That was what I concluded after my morning encounter with Ryder. Because there was no way I could have ever come that hard thinking of him. Nope. The wires of my brain short-circuited. Now that I was aware, it would never happen again.

"Think we could go on a real date next time? Just the two of us?"

"Isn't it what we're doing all day?" I asked, sipping on my water, doing my best to look unaffected.

"Nah. I want to invite you someplace else. Not my

family restaurant or hanging out with my friends. And not on a beach where my dad could walk in on us anytime or at your house where that Ryder guy could spy on us. You and me, somewhere we can be alone and enjoy our time together. Get to know each other better."

Ohmygod, Joseph was asking me out on a date. Freaking-out minute. I pinched my lips together, breathed in, and said, "I'd like that."

"What about next Saturday? We could go surfing in the morning, and I would take you out at night."

I answered without hesitating. "Sounds great."

"Awesome. Can't wait." One finger under my chin to turn my head toward him, and Joseph's lips connected with mine in a slow kiss before he rose to his feet and offered me his hand. "Come on, let's get into the water."

I removed my clothes and stood in a bikini, facing him, for the very first time. It felt a lot like being naked in front of the guy I had a crush on with nothing to cover me up. I wasn't ashamed of my body, but I wasn't that confident either. There was a big difference between stripping off my clothes while swimming with friends and in front of one boy, with his eyes caressing me. It felt oddly intimate. Even though he was the one I'd kissed. Many times now. Perhaps I could do this. Let go of my reservations today. "Avalon, I must say. If you thought I was distracting earlier, I can say the same thing about you."

I folded my arms over my chest and cursed Iris and her ideas. I should have worn a wetsuit or something when Joseph offered earlier. He promised the water wouldn't be cold, so I refused when he said he wouldn't wear one.

The same way he did earlier, he rubbed my upper arms, his touch warm and reassuring. "Hey, don't be shy. It was just a statement. I won't ogle you. You look beautiful. It's a compliment."

I relaxed a little under his palms. "Thanks. I'm not used to being barely dressed in front of guys."

"Guys?" He tipped one brow.

"A guy. You."

His hands descended to my hipbones. "I'm just teasing you. Let's get wet." He winked, and I melted inside at the way he watched me, his grin blinding.

Without thinking about it twice, I followed him, grimacing when I entered the waters, but warming up quite rapidly as Joseph scooped me over his shoulder and dropped me into the ocean, both of us laughing our hearts out.

"Warmer now?" he asked.

"Yep," I said, pushing the loose strands of the hair glued to my cheeks away from my face.

He kissed my lips before he went to retrieve a board from the beach.

On my front, I paddled with my hands the same way he taught me. When he held the board, I positioned myself.

"Remember what we practiced. You can do this."

"You won't let go of me, right?"

"Never."

I steadied my breathing, trying to smother the thundering of my heart by focusing on the sequence of actions.

It took me seven tries before I finally stood up on my two feet on a surfboard in the Atlantic Ocean. Joy flowed in my veins as I stretched my arms over my head, forgetting all about my balance and diving into the salty waters headfirst, screaming as I did.

I resurfaced, unable to hide the happiness that must have taken over my features.

"You did it." Joseph's cheerfulness matched mine.

I jumped into his embrace, my arms circling his neck. "I did it."

In my overjoyed state, I landed a kiss on his lips. His arms wrapped tighter around me, and before we could fully comprehend what we were doing, we kissed as if it was the first time. And the hundredth one.

His tongue swirled around mine, and a groan left his mouth. I could barely stand on my feet, my entire being floating from the pleasure coursing through me.

Time didn't exist anymore.

"Wanna try again?" he asked.

I bobbed my head.

With his hands around my waist, Joseph lifted me up until I sat on the board. With one palm, he adjusted his swim trunks, and I averted my eyes, pinching my lips together at the idea I was the reason for the tenseness I felt there seconds ago.

Joseph cracked his neck on each side, rolled his shoulders back, and blew out a long breath. "Okay, get into position."

"You okay?"

His throat rippled. "Trying to be." Now it was his turn to flush.

Out of the next ten tries, I succeeded at standing in the surfer stance four times, two of which lasted for more than twenty seconds, something I considered a huge win.

"Hungry?" Joseph asked when I fell into his arms after my last attempt.

"Famished."

"Come on, Amanda has reserved us the best table. Let's have breakfast."

We toweled off and put our clothes back on before carrying the boards to the surfing school premises.

"You can leave your bag here. Still up for giving me a hand during lunch hour later? You don't have to, though."

"I insist."

With our fingers threaded together we made it to Ocean Mist.

Pride wrapped around my heart. I did it. I had succeeded at something new.

I tightened my grip on Joseph's hand. "Thank you. For believing in me. And teaching me how to surf."

His smile dazzled me. A ray of sunlight in my usual tempered existence.

"Thank you for trusting me." His reply warmed my chest with a feeling I had never experienced before.

Chapter 19

"So, what's the deal with Ryder? Do you know why he acts as if he has the right to your place?" Joseph asked as we sat in front of the bonfire we lit up on the vacant land behind Ocean Mist, far away from any onlookers, after dinner. "The guy seems a bit territorial."

"I have no clue. Thus far, I haven't asked because I'm not interested in knowing. I dislike him enough as it is. I don't want additional motives to despise him."

Shivers ran through me.

"Avalon, are you cold?"

I rubbed my arms with my hands. "I'm tired, more than anything. I'm not used to doing this much exercise in a day. I predict soreness in my future. I'm usually more of a *reading a book* or *hanging out with my friends* kinda girl."

"You were amazing. I'd never lie to you. Some people can't stand up in the water even after multiple lessons."

I smiled. "I had the best teacher. All the credit isn't mine."

"Come here," Joseph said, beckoning me with a finger. "Let me warm you up."

I sat on his lap, and he wound his arms around me, making me feel cozy and protected.

I pushed my new wavy—thanks to the salty water—hair over my shoulder and angled myself to face him, my palm resting over his chest. "Thank you. For today. I had a great time."

"Our day isn't over." Joseph's fingertips drew circles over my thigh, waking up flutters deep down my core. His blue irises glimmered in the low light, filled with mischief.

I nibbled my bottom lip. "What do you have in mind?"

"Lots of things," he teased.

"Then show me."

His lips claimed mine in a languid kiss. I fastened my arms around his neck and lost myself in the feel of us.

"Can we just stay like this forever?" I asked against his lips.

"Not going anywhere, Ava."

He tugged my bottom lip between his teeth. A deep moan escaped me. He peppered kisses down the column of my throat, and I stretched my neck, loving how he caressed its flesh with his tongue and lips.

His mouth returned to mine.

For endless minutes we kissed as if we had all the time in the world, our tongues dancing and our hands curious.

Breathless, we broke apart, and a satiated curl tilted my lips.

Joseph brushed my hair back. "Avalon, you're beautiful."

I felt my cheeks warming up and nestled myself deeper into his embrace.

For the next hour, with my head buried in his chest and his arms tight around me to keep me warm, we watched the dancing flames until there was nothing left but ashes. Our connection was impossible to deny. In Joseph's arms, I felt content and secure.

"What are your plans after the summer?" I asked him when he drove me home around ten.

"I'm enrolled at Stuart University. They have one of the best marine biology programs in the country. Since their campus is on the coast, I'm hoping to join their surf team next fall. All I need is an opportunity to showcase my skills since I've never competed on the circuit before. Unfortunately, I applied late, and all the spots were already filled. I heard they sometimes hold tryouts at the start of the semester for newcomers, but you have to snag an invite to get in. That's one of my goals this summer."

"Wow, this is so exciting."

"What about you? Do you have any college in mind for next year?"

"I wanna apply to Philadelphia or Boston. They have great business programs. I haven't decided, though. All the universities I'm interested in are located on the east side of the country. We'll see."

Joseph's fingers intertwined with mine, and I relished the comfort the simple touch shot through me.

"You still have time. The internship at your uncle's garage is a great opportunity to see if you like it."

"Yep." I paused and spoke the words I'd kept inside. "Being here this summer isn't that bad so far."

We exchanged lopsided smiles.

"I agree."

Joseph parked in front of my house, just behind a tree, offering us a shadow of privacy. For the next ten minutes, we kissed some more.

Before things escalated, we both leaned back, panting. "Listen," he said, "I have a busy week, but let's make plans for next weekend. After all, we have our first official date on Saturday night."

"And my next surf lesson."

"Hell yes. You still wanna do it?"

I nodded. "I never thought it'd be the case, but I did like it. Blame it on the instructor. He's kinda cute."

"Don't tell the other kids next week, but I have a favorite student."

"Joseph Curry, am I the teacher's pet?"

"Only you."

He walked me to my door, my hand nestled in his.

"Good night, Avalon."

He was almost six feet tall, and I had to move to the tips of my toes to kiss him one last time. "Night."

The house was dark, and I didn't want to disturb anyone, so I walked to my room through the private entrance, my heart singing a happy symphony in my chest. I could hear the faint sound of the TV in the living room. A yawn passed my lips. I couldn't recall the last time I'd been so tired. My muscles were strained, and I could tell tomorrow the soreness would spread everywhere. My mind went blank, and sleep overtook me the moment my head hit the pillow before I had time to shower.

———

On Sunday morning, my day started all wrong, and by that, I meant Ryder-Wrong. The noises of construction work pulled me out of my sleep too early. I finally had a day I could sleep in but ended up sitting at the kitchen table at seven, my hair disheveled and my night clothes wrinkled, begging my uncle to put the water back on.

Ryder had cut it off, just when I was about to shower, and I bet he did it on purpose. He must have heard me mumbling to myself that hot water would do my sore muscles good while he dismantled the kitchen sink when I went to get coffee. A fitting broke, and the main valve had to be shut until it got fixed.

I cursed under my breath while I sipped on my morning caffeine, wishing it would uplift my current mood. Aunt Melinda had left to pick up bagels from the store near the garage because her kitchen had been turned into a war zone by the man I considered a second father and his jackass of a helper.

"Where's your smile, baby girl?" Ryder teased me in the mocking tone he always used with me, flashing his pearly whites at me. Right then, I had the confirmation he was annoying me deliberately. Still half-asleep, I refused to fight with him, choosing to save my low levels of energy for something that mattered.

Instead of giving him the satisfaction by joining his stupid battles of wills, I rolled my eyes and folded one leg in front of me on the chair, resting my mug on my knee, avoiding any kind of interaction with him. Acting as if I hadn't heard him or seen the winning expression taking over his features.

"Whatever," I muttered.

Once we all ate breakfast, and unable to stand Ryder's aggravating smirk, I returned to my room, plugged the buds into my ears, and decided taking a nap could help to reset my humor.

Around noon, I offered to go up to the store to

exchange the plumbing part Uncle Mason had bought in a size too big, desperate to escape the house and finally be able to take a much-needed shower.

"Ryder, could you accompany Ava?" Aunt Melinda suggested.

I froze in my tracks, turned slowly, and blinked. My eyes pleaded with him to refuse. Yeah, begging Ryder was becoming second nature to me these days.

"You could grab bags of soil while you're there. I wanna rearrange my flower beds."

"I can do it. I'm strong enough to carry a bag or two by myself." I lifted my arms as if to prove my words but stopped midway and grimaced. The pain straining my muscles due to the surf lesson made it impossible to stretch fully.

"I'd prefer his going with you," my aunt said. "You're hurting. And I want at least half a dozen bags."

"I'm not hurting."

She arched her I-know-better brow.

"Okay. Maybe a little. But I assure you I can manage. I'll do some stretching first. It's not *that* bad." Yes, it was, but I wouldn't admit it. I had some pride left. Even the smallest movement brought moisture to my eyes, and I yawned to avoid her noticing it.

"Anyway, while you're there, Ava, bring back paint swatches for the cabinets," Uncle Mason chimed in. "Melinda was thinking a shade of blue, and I was thinking more of a sage-green hue. Choose the ones you prefer, and we'll vote on it later."

"Fine. We're taking my truck, though. And I'm driving."

Ryder snickered and lifted his hands in surrender. "Suit yourself."

"I'll send you a list," my aunt added.

"Great." Cursing under my breath, I grabbed my keys and phone and went to wait in my vehicle, not in the mood to watch Ryder's smug expression any longer.

We drove in silence for a while. "Turn left at the next stop." He raised a finger, pointing at the upcoming intersection.

"I know my way to town."

"I've been living here my whole life. Turn left."

I stayed in the right lane. "My route is as good as yours."

My favorite country song played on the radio, and I turned the volume high, debating whether to sing at the top of my lungs or not in front of Ryder.

Oh, yeah, he wasn't here. If I ignored him, he didn't exist, right?

I belted out the lyrics of the chorus when my uninvited passenger changed the station. Rock music now filled the cab of my truck.

I gritted my teeth. "*Nooooo.* Why did you do this? You can't cut a chorus midway. I love that song."

"Well, I don't. I'm not a country music fan. Not even sorry."

"How can you say that?" I asked, my eyes rounded, trying to keep my attention on the road. "Know what? I don't care. My car, my music." I fumbled with the station knobs, but Ryder stopped me with his hand.

Right now, I wished this old radio had an outlet to plug my phone in.

"Don't even bother. No country whatsoever when I'm around."

"Well, I didn't invite you," I argued. "You came along, nonetheless. Live with it."

Every time I switched the station, he switched it back.

"Mind your own business," I said, an unmistakable

edge coloring my tone. "Or you can sit in the cargo box." I indicated the truck bed with a thumb.

"Not a chance. I'm perfectly fine here." He shifted in his seat and turned sideways until his back rested against the passenger door, his laser focus locked on me. "And the view is amazing."

I squinted at him and growled, uncaring that I was being blatant about it. "You exasperate me."

"You fascinate me. Your salty side is much more alluring than the sweet persona you show everyone else. Just wondering why you're desperate to tame the fire burning in you that's begging to be freed?"

"You have no idea what you're talking about." I sighed, hoping he'd just shut up once and for all.

Instead, I felt his eyes fracturing the shell around me.

"What are you hiding?" he asked after a beat.

"Nothing." My tone was clipped, not open to discussion.

"I call bullshit."

Couldn't he let go? "Think whatever you want. I refuse to talk to you."

"You act like Miss Goody-Two-Shoes, but we both know it's just a front. You're full of spikes. When I get a raise out of you, deep down, it excites you. I can tell. Your eyes light up. Stop pretending otherwise."

I kept driving, doing my best to keep my face neutral.

"Your secrets aren't as hidden as you think they are. Just sayin'," he said.

I yearned to park my truck, kill the engine, and bury his dead body by the side of the road.

My grip around the steering wheel tightened.

"My words affect you." Ryder sounded happy about it. "You pretend you are some innocent girl when you are not. Your thoughts are not just about butterflies and puppies.

Right now, you're dreaming of murdering me because you want me to stop talking. You're afraid I know too much. That I can tell how bad you are deep down."

I swallowed, keeping my focus in front of me. Ryder wouldn't get the satisfaction of knowing his words echoed inside me. That yes, I was scared he could tell things about me I hadn't said out loud.

"Stop projecting and keep that mouth of yours shut," I said through clenched teeth.

"See, you're not as much a saint as you think you are, baby girl. That much is evident from where I'm standing. You enjoy the pain. And the mind games. No matter what you try to convince yourself of. You crave darkness. As much as I do. It makes you feel alive. It gives you fuel. And ambition. It's a rush. When I fuck with you—"

I gasped.

"I didn't say when I *fuck* you… Is that what you wish for at night? My head between your thighs?"

I remained silent as a heat wave, that I'd never experienced before, pooled between my legs.

"What was I saying…? Oh yes, When I *fuck* with you, adrenaline shoots through you. You never try to leave. You always indulge, fight me with words. When you turn feisty, I can always tell when your pulse accelerates. Your breaths too. Unmistakable signs you're aroused by it. On how many occasions have you dreamed of kissing me so I would shut up because our banter excited you? Come on, tell me I'm wrong."

I fisted the steering wheel in a death grip. "You are. Everything you said is one big lie. I'm a good girl, and darkness is your middle name, not mine."

His head tilted back, and a loud chuckle devoid of humor filled the silence. "Geez, girl. You are full of shit. Stop pretending the world is one giant rainbow."

"You have no idea what you're talking about. We're not friends, and you know nothing about me. For once, just shut up. And stop interrupting my peace. Silence is a virtue where you're concerned. By the way, you're not irresistible. And the last thing I dream of is your mouth on mine. Ugh. From where I stand, it's pretty obvious you are delirious."

"Whoa. Keep lying to yourself. You're doing a great job so far." He snorted and switched the radio station. Again.

I cursed his name.

"See, this adrenaline rush when we butt heads, it's liberating. Letting the wrath out is therapeutic, I swear."

Surges of anger exploded inside me. I pressed my lips firmly, my molars about to fuse together under the pressure of my jaw. A tiny slice of me wondered if Ryder's words could be true. Was I keeping my rage inside instead of expressing it? No, he couldn't be right since he didn't know me. I talked about my emotions nowadays. I was better at it too. My past struggles had nothing to do with anger, but grief. Nah, once again, Ryder was speaking nonsense.

Praying it would bury the voices in my head, I switched the station back to the country one, humming the song. I breathed easier. Music as my coping mechanism for stress usually worked great.

I relaxed my shoulders.

Until Ryder decided to play DJ once more.

"You think you know me, but you're wrong. And if you believe riling me is the solution to all my problems, then you are even more delusional than I first thought." Tired of our tug of war, I turned the radio off, my white-knuckled grip on the steering wheel mirroring the wrath simmering inside me.

We continued for about a mile when a loud thud under my truck startled me.

My pickup truck swerved to the right, and I failed to bring it back to the center of the road. "What's happening?" I asked, panic filling my voice. "Oh God."

A strong hand gripped the steering wheel and helped me drive my vehicle to the right shoulder of the road. Relief washed through me when the hand squeezed my trembling one in a comforting gesture.

"Relax, baby girl. It's just a flat." Ryder's voice had never sounded so reassuring—or even encouraging—before. It killed some of the tension that had been strangling us since we left the house. "Breathe, you're safe."

Once I shifted to park, Ryder let go of me, and for a blip of a second, I missed his touch and the sense of security it provided me. Trying to ease my nerves, I ran a hand over my face, my overzealous heartbeat thundering in my chest.

I blew out a long breath, slipping my shaky hands under my thighs to calm the tremors.

Once a semblance of peace returned to my body, I fetched my phone to call my uncle.

"What are you doing?" Ryder asked, stealing the device from my hand before I could dial the number. Gone was the nice guy and back was the despicable jerk. "Calling your boyfriend, hoping he's resourceful enough to rescue you? Good luck with that."

"You gotta stop taking my phone. For your information, I'm calling Uncle Mason. And by the way, don't insult Joseph. You don't even know him. Not that it's any of your business. You should study his communication skills and interactions with other people. I swear you could learn a lot."

Ryder slid my phone into his back pocket as he opened the door and jumped out.

"*For your information,*" he repeated my words with a hint

of arrogance, "I fixed this truck for you *myself*. I know it inside out. So yes, I'll change the flat *myself*. Like a big boy. Happy, Your Majesty?"

I joined him on the side of the road and folded my arms over my chest and tipped my hip forward. "I'm not fucking royalty. Stop using this tone with me. It's insulting. And looking at you, I'm not certain you know what to do…or that you possess the right skills."

"Are you forgetting where I work?"

"Nah. But how can I be sure you're competent for things other than oil changes? That's all you've been assigned to since I got here. Oh, and wipers installations. Sorry, I forgot for a moment."

His mouth popped open, but I kept going before he could add something. "Tell me, *Riiidde*. Are you too afraid it will bruise your big boy's ego to ask for help? Those fingers of yours don't look that skillful."

He spun on his heels, neared me, and caged my body with his against the steel frame of my truck. The beating of my heart hastened when I felt his harsh breath against my cheek. "Careful what you wish for, baby girl. If only you knew how these fingers can rip you apart and send you to heaven, you would shut those pouty lips of yours. Unless that's your endgame." His eyebrow shot to his hairline. "Finding out how much destruction and pleasure my digits can leave in their wake. Am I right?"

I sucked in a gulp of air that burned as it made its way to my lungs.

Ryder traced my lower lip with the pad of his thumb, and goose bumps blossomed all over my skin. My eyes were locked on his. The blaze burning in them aroused the part of me I wasn't aware existed before now.

My entire being quivered under the intensity of his heated gaze.

I parted my lips, but no sound came out.

"That's what I thought," Ryder continued. "All bark and no spine. When you're ready to play with the adults, let me know. Until then, let the grown-ups do their thing."

Ryder moved away from me and peeled his T-shirt over his head in a motion so slow I couldn't stop staring at him. Standing there like an idiot, I followed each ripple of his flesh, entranced by the sight of him. Golden skin, taut muscles, and a thin layer of sweat. It took me three attempts to be able to swallow, moisture disappearing from my mouth. While he gathered the jack from the bed and rolled the spare tire to the front of my truck, I still hadn't stepped away from my spot against the passenger door.

"You gotta move. And pass me the lug wrench."

I pulled myself together, straightened my posture, and adjusted my shirt, deciding not to let Ryder witness how bothered I was by his little act. An exasperated frown crossed my face, and I asked, "The lug what?"

He mumbled something and used the crook of his elbow to wipe the sweat forming along his hairline. I was hot too but couldn't tell if it was due to the scorching hot sun above us or our interactions. My feet stayed glued to the ground as I took in every inch of him, now that he stood closer to me. His biceps, the planes of his abs, that dark hairline down his stomach.

"Lug wrench. Tire iron." He sighed. "Never mind, I'll grab it. If you can't help, just let me work."

I startled at the rudeness bleeding from his tone.

With a blink, I escaped the trance I was held under. "I'll do it. I'm not some idiot. What does it look like?"

"Toolbox behind the seat. It's shaped like a…fork. Or a chandelier. One arm on one side and three on the other. You can't miss it. I put it there myself," he said.

Rummaging through the steel box, I fetched the tool and handed it to him.

"What now?" I asked.

"Nothing. I'll lift the car and change that flat. Stay back."

"But—"

"No but. Babies are not allowed to come too close."

I sighed. "Why are you still treating me like a child? I can help change a flat tire. I'm not some stupid girl."

Ryder's eyes met mine, and we eye-fucked each other. Some unspoken words, impossible to define, passed between us. If I weren't careful, my clothes would melt just from the intensity of his stare when it traveled all over me, leaving more shivers behind.

No trace of friendliness was etched across his dark features. And still, it drew me in.

"I never said you were," he said after a long minute.

"Your actions speak for themselves. You're not fooling me."

"Whatever," he said and returned to his task, breaking the eye contact.

While Ryder was fixing the spare, I studied him, entranced by the ability and speed with which he did the job. Stupid me was now obsessed with his fingers. Images that shot through my mind the other night and his earlier words tried to invade my thoughts, but I blinked them away.

Wanting to play a part in repairing our case of misfortune and keeping my brain occupied to avoid a relapse, I rolled, or tried to roll, the flat tire toward the truck bed.

"Careful. Don't hurt yourself," Ryder warned as I bent my knees and used all my inner strength to pull it into my arms. "It's too heavy. Leave it there."

Clenching my teeth, I kept trying to lift it up. My limbs

were still sore from the exertion of the previous day, but my pride wouldn't let me appear weak in front of him.

"Gosh, you're so stubborn. Leave. It. There."

I ignored him the best I could. The sound of his voice couldn't reach me. I shut him out completely and plodded on. There was a thud behind me, and soon two muscular arms removed the wheel from my grip and dropped it down.

"Hey, I was doing it."

"No," Ryder argued, aggravation clear in his voice, every muscle of his face taut. "You were not. All you were doing was hurting your back and getting dirty."

"I don't care."

"Well, I do."

I must have lost my senses because the next thing I heard was "What if I like it dirty?" passing through my lips. In any other circumstances I would have turned neon red and run away, but facing Ryder, I relished how my words affected him.

His eyes widened. His jaw slackened. And he blinked. It lasted a millisecond, but long enough for me to witness it. Even after he schooled his expression, the sparks in his eyes were a telltale sign he heard me just right.

"Why do you feel like you gotta prove yourself to me?" he asked, choosing not to engage in my previous admission.

I rested my fists on my hips. "I don't. In case you are clueless, I'm here and can help you. Tell me what to do."

He shook his head, the devilish glints in his eyes causing me to curse my body for betraying me. "Not a good idea. You wouldn't be able to take it." A sly grin stretched his lips.

My pulse ricocheted. Our little game had turned far away from a flat tire.

"Says who?" I taunted. "Don't be cocky. It's usually an unmistakable sign you have nothing to be cocksure about."

Ryder averted his eyes and shook his head, refusing to indulge me anymore. Every inch of him tensed. "Stop it. You're out of your league with your little assumptions."

I snorted. "Says who?"

He spoke through gritted teeth. "Enough. Stay out of my way, and don't hurt yourself. I'm not doing it."

"Why are you always like this?" I asked, balls of anger bouncing inside me, as I decided to try a new approach.

"Like what?" he barked.

"Mean to me. Annoyed by my presence." I high-fived myself mentally for growing enough courage to demand an explanation for his behavior. Iris would be impressed by my new self-assurance.

Once again, we ended up in a staring contest, neither of us backing down, his eyes trapping mine.

"You speak nonsense," he said.

"No, I don't. You are rude. If today"—I motioned the air around us with a hand—"is your being nice to me, then what does not being nice look like? I agree you're kind but only with Uncle Mason and Aunt Melinda and others at the garage. In fact, everyone else except for me. And Joseph."

"Don't get me started on that boyfriend of yours."

I stepped forward. We now stood less than a foot apart. I spotted Ryder's rapid pulse at the base of his throat, and the way his chest rose and fell quickly. "What does that even mean? He did nothing to you. And he's not my boyfriend. You have no valid reason to hate him. He's funny and charming. He enjoys my company and doesn't make me feel like an incompetent fool all the time. Unlike you. He treats me well and respects me, makes sure I'm smiling when we're together. Like I said, you could learn a lot from him."

Mimicking my stance, Ryder stepped forward too, the back of his hands brushing mine and awakening shivers through me. "Glad to know he's not just a total loser after all."

"Oh, gosh, arrogant much? You make it hard for a girl not to want to strangle you," I said.

"What is that supposed to mean? Enlighten me, baby girl."

"Stop with the baby nickname. I hate it."

Ryder let out a sarcastic laugh. "Well, it suits you, so deal with it. Up until now, you haven't proved me wrong."

"You're impossible. I can't believe I'm stuck on the side of the road with you. If karma did this to me for my past sins, well, consider my penance paid." I turned away from him and spoke over my shoulder. "I'm walking back home. Good luck with your tire."

"Aren't you forgetting something?" Ryder asked in a taunting tone. More murderous thoughts flashed through my mind. Strangulation. Shovel. Grave.

I flipped him the finger and kept walking further away, feeling great for not giving him too much power over me. Finally.

"It's your truck, baby girl. Are you really trusting me with it?"

There. I knew at that instant Ryder and I would never be friends. I was done trying to figure him out and giving him chances. It was a lost cause. No matter what force pulled us together, it was a waste of my time.

Halting my escape, I stopped, breathed through my nose, fisted my hands, and tilted my head back until I could stare at the flawless blue sky. "Why?" I screamed at no one in particular. "Why do I have to go through with this?" I stamped my foot on the ground twice. Kicked dust and pebbles. Stamped my foot again. After I inhaled another cleansing breath, that I prayed would help settle my nerves, I padded back toward my vehicle just as Ryder hauled the flat tire onto the truck bed like it weighed nothing and cleaned everything up.

He wiped his dirty hands on the rag cloth he'd picked up from the toolbox. Droplets of sweat descended between his shoulder blades, following the line of his spine. Even though I hated myself for it, I savored the way his body moved. How his muscles shifted when he worked. The intensity in his eyes when he was focused.

Stop it, I begged my brain. Just stop already. Ryder is the enemy.

Snapping out of it, I threw him his T-shirt. "Better get dressed. We've lost enough time as it is. Stop parading in front of me half-naked all the time. It's just indecent."

"A *Thank you* would have sufficed," he said.

"And that too." I paused for a second to put my anger on the back burner. "Thank you. I appreciate your changing the tire."

"Anytime. You're such a fun assistant. I couldn't have done it without you. Your help was precious today."

His teasing worked its magic through me. And even though I wanted to, staying mad at someone was something I hadn't mastered well yet.

"Stop making it difficult for me not to hate you."

"Then stop making it hard for me not to battle with you," he replied.

"Whatever. Let's run those errands. The sooner we're done, the sooner we're out of each other's way."

My eyes drifted once more in his direction, and I scanned the length of him.

Stop it, Ava. Enemy. Don't give him power over you. Could my body get the message once and for all?

———

"You what?" Iris asked, bewilderment clear in her voice. "You watched him change a tire, all sweaty and hot, bantered with him, walked away, and flipped him the bird. Who are you, and what have you done with my best friend?"

I sighed and lay on my bed and braced my phone with a rolled-up T-shirt. "He always brings out the worst in me. You should see him. And hear him. He thinks he rules the world and is better than everyone else. I can't stand him. To make matters worse, he's decided to give my uncle a hand at renovating the kitchen, so now I not only see him every day at work, but also two nights a week at dinner, plus on the weekends too."

"Go to your boyfriend. Pick up shifts at his family restaurant. It will keep you busy and away from Feather Lake," Iris said.

I banged my head three times on a pillow. "If I do, all I'll accomplish this summer is work, and I like being home. Spending time with Uncle Mason and Aunt Melinda was the goal of coming here. I've missed them. It's our chance to reconnect."

"Sure, but there are things much less fun than making money. Also, you'd see that sexy boyfriend of yours all the time. Your life could be much duller."

"Iris, Joseph isn't my boyfriend."

"Not yet. It's a matter of time. Take my word for it. You two kissed more in two days than you and Lucas did in almost a year. You're all smitten when you talk about him. I can tell he's the real deal. Call him any name you want, but the next thing you know you'll both have pet names for each other, and you'll be spending the night at his place."

I sprang into a sitting position. "Nobody said anything about sex. Don't get ahead of yourself. I'm *so* not there yet. Stripping to my bikini yesterday took all my courage."

Iris shook her head at the screen. "By now, you should be aware I have witch's powers. Or maybe I'm an expert at reading you, but I've sensed a change in you in the last week. I may be wrong, but I don't think I am. You've grown a spine. You're more assertive. A, take my word for it. You and your *not-yet-boyfriend* will have *A Summer to Remember* together. He'll rock your world. I'm so happy it's happening to you. You deserve a great time."

"Don't make predictions about my life. It scares me when they turn out to be true. It's disturbing," I said with no real conviction in my voice.

"Well, when was the last time I was way out of line?"

"Never. That's what gives me the chills." A zing traversed my body from my head to my toes confirming what I just said.

"I love you," my best friend added. "Stop overthinking it. Unless it's Angry Boy who makes your heart beat faster?"

I rolled back onto my stomach and buried my head in the pillow. "No, we hate each other. Why would I want to be with him?" *Liar, you touched yourself on Friday night, thinking it was Ryder.* My brain didn't need to remind me every day about that instant of weakness.

"Wipe that sour look off your face, A. I was joking. Be with Joseph. See where it takes you."

I sighed. "Iris, what am I getting myself into?"

My journal entry tonight consisted of only four sentences.

Dear Diary

I think Ryder can see through me and knows things about me no one else does, and it gives me more ammunition to hate him with a capital H.

Why does he always awaken the murderous side of me every time he opens his stupid mouth? I don't care if he's hot and mysterious, since every time we're together, all I want to do is to kill him with my bare hands.

Would it be considered self-defense if the motive for murdering him was extreme aggravation?

Night,
Ava (who's having too many murderous thoughts lately) xx

Chapter 20

Monday at the garage went by smoothly. Every day I was getting more accustomed to my new tasks. Once I mastered the basic book-keeping knowledge, Uncle Mason promised to teach me more business management stuff so I could find out if I liked it enough to pursue it as a major in college.

During my lunch break, I sat on the patch of grass in the park adjacent to the back lot with a magazine I took from the waiting room and music pumping into my ears.

The blazing sun, high in the sky, warmed me at first, but after a while, it became unbearable, so I moved to a shaded corner until my break was up. With a light heart and a smile, I went back to my seat behind the reception desk. A message pinged on my phone before I could put my bag underneath the counter.

JOSEPH

Saw your good morning message late. Was already on the beach. The surfing summer camp started today.

On my lunch break. How is it going?

Just the sight of Joseph's name was enough to curl my lips into a permanent smile. I typed fast before he had to go.

ME

Great. Kids not being too hard on you?

JOSEPH

Nah. But they're not as good as my favorite student.

A bunch of twelve-year-olds are asking all kinds of questions. Want to know if I'm texting a girl. The grin on my face must be a telltale sign.

ME

Would love to see it. Free to talk later? When are you done for the day?

JOSEPH

I'll be home around three. I might give a hand at the restaurant later. Or watch the girls.

ME

Call me when you're free.

JOSEPH

I will. Gotta go. Two kids are fighting. Talk to you later.

How did my life change so much in a little over a week?

I resumed my work, my thoughts always drifting to Joseph and our upcoming date next weekend.

With a pep in my step and humming my favorite song, I entered the house minutes after four o'clock.

"You're in a good mood," my aunt remarked. "Is it all work-related or a certain someone on your mind?" She studied me with a knowing smile.

"Nothing special. Just had a good day. Need any help with dinner?"

"If you offer."

"I always offer."

She laughed. "I know. Just messing with you. Anything fun planned this week?"

I shrugged. "Not really. Joseph isn't available to hang out."

"Remember Tasha who works at the ice cream parlor? I'm certain you two would be a great fit. We could go there after dinner, and I could introduce you. See if you girls hit it off."

A knot coiled around my stomach. The idea of meeting a new person on a whim awoke butterflies in me, but then I recalled my motto, *A Summer to Remember*, and agreed.

Aunt Melinda pulled me into a hug. "Great. I'm glad you're adjusting to life here." She let go of me and asked, "Fajitas?"

"I'm on it," I said, gathering what we needed from the fridge.

We prepped food side by side, talking about anything and everything for the next half hour.

"Wow, it smells delicious. What are we having?" Uncle Mason asked as he walked through the kitchen door. The moment he held the door open, I realized what day it was.

My cheerful mood dissolved at the sight of him. Ryder

said something to my uncle that made him chuckle before resting his penetrating gaze on me.

His good mood seemed to evaporate too as we engaged in yet another never-ending wordless fight.

"I'll set the table," I said, desperate to escape his attention. While I busied myself, Uncle Mason joined me.

"Hey kiddo. Got a minute?"

"Sure."

He led me through the house, and we sat on the front porch swing.

"What's up?" I asked.

"I can't help but notice the tension between you and Ride. More than usual. At first, I thought it was harmless, but you guys give off some heavy vibes when you're in the same room. Anything I should know? Whatever it is, you can tell me. You're both family to us, and Melinda and I wish nothing more than for you two to get along. If you don't, or can't stand him, no problem. We'll figure something out while you're in town."

It wasn't my style to snitch on people. No matter how bad they got on my nerves.

"Just some friendly rivalry. We're different, and most times, we don't see eye to eye. He seems annoyed by my arrival. It's okay. We won't be the best of friends, but as you said the other day, we can be civilized. I'll try not to engage with him when it's not needed. Don't worry."

"Anything else I can do to ease things out?"

I shrugged. "No idea. It's been a week. Maybe I'm the one who needs to make an effort to get to know him better. Or perhaps he'll warm up to my being here before it's time for me to go back home."

"Not being cynical, I like it," he joked, bumping his shoulder with mine. "Does it have anything to do with the teasing? I can tell him to drop it or take it down a notch.

His humor is dark sometimes. The kid has gone through a lot. It doesn't excuse anything, but his heart is in the right place. You'll see, your presence will grow on him. I'm sure once you know each other better and your little rivalry stops, you'll get along great."

I jumped to my feet. "Hope so. I'll do my best to repress the desire to kill him in his sleep in the meantime."

Uncle Mason followed me as we made our way back inside. "That's my girl. I'm happy to have you here, kiddo."

We hugged and joined Aunt Melinda and Ryder back in the half-dismantled kitchen, deep in conversation about the best camping spots around the lake.

"Everything good?" she inquired when she noticed us.

"All fine," I said, my gaze drifting toward Ryder's stern expression.

Uncle Mason's words that Ryder had it tough replayed in my head, and I decided to do my best to be less irritated by his presence and see if we could one day be cordial toward each other.

"Go and sit, you guys. I'll finish up here," my uncle said. He kissed his wife, and they exchanged whispers. Even when I was young, it was clear they loved each other very much. Otherwise, they would've never survived the ordeal that had torn their lives to pieces four years ago.

Life had tested them. To the extreme. It wasn't fair, but they stood by each other through it all. In the end, it was their love that held them together.

Dinner went by smoother than expected. For the first time, Ryder and I could almost pretend we tolerated the other's presence. I was sure Uncle Mason had served him the same talk he did to me because he didn't call me on stuff or stare at me with barely contained hatred.

For now, we could call a truce. I crossed my fingers, hoping it'd last more than a few hours on a Monday night.

"You boys are on dishes duty tonight," Aunt Melinda announced as Ryder started cleaning the table. "Ava and I are going out."

"And we're not invited because…" Uncle Mason asked with one tipped brow.

"Girls' night out," I said. "We cooked; you clean. It's only fair."

"True," he said. "We may use the time to continue the kitchen tile backsplash. You girls have fun."

We said our goodbyes and climbed into her SUV.

We arrived at the ice cream parlor minutes later. For a tiny moment, a flashback of the first and last time I came here played in my head, and tension rose in my back. It was clear even back then Ryder and I were destined to be enemies and hate each other. We had nothing in common, and he acted like a dipshit from our first encounter. I should have been wiser that day and never got played.

With careful steps, I left the comfort of the car and straightened my back, shaking my head to erase the images of that night.

"Tasha, this is my niece, Ava. Ava, this is Tasha, the one I told you about," Aunt Melinda introduced us before ordering banana splits.

"Love your hair," Tasha said while she prepared our treats. We made small talk for a moment. "Tomorrow night, if you're free, there's a bonfire at the lake. We could go together. I can pick you up at seven-thirty." She offered a one-shoulder shrug. "Could be fun. Everyone will be there. Gimme your phone. I'll add my contact."

I handed her my device.

"Let me know when you decide." She glanced at the

group of people who just came in. "Sorry, gotta go, but it was nice meeting you, Ava. Text me, okay?"

"I will," I said, pocketing my phone. "Thank you for inviting me."

"See? I knew you two would hit it off," Aunt Melinda said after paying, a satisfied smile on her face. "Come on, let's walk across the park."

———

On Tuesday night, I was in my room, looking at my reflection in the mirror after I changed for the third time. Wearing ankle Chucks, a black skirt, and an aqua tank top with a gemstone skeleton printed on the front, I felt confident I'd nailed it. I braided my hair over my left shoulder and applied nude gloss and a thick coat of mascara. Yep, the image in the glass pleased me.

"You look pretty," my aunt said when I joined her in the living room while waiting for Tasha to arrive.

Could she hear my wild heart from where she sat? I rolled the friendship bracelet on my left wrist between my fingers. Whenever I felt agitated, it helped calm my nerves.

"Don't look so nervous," she continued. "It'll be great. Call me if it's not, and I'll come and get you. You have nothing to worry about." Her eyes searched mine, and I could read the compassion and seriousness in them.

I didn't want her to worry, but I loved that she cared enough to make sure I'd be all right. I nodded and shoved my hands deep into my pockets to avoid fidgeting. "Thanks."

"Ava, you look so much like your mama right now. She used to be a ball of stress every time she had to go out with a new group of people. She hated being the newcomer. Or the center of attention. She much preferred books to any social event. I always had to drag her out to meet friends."

"Mom used to be shy?" I asked, sitting on the edge of the couch, the piece of information capturing my attention. "I always thought nothing could faze her. She looks so in control all the time. As if nothing scares her and she can give anybody a run for their money."

"Well, it wasn't always the case. When she started dating Craig, she was a bundle of nerves in the days prior."

"Wow, I can't picture that. They're so perfect together. Sometimes I fear I'll never get that. I mean, find the one person you're supposed to be with. You and Uncle Mason have it. My parents have it. Things would not have been the same if bio-dad were still alive and in the picture. Or maybe, no matter what, Mom and Dad were always meant to end up together." I paused to think about how different my life would have been if bio-dad was my parent instead of Craig. "How will I know I've found my soul mate? Will I get a sign? Some sort of electric current that will pass through both of us, proof we're destined to be together? Will we end each other's sentences?"

"Honey, when you know, you know. I'm aware it sounds clichéd, but it's true. You'll just feel it. Deep in your bones. Your world will begin and end with that person. It's not rational. But it's strong. Like you've known each other all your lives. Wanna hear a story?"

I nodded.

"Uncle Mason asked me out several times before I took pity on the guy and finally said yes. After many refusals—let's just say I was scared to give him a chance back then—he came up with creative ways of asking me out, so I couldn't ignore him anymore. He had a reputation with girls, and I refused to be the latest notch on his bedpost. I had been through a difficult time, so I was a bit skittish about the whole dating thing. We'd known each other a long time, and he used to rile me up. In all honesty, we've always had a complicated friendship. After our relationship fell apart in high school, we reconnected in college. To me, he was still the infuriating boy I grew up with, and it took me a while to recognize he really had changed—for the better.

"Once he entered my sociology class, dressed as a hotdog, and asked me if I'd go out with him—in front of everybody. I said no, and the entire class booed me. I remember it as if it were yesterday. The poor guy. I thought I'd ruined his life. He looked so defeated. But when Mason has something in mind, he's relentless. It took him two weeks to find the courage to ask me out again. This time, he came to the pub where I worked and said, 'I'm desperate for a chance. Just one. You can even leave after the appetizers if I'm boring you, but please gimme one evening to show you we belong together.' This was his exact speech."

"Whoa. He said that?"

"Yes. That was the most honest and vulnerable version of him I'd seen so far. Not the cocky jock or the womanizer. He was just brutally honest and completely himself."

"Ohmygod. What did you do?"

The doorbell rang, cutting her story short.

"Please tell me before I go," I begged.

"I kissed him. Right there. I circled the bar, molded my lips to his, hoping it would prove there was no chemistry between us. And that's when I knew. It was like nothing else I'd experienced before. We lost ourselves in that kiss. So much so that my boss had to chase him away so I could return to work. Mason promised to pick me up the next night, and we've been together since." She sighed, her lips curling at the memory she'd relived before my eyes. "If I hadn't risked it, I would have missed the chance of a lifetime."

"This is so romantic. And bold," I said, my stupid heart loving the story more than it should. The bell rang again. "Coming," I said, crossing the room in four strides. Dressed in denim shortalls with a white tank top underneath, a contrast to her mocha skin, Tasha stood tall on the front porch as I opened the door. Having two inches over me, her legs looked infinite. Golden bracelets and loop earrings completed the look. She projected style and confidence. I wished I had that assurance when it came down to clothes. And life in general.

"Hi there, Mrs. Pierce," she said to my aunt. "Mom says to give her a call when we're out of here. Hey Ava, ready?"

"Yes." I grabbed my purse from the hook behind the door.

"Have a great time, you two," Aunt Melinda said, waving at us from the couch.

"We will," Tasha assured. Once outside, I forced myself to breathe to hide the nerves tightening my stomach. "Is that your truck?" she asked, pointing at my refurbished vintage teal pickup.

"Yeah. Uncle Mason restored it for me."

"It's sick. I love it."

We climbed into her white cabriolet, and before she pulled away, she chose a playlist from her phone. Jessa Hart's "Boots On You" played on her stereo.

"Country music fan?" she asked.

"Die-hard fan here," I said, and we both burst out laughing. "I *loooove* this song. And the dress she wears in that video is just insane."

"Ava, you and I, we were destined to meet. People tell

me I look like her all the time." Tasha flipped her hair with one hand, pride evident in that gesture. "She's my favorite artist ever."

Yes, I could see the resemblance. "I love her too. She's badass. It's your eyes. They look similar. A lot."

"You and I will be best friends," she announced as if she was aware of something I wasn't and was just stating the obvious.

We drove for ten minutes. The lot by the lake, the same one I drove to on my first day here, was full. Cars and pickup trucks were parked on the grass at weird angles. Tasha maneuvered her car into a tight spot in between a mature tree and a fence, and we climbed out.

"Okay, you'll meet everyone tonight. Stay by my side, and I'll have your back. Tiffany can be difficult. Don't let her mess with your head. Misty will try to scare you off. That's her M.O. She hates everybody. Other than them, stay away from William and Paul. All they'll want is to get into your pants and hope you'll forget they exist by the next morning. Also, they come with an array of free STDs."

"Oh geez. Thanks for the warning."

"Ride can be a prick too. I'm sure you're already aware since he practically lives under the same roof as you do. Not sure he'll be there, though. He tends to skip these parties nowadays. Another reason Misty hates people. She thinks Ride is her sole possession. He turns her down most of the time, but she's still hopeful they'll become a real thing." She paused. "Oh, and don't drink the punch in the red cups. Stick to beer or anything you mix yourself. I'm driving, so you're allowed to get loose tonight. Just don't throw up in my car, and our friendship will last." She grabbed my hand and led me forward. "Come on, let's go."

"Thanks for the heads-up." I smoothed my skirt with

my fingers, keeping them busy to avoid tugging at the bracelet around my wrist or scratching the skin of my forearm, the latter a habit I was working really hard to break once and for all.

The faint scent of weed mixed with aftershave and smoke from the fire invaded my nose.

Tasha introduced me to a group of girls and then to Ronald, her boyfriend, and his friends. Ronald offered me a beer, and after refusing the first time, I finally accepted.

A Summer to Remember, I repeated in my head.

I had drunk beer twice in my life, and both times, I disliked the headache that came with it the next day. And to be honest, it tasted awful too. I only indulged in wine sometimes during dinner—on special occasions.

A guy named Brandon was entertaining me with stories of his college football days when I spotted Ryder and a girl arriving. The one from my first day here and then again at the ice cream parlor. My gag reflex got triggered at their sight.

Tasha elbowed me. "That's Misty," she whispered in my ear.

Misty's eyes landed on mine, and we glared at each other. I had excuses to despise her, but other than crossing my path twice, she had no other reasons to hate me. None whatsoever.

She rose to her tiptoes and said something in Ryder's ear, rubbing herself against him. He held her closer with an arm as he spoke to a group of guys.

From over her shoulder, Misty watched me.

She ran her tongue along his neck, slow and deliberate, but Ryder kept ignoring her, chatting with whom I assumed to be his friends.

"See? She's doing it on purpose. She loves giving a

show. One advice. Pretend she doesn't exist," Tasha said from beside me. "Let's dance."

Before I could avert my eyes from the scene playing in front of me, Misty got furious at Ryder, grabbed the red cup from one of his friends, and took a sip. Swaying her hips, her dark hair shining under the moonlight, and her kohl-lined eyes menacing, she traipsed in our direction.

"Trouble," Tasha warned under her breath.

"What are you looking at?" Misty's chest almost brushed against mine as she spewed the words.

"Get lost, Misty." Tasha waved her away with a hand.

Misty's attention stayed on my face even when she spoke to my friend. "Mind your own business, Tash. This loser isn't welcome. She doesn't belong here."

"And you do?" I asked, keeping my face neutral, even though my pulse was going haywire.

"Leave or I'll make you," Misty said.

"Are you threatening me? Or are you jealous Ryder isn't giving you the time of the day?" I clamped my mouth shut when fury exploded in her eyes.

Before I could utter another word, she poured her drink all over my top. "Oopsy," she said, a hand over her mouth, barely hiding her satisfied smirk.

Standing there, I pinched the fabric away from me, the coldness of the liquid uncomfortable against my skin.

Misty invaded my personal space. "Stay the fuck away from Ride. Last warning. He's mine. Don't talk to him, don't look at him, don't think about him."

This disturbance had attracted the attention of people around us, and soon Ryder joined the crowd. The defined angle of his jaw could cut through a glacier as his gaze darted between his girlfriend and me.

He was about to open his mouth when I shook my head, not in the mood to hear his accusations. Pushing

Misty behind him, he came too close for comfort. "I gotta talk to you," he hissed through his teeth.

"No, you don't."

His posture tensed. "I do."

"Stop trying to rule my life."

Brandon neared my side. "Everything okay?" he asked.

I shook my head. "No. It's not." Feeling feisty, I chugged my beer and pushed the empty can into Ryder's chest before turning toward Brandon. "Let's dance." I spoke to Ryder over my shoulder, "Keep your guard dog under leash."

I heard a few *Ohhhs* and *Ahhhs* but chose to block them out.

From a safe distance, I noticed Ryder stood motionless, stiff as a pole, glaring at me while sipping from a bottle of water. Misty kept trying to draw a reaction out of him. In vain.

Brandon's hand lowered from the small of my back to the curve of my ass. With a skillful gesture, he flipped me until my back rested against his front, and he ground against me while my arms looped around his neck.

His hands ventured on each side of my ribcage, sending shivers through me. Someone offered me a beer, and I accepted it, taking a long swig. It didn't taste nearly as bad now that I was enjoying the alcohol buzz that numbed my senses.

Brandon's lips grazed the side of my face. I offered him a smile, and just when our mouths were about to touch, a muscular hand gripped my upper arm and yanked me away from him.

Leather and spice.

His scent hit me before we even faced each other.

"Enough," Ryder said. "What are you trying to prove? Stop acting so desperate. You're not that girl." He led me away and pushed a bottle of water into my hand. "Drink this."

"Nope. Make me."

"I swear—"

"What? Finish that sentence, *Riiidde*."

His face turned to stone.

"Let me go." I jerked away from his touch. "A girl is allowed to have some fun. Stay the fuck away from me, and mind your own business."

He remained silent, assessing me with a dark stare. I averted my eyes to avoid getting sucked into it.

"You should keep an eye on your *girlfriend*, and gimme some slack." We turned our heads toward Misty, now busy making out with some guy who was groping her. "Oops, I think she forgot about you. Or maybe she realized you are forgettable."

If looks could kill, I'd be dead.

Ryder closed his eyes, breathed out, then opened them again. The storm in his irises had receded. "Let's go home."

"Not yet. I'm having fun." I tapped his chest with my forefinger, the booze doing all the talking. For once, I was pouring my heart out to the person I hated the most in this world—other than Misty. "This summer was about enjoying new experiences. To be bold, amongst other things. My parents shipped me here without my consent. Don't steal anything away from me, more than what I've already lost, as I'm trying to make the most of a situation I resent." I wiped my emotions away with the back of my hand. "Stay out of my way, Ryder. I'm done fighting with you. It's getting old, and you're not worth it. You only make me hate it here more than I already do."

Something resembling hurt flashed in his eyes, but I brushed it off.

I stumbled away, emptying my beer in two sips.

Without arguing, Ryder watched me go, not making an attempt to stop me.

"Everything okay?" Tasha asked as she got in step with me. "I thought Ryder would crack his jaw earlier. What's his problem with you?"

I shrugged. "No idea. Wanna dance?"

Her face lit up, and she reached for my hand. "Let's get this party started, girlfriend."

I grabbed a can of beer from the cooler next to Brandon. "Okay?" I asked.

He nodded. "Sure, girl. Take what you need."

"Thanks."

Ryder wouldn't spoil my night. I would show him I wasn't some fragile doll he had to watch over. I didn't care what he thought. For once, I was allowed to have fun and let loose.

Without turning around, I felt the weight of his gaze on me. Lifting my arm above my head, I flipped a finger in his general direction and followed my friend.

Giggling, Tasha and I made our way to the truck parked on the beach that played the music. Tasha climbed on the bed and offered her hand for me to join her.

Someone turned up the volume, and together we danced as if we were alone and didn't care about anything else in the world.

"How's that?" she screamed so that I could hear her over the music.

"Perfect."

I drowned the beer and crushed the can in my fist before dropping it at my feet.

Opening my arms wide, I spun on myself, relishing the night breeze on my burning cheeks. I savored my newfound independence. Letting go was new to me. And highly addictive. All my worries vanished. I felt free. From my fears, my doubts, my insecurities. Tasha and I laughed our hearts out. Some guys wolf whistled and cheered on us, but we kept dancing the night away.

The day was yielding its place to the night, the sun low on the horizon and the sky, a piece of art with pink and orange streaks.

"Ava, come with me," my friend announced after a while. "I gotta pee, and no way am I going alone with all these creeps around, trying to catch a sight."

We jumped from the back of the truck, and soon we were replaced by another set of girls. I blinked a few times, the world spinning around me.

With our arms linked together, Tasha and I weaved through groups of people, all gathered around the bonfire. The music faded the more we neared the edge of the woods.

"Okay, you go first," she said. "I'll keep watch for you. Then I'll go, and you keep an eye out."

In a dark corner, behind lined-up bushes, only lit by the silver light of the half-moon shining over the lake, I relieved myself before switching places with my friend.

Ronald joined us, and Tasha signaled one second with her finger. "I'll be right behind you," she said when her boyfriend kissed her.

Two guys, visibly drunk, started arguing. The shorter one tackled the other, much taller than him. People gathered around them, but nobody tried to stop the imminent fight.

"Keep your filthy paws off my girl, Delaney," the tall guy barked. "And stop hitting me. I'm warning you to step back."

"This is ridiculous," a girl standing beside me said.

She walked away, and even though I tried, I couldn't avert my eyes from the two pissed-off guys.

"Don't be possessive over women," Delaney said. "Crawford, a pussy is a pussy. Find yourself another girl. I call dibs on this one."

Crawford blinked. "Are you serious? Or are you blind? Cass wants nothing to do with you. We've been dating for four years."

The sound of the small crowd drowned their replies, and a fight erupted. Other people jumped in, trying to stop the rumble.

A couple of people bumped into me, and I wavered on my feet when I was about to retreat. I hadn't even taken ten strides forward when I tripped over. The booze I drank earlier didn't help with my balance. Someone else bumped into me. Harder. This time, I landed on my knees. It stung. The fight moved closer. When I stood up on shaky legs, more people backed into me, and I got knocked over a second time.

Sand flew into my eyeballs.

Where was Tasha? I tried to spot her in the crowd but could barely see two feet in front of me.

"Ava." I heard her voice. Before I could rise to my feet, two muscular arms lifted me from behind.

"What the hell, Tash. What were you thinking when you invited her here tonight?"

"It's just a drunken fight, Ride. No need to become overbearing," she said. "It's usually peaceful here. We did nothing wrong."

"Delaney is being his creepy self. I don't understand why people keep inviting him." Ryder's tone left no room for arguments.

"I'm *saaafe*. Thank you very much. Now you can release *meee*," I said, trying to jerk away from his grip.

Instead of freeing me, Ryder tightened his arms around me.

"Let go of *meee*." No effect. I punched his hands away, with no success. "You're not the *bosss* of me."

"You shouldn't be here," Ryder warned in a cold tone. "The show is over. You had your fun, and now it's time to go home."

"Why?" I asked. "Because everyone else is allowed to have *funnn* this summer except *meee*? Why are you still treating me like a kid? You should mind your *ownnn* business. Find Misty. She's probably looking for *youuu* anyway. She was a *bittt* possessive earlier."

Ryder stilled behind me, his grip around my waist tightening. I felt his harsh breaths on my nape.

For a quick instant, I enjoyed his strong arms around me. It made me feel safe, like I belonged there. All I wished for was to lean against him and pretend he could really protect me.

"I don't care about Misty. She's no one to me. And I'm not treating you like a kid," he whispered through clenched teeth after a minute. His deep voice rippled through me. "Just looking out for you. Don't be a brat. We're leaving." Gone was the fight in his voice. He sounded…concerned. I knew better. Ryder didn't show concern when it came to me.

I broke out of the booze trance enveloping my brain and remembered Ryder and I were enemies. We didn't care about each other. His endgame was to ruin my life.

"Well, I don't need you watching over *meee*." I jabbed my finger into his arm. I slurred my words, but I couldn't care less. "I can watch over myself *jussst* fine. And I say that I'm *stayyying*." I nodded my resolve.

"How much did you drink?" he asked. "Tell me."

I shrugged. "None of *youuur* business, Mister I'm-No-

Funnn. Nothing to get pissed about. Stop pretending you care. We both know *youuu* don't."

"Fuck, you're wasted."

Oh, someone wasn't happy with me. "Oops. I am. Now let go of *meee*."

Tasha jumped in. "Ava is right, Ride. You're not her daddy. She's with me tonight. Let go of her. Until your psychotic girlfriend showed up, we were having fun. I'm the one driving her home later, so give her a break."

"No," he said at the same time I said, "*Yesss*."

"Stop arguing, Tash. I *am* driving her home." Why was he talking as if I wasn't here?

"No, you *arrre* not," I argued, trying to push away from him.

"Yes, I am."

"I won't climb into *youuur* stupid car. And it's *whaaat*? Like ten o'clock? Why would I leave now?"

"Because I said so," Ryder said, his tone almost lethal.

I blinked.

"Ride, Crawford and Cass left, and someone escorted Delaney away. Since when are you big brother material?" Tasha asked.

He huffed but said nothing. Before I could comprehend his actions, he scooped me over his shoulder. "I'm nobody's brother, Tash. Mind your own life. And just to be clear, Misty's actions are the least of my concerns, baby girl. We're leaving."

I kicked the air. "Let *meee* down. How will I ever make friends this summer if *youuu* humiliate me in front of every-one? Release *meee*."

"No."

"*Yesss*."

"Good luck." I could hear the sneer in his voice.

I lifted my head and looked at my friend. "Tasha, I'm

sorry." Embarrassment coated my words. "Can we do this again *laaater*? When Ryder here is a *nooo*-show." I punched his back, a new surge of rage pounding through me. "Put *meee* down. I'll flash everyone." I used one hand to keep my skirt in place. "I can walk. Let *meee* go."

"Ride, you're being ridiculous," Tasha argued, following us.

He continued toward the parking lot as if she'd said nothing, tightening the arm around my bare thighs to prevent me from falling as I kicked and punched in vain.

"Ava, I'll talk to you tomorrow," Tasha called after me. "Text me when you're home safe. Just in case Neanderthal Man here decides to hide you in his cave, thinking there is no other place where you'll be safer." She brought her attention back to him. "Ride, you're making a scene. I'm done with you. You used to be cool." She flicked her wrist above her head. "So much drama for nothing."

"I'm *sorry*," I mumbled. My emotions clogged my throat. My body often mixed anger and sadness. Both made me cry, and right now, I prayed the tears wouldn't come as I was about to give Ryder a piece of my mind. As soon as he lowered me to my feet.

"Where are *youuu* taking *meee*?" I asked as we approached his car.

"Home."

"Put *meee* down."

"No."

"Gosh, I was having *funnn*. I'm not ready to go."

"Well, it's not up to you, baby girl."

"How is it not? And, for *youuur* information, it's not up to *youuu* either. It never was *aaand* never will be," I replied.

"We'll see."

Chapter 21

I couldn't believe I'd been kidnapped from a party by the same guy who hated my guts because he thought my going out with friends was now a hazardous activity. Who the hell did he think he was to decide what I should or shouldn't do? As if he could read my mind, Ryder continued with the newfound rules he came up with.

"You shouldn't drink," he said.

Right there, another *shouldn't*.

"Look who's talking. Oh yeah, *youuu're* nineteen and *youuu* do, so stop being Mr. I-Think-I'm-*Perrrfect*. I won't fall for your *Do as I say, don't do what I do* bullshit. Sorry, I'm *smarrrter* than this. Try again."

"Why are you always a pain in my ass? Can't you just listen?"

Ryder dropped me to my feet, and we faced each other.

I blinked. And re-blinked just to make sure all this was not a dream. Or rather a nightmare, since it involved the devil himself.

The thick air surrounding us could be cut with a knife. The noises from the party were muffled by the distance. Only the faded beat of the bass resonating from behind the line of trees could be heard. The warm breeze carried the scent of smoke from the bonfire.

"*Meee*?" I asked, pointing my thumb to my chest, my eyes focused on my enemy. "You have *meee* mixed up with someone else. Since I came here, *youuu've* been nothing but rude and obnoxious to *meee*. Don't sugarcoat *youuur* role in this," I added, my hand flipping between us. "*Youuu* started this war. I was minding my own business when *youuu* decided to spoil my first day in town, and *youuu* haven't stopped since. Now let *meee* go. I can *walkkk* home."

"Not a chance."

"Why?" I screamed. "Why can't *youuu* back off for once?"

"Because. You're not drinking and partying under my watch. End of discussion. I let you have your fun. Now it's over."

"But I'm not *youuur* responsibility. You have no say in what I do or who I see or spend time with. None. N.O.N.E. It makes no sense."

"Well, it does to me," he said, his tone level and his gaze turbulent.

Something close to regret passed through his eyes. The wrath that had been there for the last ten minutes dissolved. Though I could still tell he was upset with me due to things I couldn't understand.

Resigned to the fact that I wouldn't be going back to

the party, I hauled myself in his car and slouched in my seat, determined to let it go.

For now.

Ryder's gaze lingered on my left forearm. Feeling naked under his scrutiny and not wanting him to see the now-faded scars just below the crook of my elbow, I folded my arms over my chest.

He moistened his lips with his tongue and looked away for a fleeting second before he fired up the engine and backed out of the parking space.

We drove in silence, the tension in the car so charged it could have exploded any second.

Once he parked in my driveway, I turned to face him after I opened the passenger door. I could read the hurt in his eyes now. Along with an expression I could not comprehend because, in reality, nothing wild happened tonight.

The part of me unable not to care for another human being took over and chased my anger away. Remaining in my seat, I closed the door and turned toward him. "*Wannna* talk about it?"

Ryder's eyes darkened before he dropped his head back. A long exhale broke the silence, and an indifferent expression painted his face when he looked at me. "There's nothing to talk about. Stay out of my personal life, and stop imagining things that don't exist."

I rolled my eyes. "Go ahead. Now lie to *youuurself* too. Nice job."

"Go to bed, baby girl. It's late."

I clenched my hands at my sides. Our fight was far from over. Whatever respite I read in Ryder's eyes moments ago was gone. He had returned to his annoying, bossy self.

Without another word, I got out of the car and slammed the door behind me, hurrying to my room, relieved my aunt and uncle weren't up and waiting for me to return.

Lying on my front, I punched the mattress, sending Iris a nine-one-one text message.

In the en-suite bathroom, I stared at my reflection. Mascara was smudged beneath my bloodshot eyes. I looked awful. The alcohol buzz had worn off, and now a cocktail of emotions churned inside me as I lingered in front of the mirror a little longer. Now mostly sober, I couldn't tell if I was angry, hurt, or something tangled in between.

Iris called me back, and I walked to my bedroom to grab my phone, feeling like the weight of the world was pressing on my shoulders.

"He what? Girl, who does he think he is? Ohmygod, I would have died of shame. I'm so sorry you had to deal with it, A. I would have ripped his eyes out."

I loved how my best friend was ready to defend me against enemy number one if she were here as I told her all about my night.

"Let's recap. He kidnapped you? Without any explanation? In front of everybody? Okay, gimme a moment here to assess all this."

"None of his excuses made sense. He carried me like a package over his shoulder. It was so humiliating. I'll never be able to look all those people in the eye ever again after what went down. They'll treat me like a kid now. And we're all the same age. Can you imagine? Who'll want to invite me to hang out now? Ryder destroyed my reputation. He killed my social life and any future opportunities to make friends while I'm here. Also, his girlfriend got jealous and poured her drink over me. This is a nightmare. All of it."

"A, it might not be that bad." I knew Iris. She was

trying to make the situation appear better than it was. We were both aware, but I said nothing. I adored her for trying to cheer me up when things had gone south.

I shook my head, tears prickling the back of my eyes now.

"It was. It is. He made a fool of me. This is bad, Iris."

"What do you wanna do?" she asked in a soft tone. "Are you gonna ask your parents to bring you back home?"

"Nah. I kinda love it here, but for whatever reason, Ryder is making my stay difficult. I don't wanna leave just yet." We said nothing for a while. "I have no clue what I should do. I hate him so much. He's a jerk, and he's pretentious and thinks he knows it all. I don't wanna fight; it's exhausting. Can't I just be happy and free for a night?"

"Do you…like…are you having thoughts about harming yourself?" she asked in the most caring voice. "I'm here. You can tell me."

I shook my head. "No. I scratched my arm earlier and fidgeted with my bracelet, but that's as far as it went."

"You'd tell me if it was more than that, right? You promised last time you'd never do it without talking to me first."

"Yes. I won't. I'm fine. I swear. I'm better now at dealing with my anxiety or when I'm overwhelmed. Those breathing techniques help a lot. I can face Ryder and his angry attitude. He doesn't scare me."

"Okay. When is your date with Joseph?" she asked, changing the subject. "You should focus on that instead."

"Saturday." I breathed out. "As usual, you're right. I can't wait." Specks of happiness returned. "He's the only one around here who understands me, other than my immediate family. From the second we met, it has been easy between us. I was kinda hoping Tasha would understand me too. Ryder didn't give me enough time to find out."

"Call her. Why don't you invite her to watch a movie or go shopping or have a sleepover?"

"I should."

"No. Scratch that. You will. This summer is all about getting out of our comfort zones. Making new friends and being brave are parts of the deal."

I sighed. "I guess." Even though I forced the words out, I couldn't find it in me to sound convincing.

We talked some more before Iris announced she had to go.

Now, on my back, I opened the text app on my phone.

ME

Home safe. Sorry R was a jerk and I had to leave. He had no right to do this.

Are you free Thursday night? We could do something together. Raincheck.

I waited ten minutes, but Tasha never answered. After I removed my makeup and changed into night clothes, I slipped underneath the covers and surrendered myself to sleep.

———

On Wednesday morning, I was still reeling from Ryder's actions the previous night.

"Morning, kiddo," Uncle Mason said as he placed a mug of hot caffeine in my hand when I joined him in the kitchen. "How was your night? You came home early."

I shrugged. "Okay, I guess."

I faked a smile, but from the way his eyes turned to slits as he studied me, I could tell he saw right through my lie.

I sighed and joined him, sipping my coffee to avoid talking.

"Whose ass should I kick now? Nobody messes with my family." He said the words with a hardened tone, but I could tell he was joking. Sorta.

"Nobody. It's fine."

If only he knew the jerk he considered a son was the reason why my sleep was troubled last night. Sure, he was aware we weren't getting along too well, but I was certain he would never approve of how Ryder dragged me out of that party last night. But also, I didn't want to be the person driving a wedge between them. After all, I was in town only for the summer. No need to create drama while I was here. And I was happy to know he and Aunt Melinda had someone to watch over them when I would leave.

"Listen, instead of having dinner at home tomorrow night, we were thinking we could go out, the four of us. There's this place an hour's drive from here that serves the best crab cakes in the country, and since it's Melinda's birthday in a few days, I thought it could be fun to have dinner there. I'm taking her to an inn on Friday for a long weekend; it's our annual birthday ritual. Anyway, the restaurant I'm talking about has a huge deck overlooking the ocean, and the sunsets are to die for. We'll have to leave around five-thirty. What do you think?"

"I'd love that."

"Sorry I didn't tell you about our weekend plans sooner. Hope it sits well with you to be home alone for two nights."

"Don't worry about me. I'll be more than fine. I have plans with Joseph on Saturday, so I'll be gone most of the day," I said. And the excitement of my upcoming date chased away the dreadful thought of spending yet another evening with Ryder.

"Perfect. Then it's settled. Bianca will work with you today and tomorrow. She'll show you what she does marketing-wise. Social media, advertising, events, promos. It should be interesting to shadow her and see that side of the business. What do you think?"

I leaped up to hug my uncle. "It sounds perfect. Thank you."

"Glad you approve, kiddo." He stood up and filled the dishwasher. "Come and say hi when you get to the garage. I'm leaving in two minutes."

"Okay. Where's Aunt Melinda? She's usually awake at this hour."

"Press conference. Some scandal happened last night, and she left early to find time to prepare. Life of the rich and famous…harder than it seems." He stifled a laugh and left as I finished breakfast on my own.

———

Home alone after my aunt and uncle met with friends for dinner, I nibbled on another slice of pizza. Spread out on my bed, I was writing in my journal and listening to music, with the half-empty pizza box set beside me. It'd been a long time since I'd been on my own for more than a couple of hours, and I enjoyed the calm it provided.

Jessa Hart's new single played on the portable speaker set on my nightstand, and I increased the volume, not caring if anyone would ask me to turn it down. Yeah, this night was perfect.

Joseph had texted me earlier, and since he was on babysitting duty, he said he'd call me later. I checked the time on my phone. Seven thirty-four. I smiled at the idea of his being in the midst of bath and bedtime stories. I loved the fact he could care for his little sisters by himself without being freaked out about it. Lucas, my ex-boyfriend, would have never been caught babysitting.

The mattress dipped beside me, and before I had time to react, a hand I would recognize anywhere grabbed a slice of pizza from the open box. Moving to my knees, I slapped it away, but it was too late, the pizza had found his stupid mouth.

Ryder watched me, amusement brightening his irises, which appeared bluer than usual tonight. "Heard you were here by yourself and came to keep you company."

He grabbed my phone and stopped the music.

"Hey," I protested. "Gimme that. And scram."

He motioned to his feet, but instead of leaving, he kicked off his shoes and jumped back on the bed, resting against the headboard, his legs stretched before him.

"Are you kidding me right now?" I pressed my fists to my hips. "Go away."

He inhaled the rest of the pizza and extended an arm for a second slice. *Ugh, teenage boys are gross.*

"I don't remember inviting you." I pushed him to the side. Too strong for me, Ryder didn't even budge an inch. I cringed as he devoured his pizza in two bites. *Yeah, super extra gross.*

"What are you doing, baby girl? I knew you couldn't resist touching me. But in your bedroom? Are you sure Mason and Melinda would approve of this?" He raised his brows, his piercing shiny under the ceiling light. Before I could remove my hands, he captured them with his. "Not so fast. Are you afraid you'll love feeling me up?"

I pushed him back at the same time he tugged at my arms, and I ended up spread across his lap, our faces inches apart.

I growled, trying to break free. The upturn of his lips

as he watched me made me see red. "I wanna be alone. This means you're not invited. You can't stay."

"Why?" His grip around my wrists slackened, but not enough for me to break free. "Nobody loves to be alone."

"Well, I do. Now go, or I'll-I'll bite you."

His head fell back, and he burst into a fit of laughter. A sound so foreign when it came down to him.

"You'll…bite me? Is that right?"

"Yes. And I'll tear off that piercing of yours with my teeth. Wanna see if I'm bluffing?"

Before I could realize what had happened, I was flipped on my back with Ryder hovering over me, my arms pressed into the mattress on either side of me, his hands holding them still.

It wasn't disdain that swam in his eyes right now, but something that got me tongue-tied, and warm all over.

He traced my features with his gaze.

His breathing picked up.

"Wh-what do you want?" I asked, my voice husky.

He said nothing, still scanning each inch of me.

I pushed my chest forward trying to shake him away, but it had the opposite effect because his eyes landed on my breasts.

"What do you want?" I repeated, more assertive this time.

"I bought something for you."

I snorted. "Yeah, right. Let me guess. A bus ticket back home? Or a leash so you can keep me in line?"

Color tinted his cheeks. Did I say something that unnerved him?

"So, it *is* a leash. I knew it. You're so predictable."

His amusement vanished, and something dark shone on his face. "If it was a leash, believe me, it wouldn't be to keep you in line. I bet we could find more uses for it that would make you scream in pleasure. Don't you agree, baby girl?"

"You're so fucked in the head. Release me." The words I spoke had nothing to do with the images invading my mind. Ryder was such a mystery to me. Did he really practice bondage and stuff, or was he just messing around to get a reaction out of me? Every time I thought I knew everything about him, he said or did something out of character that kept me guessing.

"Are you ready for your surprise now?"

I harrumphed. "If it concerns you, I think I'll pass."

"Come on, you shared your dinner with me, so I wanna share my dessert with you."

Even when he said *dessert*, it sounded like dirty sex promises. I had to stop associating Ryder with sex—it had become a bad habit of mine. Else he would haunt all my nights.

"Fine, I'll eat your *dessert*," I said, using a tone I hoped sounded desperate and hot.

He jumped away from me and landed on his feet, extending his hand for me to grab. I squinted at it and pushed him aside, standing on my own.

After he put his shoes on, I followed him to the kitchen.

"I'm not up for games, so it better be real."

"Close your eyes."

"No."

Ryder sighed. "Why are you being so difficult?"

"Look at yourself in a mirror, and you may find the answer to that question."

Rummaging through the freezer, he turned to face me with two ice cream sandwiches and offered me one.

I hesitated but only for a few seconds because I really loved those. Aunt Melinda used to keep a freezer full of them during the summer when I was a kid.

"See, it didn't bite you." Ryder smirked at me, and I rolled my eyes.

"Thanks."

"Wanna go for a walk?"

No. I should make an effort, though. I told my uncle I'd give him a chance. "Fine."

Side by side, we toured the property and stopped by the pond. I sat on one side of the bench, and after pacing the grass in front of me, Ryder took the seat on the other end.

We remained silent for the longest time, admiring the pastel-colored sky and the night falling upon us. With my head tilted back, I watched the stars, wondering if other people lived somewhere out there.

The orange glow of a flame on my left caught my attention, and my focus drifted to the boy next to me as he lit the blunt dangling between his lips.

"Why are you smoking?"

He shrugged. "Because."

"That's not an answer." Right now, I was very curious about what his reasoning would be. From what I'd seen so far, it wasn't a habit of his. I only saw him do it once or twice. Ryder didn't appear to be a junkie. Tonight, I could tell something was bothering him. He never tried to spend time with me, always warning me to stay the fuck away.

"Sometimes, it helps me to deal with shit. Memories I wish I could delete." He blew a cloud of smoke. "Why do you care?"

"I don't. It's your life. Just curious." I stretched my arm toward him. "Give it to me."

"Why?"

"Because."

He quirked one brow. "That's not an answer."

I laughed at how he used my own words against me. "I want a puff."

"No."

"Why not?" I asked.

"You don't need it."

I shook my head. "And you do?"

He stared at me, and I shivered under the intense scrutiny. "It's not the same."

"Talk about double standards. It's okay for guys to sleep around because it makes them cool, but girls do the same, and people point fingers at them. And now it's right for you to pollute your lungs and get high, but it's not for me. Are you serious?"

"Nobody should smoke this shit."

"Well, you do."

Without another word, he put it out on the ground, leaned back, and stretched one arm on the backrest of the bench.

"You should care," I said after a moment, "about your health. Numbing yourself won't help anything." As I spoke the words, my fingers fidgeted with the bracelet around my wrist.

Ryder turned to stare at me. "Why do you say that?"

I breathed out. "I have my reasons."

"Mind sharing?"

"With you?" I let out a mirthless laugh. "I'll pass."

He brought his attention back to the starry sky. "Suit yourself."

After what seemed to be hours, he took out a bag of sour gummies from the front pocket of his hoodie. "Want some?"

"Okay. Unless it comes with a catch."

He shook his head and tore the bag open with his teeth.

"My favorite."

"Yeah. Mine too."

"What?" Did he say what I thought he said? He couldn't know my favorite flavor of gummies.

"Nothing."

"Thanks." He pushed the bag in my direction, and I took a handful. "Does your pocket contain more treats?"

A small smile lifted the corner of his lips. "Nah. That's everything I've got."

"It is nice of you to share with me."

He shrugged one shoulder. "Thanks for spending time with me."

My tongue burned to ask what he meant, but I decided to keep the peace between us for a little longer. Ryder was such a confusing person, but this side of him, somehow vulnerable tonight, made me believe he wasn't all that bad underneath his layers of anger.

At some point, I realized my phone wasn't on me and asked, "What time it is?"

Ryder grabbed his device to read the screen. "Almost midnight."

"Oh shit, Joseph." I had totally forgotten about him and our night call while I was here with Ryder. And at this late hour, no doubt, he was already asleep.

Ryder's face fell, and he moved to his feet. "Let's go." The lightness slipped away, and in its place, a mask of stone settled over his features. The walls were back around him. Gone was the boy who let me see a new side of him tonight. His hand lingered on the armrest of the bench for a long minute, and he mumbled something I couldn't hear from where I sat on the other end, then waved as he sauntered away.

Rushing after his retreating silhouette, I caught up with him halfway toward the house. "Wait. Are you okay?"

Nothing.

"Are *we* okay?"

No answer.

I stepped in front of him and pressed his chest with my palms. He circled my wrists but didn't break our connection. "Talk to me. What happened back there?"

"Call your boyfriend, baby girl, and let me be." His harsh tone acted like a cold shower.

"Are you all right?"

He snorted. "I will be. Don't worry about me. Anyway, you should stay away. Night."

He pushed past me and left me alone in the dark, not glancing over his shoulder once.

"Ryder," I screamed after him. "Come back."

He turned around the side of the house, and I lost track of him. Seconds later, I heard the distinctive sound of his car as he drove away.

"Fuck. Why is it so complicated to be friends with you?"

I locked myself in my room and noticed the screen of my phone flashing with two missed calls and five texts.

JOSEPH

Hey Avalon. Girls are in bed. Call me when you get this.

I'll be in the shower, text me when you have a minute.

I tried to call you, but your phone may be dead.

Going to bed. It's almost ten. Let me know if you're ok when you read this.

You're still not picking up. Should I worry? I'll call you in the morning when I have a break. Sleep tight, bestie.

Burying my face in my pillow, I grunted. The night had been nothing like I expected.

Lifting the pizza box and other stuff from my bed, I placed my journal on the bedside table and disposed of the box in the kitchen, noticing my aunt and uncle weren't back yet. Leaving a light on, I returned to my room, climbed into bed, and tried to steer my dreams away from the guy with green eyes who looked somehow broken tonight. *Sometimes, it helps me deal with shit. Memories I wish I could delete.* What did he mean by that? What had happened to Ryder that made him like this, cold and full of thorns?

Before I could make up scenarios in my head, my lids closed, and sleep stole me away from my thoughts.

Bianca made the two days we spent together worth a million times over. I loved everything about her job. The creative side. The logical thinking. The analysis. I could see myself doing what she did as a career.

Today I had been so busy I didn't even have time to butt heads with Ryder the two times we crossed paths.

Back home, I changed into a soft-pink summer dress, curled my hair, and applied a little makeup. Sitting on the front porch swing with a book, I plugged music into my ears.

Aunt Melinda and Uncle Mason joined me fifteen minutes later, and Ryder arrived, wearing a button-up, short-sleeved, crisp slate-gray shirt and spruce-colored chino shorts with a pair of denim-colored Braxton sneakers. From the corner of my eye, I admired him. I had to admit Ryder always looked both handsome and enigmatic with his disheveled hair and dark clothing and his permanent *I don't give a damn* frown. But dressed up, with his messily combed hair and clean-shaven jaw, and the mysterious aura around him tamed, he fascinated me even more. Tonight's clothes were so contrary to his usual fashion choices.

We all got in Uncle Mason's pickup truck, Ryder and I in the backseat, ignoring each other and keeping to our far sides. My aunt and uncle exchanged funny stories about their early days for the entire length of the hour-long drive, skirting my need to make small talk with Ryder.

At the restaurant, a host led us to our table. Ryder's hand landed on the small of my back as if it was the most natural gesture and I was really his to look out for as we threaded through the tables. An electric current spread from under his palm, and I jerked away, but he didn't remove his hand, his touch getting heavier instead. Could he feel it too? More tingles enveloped my spine, but I chose to ignore them, holding my breath to avoid giving way to the sensations working through me. This meant nothing, even though my traitorous body reveled in the feeling.

"Ava, wine?" Aunt Melinda asked. She and Uncle Mason took their places opposite Ryder and me on the small square table covered with a black linen cloth and burgundy napkins. Two candles in glass jars burned in the middle, giving the place a romantic atmosphere. The whiff of garlic bread and seafood tickled my nose. My seat neighbor kicked my feet under the table, and I fixed my biggest smile, pretending to hesitate for a second, then agreed. My aunt brought her attention to Ryder. "Ride, we'll drive you home later if you drink some too."

He nodded, and she filled our glasses before Uncle

Mason raised his. "To my wonderful wife. Happy birthday, my love," he said, clinking his glass to hers, then ours. He leaned in to kiss her before his focus landed on Ryder and me. "And thank you, kiddos, for celebrating with us tonight. Sometimes, families come in different forms, but they mean just as much. I'm speaking on behalf of both of us when I say we're grateful you two are in our lives. It wasn't an easy road for any of us, but we made it to the other side. I love you all, and I wouldn't want to be here tonight with anyone else. To family."

"To family," Ryder and I both echoed.

Dinner ran smoothly, and Ryder and I did a great job of ignoring each other without being too blatant about it. We still had to talk about what happened the previous night and his bossy attitude toward me at the party, but now wasn't the time. Even if I tried to ignore it, having him so close for hours brought my frustration back to the surface.

"Slept well?" he asked in a whispered tone, a challenge in his eyes, as soon as my aunt and uncle were on the dance floor, kissing and swaying to the music, amongst other patrons.

Keeping my gaze glued to my phone, I decided to avoid any confrontation tonight. Instead, I scrolled through my photo feed, pretending to be busy.

Ryder slid his chair closer to mine. "What's wrong? You're usually feistier than this. Want me to drag you out of here my way?"

It did the trick, as my head swiveled in his direction of its own volition. I could no longer avoid his eyes.

What I saw in them sent shivers through me. I possessed no word strong enough to explain the mix of attraction and disdain I felt at that exact moment. It was unhealthy to have intense contradictory emotions toward someone else. Even though Ryder woke up something deep inside me, something I kinda liked, why would I choose darkness when light made me happy? I was done with the murky side of my existence. Once and for all. Joseph was the light I craved—the brighter, happier side of me—and I should focus on him instead.

"I'm not gonna acknowledge anything that comes out of your mouth," I said, trying my best to keep my voice steady and detached. "Now isn't the time to tell you how much I can't stand you." Gone was the friendliness we experienced last night. How did he always manage to bring out the worst in me? I barely recognized myself every time we ended up in one of our heated exchanges.

"You're wrong. Now is the perfect time to let that anger out. I'm all ears. Go ahead, baby girl. Gimme your best I-hate-Ryder speech. Wanna dance when we hash it out?" He held out his palm.

"Never." I groaned and closed my eyes, my fists clenching beside me. "Not gonna join your little game. It's childish," I said, once my eyes returned to his amused ones. He smiled, and I was taken aback by the sight. I blinked, but it was a genuine curl I saw on his lips. "Why are you smiling? It doesn't suit you. You're the broody, exasperated type. Go back to being mad at the world."

With his fingers, he cocked my head to the side. "See? They seem happy. Seconds ago, they looked our way, and they smiled. Only trying to pretend we're fine here, so they don't worry about you being manhandled by the big bad wolf. Making conversation is a social skill. You should try it sometimes. It will be useful for the rest of your life."

In one swift movement, that I never anticipated, Ryder jumped to his feet and pulled me up until I stood beside him, before leading me to the dance floor.

"I don't wanna dance. With you." My words lacked conviction even to my own ears.

He snorted. "Yeah, right. Throw a tantrum. You prefer showing your skills at a party on the bed of a truck while you're drunk. Not judging."

I tilted my head back, a loud chuckle bubbling out. "You not judging me? Yeah right. Since when?"

His lips descended to the side of my face, ribbons of venom slicing his words and sending palpitations through my entire self. "Don't be so hasty to draw conclusions when you're clueless. One day, you'll thank me."

Shivers worked through me. "No. I won't."

"Wanna bet?"

I yelped when his fingers dug into my flesh, and he pulled me closer to him. One tiny movement of my head and our lips would brush.

My palm covered his thrumming heart, and I heard Ryder's sharp intake of air. I fisted the fabric of his shirt, the only thing grounding me in the present.

The air between us thickened with unsaid words. I tried to look away but became entranced by his tongue darting out to moisten his lips.

Why was he always doing that when he looked nervous? It always sent mixed signals to my body. And I hated it.

Something tightened in my chest.

Ryder fastened his hold around my waist. Leaning in, his rough cheek brushed against mine, and the moan I tried to conceal made its way out despite myself.

A zing stirred inside me. I knew I shouldn't stay here, yet I couldn't move away, Ryder's hot and cold attitude a constant puzzle to my brain.

Our feet stepped to the side, and I realized we were dancing. Sorta.

Why did hate look and feel a lot like attraction right now?

My body had a mind of its own because no matter the thoughts in my head, I stayed on the dance floor, glued to him.

He hung his head and whispered, "Be honest with me. How was sleep last night?"

I blinked, trying to avoid the spell he cast on me. My voice sounded weak. "What does it matter to you?"

"Curious, that's all."

"Don't be."

"Interesting," he said.

I chose not to think too much about what he left unsaid. "Whatever."

We kept dancing, swaying on the dance floor, remaining silent for a long while.

After a moment, I remembered his earlier words and said, "Just so you know, I'm not scared of you." My voice sounded weak and lacked confidence.

"Well, you should be."

"Why?"

"Because. I'm not good for you."

"That I already know. I'm asking you why. Why are you being so hard on me? Why are you cold, but when you think I'm not watching, you're studying my reaction?"

"You have no idea what you're talking about. It's not that simple. Stop trying to figure me out." He groaned and shook his head.

"What does this even mean?"

Ryder pushed away from me and returned to the table without another look in my direction.

My arms dropped to my sides, and I remained on the dance floor, unable to comprehend what went down—and what didn't.

What did I say that upset him? Why couldn't we just have a normal conversation for once?

"Ready to go?" my aunt asked as she and Uncle Mason joined me, cutting through my thoughts.

On our way outside, my phone chimed in my purse, and I enjoyed the more-than-welcome distraction.

TASHA

Sorry, forgot to answer you earlier. Can't tomorrow, already have plans.

Free on Sunday afternoon? I know the best place to go shopping.

ME

Count me in.

TASHA

We could get our nails done afterward. Could be fun.

ME

I'll pick you up at one. Send me your address.

"What or who makes you grin so big?" my aunt asked.

"Tasha and I made plans to hang out this weekend."

"That's fantastic. I thought you and Joseph had that date planned?" She draped an arm around my shoulders as we exited the restaurant.

"Yes. That too."

I sensed Ryder's eyes on me. They burned the skin of my back.

"Busy weekend." Aunt Melinda pressed her free hand over her heart. "It makes me feel better since we'll be out of town for two days. I was afraid you'd be on your own the whole weekend."

"All good," I said. "I'll be plenty occupied."

She pulled me closer to her in a side hug. "So happy to hear that."

"Me too."

The wine I had drunk combined with the vibrations of the truck and the darkness outside made me sleepy. Before long, my head weighed tons. At one point, I stopped fighting, and sleep won the battle.

When the truck stopped, Uncle Mason announced, "Home, kiddo. Ride, I'll be right back to drive you to your place."

Warm and cozy, I refused to leave the comfort I had fallen into. I wished I was already lying in the warmth of my bed. Something moved against me, and when I pried my lids open one by one, I realized I'd been resting my head on Ryder's chest.

No. *No, no, no.* How could I have been so clumsy in my sleep? And why was he even sitting next to me? The last thing I recalled was him positioned on the opposite side of the backseat.

"Hey baby girl, slept well?" That crooked smile. It angered me just being on the receiving end of it.

What was with this sentence tonight? The quality of my sleep had nothing to do with him.

Fully awake now, as if I had been jolted by a ten-thousand-volt device, I jerked back.

"How? Why?" I asked.

"Your head was at a weird angle. I thought you could use a shoulder to drool on instead of getting neck pain."

"I didn't…I don't drool."

He pretended to wipe something from his sleeve while I ran the back of my hand over my mouth. Just in case.

"Guess you'll never know." He winked, and I almost lost it. If I wasn't so sleepy, I would strangle him.

Gone was the moment we shared earlier, and back was the hatred.

Ryder scooted over the seat until the length of his body pressed against mine.

"Dream about me tonight, baby girl." He winked and leaned across from me. I used both palms to keep him at a distance only to realize he was just opening the door.

"I hate you."

"That's the spirit." His cruel laughter vibrated through me. "I'll take hate any day. It's better than indifference."

I slammed the door in his face and hurried inside. Not in the mood to cross paths with my family, I entered the house through the private entrance of my bedroom. Once I was sure it was locked, I pressed my back against the closed door. When my breathing slowed to a normal pace, I shot my best friend a text.

ME

Iris, if I murder him in his sleep, will you help me bury the body?

She replied within seconds.

IRIS

Always. I'll bring the shovel. Gimme ten minutes and I'll call you. Should I grab some popcorn? Your life is always so entertaining.

ME

poking tongue out emoji Don't you dare call the devil incarnate entertaining.

You have no idea how bad it's gotten.

Chapter 23

On Friday night, Aunt Melinda and Uncle Mason left around six. They had filled the refrigerator as if they were leaving for a month, hugged me countless times, and made me promise to reach out if I needed anything.

"Don't worry about me. I'll be fine. I will barely be here anyway."

My aunt pulled me into her arms once more. "Be safe and responsible. We love you."

I hugged her back. "I love you too. You deserve the weekend off. No need to check in on me—just have fun."

"Have a great time with your friends."

I waved at them from the front porch and returned inside to call Iris.

"Hey you," she greeted me. "Alone?"

"Yep. Until Sunday late afternoon. I wish you could come over. I miss you so much right now."

She sighed. "I wish I could come too. How are things with enemy number one?"

"Same. Enough talking about him. He's not worth our time. What's going on with that girlfriend of yours?"

"Tuscana invited me to spend time with her friends tomorrow. I can't wait. I think it could be serious."

"Did you tell your parents yet?"

"Nah. I have no idea how they'll take any of this. They keep trying to match me with the son of one of my mom's tennis friends. They have no idea who I am and who I like, and I'm not ready to have that talk."

"Iris, you gotta tell them. You can't just go behind their backs all summer. You'll be miserable. Your parents are cool. They won't react to your liking a girl. Perhaps they won't approve of the age difference at first, but I'm sure if they meet her and see what you see, they might surprise you."

I grabbed a slice of cake from the kitchen and walked to my room. Sitting on the bed, my back against the headboard, I locked my phone between my shoulder and ear while I indulged in the sugary treat.

"What if they don't approve? What if they forbid me to see her? You're my best friend, and you're far away from here. I'll be all alone. I'm not sure I'm willing to risk it."

"Iris. Your parents want you to be happy. They love you. They didn't even ground you the time you tagged the school wall because you didn't agree with how the principal dealt with that kid being bullied. You do you. But think about it. It could be the begin—"

The sound of the front door opening and closing startled me.

I raised one eyebrow, hoping I'd conjured the noise in my head.

"Iris," I whispered. "Someone's here." My pulse sped up. A crippling feeling traversed my body and lodged in my stomach.

"What do you mean?" she whispered back.

"The door. Someone is in the house. I hear footsteps."

"A, are you sure your family left already? Maybe they forgot something?"

"I'm sure." I tried to even my breathing. "I even locked the door myself."

"Do you have anything around you that you can use as a weapon?"

A flashback of the time I entered Ryder's apartment with a wrench played in my mind, and I scanned my bedroom, searching for something.

"No." I paused and rummaged through a drawer. "Huh, found a pair of scissors. Think it could work? Never mind. I'll check it out and call you back."

"*Nooo*, stay on the line."

"All right. I'm putting you in my back pocket. Stay quiet."

Slowly, I tiptoed out of my room, armed with the scissors, my heart leaping into my throat, its beats deafening me.

The chime of the TV being turned on stopped me in my tracks. Grabbing my phone, I murmured, "The person is watching TV. Can a home invader be that stupid?"

Iris whispered as if she were standing next to me. "Perhaps they're using the noise to cancel theirs. It's actually smart."

"No, it's not. I'm putting you back into my pocket. Be silent."

Deciding not to let some stranger ruin my weekend, I

inhaled a calming breath and padded forward, my back straight and my eyes alert.

In the living room, I dropped the weapon on the floor when I took in the silhouette slouched on the couch.

"You?" I accused, not hiding the quakes of anger slicing my voice. "Are you for real?"

"Hey baby girl. I thought you were asleep," Ryder said with a shrug.

"It's not even six-thirty. Are you being stupid on purpose, or were you born lacking brain cells?" I fought the urge to scream. "What are you doing here?" I was two seconds away from roasting him with the fire blazing in my eyes.

"House-sitting," he replied, not even daring a look at me, surfing the channels.

"No. *I'm* house-sitting. Living here, remember?"

He shrugged again and opened a paper bag, retrieving a wrapped burger. "Want one?" He grabbed another sandwich from the bag and waved it in my direction.

"Leave. Now. I don't want your food or your company. Bribing doesn't work with me. Sorry to disappoint you."

"Too bad. I thought kids were easy to bribe. Anyway, not leaving. I always stay here when Mason and Melinda are away. It's like a mini vacation for me too. I don't care whether you're here or not. I'm not going anywhere for the next two days."

I balled and relaxed my fists, about to explode. My heart hammered in my chest. Fumes came out of my nostrils. Not really, but almost.

"No. I have plans, and you're ruining them. Please. Just leave." Why was I begging him again? I flinched, unimpressed with myself.

"Seems like you gained a roommate for the weekend, baby girl. Smile. It's a better look on you."

I folded my arms over my chest. "How would you know? You only obtain the pissed-at-you version of me every time."

He shook his head, amusement dancing in his irises, but added nothing.

I was about to storm into my room when I remembered Iris in my pocket.

"Sorry. It's that Ryder guy. Again," I said through gritted teeth, my eyes fixed on him, so he could sense the intensity of my dislike toward him.

"Oh, believe me, I heard the conversation," she said. "Want my opinion? It's interesting. The explosive banter you two have is delicious."

"Shut up. Nothing worth mentioning here," I said. "And don't say delicious ever again when talking about him."

"Your friend is curious about me?" Ryder asked without turning, his voice laced with a smile—then, a growl. "Is that useless boyfriend of yours coming to save you?"

I ignored him. "Iris, help me kick his ass out or I might be tempted to murder him. Please. I don't want blood on my hands."

"Not sure I want to. Your life is so fascinating this summer. Unless you tell me he's a threat to you or you don't feel safe around him."

"I'm perfectly able to fend for myself. He's just annoying…and staying here uninvited."

"I can hear you," Ryder said around a mouthful. I wished I could shove the burger down his throat right now.

Now I was certain. Only Ryder Dickhead could trigger my anger and that side of me I never knew existed before I met him.

I shut my eyes and returned my attention to my friend

still on the line. "Can I call you later? I need to deal with this, and by this, I mean the flea taking over the living room and infesting the couch."

"A, be nice to him. He might not have any other friends."

"Whatever. I'll text you later."

"Wait. Do you have a picture of him? I wanna see whom we're dealing with?"

Before Ryder could comprehend what I was doing, I snapped a photo of him and sent it to my best friend.

"I knew you were thinking about me at night, baby girl. If you wanted a picture, you should have asked for one."

I poked my tongue out and turned away from him.

"Oh, A. That *is* Ryder? *Ohmyfreakinggod.* No wonder you can't stay away. Even his scowl is hot."

"Shut up."

"I'll zip it now. But girl, I'll say this first. I wish I could be there to see how this whole thing, and I mean, your summer, unfolds. Joseph, the hot surfer, and Ryder, the broody—"

"Bye. Love you. I'll talk to you later."

Her clear laughter filled the line. "Love you too."

When I pivoted and faced him again, Ryder's eyes traveled the length of me and fixed on my chest for a long— too long—second.

I gasped when I remembered I wasn't wearing a bra. "Stop ogling me." I crossed my arms to cover my breasts. "For the last time, what are you doing here? And no bullshit."

"Settling myself in. Isn't it obvious?" he asked, his eyes so dark it felt they would swallow me if I wasn't being careful.

My nipples pebbled under his slow perusal of my body. I swallowed hard, trying to kill the sensations waking up inside me. Nobody had ever looked at me this way before. Almost like he wanted to eat me up alive.

When Joseph looked at me, my heart galloped in my chest. It made me feel beautiful. And giddy. When Ryder stared at me, it felt as if he could see right into my soul and into the parts I kept hidden from the rest of the world. As if he could learn every secret about me—inside and out—with no walls left standing between us.

Heat swirled in my lower belly, and I hated every second of it because it made me long for something I shouldn't want. My body felt alien to me as if it had betrayed me. I didn't want it to react to Ryder, but it always did. Despite myself.

"You're leaving," I said. "Now."

"No." He licked his fingers clean, put the burger wrapper back in the bag, and crossed his arms over his torso, mimicking my stance. "When you came to town, I promised Mason I'd watch over you. That I'd keep you safe from any harm. That's what I'm doing. Making sure you're not afraid of the dark, here all by yourself."

"Thanks, but no thanks. I can handle myself quite well. On my own. Go back to wherever you came from."

He sprawled out on the couch, kicked off his shoes, and folded one arm behind his head. "What are we watching? I'm happy to find a compromise between My Little Pony reruns and bloody zombies."

Cursing under my breath, I turned off the TV. "Nothing. Going to my room. Suit yourself. Don't let the door hit you on your way out."

"I'll be here in the morning when you wake up, baby girl. If you're afraid of the dark, feel free to *not* wake me up. I'm only camping here so you don't set the house on fire. Or call the cops because you're having nightmares.

They can do nothing about the bad guys starring in your dreams, though."

I blinked and ground my teeth. "Amazing. Once a jerk, always a jerk. Don't come to my room."

"Only in your dreams," he said with a sarcastic, smooth-as-honey voice that I was dying to never hear again.

"I eat my eggs scrambled and my bacon crispy."

"Noted," Ryder said. He wiggled the second burger in my face. My stomach grumbled. Traitor. "Take it. It's yours anyway. No pickles, extra mustard."

My gaze snapped back to his. How did he know how I liked my burgers?

"Come on, stop being stubborn. You gotta eat."

"I had cake earlier."

He looked at me with an arched brow.

"Okay, fine. Gimme the damn thing. Happy now?"

"Looking out for you. Told ya."

I spun on my heel to retreat to the safety of my bedroom.

"You can stay here. I don't bite."

Shaking my head and replaying Iris's words that he might not have many friends, which I doubted, I turned back and sat on a chair next to the couch. I had to be a sucker for idiots. Seriously, what was wrong with me?

I took a big bite, relishing the flavors hitting my tongue.

"Thanks," I waved the half-eaten burger at him, "for the food."

"You're welcome."

The chime of my phone broke the awkward silence we basked in.

Relief flooded my bloodstream when I noticed Tasha's name flashing on the screen.

I typed fast, excited at the idea I could go out and escape this weird predicament I found myself in with Ryder.

Ryder's phone went off, and his answer was clipped. "No." A pause. "I don't think so." A longer pause. "Not in the mood… Well, I'm busy tonight."

I eyed him for an instant, wondering who was on the other end of the line. His eyes were dark and his jaw, tensed. Even his posture was guarded and closed all at once.

"Yeah, another time." A longer pause. "Maybe. Bye."

He hung up, and I returned my attention to my own device, hoping he didn't notice my eavesdropping, and read Tasha's next message.

"You're not going," Ryder said, closing in on me.

The temperature of the room soared around us.

"Too bad I didn't ask for your permission."

"Well, you should." His voice lowered to a whisper. "I'm here to watch over you, and I say you're not leaving this house tonight." His fingers skimmed over mine, sending mixed signals to every cell of my body.

Something flashed in his eyes, and for an instant, I forgot what we were arguing about, stepping forward, unable to escape the pull.

My palm landed on his chest. Every pulse of his heart shook underneath my touch. Every breath he took caressed my nose. Right now, I didn't wish to be anywhere else when he stared at me with such unconcealed heat.

Time idled.

"Are you going to lock me in here?" I was acting like a brat on purpose.

"Should I? Or can you stay put for a night?"

I didn't reply. Instead, I studied the flecks of gold around his pupils and the way his lips moved.

One of his hands cupped my face, his thumb brushing the apple of my cheek.

"Can you? Stay still?"

"Not sure." Because, well… I wasn't.

"Let me convince you." He dipped his head forward, and without thinking—my brain being a jelly mess—I rose to my tiptoes, our lips so close we breathed the same air.

My wits made a comeback just in time, and I blinked, jumping back. "What the hell. Don't try to kiss me. We're not friends, you and me. And I'm not kissing my enemies."

Ryder rubbed his nape with one hand before expelling his anger on me. "Well, don't try to seduce me. I already told you. You and I, not happening. Stay the fuck away. I was just testing you anyway. To see how far you were willing to go."

Chills crept along my spine, and I recoiled. "I'm not a toy you can use when you're bored. Leave me alone," I barked. Moisture filled my eyes. Anger replaced my humiliation, burning hotter than the shame that filled me. "You're cruel. And mean. Maybe I was the one testing you. Why would I befriend someone as selfish as you?"

He remained silent.

"See, even you can't come up with some logical explanation."

"I didn't mean… You should…" Ryder must've thought twice about feeding me bullshit, because he went quiet and retreated into his jackass persona, a mask of fury covering his face. "It was about time you came to that conclusion yourself. I'm bad news for you. Doesn't mean I'll let you party all night without making sure you're safe and sound."

"Suit yourself. I'm done caring."

He raised his arm and opened his palm, dangling my truck keys in front of my face.

"Gimme those."

"I'm afraid this isn't going to happen. Under my watch, you're not going out. Already told you that."

"You're impossible. You're not the boss of me."

"Technically, I'm the adult here."

"Well, technically, I'm allowed to tell you to go fuck yourself. What's happening here? You can't tolerate me for more than two seconds, and now you want me to listen to your orders?" I shook my head. "Stop pretending we're friends, and move out of my way. I have a spare in my room."

He clutched my elbow before I could walk away. "I'm serious. Stay. Don't go out. It's late."

"I'm going. I'm not your hostage."

Ryder groaned. "If you go, then I'm going too." He paused. "And I'm driving."

"No. Tasha invited me. Not you."

"Well, I was invited me too."

I could sense the blood draining from my face. "You kidding, right?"

He shook his head.

"No. Please. This has to be a joke. Don't come."

"Sorry, baby girl. I've already decided, and you can't stop me. I'm going."

I hurried to my room and slammed the door behind me, tears of frustration blinding me. I wiped them off with my fingers while I sent a text message to my friend.

ME

> I'll meet you there. Ryder has decided to get involved.

TASHA

> Should I worry?

ME

> Nah. He's a dickhead, but he's harmless.

TASHA

> Okay. If you change your mind, gimme a call.

It took me fifteen minutes to regain my composure and get ready before meeting Ryder in the living room.

"One word of advice," I said. "Keep your crazy girlfriend away from me. I mean it."

"I thought you like a good catfight."

"Well, think again."

Chapter 24

I brought the drink to my lips, but before I could take a sip, it got switched to a cup of water. Again. Tasha shoved Ryder back with both hands. Hard. "Get lost, Ride."

He smirked but said nothing, pouring the booze at his feet and sauntering away.

The party was held at a house on the other side of the lake. Some guy from Tasha's year in high school and his older brother. People were spread all over the yard on the lakeside, a few couples making out around the bonfire or on the dock.

Tasha left to find Ronald, and I found myself alone for a total of twenty seconds before a guy I'd never met joined me. Longish, curly light-brown hair, tanned skin, and piercing chestnut eyes that bore into mine. "Ava, right?" I nodded. He held out his hand, his palm enveloping mine as we shook hands. "Chris." His eyes roamed around. "Welcome to my kingdom." A large teasing smile lit up his face.

"Oh, you live here?" I looked at the Southern mansion on my right, all white with a Juliet balcony on the second floor and its roof supported by columns that wrapped around on all sides. Black shutters, a large staircase, immaculate green lawn and flower beds, and a matching garage at the end of the large crescent driveway.

A serious expression filled his eyes, and he sounded jaded when he said, "Yeah, this is my palace."

"Well, I love it."

"Good for you. Not everything that dazzles is worth your admiration." So I was right, he really was indifferent to the mansion he called home. "I've heard you are here for the summer, and that you can serve Ride his ass on a platter. Is the rumor mill wrong about you?"

I snickered. "Pretty accurate so far."

"How do you like Feather Lake?"

"That's a tricky question," I said.

"Not from my point of view. It's either a yes or a no." He watched me with a raised brow.

I sighed. "It's a bit more complicated than—" From the side of my eye, I spotted Ryder walking toward us. Snaking my arm through Chris's, I asked, "Wanna gimme a tour? I need a drink."

His smile stretched wide, and his eyes sparkled in the low light of the early night. This boyish look fit him.

"My pleasure. Let's go. I happen to know where the good stuff is."

With red cups filled with a mix of lemonade and pomegranate vodka, we settled amongst a group of people on the back deck where a blunt was being passed around. When it reached me, I flicked my hand and refused.

"Not a fan of weed?" one girl with a throaty voice asked before coughing.

I offered her a tight-lipped smile. "Nah."

The only time Iris and I had tried pot, out of curiosity, was last year after she convinced her cousin to sell us some. The burning sensation in my lungs and fits of cough that followed were enough to deter me from ever giving it another try. The other night, with Ryder, I surprised even myself when I asked for a puff. Like every time we were together, he always made me want to push the limits. Even my own.

As if he were a magnet to my eyes, I saw him dismissing two guys and nearing the house. If he raised his eyes, he'd see me. Backing one step and pointing to the dock, I asked Chris, "Your boat?"

"Yeah. What about it?"

I pinched my lips together, trying to come up with an escape plan. Before I could tell him what was on my mind, Chris spoke up as if he'd read my thoughts. "Wanna go for a ride?"

"Sure."

"Awesome."

We walked side by side toward the water.

"The other night, I noticed you when you danced with Tash on the bed of the pickup truck, but at first I thought you were Ride's girl."

A loud chuckle tumbled out of my mouth. "Me? Nah. We're not even friends. We can't stand each other."

"I felt some heavy vibes between you two." He shrugged. "Everyone did."

"Must have been hatred. There's a lot of it where he's concerned."

"Then let's go away for a while." He helped me into the jet boat, with a red deck and a silver wave decal on the side. A wakeboard tower was mounted on the top of the hull.

"Fancy ride," I said.

"Well, my parents' latest bribery attempt so Declan—that's my brother—and I don't request some quality time with them. They're married to their work and are barely ever around. The boat is supposed to be a great diversion to forget they only care when it's convenient."

"I'm sorry. It sucks."

"Well, don't be. We've been raised by nannies. At this point, our folks are more like strangers having a sleepover one week a month than parents to us." He fished two cans of beer out of a compartment below his seat and offered me one.

"You sure it's safe to drink and drive?"

"No, but I'll be careful. I swear. And I only had one beer, hours ago."

"And the spiked lemonade before that."

"Nah, mine was water. I gotta keep an eye on the party so it doesn't get out of control. My big bro is not trustable, too busy sleeping his way around to care."

He untied the cables anchoring us to the dock, pressed the lever, and the boat drifted into the water. Darkness had almost taken over the entire sky. Just a few brushes of vibrant pink and orange decorated the blank canvas. We flew across the water until the house became just a dot on the horizon and we could no longer hear the music blasting or the loud chatter of his friends.

Seated at the front, I took a sip of the cold beer and closed my eyes, letting the wind sweep across my face. Every cell in me relaxed, and I felt at peace. And free.

No one treating me like a kid or giving me orders.

Chris decreased the speed of the boat, and I opened my eyes just when he stopped in the middle of a little bay.

His contagious smile returned. "This is my favorite spot. During the day, we can see almost the entire expanse of the lake."

"It's peaceful."

"How do you like your summer here so far?" he asked, sitting next to me.

"It depends. But somehow, it's growing on me."

We exchanged small smiles. I sipped on my beer, enjoying the sound of silence and the water lapping against the boat hull.

"What's the story with Ride? He's a complicated person, but he's not as big a jerk as he pretends to be. We used to be friends a while back."

"Nothing to tell. He can't stand me. Always finds motives to pick fights. We never see eye to eye. Nothing interesting, I swear. His jerk ways aren't a pretense around me."

Chris pondered the information for a minute, looking in the distance, before turning toward me again. "Let's say if I were to kiss you right now, I wouldn't have to be afraid of his acting out, would I?" He lifted one golden brow, the same color as his curly hair, a tentative smile stretching one side of his lips. He sat so close I could smell the faint hit of beer on his breath, and feel the heat from his body.

My heart vibrated with a new awareness. "Technically, no. But who knows? Ryder could decide it's against the rules he's playing by and could throw a fit. He forgot to share those rules with me." I swallowed, conscious of how Chris's attention moved from my mouth to my throat. "The thing is…I'm seeing someone."

His fingers pushed the rebel tendrils of my hair away

as the wind picked up. "You left a heartbroken boy back home?"

The air charged and wrapped around us.

I shook my head. "I met someone who lives here. Not *here* here, but in Medora Beach. I like him. Sorry."

His eyes fused with mine. "Don't be. He's a lucky guy. I wish we had met first."

Shivers ran through me.

"You cold?" he asked.

I rubbed my arms with my hands. "A little."

Chris moved to grab a blanket from under his seat and a bottle of tequila. "This should help."

Enveloped in the blanket, we passed the bottle back and forth. My eyes watered when the alcohol coated my tongue. Chris let out a clear laugh. "Not a liquor drinker either?"

I blinked, puckered my mouth, and wrinkled my nose, praying for the burn to dissipate.

"Not really." My finger traced the outline of the tattoo on his forearm. "Did it hurt? When you got inked?"

"Nah. For the time it lasted, I liked the sting."

"Why a mountain?" I asked.

"Reminds me of where I come from. I was born on the mountainside of the state. We moved here when I was thirteen. Left my heart there."

"I dig it. It's nice."

"Why do you look sad?" he asked, once the alcohol we drank melted some of the walls I had built around me.

"I'm not." Just his assumptions were powerful enough to tie knots around my stomach.

Chris's eyes were glued to mine. "There's sadness lingering there, deep in the recesses of your eyes. I can see it. Why do you push people away then?"

I tilted my head to the side. To avoid answering, I took

another hit of the tequila and wiped my mouth with the back of my hand.

His fingers closed around my chin, and he forced me to turn in his direction.

"Hey, you don't have to share if you don't want to." He waved his other hand around. "You're safe here. Nobody is judging you. I'm doing all kinds of stupid shit all the time, expecting my parents to react. They never do. Instead, they send me their lawyer, fill my bank account, or do just about anything to avoid admitting we don't have a relation-ship…that we're a broken family. Whatever I do, they don't care. Sometimes I feel invisible."

I recognized my pain in his. When I used to cut myself, I was trying to feel things. Because I always kept my emotions and feelings hidden from everyone else. It made me feel in control. Like I wasn't invisible, at least not to myself. It helped me remember that I was alive, not just some robot. If Chris could blame his parents for his fucked-up existence, I couldn't even blame anyone else but me for mine. And circumstances and a weak mental health or warped emotional response to stress and grief.

"You're not"—I held his hand—"invisible. Your value isn't defined by your parents' standards. You don't have to prove anything to them. Whatever you do, do it for you. To be a better version of yourself. What they think or don't think sucks, but you're not them, and they are not you."

"Wow, I didn't picture you as a deep psychology shit kind of girl."

"Well, I spent an awful lot of time in therapy. Guess I learned a few things."

I appreciated he didn't press me to explain myself, and that he respected my boundaries.

"I was right about you then," he said. "There's pain in your eyes." He shrugged. "We're not so different after all."

"I guess."

He studied me for the longest time. "Are you okay, though?"

I exhaled. "Yeah. I am. I will be. It's a long process, but I'm getting there." I watched him. "Are you? Okay, I mean?"

He busied himself ripping the label from the tequila bottle. "Nah. I'm not. Trying to be. Very much, though."

"At least you're aware."

"Yep."

We took another sip, but our conversation had somehow killed the mood.

"Wanna go back?" Chris asked after a beat.

"Yeah. I do."

The liquor had helped to wash my worries away, and I relaxed in my seat, enjoying the ride back.

We berthed at the dock, and Chris held out his hand to help me out. I hooked my arm around his, tipsier than I thought I was.

"You okay?" he asked, against my ear.

I nodded.

"I'm sorry. It was stupid to drive the boat while drinking. You were right earlier. I should do better."

"Thanks for taking me, though. I had a great time." I lost my footing, and he wrapped an arm around my waist to steady me, my body now flush with his as we stepped down the dock. "Everything will be okay. For you. Don't be too hard on yourself."

"I'll try—"

"Here you are," Tasha said, hopping in our direction and cutting our conversation short. I could tell from the exaggerated tilt of her lips she was as tipsy as I was. She grabbed my hand and pulled me forward. "So, you and Chris, huh?" she whisper-screamed, wiggling her eyebrows.

I nudged her. "Stop starting rumors."

Chris's smirk, when I caught his eye, confirmed he'd heard everything she said. His happiness faded when a tall silhouette neared us, pulling dark shadows in its wake.

My heart sank.

"Where the fuck were you?"

Chris slapped his shoulder, his bright smile back in place. Gone was the guy who shared about the emptiness in his life not so long ago. "Ryder, my man. Give Ava a break. Go and annoy someone else. She's under my watch tonight." To prove his point, he inched closer, circled my waist with one arm, and pulled me to him, away from Tasha. "See? We're best friends."

Multiple shades of red flashed across Ryder's face. His gaze bounced between Chris's arm around me and my face, finally ending on the palm still resting on his shoulder. With a shrug, Ryder yanked away. "Are you fucking drunk, Mackenzie?"

"Not your business," Chris said. "Now leave us alone. We're still getting to know each other, and you're in the way."

Ryder pushed him back, both hands hitting Chris in the chest. "No fucking chance."

I sighed as my eyes met Tasha's rounded ones.

"What's your problem, Ride?" Chris asked in a calm tone, trying to disarm the situation. "Are you jealous?"

Ryder clenched his hands at his sides. "Don't provoke me, or you'll meet my fist. I swear, Mackenzie, don't start."

"Ava and I are having a great time. Stop interfering in her business. Now move, or get the hell out of *my* property."

I straightened and stepped forward before speaking into Chris's ear. "Thanks. I can fend for myself. He's just being his usual jerk. Warned you. Don't worry. I'll take care of him."

Both his arms wound around me. "You sure? I can kick him out if you prefer. Your call."

Without looking in Ryder's direction, I could feel the smoke coming out of his nostrils.

I dropped a chaste kiss on Chris's cheek. "Thanks for tonight. I had fun. I'll see you later."

"I had fun too. Thanks for listening."

I followed Ryder to a corner of the yard, where two guys were smoking weed. Ryder took the blunt and sucked on it until the tip lit red, then blew the smoke away before ordering them to get lost.

"Getting high to discuss something with me. Wow." I clapped my hands. "Real mature. I thought we had concluded it was a shitty habit the other night. Go ahead, get zonked. It makes everything so much better."

Ryder squinted but said nothing for a while, ignoring me.

"Talk or I'm going back out there," I said, motioning to the house behind me with my thumb. "Unlike you, Chris is a decent guy."

Ryder remained silent. I rocked back and forth on my heels, fidgeted with the bracelet around my left wrist, and rolled my eyes as the first stars shone upon us, erasing the pinkish stripes decorating the sky.

"Okay, never mind. I'm gone." Before I could put too much distance between us, his digits clutched my wrist, and he tugged me back to him.

His eyes were menacing. Gone was the aquamarine hue around his pupils. Instead, they looked black and deadly. "You're not."

I wrenched my hand away from his hold and threw

both arms over my head. "Change your music. This song has been played too many times. I'm done."

Ryder's shoulders dropped, and the anger in his eyes ceded its place to impatience. And something resembling fear.

"You went on a ride with him after he'd been drinking. Chris is always drunk as fuck. Everybody knows that. It was reckless."

"First, Chris is a nice guy. Stop trying to insult his character. Second, none of this is about you. Third, I was never in danger. Stop meddling in my business."

He took another puff of the joint still clamped between his fingers. "Drinking and driving is a big no. I don't care whether it's a spaceship or a boat, it's dumb. I figured you were smarter than this."

"Stop trying to solve me. Chris was being my friend. Unlike you. All *you* do is piss on my parade, pretending you care when we're both aware you don't. You get hard on the power it gives you to boss me around."

My words hit him where it hurt because Ryder flinched. "You're clueless." His annoyance was fully back.

"You infuriate me, and this conversation is leading nowhere. I'm—"

Misty walked over to us and put an end to our argument.

"What?" Ryder barked, his fingers returning to my wrist to prevent me from leaving and securing me next to him, as if to protect me from some invisible danger. His eyes said, *Just a sec. I'll deal with this. We're not done.*

"Ride, I gotta talk to you." Misty used her most syrupy voice, the one grating on my eardrums. If I didn't know better, I would think she looked preoccupied with something.

"Not now. I'm busy. Later."

She grimaced and sent an annoyed expression my way. She stole the joint Ryder was still holding and brought it to her lips. "It's kind of important. I think I might be… Well, I'm late."

Ryder coughed, and his hold on my arm tightened.

"And here you are. Getting high," I said, sarcasm clear in my tone. "Impressive. Keep leading by example. Your baby will be a lucky one."

Misty murdered me with her eyes.

Ryder's attention ping-ponged between the two of us, and he looked torn.

He released me and jabbed a finger in my face. "Wait here. Don't think about pulling another one of your disappearing acts. I'll be right back. We. Are. Not. Done."

"Yes, we are."

"No. I'm fucking serious. Stay here. Listen for once."

Yeah, yeah. As if I'm about to start doing what you order me to.

"Tash," I called out to my friend after Ryder left me to my own devices. She spun on her heels, Ronald by her side.

"Hey girl. Where have you been?" Her gaze perused the area around me. "Did you ditch Ride? He's usually wherever you are."

"Nah, I have Misty to thank this time around. Wanna leave before he comes back and tries to rule my actions?"

"Oh, let's get out of here. Like *super spies*. Sleepover? You could stay at my place."

I joined my hands in prayer. "Yes, please. Knowing Ryder, he'll carry out his guard duty outside my bedroom door all night to make sure I don't leave the house."

She linked her arm with mine. "Ro," she addressed her boyfriend, "mind driving us?" She turned to me next. "He only drank soda all night."

"Follow me, you two." Ronald grabbed the car keys from his pocket and led us to our exit.

Once again, Ryder was about to ruin my night, but time I wouldn't let him.

Take that, jerk.

———

"Chips or popcorn?" Tasha asked after I cleaned up my face and changed into the night shorts and T-shirt she lent me.

"Huh…popcorn. Are we watching a movie?"

"Depends. We could also keep drinking. I make an incredible punch, and it so happens my parents are out."

"Sounds good."

After we split the punch in two—she didn't lie about it tasting like cranberry juice with an edge—we ended up in her bed.

"What are we watching?" my friend asked, surfing our options.

"A horror flick?"

"Oh, you like to be spooked? I prefer romcoms."

"Nah, I like it when everything isn't just a colorful happily-ever-after with no substance. Sometimes, I enjoy the shades of gray. Nobody's life is only fun and kittens. We all have darkness inside ourselves. We all hide secrets. Being cheerful all the time is a pretense, not real life."

But then Joseph's face appeared in my mind, and it discredited my own beliefs. Still, he was an exception. An abnormality. I was sure he had bad days too. He just chose not to let them affect him. Something I couldn't figure out how to do just yet.

"I enjoy easygoing love stories with no real plot," Tasha

said with a sigh. "Easy peasy love stories that make you believe in fairytales."

"Me too. Sometimes. But if I have to watch a romantic movie, I'll choose one with drama. And a lot of tears." What I didn't tell her was that watching movies that triggered emotions in me was a great coping mechanism to deal with my own feelings. It helped force out stuff I would otherwise keep in.

"Do you miss your parents?" she asked after we settled on a horror comedy.

"Not really. We haven't talked that much since I landed here. I need the break."

"You would tell me the truth, right?"

"Yeah."

"Did you kiss Chris earlier? You two looked cozy when you came back from your little boat ride. I don't know… There was a spark there."

My face warmed up, and I placed my hands over my cheeks. "I didn't. He asked if he could, though. For a brief instant, I wanted him to. We were sharing stuff, and it would have felt right. But I'm already kissing Joseph. I want to see it through with him. Kissing another guy felt wrong. Joseph and I, we're not dating and haven't had the talk about exclusivity or whatever we are yet, but he cares about me and has always been nice to me. I wouldn't kiss someone else behind his back."

"Oh wow. You're a saint, Ava."

I threw a handful of kernels at her. "I am not. I swear. There's a lot of darkness in me sometimes. And I've said terrible things to Ryder. When we fight, it's so intense that sometimes I don't think about my words before speaking them out loud. And then when I'm alone, I'm mad at myself for not shutting up before it escalated."

"Ride loves to get a rise out of you. I'm sure it makes him hard when you two banter."

I fanned a hand over my face. "Don't put Ryder and sex in the same line, Tash. It's wrong. Ugh. The last thing that I need is a visual of his dick."

If only she knew he had appeared in every fantasy I had since moving here, she would have a blast. But that was secret information, not meant to be shared, even with my girlfriends.

"What did he say anyway when he cornered you earlier?"

"Something about not letting Chris drive the boat because he was drunk and I shouldn't trust him."

My friend gasped.

"What?" I asked.

"Drunk driving is a sour subject when it comes down to Ride. I bet you triggered memories he would prefer to forget."

His words from the other night replayed in my head. *Sometimes, it helps me deal with shit. Memories I wish I could delete.*

"What happened?"

She mimicked zipping her lips. "Sorry, not my story to tell. You've heard nothing about what happened since you moved here?"

I angled my upper body to face her. "No. Tell me. Everybody always keeps me in the dark. Ryder keeps telling me I have no idea, and so far, I understand nothing he says."

Tasha sighed and grabbed my hands in hers. "Ava, I really would tell you, but if nobody told you, I don't want to be the one to do so. Sorry. It doesn't concern you, okay? Trust me. I'm sure when the timing is right, you'll learn about it. But it won't be from me."

My pulse sped up. "Why do I feel like it's about me somehow?" My voice had lost its previous zest.

"It's not. We should catch some sleep. It's almost three."

"Tash, please. I won't tell anyone you told me."

"Ava, I swear, it doesn't concern you. If you ask Ride, maybe he'll tell you. Let it go for tonight, okay? You have nothing to worry about."

When I closed my eyes after Tasha turned off the light and we slid under the comforter in her bed, the feeling that people in my life were hiding something important crept up on me.

Ryder, my parents, Uncle Mason and Aunt Melinda, and now Tasha.

Something had happened, and they thought they were protecting me by keeping the truth from me. But it did the opposite. Anxiety crippled me, and I scratched the flesh of my left forearm until it burned. The exhaustion of the day and the booze I drank finally won the battle of wills, and I surrendered myself to nothingness.

Tasha dropped me off at ten to six the next morning. With a pep in my step, I walked toward Joseph, who was leaning against his truck. He lowered his head until his mouth molded to mine. "Had a great night?" he asked against my lips.

For the most part, last night had been fun.

"Yes. How long have you been here?"

"A few minutes." He intertwined his fingers with mine and smiled, reminding me I'd been right when I refused to kiss Chris the night before. Joseph and I could be more than just a summer fling. Yeah, it felt real. More real than anything else in my life.

When I unlocked the front door, I had no idea what we

were walking into. The moment my feet landed on the kitchen floor and I closed the door behind us, a new surge of anger washed through me.

I sighed. "Seriously, are you kidding me?"

Chapter 25

"You're asking me this question? After you went missing for hours? Where have you been?" Ryder asked, his tone icing my blood. "Last night, I told you to wait for me. When I came back, you had vanished."

I blinked. "None of your business. Again, why is it your problem?"

"Because I promised to watch over you, and your going MIA isn't making the job easy on me."

"You're impossible. I was tired of being bossed around by you, and I left with Tasha. Since when am I supposed to report my whereabouts to *you*?"

Joseph, still holding my hand, walked between Ryder and me. "Enough with this, you guys. Can you talk to each other without trying to rip your heads off? This is getting ridiculous. Stop. I'll lock you two in a room until you can figure your shit out."

"You don't want to do that," Ryder said, the venom unmistakable in his tone. His eyes were fixed on me. "Believe me, that's the worst idea you can come up with. Never say I didn't warn you."

"Then mind your own things. Ava is old enough not to have to explain her actions to you. She owes you nothing. You're what? Like twenty at the most. Who are you to barge into her life and pretend you care about her? All you do is complicate things—for her—when you can't even stand being around her for more than a minute."

"Hey surfer boy, you sure you wanna get in the middle of this?" Ryder asked, his hand gesturing to me and him. "You sure it's a good idea? If I were you, I'd stay out of it. Don't get involved in our family business."

"Family?" I clenched my jaw and breathed in through my nose, trying desperately to keep it together. "Unbeliev-able. Stop. Just stop. God, how do you think it's even possi-ble? We're not family. No. Never been one. We're not related. And anyway, you want nothing to do with me," I said, unable to bury my exasperation under nice words. "I'm not yours to care for. Not now, not ever. Find someone else to annoy. Misty looked like she could use your help last night. Oh no, my bad, you already did enough."

"Don't get in the middle of this." His tone sounded like a cruel warning.

"Or what, *Daddy*?" I used my most condescending tone.

He cursed under his breath, his eyes becoming weapons ready to vaporize me.

"Whatever. I'll be out of here in ten minutes. Leave me alone, Ryder."

He dragged in a long breath. "Baby girl, you have no idea, do you? You have no clue about anything that happened. And here I thought you were smart. Guess I was wrong all along."

"Why are you talking in puzzles that I can't understand? It has nothing to do with intelligence. Nothing you say ever makes any sense. Why can't you tell me what it's about once and for all? Even Tasha refused to say anything. I'm tired of being lied to....or kept in the dark about everything."

"Never mind. Go and play with your toys and stay out of it."

"Ohmygod. You're such a pain in the ass. Is your only goal in life to infuriate me?"

He crossed his arms over his chest. "I can't help it if you're acting dumb. You can't even see what's right in front of your eyes."

A loud grunt passed my lips. "Speak. English."

"Sorry, baby girl. You're not ready for what I have to say. Grow up first. Then we'll talk."

I stamped my feet. "Gosh, I hate you. How is it that every time you open your mouth you exasperate me to no extent?"

A smirk tilted his lips. "You're welcome."

Joseph stepped forward, reducing the space between the two of them. His back was firmed, his stance rigid. He never let go of my hand as I stood behind him. Both guys stared at each other, neither of them backing down. "Respect. Ever heard of it?"

Ryder snorted, not breaking his stance. "Go chase waves, surfer boy, and leave us the heck alone."

Moving into the small space in the middle, I pushed their chests with both hands, forcing them to step back.

"This is getting out of hand. Ryder, stay here. I'm not done with you." I switched my attention to Joseph. "Wait for me in the truck. Please. Let me deal with him. You don't have to get mixed into this. If he's not worth my time, he's not worth yours either."

Joseph spoke to me in the soft voice he always used around me, his gaze still locked on Ryder. "Avalon, you don't have to waste your energy on him. We can just go. Let me help you gather your stuff."

I framed his face with my palms, forcing him to look down at me. "I gotta settle whatever this is once and for all. Don't worry, he's harmless. Just being a prick and can't help himself. And by the look of it, it is possible he is about to become a father."

"What?"

"Long story. Misty isn't a trusted source. I'll explain later."

"I'll wait on the front porch. Come and get me if he's being out of line."

I nodded and watched him exit the house, not before pointing an accusatory finger in Ryder's direction. "Don't hurt her, you hear me? You touch her, I'll end you."

I closed the door after him and faced Ryder, irritation still clung to his features like a mask, and his eyes so dark I couldn't look elsewhere, mesmerized.

"The fuck you couldn't have called," he said with a stride forward.

"I turned off my phone. Spies don't leave traces about their whereabouts," I said, trying to ease the escalating tension in the room with a half-joke.

"Spies?"

"Forget it."

Ryder remained silent. My heart leaped in my throat. I tried to swallow, but I could barely take a full breath in.

Something shifted between us.

Tingles spread all over my skin.

Under a spell I couldn't escape, I studied his profile. In that instant, it wasn't hate radiating from him, but something far deeper that I couldn't define. It was more potent, more intoxicating, and it made my entire being vibrate with awareness.

As if linked by an invisible thread, we came closer together, halting when only a foot separated us. Ryder's hastened breathing matched mine. Whatever mind games we were playing, I couldn't escape its grip on me.

"Did you spend all night waiting for me to get back?" I asked, my voice rough as if I'd cried for hours.

"I had no idea where you were. I drove all over town. Even broke into Chris's bedroom. Just in case."

"You did? Why?"

"Because."

"It's not a good enough answer. Why?"

He said nothing. His fingers circled my left wrist, and he flipped it around, exposing my forearm to his scrutiny. One of his digits traced the length, shivers rising in its trail. He watched my flesh for a couple of seconds before I freed my arm, once again afraid he would notice the marks I put there.

"You don't get it. You just don't get any of it, do you?" he asked.

"What am I missing? Enlighten me. I can't keep up with anything you say. For once, tell me the truth. About everything."

He averted his eyes, looking in the distance, breaking the daze we had fallen under.

"Why can't you be honest with me for once? Whatever

I did to enrage you, I can't fix it if I'm not aware of what the problem is. What did I ever do to you?"

His throat rippled, stealing my attention. Ryder was such a mystery. One I wasn't sure I really wanted to uncover. Whatever it was, I had a hunch I'd never recover from it. Not fully at least.

"Don't go with him." He broke the tensed silence, his tone softer. "Stay here."

"I'm going. We have a surf lesson. Nothing you say will stop me. Unless it's something I need to hear. Unless it explains why you hate me so much."

He shoved his hands into his pockets, balancing on his heels.

"I don't hate you."

"Well, you have a funny way of showing it. One day you tell me I should be afraid of you. That I should never come to your place without an invite. Then you bring me coffee and say you are sorry, only to start again with the mind games the next day. I never catch a break. Something is wrong with you. It's not normal to be possessive of someone you barely know."

We faced each other, breathing the same air, our bodies so close that if I took a big enough inhale, our chests would collide.

"Don't go." Ryder pleaded once more, his voice lower. The storm in his irises lessened, like clouds parting to give the sun the attention it deserved. The green color returned. Precious aquamarine.

My lips separated, but no sound left my mouth. I had never been on the receiving end of Ryder's intensity when it wasn't mixed with hatred.

"Joseph and I have a full day planned. I gotta go."

The armor Ryder kept around himself returned right

before my eyes. He stepped back, something resembling hurt filling his features.

I sucked a breath in. "Well, in that case, if you have nothing to tell me, enjoy your day. Don't wait for me. I have a date later." I swiveled on my feet and went to my room to pick an outfit for tonight and everything I required for the day.

After a quick shower and dressed in a pair of denim cutoffs and a cream tank top, I returned to the living room. Ryder still hadn't moved. Passing by him, I leaned over to grab my purse I discarded earlier by the door when he reached for my hand.

"What?" I asked, trying to keep my tone neutral, void of emotions.

He said nothing. Instead, he glared at me as if I should be able to read his inner thoughts without any explanations. As if his face contained the answer to all the secrets he kept from me.

We stood there for a minute, neither of us saying anything.

"That's what I thought," I said after a long beat. "When you're brave enough to tell me the truth, to be honest, then we can have that conversation. In the meantime, mind your own stuff and leave me out of it."

With a sharp intake of air, he let go of me, and I sensed his eyes on my back as I made my escape.

Chapter 26

"Ready for lesson number two?" Joseph asked once we changed into bathing suits and carried the boards to the beach.

I sucked in a deep breath. "I think so."

"Ava, you were a natural last week. Let's practice on the sand first, then we'll get into the water. Turn around. I'll put sunscreen on your back."

His warm palms traveled along my spine and shoulder blades, his calloused fingers waking up tingles across my skin. When he rubbed the lotion on my lower back, I shivered—in the best possible way. Electricity spread through me. He sampled the flesh of my neck with his hungry lip, and I stepped back to press against him, eliminating every inch of distance between our bodies. I wasn't used to inti-

mate touches from someone, but with Joseph, it felt familiar, right, and addictive. Deep down, I was aware I'd never
get enough. It was as if he knew exactly what I liked and
what made me feel good.

His hands worked over my shoulders and the sides of
my ribcage.

I turned around, and he handed me the sunblock so I
could finish applying it all over my face and abdomen
while he did the same. When I was done, I applied some to
his ripped back and loved the feel of his muscles undu-
lating under my touch.

When he pivoted to face me, Joseph's forehead met
mine. "Good to go?" he whispered. Right there, I was
melting, and the sun wasn't even at its zenith yet. Every
inch of my skin blazed with a newfound awareness.

I nodded with an exhale, pushing my shoulders back,
ready to ride the wave.

"That's my girl."

Happiness bubbled inside me when he said those
words. Yes, I loved the idea of being his.

We were one hour into the surf lesson when I lay flat
on the board. For the last five minutes, we'd been paddling
for fun beside each other. "I'm done. My arms are
spaghetti. I'm hungry. And I feel like I haven't slept in
weeks. Can we go and grab some food?"

Joseph tugged my board to his so the waves wouldn't
move us apart and claimed my lips. "I was hoping you'd
say that. I'm starving."

Under the shadow of mature trees, we spent the afternoon napping on and off in a hammock behind Joseph's
house after our lunch shift at Ocean Mist. It was a small
cottage with an attached garage his stepmom, Amanda,
kept after her divorce from Kelly's father. It had baby-

yellow siding, white shutters and trims, and beautiful flower beds all over the front lawn.

"Hey Avalon, wake up," Joseph said, peppering kisses all over my face, his fingers tickling me at the waist, sometime later. "It's date night. We gotta get ready. Or we can also forfeit the entire thing and stay here all night. I won't object. Whatever pleases you the most."

My eyelids popped open, and I part-laughed and part-screamed, writhing against him, unable to take the torture of his digits any longer. "Fine. See? I'm awake. Let go of me."

His lips descended to mine in a slow torturous kiss. We broke apart, and a loud yawn passed the seam of my mouth.

"Sorry. All week, I have been looking forward to tonight." I stretched my arms over my head. "I'm just so tired right now. Gimme fifteen more minutes."

"Am I allowed to kiss you while you wake up?"

I bobbed my head fast.

"Oh, I love this game. You can't open your eyes too soon," Joseph murmured, his lips molding to mine. "Take your sweet time."

He moved over me, steadying the hammock so we wouldn't tip over, careful not to crush me under his weight.

He toyed with the flesh of my neck with his tongue and teeth and followed the column of my throat before tracing my collarbones. A ache built inside me, and I trembled underneath him. "It feels so good. Please, never stop."

"I don't intend to," he said, more breathless than usual.

I arched my back, relishing every sensation invading me, some of those I was feeling for the very first time. My skin heated up. Sounds I never heard before tumbled out of my mouth. I wrapped my arms around his neck, holding him as close to me as possible. The need to rub my lower self against the bulge in his shorts became unbearable.

Stars shone behind my closed eyelids.

A low grunt escaped Joseph's lips as he feasted on mine

Soon our make-out session turned steamier than it'd ever been.

"Fuck," Joseph said, lifting himself on his arms and breaking the connection of our bodies. "We can't keep doing this, or I'll embarrass myself and come in my shorts."

I pinched my lips together to avoid laughing. I had no idea if I looked as aroused as he did right now, but this was a good look on him. Reddened lips, tousled hair, flushed face, and eyes filled with twinkles. He really was beautiful inside and out.

I twisted the wild strands of his hair around my fingers as he evened his breathing.

"It was kinda hot," I said, once the palpitations in me lessened. I chewed my bottom lip, daring myself to ask the questions on the tip of my tongue. "Did you ever…huh… have sex?"

His eyes found mine and settled there for a moment. Softness filled his gaze. "Three times. First time was awkward. Second and third, much better. That summer, we thought we loved each other. Turned out she started dating one of my friends behind my back weeks later." He cupped my jaw, his eyes trained on me. "Have you?"

I shook my head, feeling my cheeks warming up. "I had a boyfriend. We broke up before I got here. I think we're better off not dating. The breakup was a mutual decision. We were more like good friends hanging out. There were no sparks. Now I'm certain. Nothing like what you and I have. We talked about it, but it felt wrong."

"Ava, I'll never force you to do things you're not ready

for," he said. "I hope you know that. I'm not that kind of guy."

"I know. Up until this instant, I've never felt the ache to do it. I'm still not ready, but I might get there soon if we keep things this heated between us."

We exchanged timid smiles.

"No pressure, okay? We'll take things slow and see how it goes."

"Anyway, we're not even dating. Not officially at least," I teased, laughing at Joseph's shocked expression.

"Well, huh, you beat me to it. I had planned to ask you tonight, but since we're talking about it, Ava Pierce, would you officially be my girlfriend?"

Tugging at the hem of his tank top, I pulled him down to me and met his mouth. "Yes. If you hadn't asked me, I would have tonight," I said with a wink. "You looked too handsome—and sexy—earlier today on that board. How can a girl resist?"

"I did?" His brows reached his hairline, and I nodded, deepening the kiss in the same breath.

His tongue danced with mine as we lost ourselves in yet another breathless kiss.

"The truth is, I couldn't look anywhere else. Focusing on the lesson was impossible. The shirtless version of you is pretty tempting. The dressed version too, but those abs? Total distraction."

"Now that I have learned you have a weak spot for me, I know how to torture you. The thing is"—he pulled at my lower lip with his teeth—"you looked pretty sexy yourself in that tiny bikini, Avalon. I may have threatened three guys with my eyes who watched you a little too closely."

"You did? For me?"

"Yes. Now let's go before we can't move from this hammock." He jumped to his feet and lifted me over his shoulder while I laughed my heart out. Joseph's palm smacked my ass, and my laughter doubled. Images of Ryder carrying me the same way, but without an ounce of cheerfulness, invaded my mind, and I pushed them away. *Stay out of my mind, Ryder. I swear you're not invited.*

Joseph lowered me to my feet, but I locked my legs around his waist before he could put me down.

"I love it when you're in my arms," he said, his palms gliding over my back.

"And before I don't have the guts to tell you, you're allowed to touch me, okay? If it gets too much, I'll tell you."

His excitement died down. "You sure?"

"Affirmative. It felt good earlier when you put the sunscreen on my back. And minutes ago, it felt incredible." I shrugged. "We could start there."

He studied me for a full minute. "Okay, I might take you up on your offer."

My lips pouted a little. "Please. I promise I'll be honest with you."

———

"Where are you taking me?" I asked, my heart doing happy flips in my chest at the idea Joseph and I were going on our first official date together. Wearing beige cargo shorts and a blue polo shirt that made the color of his eyes pop, I couldn't seem to stop looking at my *boyfriend*—I loved this word. We rode in his truck, and since we had left his house, he hadn't released my hand once.

Every few seconds, we exchanged heated gazes and stupid smiles. Yep, we'd be one of those couples.

"Who knew the angry girl I met on the bus that morning would turn out to be the one I can't stop thinking about?" he asked after he stopped at a red light and leaned over to kiss me.

"Your smile was blinding me that day. I couldn't understand why you were so cheerful for nothing. Who's excited about a two-day bus ride with a bunch of strangers? I'm glad your optimism bled on me. And that you declared us besties. You make this whole summer worth it." I squeezed his hand.

"If I only get you for the summer, I better make the most of it."

We drove in a comfortable silence.

"Please don't talk about a deadline, okay? Just thinking the summer will eventually be over gets me all emotional," I said, fidgeting with the bracelet around my wrist. "I'm not good with separation."

"How so?"

"It's complicated."

His hand caressed my thigh. "I won't bring it up. Let's just enjoy our time together and see where it takes us. I'm not ready to think about *after us* yet."

I nodded, my conflicted emotions sticking down my throat.

"Hey Avalon," Joseph said, his fingertips tracing my cheek, awakening butterflies in my stomach. "I'm sorry. Don't be sad. It wasn't my intention to make things awkward."

He pulled into a gravel road and stopped the engine at the end of a driveway. "Come here, you."

Unbuckling my seatbelt, he pulled me to him after he pushed his seat back. I straddled his lap, my back pressing against the steering wheel. His scent, ocean and something exclusive to him, filled the cab. I gasped when his large hands framed my face. "We're in this together, and we'll figure it out. Let's enjoy our summer together for now."

"About what we discussed earlier..." I felt my cheeks burning up under his attention. "Can we continue where we left things off?"

"Avalon, we don't have to rush into anything. Let's go slow."

I combed his hair back, massaging his skull with my fingers. "My best friend from home and I decided this summer would be one to remember. Try new things. Like surfing. Meet new people. Get out of our comfort zones. When I'm with you, I really want this summer to be special because you kinda make me want to embrace it all. With you. And if you desire it too, even though I'm not ready to have sex yet, we can still enjoy other things. I'm not super experienced, but the sensations I felt earlier when we were kissing made me feel good. I want them back. If you're the one providing them."

My lips descended to his, and Joseph kissed me back.

"I love it when you speak what's really on your mind and are honest with me."

Joseph was right. I usually didn't open up that much about myself around him.

His mouth returned to mine, and we took our time. His lower self swelled underneath me, and I couldn't help myself from rubbing against him. He broke the kiss, panting, and nestled his face in the crook of my neck.

"Okay, let's make a deal. We'll wait until after dinner. If you haven't changed your mind, I know a few tricks that could get you back there."

"Thanks," I said, unable to control the heat wave traversing me. "Can we do something first? To see how it feels?"

"What do you have in mind?"

I knitted our fingers together and brought his hand over my chest until he could mold his palm to my left breast. We both sucked in a breath as Joseph touched me in an intimate manner for the first time.

"You good?" he asked, barely able to look at me, his face flushed.

"Perfect."

Holding on to each other, Joseph's chin rested on the top of my shoulder. We stayed in each other arms while his hand went back around my waist.

"Hungry?" he asked, breaking the symphony of our combined heartbeats.

"Famished."

"Perfect because we happen to be at one of my favorite spots around here."

We exited the truck. With one hand, I pushed the back of my white A-line summer dress down as the breeze lifted it up. "You're gorgeous tonight," Joseph said. "You always are, but there are sparkles in your eyes now that weren't there before."

I mirrored the tilt of his lips. "It's all you. You put them there."

He grabbed a bag from the backseat and locked the doors. "I prepared a picnic last night. There's a field, and the sunsets are beautiful there. The property belongs to Amanda's great-aunt, so nobody will disturb us. You'll see, it's amazing."

We walked through the high grass for ten minutes before we arrived at a fence made of old hemlock trees. "Let me go first." Joseph jumped over the four-foot height structure like it was the easiest thing he ever did. "Gimme your hand. When you're high enough, swing your legs over the railing."

I did as he said, but soon Joseph lost his balance, and I landed on top of him, both of us giggling like little kids.

The air surrounding us heated up with promises we

hadn't defined yet. A warm breeze swept across our faces. Spellbound by each other's gazes, we didn't move or speak.

Before I lost my boldness, I kissed Joseph like the starving girl I had become since our little make-out session in the afternoon.

Straddling his hips, I sucked on his tongue and glided my hands under his shirt, grazing the skin of his abdomen for the first time. A loud growl broke the silence as he kissed me back, claiming my mouth like he was starving too.

His sex hardened right where it felt good, and I rocked my hips over his, desperate to increase the friction. Joseph's hand pushed the hem of my dress up, and his rough palms made their way to my thighs.Every piece of me combusted under the delicate touch.

Without a warning, he flipped me over until I lay on my back. "You really wanna do this?"

I nodded, unable to form coherent words, lust having taken over my mushy brain and transforming it into a ball of jelly.

One finger ran across the crotch of my panties. His simple touch electrified my core like never before. "Like that?"

I drew in a short intake of air, trying to hold on to the little composure I had left, and nodded again.

"We better eat then, or I'll feast on you. We did say we'd take things slow." He stood up and kicked his legs, probably trying to shake off the tension I felt there seconds ago.

Panting and aroused, I moved to my feet too, and grabbed the bag. "Show me the way."

Joseph shook his head, his smile now a permanent fixture on his face, and led me to the side of a small hill from where we could admire horses and miles of pasture ahead.

"Wow, it's so peaceful here," I said, savoring the fresh air as it filled my nostrils.

"I knew you'd love it. I come here when my life feels overwhelming or I gotta think things over."

Sitting on a blanket, he fed me bites of everything as my head rested in his lap. Aware of how much I liked music, he had also brought a portable speaker on which he played all my favorite country music playlists that we'd shared during our bus ride from Michigan to North Carolina.

He fed me a strawberry before swallowing the second half, and I was mesmerized by the shape of his lips as they closed around the juicy berry. It reminded me of how they felt against mine so many times today, and how good they would feel around other parts of my body if I let him explore each centimeter of my skin.

New tingles woke up inside me just at the thought we could be intimate if I were ready.

"'Tell me something nobody knows about you?" Joseph asked.

"Like what?"

"You're always super secretive about yourself."

"Nothing that interesting to share. Life as usual." I paused, feeling bad about keeping him at arm's length when he always volunteered pieces of him to me. "When I was little, I took in a stray dog and hid it in my room for almost a week without my parents noticing."

"See, I could tell you had the biggest heart out there. Did you end up keeping it?"

"No. Collin is allergic. We found a great family to take care of it, though."

Joseph popped two grapes into my mouth and leaned forward to kiss me, stealing one in the process.

"Hey," I called out in fake accusation.

"Yours taste better than mine."

My hand shaped to his neck, and I pulled him forward, thirsty for his lips on mine.

The sun had descended upon the horizon, and the sky was a display of purplish shades of watercolor. I admired the scenery around us, spellbound by the sight of the field under the low golden light.

"I'm happy," I said. "Back home, I thought I was, but being here with you makes me realize I was missing out on so many things in my life. I never did anything just for the sake of it. I've always played it safe. Now I'm done being Ava Pierce, the girl who never challenges herself, the one always saying yes, even when she wants to say no. Every day, I wanna feel alive like I do now. With you. Except with my friend Iris, I'm more myself around you than with any other person."

"And it's a good thing, I suppose?"

"Yes. You make me wanna be brave. And try stuff I never thought possible before. Like surfing. Or being here, in this field, with you."

Joseph lay beside me, and I nestled in the crook of his arm, relishing the scent of salt water and clean man emanating from him.

We stayed there, enjoying each other's company and the silence around us. When he turned to his side, taking me with him so I was on my back, his finger traced a line from the valley of my breasts to my lower belly. I quivered from head to toe, my cells shaking with delight.

He nuzzled my neck, the roughness in his voice spreading goose bumps over my arms. "Still want me to touch you or have you changed your mind?"

I swallowed, anticipation thickening my vocal cords. "I-I haven't."

His hand continued its descent, his fingertips painting my skin with unknown sensations I could easily get addicted to.

"You like?" He sucked on my earlobe, his teeth nibbling the delicate flesh.

I was becoming a puddle of molten clay on that blanket, and I didn't even care anymore. When his digits traced the side my thigh, I tensed.

"Want me to stop?" he asked

I shook my head. "No. I'll tell you if I'm not comfortable."

"Relax then. It's me. I'll never hurt you. All I want is to make you feel good."

In the most torturous sensation I had ever felt, Joseph's fingers traveled to my collarbones before grazing the swell of my breasts and returning to my legs. His fingers pushed under my dress, caressing my thighs up to their apex. Over my underwear, he drew a line with his fingertip, spreading my wetness all over the now-drenched fabric.

Tremors shook me. The foreign sensations, like a tsunami, washed through me, leaving tingles in their wake.

"Oh geez," I gasped, digging my fingernails into his biceps, unable to stop the unraveling happening inside me. One of his thick fingers pushed the material of my panties aside, and he rubbed my clit in slow circles.

I grew rigid, trying to relax, but barely able to, overwhelmed with the stimuli shooting in all directions deep in my core.

A gazillion stars now shone behind my eyelids. I couldn't keep my eyes open even though I tried. I had no idea how every cell in me could be so sensitive and so receptive to Joseph's touch. His lips searched my mouth, his tongue cherishing mine in slow strokes. It took me no time to detonate under the pads of his fingers, unable to stay put any longer.

My head shot back.

My back arched.

My toes curled.

My teeth sank into my bottom lip.

And a soft cry passed the seam of my mouth.

The coils around my wild heart loosened. I could take a full breath in only when the surge of pleasure lessened.

My heart tumbled in my chest, and I kept my eyes closed, uncertain how to face my boyfriend now.

He combed my hair back. "Look at me."

One by one, I peeled my eyelids open and met the content expression bending his lips.

"Want to keep going?" Joseph asked, his voice dripping with raw, uncontained desire.

I inhaled, barely able to stay still, the need building up inside me. "Yes. Please."

In the most delicate manner, one of his digits found its way inside me and slid in and out of my warmth at a steady pace. I yelped at the intrusion at first, but soon it wasn't enough. I had to move, to roll my hips over his hand, to increase the contact, unable to stay still, the friction igniting my core. My own hand enveloped his because I feared if he stopped, I would vaporize and never recover. My hips buckled from the ground, chasing those rousing frissons waking up in the depths of me. This was the most intoxicating state I'd ever been in. Even though I tried, I couldn't stop writhing underneath Joseph as I pressed his hand firmly against my center. My hips rocked back and forth, increasing the tempo of our connection.

Muffled whimpers escaped my mouth. Joseph's lips returned to mine, his tongue taking charge, increasing the whirlwind seizing each of my cells and erasing the embarrassment of becoming a ball of needs about to rupture into a kaleidoscope of colors before his eyes.

I didn't belong to this world anymore. I was floating, light, blazing with heat.

My body had a mind of its own.

Joseph kissed me with a new passion I never experienced before.

I cupped his nape, keeping him close as we devoured each other's mouths.

"Joseph, I will… Oh. I can't… Yes… No… Keep going." His movements became less precise as he accelerated the pace. My vision blurred. I lost all sense of time.

Something clenched in my core. A bright light flared behind my closed eyelids.

"Let it go, Ava. I'll catch you on the other side. I'm right here. With you."

A buzz started in my belly and expanded through my being. My head spun. I breathed faster. When I thought I'd die, a sensation I couldn't describe erupted inside me, swallowing me whole before I fell over the edge in a bliss too strong for words.

I tried to catch a full breath, but every cell in me shuddered with the release that shook me to the core. Never on my own had I achieved such a powerful relief.

"Ava, look at me," Joseph pleaded. I could feel the rigidity of his manhood against the side of my leg. "Open your eyes. Let me see you."

I cracked my eyelids open, and my gaze met his. I blinked some of my shyness away, deciding to trust him fully.

A satisfied grin curled his lips. "Are you okay?"

I nodded.

"How was it?"

I blinked, trying to reboot my brain to form thoughts—and sentences. "Amazing."

"Got those butterflies back?" he teased.

"More than I bargained for." I swallowed, my body slowly making its way back to earth, sensations returning to my limbs, and the fog around my brain evaporating. I put a hesitant hand over the crotch of his shorts. "Can-can I touch you?"

His throat bobbed a few times. "You don't have to."

"But I want to. Just tell me what to do. What you like."

He positioned my hand over his erection, and blanketing my hand with his, he moved them over his shaft in long, slow strokes. Once I got into the rhythm, he removed his hand. His hard-on twitched underneath my palm, and I tightened my grip around him.

"Like that?"

He nodded, his eyelids hooded, and his teeth sinking into the tip of his tongue.

I worked him a couple of more times, then asked, "Can I feel you?"

"You sure?"

"Yes. I want to."

Joseph unzipped his shorts, and when he lowered the waistband of his boxer briefs, his length saluted me. I blinked at the first fully erect penis I'd ever seen. With a tentative gesture, I fisted the heated part of him and motioned my hand up and down like he showed me, relishing the softness of his flesh and the hardness it covered.

A string of loud curses tumbled out of his mouth. "This feels too good. I won't last long."

I accelerated my movements, enjoying how Joseph fit in my fist. His eyelids fluttered. His breathing kicked up a notch. He tried to stay still, but his hips increased the tempo, and he was now fucking my fist. Our eyes stayed locked, and I could read the pleasure lighting up his irises under his heavy eyelids. Just then did I realize he had surrendered himself to me. With no restraint.

Something I had yet to achieve. Because even when I let him finger me earlier, a part of me was still holding back.

He put a hand over mine to stop me. "Ava, if you keep going, I'll come."

"Then do. You made me come twice."

Focused on my task, I tightened my grip around him and pumped him as fast as I could. Joseph lifted his shirt, exposing his chiseled abdomen, and at the same time, he shot his semen over his taut stomach in powerful jolts.

He exhaled. Then breathed in again before meeting my eyes.

I watched him, transfixed.

"Come here, you," he said, pulling me to him and kissing me as if I'd just rocked his world. In a sense, maybe I had. Because he sure had rocked mine minutes ago.

I lost myself in the kiss, still floating from the orgasms that had rippled through me. For the next hour, after we cleaned ourselves up with napkins, and until darkness had almost fallen completely upon us, we cuddled on the blanket, no words necessary to express the connection and contentment that now bound us.

On the way back to my house, we both barely said a word, the width of our smiles betraying, without a doubt, the level of intimacy we had experienced. This felt right. Everything about Joseph felt like it was meant to be. I scooted over the seat until my head rested on his shoulder, enjoying the feel of him next to me. Catching me after I fell, like he promised.

The entire ride, our hands were linked together, resting on my thigh.

"Are you all right?" he asked after a while.

I nodded. "Are you?"

He nodded and kissed the top of my head. The vibrations of the vehicle tamed the flames still burning strong inside me.

When I climbed out of his truck twenty minutes later, I was unable to get rid of my grin.

"You look happy. Satisfied," he said.

"Yes. Still surfing a high. All pun intended," I said with a wink. "Not sure how I'll even sleep tonight."

His fingers connected with mine as we made our way toward the house.

"Me neither. Can I see you tomorrow?" He inched closer and kissed me one more time, pressing my back against the wall.

"I have a girls' day out." I grimaced. "Right now, I wanna cancel my plans and keep experimenting with you instead. It's a shame because I have the whole house to myself for another day."

"Tasha?"

I nodded.

"Enjoy your day with her. Don't worry. We'll have more occasions to be together. Don't cancel for me. I'm glad you're making friends in town."

We kissed a dozen times more before I begged him to drive away. My gaze followed his taillights as he disappeared into the night. My mind was still with the boy who had changed me for the better tonight. The one I didn't wanna wash off me in case all of this was just a naughty dream.

I landed back into reality when I noticed Ryder's truck parked in the driveway. Inhaling some much-needed peacefulness, I entered the house, hoping he was already asleep in the guest room.

"Hey, where have you been? It's past midnight."

I raised a finger to stop his comments as I walked past him. "No. Not tonight, Ryder. Keep your nasty comments to yourself. I won't let you steal my happiness away. Night."

I retreated to my room. Soon the sound of footsteps resonated behind me. Closing my eyes, I prayed he wouldn't follow me because I wasn't in the mood for another altercation today. All I wanted was to never escape the state of bliss I was basking in.

At the threshold of my bedroom, I whirled around, readying myself in case he didn't get the message.

Chapter 27

Ryder folded his arms like he always did when we disagreed about something and offered me a sour look. "Explain."

"No."

"Why are you smiling? What's so funny?" he asked with quirked eyebrows.

"As I said earlier, nothing that concerns you. Can't you get a life of your own?"

"It's not that simple."

"It is. If you were nice, or at least decent, with me, I would be happy to tell you where I've been. But since neither applies to you, I won't. We're not friends. You've reminded me multiple times already. I owe you nothing. Good night."

I pivoted, but he clamped his fingers around my elbow.

"What now?" I huffed as Ryder studied me.

"What happened? You look…huh…you look different."

I shook my head. "Stop thinking you know me. I'm happy, and happy people smile. You should try it sometimes. You may love it."

"The fuck. You're lying. When you do, your nose twitches."

"No, it doesn't."

"Wanna bet?" he asked.

"Since you're about to become a daddy in less than nine months, you should focus on that. Learn how to change diapers." I was aware bringing up Misty's possible pregnancy was a cheap shot, but I couldn't just shut up. If Ryder was allowed to rile me up, I was allowed to mess with him too. There were no rules in this fight of ours. And for once I possessed bits of information about him no one else did.

He snorted. "You wish. If Misty is pregnant, I can assure you it isn't mine."

"Yeah, right. Keep telling yourself that. This explains why so many babies are being born without a daddy in the picture."

From the look in Ryder's eyes, I had touched, once again, a sensitive cord because he flinched.

I blinked, and my need to win our argument ebbed. "Sorry," I murmured.

His composure came back, and he spoke through clenched teeth, his posture rigid. "Nobody is pregnant with my baby. End of discussion. And if someone was, for the record, I wouldn't walk away from my responsibilities."

We stood there, inches apart, and something in Ryder's face soothed the agitated half of me. His proximity calmed the remnants of the battle that had raged in my core seconds ago. His fingers skimmed mine, and a warm feeling crept up my arms and spine.

Desperate not to show him the transformation happening inside me, I offered him a pointed look while folding my arms. "Can I go now? I'm exhausted, and I'm done fighting for the day."

And also, I wanna relive my night over and over again until I can't keep my eyes open anymore. The segments that don't involve you.

He murmured something I didn't catch, turned on his heel, and stomped away.

Speechless, I watched his retreat. Hurrying to my room, I showered in a rush before slipping under the covers, ready to bring back the fantasy of the shivers that had invaded me earlier.

Alone with my memories, I closed my eyes, wishing images of my boyfriend would appear and play with my body, in the same manner he did tonight, till the morning.

When stormy aquamarine-green irises popped into my mind instead—threatening to mess up with my fantasies again—I squeezed my eyes shut and decided to forfeit the idea of sweet dreams tonight. In the middle of flipping to my side, counting sheep, and replaying my night in my head, I fell asleep.

When I got up around nine the next day, Ryder was nowhere to be seen, and all his shit was gone. For a fraction of a second, I even wondered if last night's encounter had really occurred or if my mind had fabricated the entire thing. By now, I was aware I was sick or suffering from an unknown ailment, because my brain thought having sexual dreams about my nemesis was the way to go. Anything could have happened. But this? This was real. He had been here last night. I hadn't imagined it.

Sitting on the front porch swing, I video called Joseph the first chance I got.

"Hey you. I was wondering if you were already awake," he said, his lips stretched and his eyes sparkling. He lay in the same hammock where we both had been resting the previous afternooon. "Slept well?"

I shook my head, feeling more self-conscious in the bright light of the day. "Not sure if I did. I was hot and bothered. I tossed and turned for a long time before I found a soothing position."

"At least I'm not the only one who had a restless mind. And body. Glad to know my girlfriend and I were on the same page."

"Say it again," I asked, warmth heating my cheeks.

"What? Girlfriend?"

I nodded. "I love when you say it."

"I'll miss my girlfriend today. I wish it was tonight or tomorrow already so I could visit her."

My body and my mind hummed, relishing the underlying happy notes in his voice when he said it.

"Wanna come over for dinner? I promise to kick you out before eight since you gotta wake up super early for surf camp."

"Your aunt and uncle will be back. You sure they won't mind?"

I shook my head. "The other day, they said they wished to see more of you. What do you say?"

His face illuminated with glee. "Let me check if I'm required here, and I'll text you later."

"Awesome."

We talked for over an hour. Until Joseph had to leave to give a hand at the restaurant.

"Have fun with your friend," he said.

"I'll do my best. Message me later when you know if you're coming over."

"I will."

Our eyes fixated on each other through the small screen, neither of us brave enough to terminate the call.

"Okay, I'll do it," I said. "Only because you'll be late if I don't."

"Not my fault. I kinda love watching you. That blush on your cheeks is adorable."

"See you later," I said, tugging my lip between my teeth as I ended the call. My heart cartwheeled in my chest, and my body heated up with flashbacks of last night's date.

I was happy. Joseph made me happy.

Next, I called Iris because I had so much to tell her and I couldn't stay still for more than a minute without confiding in someone.

"Hey A, can I call you later? I'm working all day," she said.

"Sure. A lot happened. So much to tell you. I'm busy all afternoon. Text me when you're available tonight."

"Cool. Have a great one."

"You too."

We hung up, and after I scrolled through my phone and smiled at the pictures Joseph and I had snapped last night, I returned to my room, ready to jumpstart my day. Through the ajar drawer of my bedside table, I spotted the teal and dark pink cover of my journal. I took it out and spread it open on my bed. I usually wrote at night, but right now, I really felt like confiding in my paper friend. So much stuff had happened in the last few days, and I still had a hard time wrapping my head around all of it.

Dear Diary

This summer will probably be one to remember after

all. When my parents cast me away, I thought they were screwing with my entire vacation, but now I'm thankful they did.

Sure, Ryder is still the biggest pain in my existence, but if I learned something over the last few days, it is that I somehow (don't tell him or I'll deny it, even under torture) need him in my life right now. I can't explain it, but I have come to enjoy our banter. Because it starts a fire inside me, and I love how alive I feel. It forces me to assert myself, and I think that could be a good thing. Iris thinks he doesn't have any friends. I wish he was nicer, and we'd get along, though. He doesn't want to, so his loss, right? Anyway, enough talking about him. He's still not worth my time.

Now the biggest news of all. Joseph asked me to be his girlfriend. Officially. I've never felt like that with a boy before. When we're together, his contagious happiness spills on me, and I can't stop smiling. Even when I don't feel like it. It's still brand new, but he makes my summer here so worth it. I can already predict I'll be heartbroken when I move back home once my stay is over. We decided not to talk about it for now and see how it goes instead and enjoy our time together.

Yesterday, he took me out on a date, and the way he kissed and touched me, I couldn't get enough. I just wanna keep experimenting with him. All the time. He makes me feel special, and when he looks at me, his blue eyes sparkle. I really think he could be the guy for me. I'll keep you updated.

I gotta go because I'm spending the rest of the day with Tasha. She's my best girlfriend in town, and we have so much in common. She's funny and kind, and today we're going to the mall.

In a few days, I'll tell you all about it.

Have a great day
Ava (who wears the biggest smile her face can contain right now) xx

———

To be continued in ***Ride for a Fall***, the second book in the **Wrecked** series. Get your copy **here**

emmanuellesnowshop.com/products/ride-for-a-fall

———

Thank you for reading the first part of Ava's story.
Keep reading for an excerpt of ***Snowbound***,
a coming of age, stranded, airport love story
Snowbound
emmanuellesnowshop.com/products/snowbound

ACKNOWLEDGMENTS

Oh, Ava, I love you so much, and I wish I could hug you for real. I know Ryder is hard on you, but don't lose hope. In the end, he might surprise you.

For now, let Joseph's light shine on you. You deserve the happiness. And he's good for you.

I've written a lot of teen characters (some in published books, some in works in progress), but there's just something about these three that speaks to me. The duality. Ryder and Joseph. Light and darkness. Hardships and happiness. I wish the characters could see that everything happens for a reason, and life has bigger plans for them all.

Medora Beach is my new universe, and I'm so excited you're going to experience it too. Summertime, beach, waves, bikinis, what's not to like, right? And I fell in love with the Pierce family, and I can't wait to tell more of their stories.

I want to thank my children. The four of you are my inspiration for writing YA novels. I'm watching you turn into future adults, and it makes me so proud. I love writing younger characters who don't have everything figured out yet. Being a teen is confusing and even more in the world we live in. It's okay to make mistakes. And to be wrong. It's also okay to try stuff. Nobody gets it the first time anyway. I want you to live and love, to dream big, and to reach out for them. I'll always hug you and help pick you up when you fall apart, and I'll always cheer you on when you get back up on your feet and give it another shot. I love you, babies.

To my husband. We were those teens once, the ones with big dreams. I'm glad we're still reaching for them and showing our kids everything is possible. I wouldn't want anyone else but you on my team. I love you.

To Shalini. I know I've been working on five projects at the same time, and my life got crazy again for a little while, but we did it. This book was a long time coming, and I'm happy it's finally out in the world. Thank you for helping me make my books shine.

To my Snowmate team, thank you from the bottom of my heart. I love your contagious excitement, and I'm happy you're on my squad.

To the Bookstagrammers, YouTubers, TikTokers, bloggers, and everyone else who spreads the word about my books, I wanna thank you personally. I am sending a big virtual hug your way, and I hope one day, we'll be able to meet in person.

To my readers. You make each of my books feel special. And I can't tell you enough how much you mean to me. Thank you!

To all of you who have dreams, don't let anything or anyone stand in your way.

Ava, Joseph, and Ryder's story is not over. Life isn't done testing them, but I swear, even if their journey is bumpy, love will always win. Or I wish it would.

Thank you for your support. With all my love,

Emmanuelle

ABOUT THE AUTHOR

Soulfully Beautiful Love Stories

USA Today Bestselling Author Emmanuelle Snow is an author of contemporary YA and women's fiction love stories, who gives life to strong characters who'll fight with all they have to reach their life goals and find their own happiness. She loves her characters to be relatable and realistic.

Emmanuelle is in love with love. Especially complicated, deep, and passionate feelings that make a relationship extraordinary and complex all at the same time.

In her spare time, when she's not writing or reading, she likes to go on road trips—with her four kids and her own soulmate—watch movies, paint, or do some DIY, always with a cup of green tea in her hand and listening to country music.

She splits her time between beautiful Canada and the small US towns she adores.

Find all of Emmanuelle's books here:
emmanuellesnow.com

———

ALSO BY THE AUTHOR

CARTER HILLS BAND UNIVERSE

(suggested reading order)

Carter Hills Band series

False Promises

HEART SONG DUET

Blindsided

Forevermore

Whiskey Melody series

Sweet Agony

SECOND TEAR DUET

Cruel Destiny

Beautiful Salvation

BREATHLESS DUET

Wild Encounter

Brittle Scars

Upon A Star Series

Last Hope

Midnight Sparks

Love Song For Two Series

MEDORA BEACH UNIVERSE

Wrecked series

Touchdown series

READ THEM ALL

emmanuellesnow.com

All available on author's bookshop

SNOWBOUND
ABIGAIL

Present

All my life, I'd dreamed of working in the music industry, and after everything that had happened, I never thought this day would come—or that my dream could ever become tangible one day. For more than three years, I'd worked my ass off as a virtual assistant while juggling home, college, and all the other responsibilities a twenty-three-year-old woman shouldn't have had to deal with all by herself. But hey, I was ready now to prove to Mr. Burns that I could be the assistant he was looking to hire.

Three months ago, I had finally graduated with a dual degree in business administration and music management. One I'd worked my ass off for. Days and nights. Literally. I was overqualified for this position, but I didn't care. I would be an assistant any day if it meant proving my value. Climbing up that career ladder until I reached my ultimate goal. Yeah, anything to bring me closer to my dream job.

In the full-length mirror in the entryway, I glanced at my power outfit one last time—white blouse, red pencil skirt, along with matching heels. It had been my first impulsive buy and the most expensive one to date. Money had been scarce these past few years, but somehow, I'd always made it work. I smoothed the fabric over my thighs with trembling fingers, doing my best to calm the jitters invading me. Yes, I looked the part.

I admired my reflection for little longer. Tears pooled in my eyes, and I felt a little pinch in my heart.

"I can do this. I will do this. I deserve this." I repeated my mantra over and over. Nothing like a little pep talk to put me in the right mindset.

I blinked hard to chase away the moisture. Now wasn't the time to dwell on every bump in the road or all the things that needed to be done to get to where I was today. Instead, I focused on Aisha Jones's country song "In Your Dreams" playing on the radio in the background. A reminder that the Holidays were seven weeks away. And a nod to the best night of my life.

Two weeks ago, I had celebrated my birthday with Mixchos—reinvented nachos—and the biggest mug of hot chocolate I could find. Ellie, my best friend, had sent me the new pair of heels I was wearing today as a present and told me they would bring me luck. I hoped she was right.

From my spot near the front door, I surveyed my small apartment. The single main room, the two closet-sized bedrooms off to the side, and the open kitchen. My eyes lingered over the furniture and the mess surrounding it, caressing it lovingly. It had been hard, but totally worth it.

A smile peeked on my lips. If I'd come all this way, the interview would be easy-peasy. I crossed my fingers, hoping it wasn't just wishful thinking on my part. I'd been learning all about CB Music for the last month, from the awards Mr. Burns won over the years to each page of their corporate website. A girl couldn't be prepared enough. The guy was a household name on the international country music scene, but I wouldn't let his credentials and achievements intimidate me. I would be the professional he expected me to be. Even though, deep down, I was kind of amazed by his career.

Every day, I'd listened to each one of his songs. Just in case they quizzed me on those.

Back when I was nineteen, I used to be a music encyclopedia. I knew every artist, even the emerging ones, and could tell by heart every award they had won in their careers and their best hits. I could tell which songs would be chart-toppers from the first listen, and which ones would be misses. Over the last few years, I had lost my magic touch, too busy with the numerous curveballs life had thrown at me. But now, I was ready to take my power back, to get to the top of my game, and dig up that version of me I'd somehow lost along the way.

In the entryway mirror, I wiped away the tears with my fingers and swiped a hand through my hair. I was ready. I would get this job. I could feel it. Today was the day my life would change for the better. It was about time. I huffed. Yes, the stars would finally align themselves. It was my time to shine.

At the front door, hand wrapped around the doorknob, I closed my eyes. This job, this opportunity, would mean the world to me if I got it. I believed in the magical power of the holidays. A girl could always hope for the best. My grandma told me, while growing up, that all the best things happened around this time of the year. I could tell she spoke the truth because I had already experienced a Christmas miracle four years ago. Now I craved a second one. If it wasn't too much to ask.

Locking the door behind me, I exited the building with a pep in my step. All week, I'd been walking around my

apartment in heels to get used to their feel and look confident wearing them.

On the sidewalk, I let a full breath out as I glanced at
the sky, immaculate blue canvas glittering with sunshine.
Yes, today would be a good day. A great day. One to
remember.

A prayer to the Gods above and I climbed into the
backseat of the idling cab that would drive me to Nashville's tallest building where I would meet some of the most
important music executives in the country.

Wish me luck. No, not luck. I knew I'd be the best at
that job.

Go, get them, tiger. Yeah, much better.

I exhaled. This position was mine. I was ready to hustle
for it. Whatever it took, I'd be the new CB Music
employee. I, Abigail Peña, would be a rising star on the
Nashville's music scene. One day, I would sign the biggest
artists under my management and would become a household name in this industry.

———

One breath in. I passed through security, signed the
logbook, hung the visitor pass around my neck, and made
my way to the twenty-sixth floor. Yes, I belonged here. I
could feel it deep in my bones. Goose bumps spread on my
arms, and excited flutters danced around in my stomach.
This was my chance, and I wouldn't miss it.

I checked my outfit and makeup one last time and
smoothed a hand over my hair in the elevator's mirrored
wall. Satisfied, I rubbed my clammy hands discreetly on
my skirt and squared my shoulders.

A woman in her fifties, with a businesslike demeanor,
gave me a not-so-subtle once-over as I exited the elevator.

I cleared my throat softly before approaching her, hoping my voice wouldn't squeak.

"Welcome to CB Music. May I help you?" she asked, lifting a dark brow.

I breathed out. "Yes, I'm here for the interview. For the assistant's position. I'm meeting with Mr. Burns and Mr. Jacobson at ten."

The woman tapped away at something on her computer before bringing her attention back to me. "Ms. Peña. You're early. That's good. Just take a seat. I'll call out when they are ready for you."

I nodded and sat on a white leather chair in the small waiting room, crossing my feet at the ankles.

To avoid freaking out, I grabbed a magazine and pretended to flip through it.

I had an interview with Curtis Burns, one of Nashville's most famous country music stars, turned music manager.

If he was as good a manager as his son Riley, this was promising. Riley Burns had signed many upcoming country rock stars over the years. He was as famous as his dad, even though they chose different career paths. One day, I'd play in the big leagues. Just like him.

The receptionist called out my name, and I jumped to my feet, adjusting my top before following her to the conference room. My breath hitched as I took in the view. The room had a floor-to-ceiling glass wall, offering the best view of the Cumberland River and the football stadium on the opposite shore.

Curtis Burns and Gregory Jacobson rose to their feet to shake my hand as I entered, then gestured for me to take the seat across from them. A genuine smile tugged at my lips. I finally had my chance to shine.

Deep down, I urged my throbbing heart to take a rest.

Confidence spread through me, pushing me to speak slowly, to show them I was the real deal. That I was the perfect—no, the only—valuable choice for this position. The interview passed in a blur.

If someone had requested me to write down the questions they'd asked, I wouldn't have been able to. The words had flowed from me effortlessly before I could even think them through. Every time the men exchanged nods and jotted down notes, I high-fived myself in my head. I could do this. I could excel and take the first step toward making my dreams a reality.

"Before you go, Ms. Peña, I want you to meet the first artist we've signed under our management," Mr. Jacobson said. "Being Mr. Burns's assistant means you'll work closely with our artists." He pressed a button on the speaker kept in the middle of the table. "Laura, please send Mr. Ford in. We're ready for him."

Laura said a few words and hung up as we waited.

Moments later, a discrete knock resonated through the room, and the door opened to let the man in. I moved to stand up, ready to greet him and introduce myself.

Longish brown hair, dark enigmatic eyes, nonchalant gait.

Our gazes met, and the air froze in my lungs.

"Ms. Peña, this is Anderson Ford," said someone in the background.

I tried to speak, but the words refused to come, my feet glued to the floor and my arms hanging limply at my sides.

Then a rush of air, followed by a single word: "You?"

The man's jaw dropped, and he blinked, an expression crossing his face that I couldn't quite decipher.

Mr. Burns cleared his throat. "You two know each other?"

I nodded, still unable to speak.

"Well, let's all sit and discuss, shall we?"

Neither of us moved, unable to break eye contact as my insides burned and melted, hurting me until I couldn't seem to breathe.

As I closed in on myself, I heard, for the first time, the faint strains of country Christmas music drifting from a speaker in the ceiling. Ironic, right?

Santa had mixed up my wishes—or was just late delivering them—because it had been two years since I last wished for this man, the one whose full name I hadn't even known until today, to walk back into my life.

Anderson.

Not Andrew.

Now that he was here, I had no clue what to do.

Read Anderson and Abigail's story,
Read SnowBound now

emmanuellesnow.com/products/snowbound

Author's bookstore at emmanuellesnow.com

"I'll tell you this; if you're looking for a book that will make you ugly cry but leave you with your heart full – look no more; Emmanuelle Snow is the right author for you." (Tanja, OMGreads)

"Be ready with a box of tissues because this is gonna tug at your heartstrings from every possible direction. I was ugly crying so much the whole day and even now." (OhMyWordMelly)

SnowBound is book one in the **Two Of US** duet.
Read the first part today
emmanuellesnow.com/products/snowbound

SURFER BOY

SUMMER LOVE!!!

...T THE AUTHOR

MEDORA BEACH
SUMMER NEVER
SURFING DAY